Copyright © 2023 by Melody Tyden

All rights reserved.

Cover design by: GetCovers

OUT OF MY DEPTH

MELODY TYDEN

PROLOGUE

~Tanith~

My sleepy hometown looked sleepier than ever on the Tuesday before Thanksgiving. Although flags and fake fall leaves decorated Main Street, the real leaves had mostly fallen from the trees already, leaving the trees as empty as the streets. The next day would be the high school football game and homecoming, all leading up to a weekend full of family, food and friends, but on Tuesday, most people were either still at work or in school. As I pulled up to my boyfriend's house on a lifeless-looking residential street, I should have actually been at a college class myself, but feeling even more homesick than usual, I ditched the class and decided to go home a day early.

College hadn't exactly been the fresh start I'd hoped it would be. If it weren't for my online friends, I wouldn't have any friends at all, and I'd begun to think the problem had never been my hometown at all. Maybe I just wasn't very interesting or special, at least not to anyone other than my boyfriend.

Blaine had night shifts all week at the job he got right out of high school, so I figured he would still be resting. I hadn't let him know about my change of plans, hoping to surprise him, and the thought made me smile as I grabbed my weekend bag from the passenger seat of my truck and headed up the path to the house. He'd seemed a bit distant whenever we talked recently, so a little extra time together would do us good. We both knew long-distance wouldn't be easy, but he hadn't been interested in college and everyone expected me to go. I'd always hated letting anyone down, even though lately, it felt like nothing I did was quite good enough.

The doorbell echoed through the house, filtering out to where I stood on the front step, and my heart beat a little faster as I waited for Blaine's handsome face to appear. Even two years on, I could barely believe he'd agreed to go out with me in the first place. The girls in my college dorm thought I lied when I said the cute guy in the picture on my wall was my boyfriend. He might not be perfect but at least he was mine, and after a rough first semester, I needed that feeling of belonging *somewhere* more than ever.

A few seconds went by, and a few more, and still, no one came to the door. Frowning, I glanced over at the driveway where his car sat. His pride and joy, he didn't go anywhere without it, so he had to be home.

Maybe he had his headphones on, in the middle of a gaming marathon or something. Trying the door, I found it unlocked, so I let myself in, calling out as I walked in so I wouldn't scare him. "Blaine? It's me."

No one answered me, but I could hear noises from upstairs, including a familiar-sounding laugh that sent a shiver down my spine.

It had to be my imagination. Someone in the game he was playing or the TV show he was watching happened to sound just like Amanda, the woman who had been making my life a living hell at college for months. Nothing else made sense, because there was no way in hell she would be in Blaine's house. She *couldn't* be.

As confident of that fact as I possibly could be, I headed upstairs to Blaine's bedroom, sure I would find him with his headphones on in front of his computer or TV.

I had one part right, at least. Blaine *did* have his headphones on, but the rest of him was completely naked, lying back on his bed while the equally naked body of my college bully bounced up and down on top of him.

"You've got to be fucking kidding me!"

The words exploded out of my mouth, loud enough that Blaine's eyes opened and he caught sight of me for the first time. The colour immediately drained from his face as he tried to disentangle himself from Amanda, who simply smirked over at me, almost as if she'd been expecting me.

"Ta-Tanith?" he sputtered in disbelief. "What are you doing here?"

"*That's* what you have to say?" I'd never been much for confrontation before, but my indignation gave me courage as I stared at the man who had been the one good thing in my life until then. Until *she* got to him.

"No. I mean... you weren't supposed to be here... I mean... shit."

That pretty much summed it up. He looked dejected as he finally managed to sit up, pull the headphones off and cover himself with a pillow. Amanda hadn't said a word and didn't look like she intended to, nor did she bother to cover her nudity.

I had no idea how or why, but deep in my gut, I knew she planned this. She'd hated me from the moment she laid eyes on me, for no earthly reason I could think of, and somehow, she set this up to destroy me.

Maybe it should have. Another day, it might have. But as I turned on my heel and headed back to my truck, driving straight out of town and back onto the highway to go back to college and nurse my broken heart in private, I had a sudden flash of inspiration.

All those lonely nights in my dorm bed over the past three months, my one companion had been my phone and the reading apps I found on it. Yes, the stories were ridiculous, but they were also fun and satisfying. The normal girl that everyone underestimated turned out to be something special. The guy who rejected her came to regret it. The bitch that tried to hurt her got what was coming to her.

Maybe that didn't happen in real life, but maybe I could write my own version that worked out the way I wanted it to. I'd tried writing a book of my own before, back in high school, but I never got past the first chapter or two. The world I created was always the same, a fantasy realm with magical, mythical creatures, but I never found the inspiration to decide what happened next.

That shouldn't be a problem this time, since I knew *exactly* what I wanted to write about. The Tanith I would create didn't need Blaine. She'd have a much better man of her own, or even two. Maybe three, or four? Why stop there?

As soon as I began to imagine it, the characters began to pop into my mind, almost fully formed. I could see them all so clearly, as if I knew them already, and by the time I got back to my dorm, I was bursting with so many ideas, my fingers could hardly keep up as I began writing them all down.

As long as I stayed in the story I created, I could control how things would end, and no one would ever make me feel unimportant again.

CHAPTER ONE

Three weeks later
~Tanith~

As the professor droned on about behavioural economics, a flicker of light in the corner of the room caught Tanith's eye. Looking up from the laptop in front of her, she glanced around at the other students to see if anyone else had noticed it. No one seemed to; their gazes remained fixed on either the professor, their laptops or their phones.

Convincing herself she must have imagined it, Tanith tried to focus back on the lecture, but the light flashed again. That time, when she looked over, she thought she saw a glimpse of something beyond it: a bright, green meadow on a summer's day, despite it being the middle of December. It almost looked like a window to another place; another dimension, perhaps, or another reality.

It should be impossible, but she saw it, clear as day, and yet no one else in the room reacted.

The light faded, the window closing with it, and the room immediately felt colder. Tanith shivered despite the expensive cream cashmere sweater she wore. Blaine had bought the sweater for her for her last birthday, but she couldn't bring herself to throw it away like she had the rest of her mementos of him. Her ex-boyfriend may have turned out to be an ass, but cashmere was still cashmere.

She must not have gotten enough sleep the night before, she figured. That explained the hallucinations, and her chill. She hadn't been sleeping well for the last few weeks. Maybe she had some kind of lingering bug, or maybe the stress of the upcoming midterms was responsible, but her friends insisted a good date followed by a good fuck could cure anything that might be wrong with her. She'd be tempted to put it to the test if only she could find the right man, the kind that didn't seem to exist in real life. The kind who would fulfill her every fantasy and thank her for the opportunity to do so.

Suddenly, the light flashed again and...

"Tanith?"

At the sound of my name, my fingers froze over the keyboard, and I looked up to find the whole of the Economics 101 class at Hycomb College staring at me while the professor, a dour, serious man in his 50s, raised his eyebrows expectantly.

"Yes?" The word came out as a squeak as I tried to guess what I'd missed, my heart racing at finding myself so unexpectedly on the spot.

The professor's lips pursed in displeasure at having to repeat himself. "Choice overload," he repeated slowly. "Can you give us a real-life example of where choice overload could occur?"

"I... uh, I'm not sure," I stuttered, my body flushing as every eye in the room remained on me. I *hated* being the centre of attention. Flying under the radar and not standing out in any way suited me much better.

"Look back at your notes," he suggested impatiently.

My notes?

My eyes flitted back to my laptop and the scene I'd just been editing for my book. Nothing on the screen had anything at all to do with that day's lecture. Frantically, I wracked my brain, trying to remember something, *anything*, about choice overload.

"It... uh, it happens when people have too many choices," I managed to pull from somewhere deep in my subconscious. "So they end up not making a choice at all, or changing their mind, or getting more things than they need?"

I could have sworn I had it right, but my answer didn't make him any happier. "I didn't ask for the definition," he reminded me as some of my classmates began to titter. "I'd like an example."

I *could* have said anything. I could have talked about all the different colours of paint that can overwhelm people and make them put off a painting project, or the plethora of menu choices at a new coffee shop where you don't already know what's good. Tons of reasonable, everyday situations were right there for the taking, but in my panic, as I looked back over the lines I'd written for my book, I could only think of one, and I blurted it out without properly thinking it through.

"In a why-choose romance, the main character has several different men all interested in her, and she likes all of them for different reasons, so rather than just choosing one, she decides to be with all of them, sometimes at the same time."

The professor's eyes widened in such surprise that it would have been funny... if I hadn't been the one to cause it. Laughs and whispers circulated around the room, and as the full reality of what I'd just said sank in, I wished that portal to another dimension really *would* open beneath my seat and swallow me up. I didn't even care where it took me, so long as I didn't have to show my face in that class again.

After blinking a couple of times, the professor cleared his throat to quiet the rest of the room. "That is... not entirely incorrect, but as there's no exchange of money, it wouldn't quite fit our current discussion. Does anyone else have an *economic* example?"

Hands shot up around me while I slumped back in my seat, my cheeks burning even hotter in embarrassment. That cinched it: definitely no more working on my book in class.

As soon as we were dismissed, I slammed the top of my laptop closed and tried to push my way out of the room, but I didn't quite reach the door before I heard the grating voice of my least favourite person in the world. "She spends all her time reading smut since there's no one who would actually want to sleep with her."

She had to be referring to me, and she had to know I could hear her as her group of hangers-on laughed at her insult. Stealing my boyfriend hadn't dimmed Amanda's hate for me one bit, though I still had no idea what I'd done to earn her enmity. We were polar opposites: her with her sleek blonde hair, designer clothes and sorority membership, and me with my frizzy red hair that refused to choose a direction and hand-me-downs from my older sisters. The closest I came to being in a clique was the online chat groups I'd joined with other wannabe authors in the last few weeks.

Amanda and I weren't even in the same league, so why she had decided to make me her personal nemesis, I really couldn't understand. The rest of the world seemed to have figured out I was nobody worth caring about, so why hadn't she gotten the memo?

In my book, my character would have the perfect retort, the perfect put-down that would make Amanda feel foolish while allowing me to walk away with my head held high. In real life, however, I could never think of what to say until several hours later.

Case-in-point: rather than saying anything at that moment, I simply put my head down and slunk the rest of the way out of class. Or, at least, I *tried* to. Not even that went my way. My phone fumbled out of my hands as I passed them, dropping to the linoleum floor with a clatter, and Amanda herself picked it up.

"You wouldn't want to forget this. All your fictional boyfriends live in here."

She tossed it over to me with a smirk as the others laughed again, and my cheeks burned as I finally made it out the door.

By the time I got back to my dorm room, my head swam with new ideas for the villain in my book, not-so-loosely based on Amanda: a capital-B bitch who loved to harass my main character. I hadn't quite figured out her motivation yet, just as I hadn't figured out Amanda's, but I could worry about that later. To start, I simply wanted my readers to hate her as much as I did.

Not that I actually *had* any readers just yet, but that was about to change. My online friends had been pumping me up for days, telling me I was ready, and I had agreed to publish the first ten chapters of my book that night, the night of my 19th birthday.

Ten chapters felt safe. People could get a feel for the characters and the plot, but I could still adjust and tweak things if necessary before I shared more. No one outside my small circle had read any of my writing before, but my fellow authors all promised me it would be okay. It might not be perfect, but better to have an imperfect, published piece than an almost-perfect book sitting on my computer that nobody besides me ever read.

Before I could get to that, a few emails needed my attention, mostly from my family wishing me a happy birthday. When they asked about my plans for the evening, I lied. I said I'd be going out with friends, but my night actually looked like every other night since Blaine and I broke up: sitting home alone and escaping into the fantasy world I had created in my head.

Real-life men sucked. The men in my book were so much better, and soon, hopefully, the rest of the world would fall in love with them too.

After rereading my chapters another five times, checking for typos and agonizing over my word choice, I finally did it. With my heart pounding, I pressed the 'publish' button... and immediately closed my laptop and got ready for bed so I wouldn't be tempted to change my mind.

A new year of my life had begun, and with it, my new life as someone who actually mattered. As I drifted off to sleep, I couldn't help feeling that my whole life was about to change.

As soon as I woke up thanks to the winter sun streaming in the thin curtains of my dorm window, I grabbed my phone from my bedside table. A few more belated birthday wishes had come in, but that wasn't what caught my eye. Mixed in with them, I found a message from one of my online friends:

Don't freak out, but Melissass made a post about your story last night.

Don't freak out? Melissass was the pen name of one of the most popular authors on the online platform where I'd posted my book's opening the night before. How on earth had my little story got her attention? I had no idea, but with a following as huge as hers, if she liked my book and told her followers to read it, my dream of having people know my name might actually have a chance of coming true. My heart immediately kicked into a completely different gear, sending excitement racing through my veins as I pinched myself to make sure I had actually woken up.

"Ow!"

The pinch hurt, so I took that as a good sign.

My friend's message went on, but the words swam together before my eyes, making it impossible to focus. I needed to see Melissass' post before my heart beat right out of my chest.

Since I already followed her on every social media channel imaginable, it didn't take long to find, especially since she even included a picture of the cover I'd spent a week making. My face didn't know what to do with itself as my lips twitched, my eyes watered and my eyebrows got a complete workout.

Taking a deep breath to keep calm, I started to read.

For any aspiring authors out there looking for a quick cheat sheet of all the things **not** *to do in your book, take a look at this.*

Dread immediately washed over me, its cold tentacles reaching into every part of me, chilling me to the bone and turning my stomach to ice. Blinking a few times to make sure I could see correctly, I reread the first sentence, but unfortunately, I'd read it right the first time. She meant it exactly how it sounded.

Her post went on to highlight all the things I'd done wrong. From starting the book with my main character waking from a dream to jumping into the fantasy world without enough context, from 'white room syndrome' to clunky dialogue, nothing went unscathed.

She ended the post with a half-hearted qualifier: *I don't want to single out this one author in particular, but I get asked a lot about how to write popular books, and sometimes it's easier to point out what not to do. So, here you go.*

Though I knew I shouldn't, I glanced through the comments anyway. It didn't feel like things could get any worse, so what harm would it do?

Does anyone understand why any of the characters are doing anything they're doing? Just wondering because I don't think the author does.

When is the plot actually going to make sense?

An immature heroine who does immature things with a bunch of immature heroes who all immediately adore her for no reason. The worst kind of self-insert.

When would I learn? It could *always* get worse.

Putting my phone back down, I curled up into the fetal position and pulled the covers over my head as tears of bitter disappointment stung my eyes, all my feelings of rejection and loneliness mingling together and weaving a whole new tapestry of sadness.

An average middle child from an average middle-class family, going to an average college with a B- average, absolutely nothing about me felt special. When I arrived at the dorm at the beginning of September, I honestly tried to fit in. In high school, I'd been teased as the awkward bookworm, but I figured there would be others like me at college. I just needed to find my people, everyone said so, but instead, I found Amanda, who took an instant and intense dislike to me.

Maybe that was why I'd got so caught up in the idea of writing this book, because the Tanith in my book wasn't average at all. She seemed that way at the start, but only until she ended up in the alternate reality where people started to appreciate her true value. She got cheated on too, but she didn't sit around crying about it or feeling sorry for herself. She got right back on the horse - or centaur, in her case - and a few other men besides.

My book had been the only thing making me feel like my life hadn't completely gone adrift, and with that dream knocked out from under me, all the other pain and loneliness found its way back in too. My tears were for my book, but for Blaine too, and every sad, lonely minute I'd spent feeling like I didn't belong.

Spending the rest of the day curled up under the covers and pretending the rest of the world didn't exist sounded like a really good plan, but unfortunately, someone had other ideas, which they made clear by knocking loudly on my door.

With a frown, I poked my head out from the covers. No one *ever* came to my dorm room to visit. They must have the wrong door, so I decided to pull the covers back up and ignore it.

The knock came again a moment later, followed by a deep, male voice. "Tanith?"

Who on earth could that be? No other girls on the floor shared my name, so the stranger had to be looking for me, as unlikely as it seemed.

Still in my pajamas, with my hair a mess and no makeup on my tear-streaked face, I couldn't have looked like more of a disaster. "Give me a minute," I called back as I hurried out of bed, shoving my phone into the pocket of my pajama pants.

"I might not have a minute."

The muffled voice on the other side sounded rather desperate, and I frowned again. What did *that* mean?

With time of the essence, I ran my fingers through my frizzy red hair and crept over to the door, opening it just a crack to reveal as little of myself as possible.

As soon as I did, my jaw nearly hit the floor.

The man on the other side had to be one of the most handsome men I had ever seen in my life. He looked a little like the grad student in my history class, the one I had a slight crush on and had written into my book as one of the love interests for my main character, except that he looked even better. Bright, green eyes shone from beneath his thick, dark eyebrows, and thick, dark, glossy hair. Red, full lips drew my attention to his mouth, but I quickly raised my gaze again, trying to slow my racing heart.

From crying one second to my body throbbing with lust the next, I would give myself a heart attack with these kinds of mood swings.

"Yes?" I asked when he simply stood there, staring at me in almost as much wonder as I looked at him.

"I'm sorry." He shook his head, his hair flopping back into place perfectly when he stopped. The long, tan trench coat he wore made him look like a spy from a black-and-white movie, elegant and timeless. "You're just... more beautiful than I imagined."

Immediately, my back went up. No one had ever said anything like that to me, and in my present state, it sounded like a cruel joke, or at least some kind of set-up. "Did Amanda put you up to this?"

"Who?" Confusion darkened his expression before he shook his head again. "No, there's no time. You have to come with me."

"Go with you? Where?" I had no idea who the man was or how he knew me, but no matter how good-looking he might be, I would not be going anywhere with him. I'd read enough horror stories to know how *that* scenario ended.

"There," he answered simply, pointing down the hall. Tentatively, I opened the door far enough that I could stick my head out and turned to look in the direction he pointed.

At the end of the hall, past all the other identical dorm room doors and hovering in the space above the stained grey carpet, sat a shimmering oval of light just like the portal between dimensions in my book.

CHAPTER TWO

An hour earlier

~Cadriel~

The bright sunshine amplified the pounding in my head, as did the hard surface beneath me. A human hangover must feel similar, based on everything I'd heard about them, but I'd never experienced one before and couldn't imagine what brought it on at that moment. Certainly not anything alcoholic. I *never* drank anything alcoholic.

"Where the fuck am I?"

The annoyed groan came from next to me and, squinting against the brightness, I turned my head towards the sound just in time to see my half-brother, Zolgozig, stumbling to his feet. His horns were hidden that day but they would still be there, just beneath the surface.

"Language," I reminded him as I groggily pulled myself up too. Without his horns, we looked an awful lot alike, sharing the same dark hair, green eyes, six-foot height and lean build. Some of our mannerisms even mirrored each other as we both brushed ourselves off.

Zol, however, wore a scowl on his face. "Why the fuck are you here, Cad?"

So much for watching his language, but the bigger question to me was where 'here' might be. "I have no idea. Do you know where we are?"

We both looked around at our surroundings, searching for anything that looked familiar. An unnaturally green meadow stretched out in all directions, and to the east, I could just make out what looked like a small settlement.

"It's not hell," Zol grumbled. "And it's not heaven either, so I guess it's Earth?"

"That doesn't really narrow it down." I gave my wings a stretch, flexing them out since they'd been ruffled by whatever happened to bring me there. Double my height when outstretched, they made an impressive sight, and I would have been proud of them if I allowed myself to feel pride in anything.

"Show-off," my brother muttered.

"You chose to give yours up," I reminded him, flapping the wings lightly until the feathers all lay flat before tucking them in against my back. "But to the question at hand: why have we been brought here?"

Angels didn't just visit Earth for no reason. We had a strict set of rules to follow, and normally, I would have been briefed on my assignment ahead of time. Perhaps it had been an urgent matter. I examined our surroundings once more, looking carefully for any signs or hints I'd missed, but nothing jumped out at me at all.

"You didn't receive any assignment?" I asked Zol when I came up empty.

"I don't get 'assignments'," he replied, mimicking my tone. "I make deals. And no, I didn't take one on. I'm supposed to be on holiday."

"Holiday from being a demon? So instead of being lazy and self-indulgent, you actually help someone else for a change?"

His eyes rolled. "I'm always helping others. I help them to help themselves. My conversion rate is triple yours and you know it."

The path to temptation had always been an easier sell than the high road. "Well, that town over there looks like the only civilization around. Let's go and see where we are, and maybe we can figure out why we're here at the same time."

Just as Zol had hidden his horns, I cloaked my wings so that to anyone passing by, I looked like any other man, and more like my brother than ever. If it weren't for the way we were dressed, we might have even passed for twins. Zol's cargo boots, black leather pants, half-unbuttoned black shirt and black leather jacket smacked of rebellion. I could have sworn he even had eyeliner on. Meanwhile, I wore a white shirt, tan khakis, and sturdy, sensible walking shoes, along with my tan trench coat, as usual for my earthly visits.

The only thing missing was my purpose in being there.

The warm sun and light breeze felt pleasant and peaceful as we walked through the tall grass. Usually, I got sent to slums or grimy, downtown streets, places where people were desperately in need of help rather than this type of idyllic setting.

Zol kept quiet as we walked, obviously as confused as me about what we were doing there, and especially what we were doing there together. We'd been sent to the same places before, him by his superiors and me by mine, but we always knew why and what we were meant to do. It had been a very long time since we'd just 'hung out', as the humans called it.

Not since he fell.

Once upon a time, we were close, but he chose his path and I chose mine, and since then, we were hardly better than strangers. Some days, we were enemies. That day, I didn't know for sure yet.

"Cad?" Zol's surprised tone of voice pulled me out of my thoughts and I looked over at him curiously.

"Yes?"

"I don't think this is Earth."

He stared straight ahead as he said it, and I turned to follow his gaze, my eyes widening as I did. The town in front of us had started to come into view, and as Zol suggested, it didn't resemble any town I'd ever seen before. The buildings were all white boxes, square and squat, and the people... well, that was just it. They *weren't* people. Not humans, anyway. Magical creatures of all kinds sat around, creatures that had long since gone extinct or ones that had never existed as far as I knew, at least not on Earth.

"What the hell?" The words were out of my mouth before I realized what I'd said, and Zol shot me a smirk.

"I thought that was my line."

Some kind of dragon flew overhead as we made our way into town where an argument had broken out between some elves and some fairies. They all looked vaguely similar, the lines of their faces not clearly defined. Even when I squinted, I couldn't tell the difference between them.

"They're minor characters," a voice behind us said, and Zol and I spun around to find an elderly wizard standing there. Tall and thin, he wore a pointy hat, exactly like I would have imagined a wizard to. "They don't matter."

"All of God's creatures matter," I pointed out as Zol rolled his eyes again.

"Well, that confirms my suspicions. I guess you're the angel." He pointed at me before turning to Zol. "And you're the demon. The clothes were a bit of a giveaway too."

"How do you know what we are?" I kept my voice low so we wouldn't be overheard. Revealing our identity on an assignment was a major violation, at least for an angel.

"We've been expecting you," he replied vaguely. "The text predicted it."

"Text?" Zol and I repeated in unison.

The wizard just smiled. "Come and see."

He led us through the streets of identical white buildings, each with a door and two windows, until he reached one in particular and led us inside. The interior looked just as nondescript as outside, the walls white with only a table in the centre of the room.

On the table lay an ancient-looking book.

"This is the story of our creation," he explained. "It's been here as long as I have. It explains everything about our location."

"How long have you been here?" I wondered. It didn't sound like he was a native of this place either.

"Years, I think. I simply woke up here one day with no memory of arriving. It's the same for everyone. The text mentions us all, at least vaguely, but you are almost the last to arrive. Soon, *she* will come here, and then..."

He trailed off and Zol and I leaned forward in anticipation. "Then what?" Zol demanded.

The wizard shrugged. "We don't exactly know. That's where the text ends."

"Let me see it." Picking up the book, I started from the beginning. Not very long, and with many of the details frustratingly vague, it did describe a place very much like the one where we found ourselves.

The wizard was mentioned for the first time near the beginning of the book, arriving in the small town to help its inhabitants protect themselves against the evil witch who lived in the forest to the south.

Only two pages from the end, it described the arrival of an angel and demon.

The last page mentioned the arrival of a girl, a red-headed young woman by the name of Tanith who would save the world from imminent destruction.

"Destruction?" I looked back up at the wizard in alarm. "What kind of destruction?"

He shrugged again. "I don't know. Though the text mentions the witch, we've never seen her. If she's planning something, I don't know what it is."

"Why haven't you gone to find her?" Zol asked. He'd been reading over my shoulder, taking it all in with me. "If you knew she was going to cause trouble, you could have eliminated her already."

"Or tried to show her a better path," I countered. "Perhaps she simply needs acceptance or friendship."

"We've tried, but we can't get to the forest. No matter how far we walk, it never gets any closer. The boundaries of this place seem fixed and set. None of us know how we got here, and none of us can leave."

I didn't like the sounds of that at all, but one thing seemed clear: we needed to find this Tanith. If imminent suffering lay on the horizon for the town, stopping it would be my duty. Perhaps that explained why I'd been sent there.

Quickly, I reread the final few paragraphs. "It says the angel, which is me, is meant to bring Tanith here. How would I do that?"

"There's a portal that appears," the wizard explained. "It opened over the meadow just before you two fell in. People only come in the portals though, they never go out."

Zol and I exchanged glances. "Have you ever heard of anything like this?" I asked him and he shook his head. In the movement, I could see the bumps of his horns starting to poke through, telling me that he felt as uncertain as I did about the whole situation. Fear made them come out, whether he wanted them to or not.

At that moment, we only had questions, but based on the text, it seemed that Tanith should have the answers.

"Where do I find the portal?" I asked the wizard.

"It will find you," he answered enigmatically, and no sooner had the words come out of his mouth than a flash of light appeared next to us, creating what seemed to be a doorway between our location and another. I glanced over at the wizard and Zol, both of whom gestured to the portal in encouragement.

"Better you than me," Zol said, but though he tried to play it cool, he didn't fool me. He felt just as confused as I did.

What choice did I have? Nodding at them both, I stepped through the boundary, finding myself in a long hallway. Identical doors stretched ahead of me on either side, and I had no idea which one to try until I remembered that the last page of the book, the one that said I would go to find Tanith, was page 24. A door with the number 24 in brass numbers sat just ahead on my left, so I went to that one and knocked on it. When no one answered, I called out Tanith's name, hoping I had the right place.

A moment later, the door opened just a crack, and my breath instantly caught in my throat.

Through the practice of long centuries of self-denial, I'd become mostly immune to the beauty of humans. They were all beautiful in their own way, but I appreciated it as someone might appreciate a work of art, something to be admired from a distance but not engaged with in any sort of visceral way. However, at that moment, something inside me pulled me towards Tanith in a way I had never experienced before. She felt both familiar to me and altogether new at the same time.

For a moment, I could only stare at her in surprise, but eventually, I forced myself to remember what I had gone there for.

When she asked if Amanda put me 'up to this', I had no idea what she meant. What I did know was that the destruction mentioned in the text would begin soon and she needed to come with me to stop it, even though I had no idea what 'it' was or how to prevent it.

When I pointed at the portal where we needed to go, the one that remained open in the hallway waiting for our return, Tanith stared at it for a moment before turning back to me, her eyes wide with shock.

"It... can't be. This isn't... I don't... who are you?"

"My name is Cadriel," I introduced myself, holding out my hand to her. In her warm cotton pajamas, fresh-faced and wide-eyed, she looked even more appealing than before. "I'm so pleased to meet..."

I didn't get a chance to finish my sentence before she fainted straight into my arms.

~Zolgozig~

As Cadriel stepped through the portal, leaving me alone in the bizarre town we'd somehow ended up in, I shot the wizard a wary glance. I'd seen a lot of weird shit in my time, but this place had to be right up there at the top of the list. "What's your deal?"

"My 'deal'? I don't consort with your kind." The wizard looked down his nose at me just like Cad always did, and so many others, as though being a demon made me less than them. At the end of the day, I simply did my job, like everyone else. Just because I had more fun doing it shouldn't make them so jealous. Most humans were destined for hell anyway; I just helped them enjoy the ride.

"Not that kind of deal. I mean: where do you come from? You said you don't know how you ended up here, so where were you before?"

His posture relaxed as I explained my question. Everyone always liked to talk about themselves, it didn't matter what kind of creature they were. "I lived in the realm of Lautherol."

"Never heard of it."

"I'm not surprised," the wizard answered with a little too much pride. "It's an alternate dimension that my kind created a few thousand years ago when humans became too numerous. We exist in the same space they do, but they're completely unaware of us."

"So, it's on Earth?" I still didn't really get it.

"It's part of the same reality, much like your heaven and hell are, but visible only to those who know about it. It's home to many different kinds of magical creatures: the fae, the elves, the unicorns. Sometimes, one will break through and be seen by humans, but generally, we exist outside their experience."

That really didn't clear things up, but I'd lost interest anyway. "Do the other creatures out there all come from this Lath place too?"

"Lautherol," he repeated, enunciating it slowly, as if I cared. "Some of them do, but others, I've never seen before. Creatures like the merman, for example."

Merman? Now, *that* sounded interesting. "I thought those were a legend. Are there women too?"

A little mermaid sex could spice this adventure up considerably. I would take a man, certainly, but women were my preference if I got my pick.

The wizard gave me an unimpressed look. "I've only seen the man. None of us are here for a vacation."

"You don't know why we're here," I reminded him. "This book certainly doesn't say why."

As I picked it back up off the table and flipped through the pages roughly, the wizard squealed, running forward to grab it from my hands. "Don't manhandle it. Without it, this place might cease to exist at all, and then what happens to all of us?"

I had no idea and wasn't entirely sure I cared about that either, but before I could answer, Cadriel called out to me through the portal. "Zol? I need some help."

Help wasn't usually something I gave freely, but in this case, I wanted to move this whole thing along so I could get back to my *actual* vacation. Stepping closer to the portal, I could see Cad on the other side, holding a woman bridal-style in his arms.

"Is that her?"

He nodded, looking down at her with a soft smile. "Yes, but she's unconscious."

I didn't see what he needed me for. "What's the problem?"

He shot me an exasperated look. "I can't just take her from her home without her consent."

With an irritated sigh of my own, I stepped through the portal after him. "Fine. I'll do it then."

He tried to turn away from me, still cradling the human woman in his arms. "That's not what I meant."

"What do you want me to do, then? Stand here and keep you company until she wakes up? We don't know how much time we have or how long that damn portal's going to stay open for."

Without giving him a chance to protest further, I took the girl from him, pulling her into my arms instead. He let go, more out of concern for her than because of any show of strength on my part, and trailed after me back towards the portal, which seemed to be closing in front of us.

"Look, I was right. Hurry." I picked up my pace, stepping through the portal with the sleeping woman in my arms with Cadriel right behind me. As soon as we were back in the white room with the wizard, the opening disappeared, as if it had never been there at all. "That was close."

As soon as I said the words, a new thought occurred to me, and I groaned out loud.

"Wait. Was that Earth?"

"I think so," Cadriel answered, stepping around me to look at the woman again. "Why?"

Was he serious? "Because we could have just stayed there! We didn't have to come back here at all."

Cadriel didn't see it that way. "But the others here will die without Tanith's help."

"We don't know that," I argued. He'd bought into the whole scenario way too quickly. It all sounded like bullshit to me. "We don't know anything about any of it. And even if they do die, it's not our responsibility."

No matter what I said, we couldn't do anything about it since the portal had disappeared. Exhaling in frustration, I took a proper look at the woman in my arms for the first time. She wore some kind of cat pajamas, completely out of place not only there, but anywhere. Though her red hair partly obscured my view, she had a fresh-faced, innocent quality that appealed to the naughty side of me. If we were going to be stuck there for much longer, she might prove a useful distraction.

"Put her down," Cadriel instructed. "And stop looking at her like that."

"Like what? Like a man with a working cock?"

Cadriel's jaw clenched. "Just because I don't use mine the way you do doesn't mean it doesn't work. Let her go."

"Where am I supposed to put her?" The table remained the only piece of furniture in the room.

"Give her back to me, then." He held out his arms and I raised my eyebrows, my horns starting to poke at my forehead as I put the pieces together, and a wicked smile spread across my face.

"You *like* her, don't you?"

"I just met her," he demurred, which didn't answer the question.

"That doesn't matter. The text said the angel would fall in love with Tanith at first sight."

I hadn't put too much stock in that line since Cadriel had never loved a woman, not in that way. He loved 'all God's creatures', as he put it, but real, romantic love? He'd never felt that before.

However, it appeared I'd been mistaken. He actually *did* feel something towards her, I could have sworn it from the protective, almost possessive way he looked at her.

"And it said the demon would have lustful desires towards her," he reminded me, his eyes narrowing in challenge. "I'm asking you for the last time, Zol: give her to me."

We stood face-to-face, neither willing to back down, until Tanith began to stir in my arms and Cad immediately took a step back, giving her some space.

"What the..."

Her eyes opened groggily, blinking as she tried to focus her vision. As soon as she had, her eyes darted back and forth between me and Cad for a moment, and soon, she began to scream.

~Tanith~

The two men staring down at me both winced as the scream came out of my mouth. When I tried to back away, I realized one of them was actually holding me, and that only made me shriek louder as I writhed and wriggled in his arms, trying to get away.

"Tanith, it's okay, no one's going to hurt you." The man who had been at my door held out his hands to try to soothe me, but I had passed the point of being soothed. Did he kidnap me? Where was I and why had he brought me there? This couldn't be happening!

The other one looked decidedly less comforting as he grimaced, tightening his grip around me. "Just calm down. Stop struggling, for fuck's sake!"

Not likely. Whatever they had in mind, I wasn't going down without a fight. I'd taken some self-defense classes when I started college and I tried to remember what I'd learned as I struggled harder, still screaming, hoping someone might hear and come to my aid. Finally, more through luck than any kind of skill, I managed to elbow the man holding me directly in the groin, and he dropped to his knees, letting me go. My backside hit the ground hard, temporarily cutting off my scream as my teeth clattered and I bit into my tongue.

Fuck, that really hurt.

"God damn it!" the man in black growled, also in pain. "I did not sign up for this."

Did he expect me to feel sorry for him? Despite my sore tongue, I opened my mouth to scream again, but the man in the tan coat held out his hands, and almost instantly, a feeling of calm washed over me. All the will to fight left my body as I sank into a deep pool of contentment and peace, unlike anything I'd ever known before. Even my tongue stopped hurting.

"Why didn't you just do that in the first place before she went all nutcracker?" the man in black grumbled, wincing as he got back to his feet, leaving me on the ground.

"It's a last resort," the other man told him. "Free will is important, and she's entitled to freak out a little bit. She's afraid, Zol, just like you are, even if you won't admit it."

Zol? My eyes went wide again as I stared up at the man in black. He did look an awful lot like the first man, now that I really stopped to take a look at him, and that man had told me his name was Cadriel...

But it *couldn't* be. Cadriel and Zolgozig were characters in my book. I made them up. They did *not* exist, and they most certainly could not be standing there arguing about the best way to calm someone having a panic attack.

"Allow me, Miss Tanith." A new voice spoke up from behind me, and I turned my head enough to get a view of the twinkling blue eyes, silvery hair and pointy grey hat that could only belong to one man. Or at least, only one who would be hanging out with Cad and Zol.

"Athar?"

He smiled at me in delight. "You already know me! How wonderful."

He bent down to offer me his arm at the same time that both Cadriel and Zolgozig came forward too, each of them stretching out their hand at me as well as they tried to elbow each other out of the way, and I immediately shrank back.

"Back off, both of you," Athar scolded them. "Arriving here is disorienting, you should know that better than anyone. Give her a minute to adjust."

"Here?" I repeated, taking Athar's arm as the other two men reluctantly took a step back. I hauled myself shakily to my feet and took a quick look around, which revealed absolutely nothing. The walls were white, the floor and ceiling too, and the only furniture was a small table with a book on it. "Where is this?"

"We don't know its name," Athar told me apologetically. "Everything we do know is written in this book."

He picked up the book from the table and handed it to me almost reverently. I glanced over at Cadriel and Zolgozig, one of them smiling at me and the other scowling, a perfect contrast of light and dark, before I turned my full attention to the book, flipping open to the first page.

It was always summer in the small town by the meadow...

The panic that Cadriel had somehow managed to quell came roaring back as I slammed the book shut and looked up at them all, my eyes so wide that they began to water. "Okay, whatever game this is, it really isn't funny. Who are you all, really?"

"What's wrong?" Cadriel asked, his eyebrows drawn in concern above his bright, green eyes.

How did I answer that? Absolutely nothing made sense.

"This is my book," I started, holding up the text for them. "I wrote this. No one saw it before last night. How is it here, in print? How did you have time to get costumes and build this soundstage or whatever this place is, and most of all, why? Why are you doing this?"

"We aren't doing anything." He stepped towards me, placing his hand gently on my forehead, and again, my anxiety melted away. I could get used to that, but *how* was he doing it? People didn't have those kinds of abilities in real life. It had to be a dream, the most elaborate, detailed dream I had ever had. "Tanith, Zol and I just arrived here ourselves. We know no more than you do. I came to find you because the book said I was meant to."

That much was true in the context of my book, but there, Cad came and found me in class, not in my dorm room. And he wasn't supposed to find *me* anyway. My character, who didn't actually exist, was the one meant to be found, by another imaginary character.

"Can we skip over the 'this can't really be happening' part?" Zol asked, sounding bored as he adjusted himself in his pants, wincing at the soreness my elbow had caused. "What will convince you? Do you want to see my horns?"

That was a line from my book. Zol used almost exactly those same words to Tanith when she first arrived and found out he was a demon. My eyes flew to his forehead, and, sure enough, two long, curved horns sprouted from just beneath his hairline, just as I'd imagined them. I'd even written about holding onto them while he was on top of me and I needed something to keep my balance while he...

Nope. I shut down that train of thought immediately. I didn't need to make this *any* weirder than it already was.

"Maybe my wings will help?" Cadriel suggested almost bashfully, and he took a step back before two large, white feathery wings grew from his back, flapping out gracefully before folding together again.

If these were special effects, they were very impressive ones, and I couldn't imagine anyone would go to the trouble and expense of putting together such an elaborate charade as a prank. Nobody hated me *that* much, not even Amanda.

Looking around again at the room, the book, and most of all the three men in front of me, I remembered the words of Sherlock Holmes, as written by Arthur Conan Doyle: when you have eliminated the impossible, then whatever's left, no matter how unlikely it seems, must be true.

Which left me with only one conclusion: whether it was all happening in my head, a dream or not, at least for the moment, I had found myself in my character's place, in a very literal self-insert.

Somehow, I'd ended up inside my book.

CHAPTER THREE

~Aiqen~

The portal closing sent a vibration through the air, rippling through my wings and throwing me off balance as I circled the air above the town, trying to get my exercise in the limited space available to me. Those vibrations happened every time someone new arrived, but it had never happened so many times in such quick succession. Something must be up.

Tucking my wings back, I headed for the ground, opening them at the last minute like a parachute to soften my landing. As soon as my feet were on solid ground, I shifted back to my human form. My clothes were still where I'd left them, thankfully. Though it had taken a few days to get my message across, I'd finally convinced the fairies to stop swiping my pants every time I left them behind. Threatening them with my claws seemed to help when asking them nicely hadn't.

Once I had dressed, I headed for the 'library', for lack of a better word. The building that held the book, the building where Athar hung out, was usually the best place to pick up gossip on anything happening in the town. I didn't know any more than anyone else about where we all were. I'd been there for a week and so far, I'd tried to make the most of it. A very important competition was coming up at home, one that would determine my whole future, so the time to train, uninterrupted, had been useful and I did my best to simply appreciate it.

After a week, though, I was ready to go home, so when I stepped over the threshold into the library, I hoped there would be some good news.

Athar stood there, as I expected, and he had three people I'd never seen before with him: a pair of brothers, if I had to guess, one in light colours and the other dark, and a red-haired woman wearing the strangest clothes I'd ever seen. They seemed to have pictures of small, furry animals all over them.

The men were both good-looking, though not as good-looking as me, I quickly assessed. With my golden blond hair, blue eyes, six-foot-five frame and hardened muscles, few had matched me in appearance at home, and so far, I hadn't found my equal in this new place yet either.

"What's going on?"

All four people in the room turned to look at me, the three newcomers with curiosity, and Athar with an air of weariness.

The feeling was mutual.

"You're not needed here, Aiqen," he tried to tell me. "We've got it under control."

"There's something that needs to be controlled?" He always tried to box me out, not recognizing what had been obvious to me the first time I read through the book he guarded so religiously: I was the hero of the story. Excluding me from the action made no sense.

"Aiqen?" The woman repeated my name as she moved closer to me, staring at me curiously. "You're Aiqen?"

I bowed low to her as my princely manners dictated. "At your service, my lady. May I ask your name?"

She smiled as I raised my head again. "I'm Tanith."

Excitement raced through my veins as understanding set in. This was the woman we'd been waiting for, which meant the real adventure could finally begin.

A mere bow wasn't enough for a woman of such importance. I fell to one knee instead, crossing my arm across my chest. "Lady Tanith, I pledge myself to assist you however I can. Anything you require of me, you need only ask."

The man in black snorted, turning to the other one next to him. "If he doesn't knock off all this chivalrous crap, I'll show him what achin' really means."

"No violence, Zol," the other man replied, shaking his head as he stepped forward to offer me his hand. "I'm Cadriel. You're the dragon we saw outside?"

"Wyvern," I corrected, getting back to my feet and shaking his hand firmly. I recognized his name from the book. "You're the angel, then. And that must make you..."

The man in the black didn't let me finish. "Zolgozig. The demon, the black sheep. You can call me Zol. What the hell's a wyvern?"

"We are... similar to dragons," I admitted. It irked me that people always seemed to have heard of dragons but not my own kind. "Dragons have four legs in their animal form, plus their wings, while wyvern have two."

"So, dragons are better," Zol summarized.

"Certainly not." I couldn't let his pithy conclusion influence Tanith's opinion of me or besmirch my whole species. "Dragons are brutes. Wyverns are clever. Rather than breathing fire, we..."

"You can't breathe fire either?" Zol interrupted, shooting Cadriel an unimpressed look. "What use are you then?"

"Gentlemen." Athar interrupted before I could defend myself any further. "Since Aiqen is already here, we should make the rest of the introductions as soon as possible. Tanith is meant to meet all of you before the destruction begins."

"Do you know what destruction we face, my lady?" The little human woman's petite stature and frailty only made me feel more protective of her. I had sworn her my oath and I would protect her, no matter what dangers we might encounter.

Still, knowing what they were in advance would be helpful.

"Well... yes," she replied. "I mean, I know what happens next in my book, so if all of this is the way I wrote it..."

"You wrote it?" She'd lost me, and it didn't help that she looked confused as well.

"Go get the others," Athar instructed. "Make yourself useful, Aiqen. Bring Tymanus and Leith here so Tanith can tell us all what she knows."

Although it felt like he just wanted to get rid of me, he also had a point. The five of us: me, the angel and demon, and the two men Athar just mentioned were the ones specifically named in the book, the ones meant to help Tanith stop whatever destruction was about to be visited upon this unusual place, so bringing them there would get us closer to that goal.

Tymanus wasn't a problem. I knew exactly where he'd be: in the little pub at the edge of town, the only building that wasn't simply white inside. It actually had some character, and the centaur had taken up residence there, keeping everyone's spirits up as they came to drown their sorrows or simply pass the time in this bizarre limbo we'd all fallen into. Most people seemed to find him funny, but his appeal eluded me.

"Tymanus!" I called out to him when I opened the door, figuring that would be the most efficient way of getting his attention, and a groan went up around the room. Usually, when I came to the pub, I was looking for anyone willing to train with me. It hadn't made me particularly popular. "Are you here?"

"That depends," came his reply from the back of the room. "If you're here to have a drink and chat, then I'm here. If you want someone to ride, I haven't seen him."

"I already apologized for that." We didn't have centaurs where I came from, and I hadn't realized asking to ride him would be an insult. I had no problem taking passengers in my animal form, and Tymanus was big and strong. He certainly would have been able to carry me. His upper body strength probably matched my own, and his horse half was even stronger. Both halves were the same deep brown colour, making it nearly impossible to tell where man ended and horse began. "Come. Athar wants you."

"Tell him you couldn't find me," Ty suggested. "Tell him the witch ate me."

The others all laughed with their blurry mouths, some more nervously than others. No one knew what the witch wanted with us. "It's actually about the witch," I told him, walking straight over to his table and lowering my voice so we wouldn't be overheard. "Tanith has arrived."

"Well, why didn't you say so?" He immediately got to his four feet, standing up from the low table the pub's landlord had set up for him to recline on. His usual grin fell away as he took on a more serious expression. "Maybe we can finally find out what all of this is about."

I followed him back outside, but when he headed to the library, I stopped him. "Wait. We need Leith as well."

Ty gave me a suspicious look. "You aren't just bringing me to help carry him, are you?"

"No, Athar asked for you both. But, to be honest, I got you first so you can help me carry him."

"I should have guessed." With a sigh, Ty turned towards the small house at the edge of town where the merman would be. It had a small pond in the backyard, so when Leith had appeared in the middle of town from the portal three days ago, choking on the air, the town's inhabitants quickly took him to the small pond where he had remained ever since. "How are we meant to keep him alive? Why don't we just have the meeting at the pond?"

The merman needed water to breathe, but I had come up with a solution for that. "If you carry him, I'll worry about the water."

Leith had a small group of people with him when we arrived. Endlessly cheerful, the merman seemed to attract people, especially women, even if there was very little going on between his ears. It might have something to do with his looks, I had to admit. Though I was more classically handsome, Leith did have a certain appeal. His bronzed skin shone beneath the sun, his brown hair longer than mine, and his eyes a pale shade of green.

"Athar wants you," I announced, just as I had to Ty, but unlike him, Leith's face lit up in anticipation.

"That sounds exciting! How are we going to... oh!"

He didn't get to finish asking his question before I reached into the water and lifted him out, handing him to Ty.

"Oh, okay, but I can't stay out too long..." Leith tried to remind us, but Ty was already on the move. Left behind, I went to the hedge behind the house where I had stored the small, portable container I'd crafted the other day in anticipation of a moment just like this. Dipping it in the pond, I filled it with a small layer of water, enough to help Leith breathe. Once satisfied, I followed the centaur back to the library, eager to hear exactly what Tanith had to say.

~Tanith~

"How long is this no-violence rule of yours going to last?" Zol asked Cadriel once Aiqen had left. "I don't think I can be around that guy more than a few minutes without punching him in the face."

Some of the complaints about my book immediately popped back into my head, making me wince. In Melissass' criticism and the comments from her followers, there had been a lot of negativity about Aiqen. Personally, I found his conviction endearing, and his god-like good looks didn't hurt. I almost forgot how to breathe when I saw him in person. Cadriel and Zolgozig were good-looking, no question, but Aiqen was *exactly* my type, at least physically. He looked a lot like my ex-boyfriend, Blaine, if I were being honest, although Aiqen looked even better.

In the book, Aiqen was the last of the men to fall for Tanith, simply because his focus remained so firmly on the task of keeping the world safe. He put duty first, which, to me, seemed rather heroic.

However, it seemed others found him arrogant and a little overbearing, including Zol, even though they'd only just met.

"He hasn't done anything to you," Cadriel answered his half-brother mildly. "Don't let him bother you. Now, let's do something productive while we wait. We should have somewhere to sit and talk."

We all looked around again at the empty room. Where were the tables and couches I imagined in the wizard's house? The characters all looked very close to how I pictured them, so why didn't the room? With a frown, I opened the book to where the wizard's house was first mentioned, and to my frustration, I realized just how little I had actually described it.

Athar could frequently be found at his table, looking over his favourite book.

That was literally all it said and a dissatisfied sigh slipped through my lips. Maybe those criticisms about 'white room syndrome' were valid after all. I could see it so clearly in my head but I hadn't written it down in enough detail to share that vision with my readers. If nothing else came from this incredibly bizarre experience, maybe I would pick up some writing tips?

As soon as that thought crossed my mind, I realized I had my phone with me. I'd shoved it in my pocket when I answered the door, and I quickly fished it out.

"Wait, you've got a phone?" Zol asked in disbelief. "Why didn't you say so? We can call for help."

"Who exactly are you going to call?" Cadriel asked. "And where would you tell them to come?"

"There's no signal anyway," I told them both, holding it up in the air to see if I could find anything but the setting didn't change. "Besides, I just wanted to make a note."

While they continued to argue, I quickly went into my book and added a few extra lines to the scene where Athar's home was first described.

Long couches lined the walls, their cushions deep and soft and red. In the centre of the room were two tables, one where the wizard did his reading, and a larger one with chairs that he used to meet with guests. Despite it being summer, a small fire burned in the stone fireplace, but the breeze through the open windows kept the house cool and comfortable anyway.

"What the hell?" Zol's favourite expression echoed around the room and I glanced up to see what had brought it on. As soon as I did, my mouth dropped open in disbelief.

The room was now full of furniture, exactly how I'd described it.

You've got to be kidding me.

I looked back down at the phone in my hand and back up again, catching Cadriel's eye as I did so. "Did you do this?" he asked, gesturing to the room around us.

"I think so?" I had no other explanation. One minute, it hadn't been there, and the next, it was. The only thing that had changed was that I'd added a few lines to my book.

Athar looked around curiously, inspecting his new belongings. "Not bad," he said appreciatively. "Although blue is more my colour than red."

Could I? Only one way to find out, so I moved my cursor back to where I'd described the couches as red, and changed the word to blue instead. By the time I looked back up, their colour had changed.

No fucking way.

"Perfect!" Athar exclaimed in delight. "This is wonderful magic."

It certainly felt like magic. How could this be happening? How could *any* of this be happening?

"Your phone can control this world?" Cadriel asked, connecting the dots quickly, his green eyes watching me intently and with no small degree of admiration.

"It seems that way. At least physically." Whether it would extend to controlling people or actions, I had no idea.

"That could come in very handy," he said, which seemed like a huge understatement. However, since I hadn't seen a charger or any kind of electrical source since getting here, and I certainly hadn't described any in my book, I better not waste the power I had left. For the time being, I turned my phone off and put it back in my pocket.

Now that we had a place to sit, we all moved over to the large rectangular table, but no sooner had we sat than a loud pounding at the door made us all jump.

"I'll get it," Cadriel offered. In a moment, he had the door open, and a large brown centaur entered the room, carrying a merman with a shiny blue tail in his arms.

"Ty! Leith!" I jumped to my feet to greet them both with a warm smile on my face. With the shock beginning to wear off, the thrill of getting to meet my characters face-to-face was taking over, and those two had a special place in my heart. Well, they all did, to be honest, other than the witch, but each of these men were particularly endearing in their own way, and they looked just as I'd imagined them.

Tymanus' height and bulk could be intimidating at first sight. With his long horse's legs, he stood almost seven feet tall. His dark hair was cut short and he had a number of tattoos on his human half and a brand on his horse end. Even the normally cocksure Zol kept his mouth shut as he looked Ty over, not wanting to get on the centaur's bad side. He didn't know, like I did, that Ty was a sweetheart and a joker at heart.

Meanwhile, Leith was the innocent one of the bunch, an endless ray of sunshine no matter how bad things got. He'd never left the ocean before, so everything he saw intrigued and excited him. I was no exception.

"What beautiful hair you have!" he croaked, reaching out to try to touch it. "It's like the copper wire Ty showed me."

Zol snorted, but I knew Leith meant it as a compliment. He didn't have a mean bone in his body, and besides, I wrote that line in my book. At that moment, I had other worries anyway.

"What's wrong with your voice?" I asked the merman in concern. Although he looked just like the Leith I imagined with his tanned skin, pale green eyes and childlike delight, he didn't sound like him.

"He needs water to breathe," Ty explained, his hooves clopping loudly on the wooden floor as he stepped into the room and placed Leith down gently onto one of the couches. "Aiqen is supposed to be bringing something."

Sure enough, Aiqen appeared right behind him with a round wooden container, similar to a kiddie pool, filled with a layer of water. However, as soon as he reached the door, he realized he'd forgotten something in his calculations: the pool was too wide. It wouldn't fit through the door.

"Maybe if I…" He started to tilt the pool to one side, but naturally, the water began to spill out.

"Wait, stop!" Cadriel called out and went outside to try to help.

My mind raced as I watched them. I hadn't ever considered in my book how a merman would breathe outside of the water, or how he would get around either. Having Ty carry him everywhere wouldn't be particularly efficient. And Leith did have lungs in his human half, so he *should* be able to breathe. I must not have explained it properly.

But perhaps it wasn't too late. Grabbing my phone back from my pocket, I revisited the page where Leith first came to the town and added a few more lines.

Although he'd never been out of the ocean before, Leith's parents had prepared him for it. They made sure he could survive using only his lungs when he couldn't use his gills, and they taught him how to pull his tail back to reveal the human legs beneath. He hadn't had much practice walking on them yet, but that would be sure to change soon.

As soon as I hit 'save', I looked back up at Leith, and sure enough, his tail had receded. It still covered his midsection, stopping mid-thigh so he wasn't completely naked. Beneath that were actual thighs, knees, calves and feet, and Leith looked down at them in awe, wiggling his new toes.

"Oh my gosh! Look! I have feet!" His voice sounded stronger, much more as it should, and he took a deep breath. "And I can breathe! This is wonderful!"

I could almost see the exclamation marks after every sentence and his enthusiasm seemed to bubble inside me too, making me grin. As the other men all gathered around to examine the changes in him, Cadriel came over to me, looking again at the phone in my hand.

"You did this?"

I nodded truthfully. He still looked impressed, but also a little concerned. "You'll need to be careful not to overuse this power. Playing God can cause trouble, and we wouldn't want that phone to fall into the wrong hands."

He made a very good point. It would be better not to flaunt this particular gift, particularly if the witch had any spies around, so I turned the phone off and returned it to my pocket. "Only when necessary, like helping someone breathe," I promised him, and Cadriel nodded in acceptance.

He turned to the rest of the room, assuming the leadership role that came so naturally to him. "Now that we're all here, let's have a seat. We have a lot to catch up on."

~Tymanus~

When I got up that morning, I expected the day to unfold like pretty much every other day since I arrived in the strange little town, but as everyone took a seat around the table, I could see I'd been mistaken. We had several more new arrivals, and Athar and Aiqen were almost vibrating with excitement. Something big had happened.

There was no easy way for me to sit in the chairs designed for bipeds, so I pulled the chair away from the end of the table and sat down on the floor instead, tucking my four legs beneath me. Even that way, I was still roughly the same height as the men that were sitting.

The little human woman watched me with concern. "Are you comfortable, Ty?"

How she knew me, I wasn't sure, but I liked the fact that she didn't seem to be afraid of me like so many others were when they first met me. Her warm expression made a welcome change.

"I'm fine," I assured her. "Not everyone can be their own chair, it's a special skill I have."

Though she smiled, apprehension still lingered in her eyes. "Do you need some kind of cushion? I can..."

She went to pull something from her pocket, but the man next to her, the dark-haired man in the light clothes, placed his hand on her arm gently and shook his head. With a guilty look, she nodded and glanced back at me apologetically.

"I'm fine," I repeated. "Don't worry about me."

I wasn't sure what all that was about, but Athar cleared his throat before I could ask and we all turned to him. He held the book in front of him, the book he claimed told the future and the story of this place, but so far, all I'd heard from anyone was a whole bunch of confusion. No one knew where we were or why. Some people were taking it better than others. Personally, I found it all rather amusing, especially since I had no reason to want to go home anyway.

"Finally, we're all here," Athar announced, looking around the table at each of us in turn. "We all have a part to play to defeat the witch and save this world from destruction, but first, it could be useful for each of us to introduce ourselves. I'll go first."

Of course he would. The wizard loved the sound of his own voice almost as much as Aiqen did. It explained why the two of them rubbed each other the wrong way so much: they were just as self-absorbed as each other.

"My name is Athar, as you all know. I'm from the realm of Lautherol, the same as Tymanus."

Everyone's eyes darted over to me and I offered them all a rueful smile. "Don't hold that against me."

The man in black snorted in amusement and the human woman smiled again as everyone turned back to Athar.

"I am four hundred and twenty-seven years old and my primary form of magic is in teletransportation. I can move things across distances, and normally I can move things between Lautherol and Earth as well, but I don't appear to be able to move anything in or out of this realm, only within it."

To demonstrate his ability, the book disappeared from his hands and reappeared in mine. Leith began to applaud enthusiastically, until he realized no one else was joining in, and he slowly stopped. Just as quickly, the book disappeared from my grasp and rematerialized back in front of Athar instead.

"Who wants to go next?" Athar asked, and Aiqen immediately raised his hand.

"What a surprise," I muttered under my breath and the man in black shot me another amused look. Though I didn't know who he was yet, I had a feeling he and I might get along.

Aiqen ignored the both of us as he straightened in his seat, addressing the room firmly. "I am Aiqen von Serpia, prince of the western kingdom of the Regal Plane. I am a wyvern, meaning I can shift into my wyvern form and fly. I have already pledged my service to the Lady Tanith and will be honoured to lead us into battle against the witch to free this land from whatever enchantment lies upon it. The sooner we can complete this quest, the better."

"You have somewhere else to be?" I asked sarcastically, but as usual, Aiqen completely missed my tone.

"I do. I am one of 17 princes of my kingdom and in two weeks' time, there will be a competition amongst us to determine who takes my father's throne. I must be there."

"Seventeen? Damn, your parents must have been busy."

The man in black snorted again while Aiqen lifted his head higher, though it shouldn't have been possible. "Wyverns do not give birth to live young. They lay eggs, so it's possible to have many children at once.

I actually have 68 brothers and sisters, but only 17 of us are designated princes."

"So, that makes you number 69?" I wondered out loud, and the man in black laughed, earning him a glare from both Aiqen and the other man in white. Leith laughed too, though, as usual, I suspected he missed the joke. I leaned over to him and gave his shoulder a pat. "I'll explain it to you later."

"Thank you," he whispered back in relief.

"I'm confused," the human woman spoke up, and we all turned to give her our full attention.

"You're not the only one," I promised. "Wyverns have a lot of strange behaviours."

"We are not strange!" Aiqen protested, but the woman shook her head.

"That's not what I mean. I just... I didn't write any of this. I didn't really give you guys a backstory at all. That was one of the criticisms I got, so I don't really understand where all of this is coming from."

The man in white next to her placed his hand on her arm again. "We all had lives before we came here, Tanith. We didn't just come into existence when you showed up."

"Before you came here?" she repeated in confusion.

"Yes. We all came here from somewhere else, just like you did."

"But... I wrote you," she tried to explain. "I made you all up."

That time, we all chuckled. "Look around," I encouraged her. "You're the youngest one here, and you're only a human. How could you have 'made us up'?"

"I don't know," she admitted. "But how could I have written about you if I didn't?"

"We'll get to that," Athar interrupted. "Let's continue the introductions, please. Keep it short, gentlemen."

Leith was next. "I'm Leith and... I have feet!"

Athar put his fingers to his temples as the rest of us smiled. "Yes, we all saw you get feet, Leith. What else can you tell us about yourself? What are your skills?"

The merman thought very hard before coming up blank and shooting me a beseeching look.

"You can swim," I reminded him in a whisper, and his face lit up.

"I can swim!" he announced to the room.

"Good enough." Athar quickly moved on. "Tymanus?"

All eyes in the room came to me. "I'm Tymanus, you can call me Ty. I'm a centaur, as you can see. As for skills, I'm pretty strong. I can run pretty fast if I have to, though I prefer not to most of the time. That's about it."

The man in black introduced himself as Zolgozig and a demon. "My skills lie in helping people get what they want most, even if it's not what's good for them."

The man next to him cleared his throat. "And I'm Cadriel, an angel and Zol's half-brother. We've both been around for a few thousand years. My skills are helping people do what's good for them, even if it's not what they want."

Zol rolled his eyes, and I had to admit I liked the two of them right off the bat. Cadriel was clearly on the straight and narrow, but not as obnoxious about it as Aiqen, while Zol seemed like a lot of fun.

At last, the woman got her turn. "I'm Tanith," she introduced herself. "I'm a human, I guess, and a college student. I started writing a book that somehow has all of you in it, apparently, though I still don't really know how that's possible."

Athar was about to say something else, but as he opened his mouth, the book dropped from his hands, hitting the table with a thud, and he looked down on it in consternation. "That's odd," he muttered almost to himself. "It just got heavier."

He flipped the pages open to the back, and his eyes widened in surprise.

"Look, there's another chapter!"

He began to read out loud: *It took Tanith some time to accept that the town on the other side of the portal was real. Everything seemed so strange and unfamiliar, yet she didn't feel uncomfortable there. Everyone welcomed her kindly, and she soon found herself at ease.*

"That's my next chapter," Tanith interrupted before he could go any further. "It was scheduled to post this morning and I didn't get a chance to cancel it after the negative review."

Her words didn't fully make sense to me, but Cadriel seemed to understand. "More of the story is now written?" he asked, and Tanith nodded. "And you know what will happen next?"

"I do," she agreed, her brow clouding with worry. "Now that I'm here, there's going to be an attack..."

She didn't get to finish before a loud scream echoed from outside and we all immediately headed for the door.

CHAPTER FOUR

~Tanith~

Just when I thought things couldn't get any crazier, a scream from outside made us all jump. Everyone scrambled to their feet, some more gracefully than others as Leith nearly tripped over his new feet, and we all made our way out into the streets.

The little town spread out in front of me just as I'd imagined, except that every building looked exactly like all the others, all white and blank and nondescript. I really *did* need to work on my descriptions, apparently. My fingers itched for my phone, wanting to fix it while I had the thought fresh in my head, but I forced my hand to stay down. We had more immediate concerns.

A small crowd had gathered not far away on the edge of the town and we could hear them all murmuring amongst themselves, the hushed whispers growing louder as we got closer.

"Out of the way," Aiqen ordered, pushing his way through the crowd. "Let me through."

The townspeople reluctantly did as he said, and as they turned to look at us, their blurred, indistinct faces made me recoil involuntarily. Why did they look like that? The men I'd just been speaking to all claimed to have lives and pasts that went far beyond this place, though I didn't understand how that could be possible. But if it were true, if everyone came from somewhere else, including the fairies and the elves and the gnomes that made up most of the background characters, why wouldn't they have fully formed faces?

None of it made any sense to me.

At the centre of the crowd lay a gnome in his red hat and shoes, green pants and yellow shirt, just like the garden gnomes I'd based him on, but this one had an arrow sticking out of his chest with a note attached to it.

I knew exactly what the note was going to say. After all, I'd written it myself.

What I *hadn't* written were the laboured gasps of the stricken gnome, coming from his indistinct face. He wasn't really going to die, was he? The character in my book did, but he hadn't meant anything to me. He wasn't real, not like the man in front of me. I'd killed him off without a second thought.

"Is anyone here a doctor?" Aiqen called out, but the silence that answered him wasn't a surprise to me. I hadn't written a doctor into the book, which had obviously been an oversight.

Eventually, Cadriel stepped forward. "I'm not a doctor, but I have some healing ability," he explained, kneeling next to the gnome on the ground and laying his hand on the man's head. "Stay calm, my friend. We'll do all we can for you."

The gnome immediately stilled, his breathing becoming less intense, and I remembered the calming rush that Cadriel had sent through me. Did the gnome feel it too? Could Cadriel actually heal him, or was he simply bringing him comfort in his final moments?

He looked up at the rest of us with an apologetic look which confirmed my worst fears. "There's nothing I can do. Removing the arrow will cause too much blood loss and we don't have the equipment to do a transfusion."

More terrified murmurs swept through the gathered crowd, and Cadriel whispered what must have been a prayer, keeping his hand on the man's head until his body stilled.

As his life left his body, the gnome's face came into focus, sending another gasp through all of the crowd, including the men next to me. Deep lines creased his face, his lips rough and chapped, and his blue eyes lifeless as they stared up at the sky.

"What does that mean?" I asked Tymanus, who happened to be standing next to me.

"I'm not sure," he admitted, with no hint of his usual smile on his face. "But I suspect that's his real face. The blurriness before must have been an illusion caused by this place."

So... the gnome had been a real person from another place, brought there because of my book, and he actually died? Because of me? My stomach heaved as the weight of that responsibility bore down on me and I honestly thought I might be sick. I had never ever seen someone die before, let alone been the cause of it. I didn't mean for it to happen. I didn't mean for *any* of it to happen. I only wanted to write a story to help escape from my boring, ordinary life, but at that moment, my normal life actually seemed pretty darn good.

At least it would be safe there.

"Tanith?" Leith watched me closely, his pale green eyes full of concern. "Are you okay?"

"I don't know," I answered truthfully, and without another word, the merman wrapped his arms around me, pulling me into a firm embrace. He smelled of salt and sea, his bronzed skin warm beneath my cheek as my head rested against his chest, and I could almost hear the swell of the sea next to the beating of his heart.

"What does the note say?" someone else in the crowd called out, and Aiqen quickly pulled it off the arrow to take a look.

He read it out in his strong, confident voice. "It says: 'It doesn't have to end this way for all of you. Turn over the girl and no one else will be hurt.'"

All eyes moved to me and Leith's arms tightened around me in support as my heart raced, my mind whirling.

The note wasn't supposed to say that. Those weren't the words I wrote.

I didn't have to point that out since Athar did it for me. The wizard still held the book in his hands as he stepped up to Aiqen and Cadriel. "That's not what's written here."

"Are you suggesting I'm making it up?" Aiqen asked defensively, and before the two men could argue any further, Cadriel plucked the note from Aiqen's hand and compared it to the book.

"They are different," he confirmed to the crowd. "This is useful to know. It means things won't always play out exactly as they're written."

I could have told him that since my own arrival hadn't been exactly as written either. What it meant, though, I had no idea.

"Cadriel?" Though I said his name quietly, he came over to me immediately, his steps slowing as he realized Leith was holding me. I beckoned him even closer and he leaned down until his handsome face was right next to mine. "Do you think I can rewrite this so the gnome doesn't die? That would be okay, wouldn't it?"

His deep green eyes were full of sympathy. "It's upsetting, but people die, Tanith. It is a part of life. Writing it in your book didn't make it happen."

"How can you know that? I changed those other things and gave Leith legs. I helped him breathe."

"I think Leith always had legs and lungs, you just helped him figure out how to use them," Cad countered. "I suspect you have less control here than you think you do, but if you would like to try and rewrite it, I won't stop you."

That was all I needed to hear. As he and Leith shielded me from the rest of the group so no one could see what I was doing, I pulled out my phone and went into the book to edit the passage where the gnome died. When Cadriel offered to help, he was able to heal and save the unfortunate man.

As soon as I hit save, I looked back up eagerly, full of hope, but my optimism quickly faded. Nothing had changed. The man still lay dead on the ground.

"I don't understand," I told Cadriel honestly, frustration and disappointment running through my veins.

"I don't entirely either," he admitted. "But I think that although you may have created this physical space somehow, you don't control anyone's actions. Perhaps you wrote about things that were always going to happen, like a prophet does. That might be why you knew about all of us even though we'd never met before. You didn't will us into being, and you can't change things that have already happened."

I glanced up at Leith to see if he understood this any better than I did, but his handsome face was lined with confusion as he tried to follow along.

"So, what do we do now?" I asked.

Cadriel scanned our surroundings, thinking things over, before turning back to me with determination. "The note says they want you. That's a good thing, since it gives us a motive. Now, we just need to figure out *who* wants you, and why."

~Cadriel~

Things were quickly becoming clearer to me, and the more I saw, the more concerned I became. As the others continued to speculate over the note, I pulled the wizard aside, away from the crowd.

"We need to take Tanith out of town. We're sitting ducks here, all of us. We need to get her somewhere safe, which should protect the rest of the townspeople at the same time. If they know she's gone, they shouldn't come back here to find her."

"That's exactly what it says here," he confirmed, jabbing at the new pages of the book with his bony fingers. He'd barely looked up from the text since the new pages appeared. "You're all meant to go on a quest together, the six of you, to track down the witch."

I didn't know anything about the witch, but it seemed pretty clear that whatever was happening here involved magic. Whoever sent that note must have known Tanith would be arriving that day and they timed the attack and the delivery of the note to coincide with her arrival.

"I thought you said no one could go into the woods," I reminded him.

"They couldn't before," he confirmed. "But now, the book says you do, so I suspect things have changed."

It wouldn't surprise me. Things were changing quickly. "You're not coming?"

He quickly shook his head. "I'm too old for these kinds of quests."

I resisted the urge to point out that I was several millennia older than him. People often forgot that fact since I still looked like a young man.

"Besides, I need to keep an eye on things here and make sure everyone is protected," he added. "I can keep the others safe."

It felt like an excuse to me, but if he didn't want to come, forcing him wouldn't accomplish anything. I stuck to practical matters instead. "Take care of the gnome's burial and tell people to stay off the streets, at least for now. I'll get the rest ready to go."

I glanced over to where Tanith still stood with Leith's arms around her, my jaw clenching in frustration at the easy bond they already seemed to have formed. She'd just met him. Why did she look to him for comfort instead of me?

And why did it mean so much to me that I be the one to provide support for her?

"It's really kind of funny to see you jealous." I could practically hear Zol's smirk before I saw it. "I didn't think you had it in you."

"I'm not jealous."

He raised his eyebrows in amused disbelief, saying nothing else.

His silence was more unnerving than his needling, and I found myself speaking again. "I just find it interesting that out of everyone here, she went to him for comfort."

"Makes perfect sense to me," Zol said with a shrug.

"Why?"

"Look at the guy. He's like the marine equivalent of a puppy dog. You couldn't get any less threatening."

He had a point, but I didn't like the wider implication. "And the rest of us are threatening?"

"Of course. Our sexual magnetism is harder to ignore."

"Why do I even bother…"

I walked away from him, shaking my head, and went over to Aiqen. He might be a little overbearing, but at least the wyvern was a man of action.

"We're going to go find the witch and see if she's the one behind this threat. We'll need supplies for the journey. You've been here longer than I have so I hope you know where to find some?"

He nodded, sizing me up. "Of course. And as you say, I've been here a while, so it makes sense that I be the one in charge of this expedition. I also have a great deal of experience in…"

"Fine." I cut him off before he could give me his full resumé. "You're in charge, Aiqen. I'll round up the others and meet you at the edge of town by the path to the woods."

Pumping his fists in delight, Aiqen recruited Tymanus to help him arrange the supplies. The centaur lacked the same level of enthusiasm, but he followed after Aiqen with no complaint.

Lastly, I needed to bring Tanith and Leith up to speed. That time, when I walked back over to them, she removed herself from Leith's arms, giving him a warm smile before turning to me. "What's the plan?"

She sounded convinced I would have one, and I did. "We'll be leaving, just like in your book, apparently. The witch may or may not be the one behind the note, but she seems a good place to start. Aiqen and Ty have gone to get us some provisions, and you'll need a change of clothes."

She looked down at the pajamas she still wore with a look that suggested she'd completely forgotten how she was dressed. "Where can I get more clothes?"

"In this case, it would probably be easiest if you use your phone to change them," I admitted. Based on how quickly she'd changed the furnishings in the wizard's house, it seemed the physical parameters of this world, at least, were in her control. "And Leith could use more clothing too, with good, sturdy walking shoes. It will probably get cold in the woods overnight."

The thought of spending the night outdoors made her shiver as she took the phone from her pocket and quickly typed in a few lines. As I watched, clothing appeared on Leith's body and Tanith's pajamas changed to far-more-suitable attire: a long-sleeved shirt, hiking pants and boots. A clip pulled her hair half-way back, off her face, and she looked even prettier once I could see her better.

"I didn't get a chance to brush my hair this morning," she explained with a sheepish shrug as she put the phone back into her pocket. "That feels better."

"You look... wonderful." I had very rarely had a need to pay a compliment to a human woman before and it sounded slightly awkward coming out of my mouth. Tanith smiled, though, which seemed to be a good sign. I flashed her a quick smile back before calling out for my brother. "Zol, let's go."

The four of us made our way to the edge of town where Aiqen and Ty soon joined us. They had secured some food and drink, and a few blankets which Ty had strapped to his back.

"Well done," I praised Aiqen sincerely. Having someone who could be relied on would be a huge help. He nodded at me, but with a hint of defensiveness, and I thought I knew why. He wanted to make sure I intended to let him lead, so I did exactly that to set him at ease. "Which way should we go?"

His eyes lit up and his chest puffed out as he surveyed the landscape ahead of us. "This road is the only road into the woods. I say we follow it until we have a reason not to."

None of us had a better idea, so our unlikely band set off together down the dirt road towards the forest as the sun began to set.

~Leith~

I was having the best day of my life.

I knew that some of the other people in the town were upset or frustrated when we all ended up stuck there, but I didn't really understand why. Nothing so interesting had ever happened to me before. My whole life up until then had been spent in the depths of the ocean where the only people to talk to were other merpeople, and not really much to talk about other than what the current had brought in the day before. I could talk to the fish but they didn't answer back. Sometimes, it got a bit lonely.

But in the town? All kinds of new people were available to talk to, and they were all so different from each other. They all had such amazing stories to tell about the places they came from, and I didn't miss my home at all.

Well, to be completely honest, when I arrived and couldn't breathe, that scared me, but everyone took care of me. Even better, Tanith gave me legs and helped me breathe even without the water, and since then, I'd found it all a wonderful adventure.

Everyone I met fascinated me, and I liked them all, though Ty was probably my favourite. Despite looking a little scary, he actually had a very kind heart. Even when I didn't understand the jokes he made, he explained them to me afterwards so I didn't miss out.

Some of the other people in town didn't like Aiqen, but I did. He was very brave and clever, and he often told me so, to make sure I didn't forget. I especially liked to watch him fly when he took his wyvern form. It looked like fun to fly, even more fun than walking, and I hoped I could try it someday.

The other people in our small group, I didn't know very much about yet, but so far, they seemed very interesting too. Cadriel had a calming presence about him and Zolgozig seemed a bit dangerous, in an exciting way. I could tell Ty liked him, which made me like him too.

Last, but certainly not least, was Tanith. Everyone else in this place was male like me, so a woman made a welcome change. Aside from that, I had never seen such a beautiful woman.

To be fair, I'd never seen *any* women outside of the mermaids I grew up with, but it didn't change the fact that Tanith made my heart beat faster just by looking at me. Her kindness in helping me and the way she turned to me for comfort only made those feelings stronger, and although we'd only met and exchanged just a few words, I had already fallen in love with her.

Merpeople were like that. Things moved faster underwater, but I'd been told other creatures were different so I hadn't told her yet just how I felt. Besides, we were walking too fast and there were too many other people around to have a proper conversation anyway, especially since I needed to pay extra attention not to trip over my new feet. They took a little getting used to on the bumpy and uneven road that grew narrower as we approached the edge of the forest.

"You doing okay there, Leith?" The four strong legs that came up beside me gave away who asked the question even if his voice didn't. Although Tanith had given me new clothes and shoes, Ty wore only the same pants he'd worn ever since he arrived, special pants that covered all four of his legs and his lower body. He had no shirt or shoes, although his hooves wouldn't have fit in shoes like mine anyway.

"I'm okay," I assured him with a bright smile. "But aren't you cold?"

He shook his head. "Centaurs have a higher body heat than other creatures. We sleep outside all the time. This is normal for me."

"Are there witches where you come from too?" I'd heard the others say we were going to find one.

"A lot of them," Ty told me with a grim grin. "Too many, really. Trust me, you don't want to get in the middle of a witch fight. I had a buddy who lost part of his tail that way."

I had to take his word on that, mostly because I didn't entirely understand. I leaned a little closer so no one else would hear me. "What *is* a witch, Ty?"

Everyone said the word like I should know, but I'd never heard of them before. There were a lot of creatures I'd never heard of before. Although Aiqen sometimes got impatient with my questions, Ty never made me feel bad for them.

He didn't act like that question surprised him either. "You know how Athar is a wizard and he can work magic?"

Since Ty had explained that to me a few days earlier, I nodded.

"Well, witches are just like that, except they're female."

Another female? That was exciting too, although I already knew I couldn't love her more than I loved Tanith. My heart had already been claimed.

"And why are we going to find her?" I asked next. I might as well get all my questions answered at once while I had Ty to myself.

"They think she might want to hurt the people in the town. We want to go talk to her and find out who she is and what she wants."

"Oh!" I gasped. I hadn't imagined anything like that. "Witches can hurt people?"

Ty gave me a wry smile. "Everyone can hurt people. Remember that. It'll save you a lot of heartache in the end."

Everyone? That felt like an exaggeration. All the creatures I had met so far had been so kind. "Even you?"

His lips tightened for a moment, a haunted expression flashing across his face for just a second before it disappeared and his usual easy grin returned. "Especially me. Now, pay attention to where you're walking. It's going to get a little trickier."

He pointed ahead to the path that led into the trees, and I could see what he meant. It narrowed so much that we would only be able to walk through it single file, and as soon as we entered the forest, the thick trees blotted out most of the sun's rays, making it colder and darker almost instantly. The scent of the grass in the meadow was replaced by a new smell, warmer and heavier, and the sounds of the birds and buzzing insects vanished. It almost felt as if we'd entered a whole new world.

That wasn't all that changed either.

"Does anyone else feel... different?" I asked the group in general, my voice carrying more than I expected through the still forest air.

"It's darker and colder," Aiqen confirmed from the front of the group. "You'll get used to it."

I believed I would, but that wasn't what I meant. "I mean, does anyone else feel different... down here?"

Those in front of me turned to look as I sheepishly gestured to my groin. I didn't know what words the other men used to refer to their genitals and I didn't want to say the wrong thing, but in the short time we'd been in the forest, mine had begun to swell within its sheath. It was starting to get uncomfortable.

Aiqen looked horrified at my question while Zolgozig stifled a laugh.

Cadriel, however, came to my defense from his position at the rear of the group. "I feel it too. As soon as we stepped into the forest, my heart rate increased and the blood flow with it. It feels like sexual arousal."

"How would you know?" Zolgozig called out to him, looking amused.

Cadriel refused to be baited. "You don't feel it, Zol?"

The demon shrugged. "I'm always horny. I don't feel any different."

"I think I know what's causing it," Tanith spoke up. She walked near the back of our train of people, just ahead of Cadriel. "It's the trees."

We all looked around at the trunks surrounding us and the towering branches overhead, as if they might provide an explanation.

"In my book, the scent they give off is an aphrodisiac," Tanith admitted. "I didn't think it would actually affect us."

She rubbed the back of her neck, suggesting she must have been feeling it too, in whatever way arousal manifested itself for a human woman. I would like to find out, and from the looks some of the other men gave her, I had a feeling I wasn't the only one.

The journey ahead suddenly felt like it could be very challenging indeed.

CHAPTER FIVE

~Tanith~

How could I forget about the sex forest?

That wasn't its official name, but my online friends and I jokingly referred to it that way when they proofread the relevant chapter. We were all aware that a lot of readers didn't like to wait to get to the dirty details, so I had tried to come up with a way of shoving some erotic action into my book early on, even though the characters had just met. Making them uncontrollably horny through circumstances beyond their control seemed like a fun way to do it.

As my whole body heated and began to throb, lust running rampant through my veins thanks to the potent chemicals in the air, I both regretted it and maybe, if I were being entirely honest, felt a stirring of excitement too. Alone in a forest with five handsome men, men that I had literally designed to be irresistible, the possibilities seemed endless. I'd had sex before, but only with Blaine. Never with someone I just met, and never with more than one person at a time. Tanith the character did those kinds of things, not me.

Maybe I should be more like her, though. Maybe that was what this dream, or whatever the hell was happening, wanted to tell me.

In my book, Zolgozig made the first move, but we'd already established that things wouldn't necessarily play out as they did in my version of events. Leith was the one who kept glancing back at me as we walked further into the forest, all of us trying to ignore the rising tension and none of us succeeding very well.

"Should I try to change it?" I whispered to Cadriel who walked just behind me. "It's part of the physical environment, so I should be able to control it."

"I don't want to overuse that power," he reminded me, rubbing the back of his neck uncomfortably. "But in this case, perhaps you should."

His agreement brought me both relief and a tiny bit of disappointment. It looked like I would *not* be getting railed in the woods that night after all, and I tried my best to see that as a positive thing.

"Stop for a minute," Cadriel instructed the group, and everyone slowed down so I could pull out my phone. The screen seemed brighter than usual in the surrounding darkness of the trees. As quickly as possible, not wanting to waste battery power, I found the first mention of the forest and the trees and simply deleted any mention of their aphrodisiac qualities. That should do it.

However, when I looked back up, I still felt the same and several of the men were giving me far more heated looks than they had earlier. "Didn't that work?" I asked Cadriel.

"I'm not sure," he admitted. "I still feel it, but it's possible it just got into our blood and will need some time to work itself out. Let's keep walking and hopefully it will wear off."

I might have been hoping for it a little less than him, but I nodded in agreement anyway.

We walked for another half hour, mostly in silence as our single-file formation made conversation difficult. My body continued to throb in its heightened state of sexual tension, and to distract myself, I focused on the forest around me: the snapping of twigs beneath my feet, the chill in the air that made my skin prickle, the heavy, earthy scent of the trees and the dark shadows that formed between them, capable of hiding any number of dangers. How could I describe those things to my readers so they truly felt like they were there? I composed and edited a dozen different descriptions in my head, getting so lost in it that I almost ran into Ty's strong rear end when we stopped moving again.

"We should stop here and set up camp," Aiqen announced. "It's getting dark and we don't want to lose the path."

Nobody complained. I hadn't eaten anything yet that day, and though I had no idea how long it had been since Cad appeared at my door, my limbs felt heavy and tired too. The prolonged state of arousal certainly didn't help. Some food, drink and a rest sounded perfect.

Aiqen had chosen the spot because of a clearing nearby, and he and the others quickly set to work turning it into a makeshift camp with the supplies they had brought.

Well, all the others except Zol, who came to stand next to me as I waited for someone to tell me what I could do.

"Why aren't you helping?" I asked the demon.

"They never let me in the Boy Scouts," he replied sarcastically. "Besides, I thought *you* might need some help."

"Me?" The way he looked at me had my body throbbing all over again. "I don't need any help."

He brushed my hair to the side, his hand trailing across the back of my neck as he leaned in to whisper in my ear. "I think you do. We're all still feeling the effect of those trees. I think you're unsatisfied and you know all these do-gooders aren't going to do anything about it. Do you want to try to sleep tonight while you're still aching, or do you want a quick, easy release? You know I can give it to you."

I did. Or at least, I knew how well the Zol in the book could. No fuss, no strings, just taking care of each other's needs as the rest of the men slept. That was exactly how I'd written it.

"You know where to find me if you want to take me up on the offer." With a wink, he moved away just as Cadriel came over to me, giving Zol's retreating back a suspicious look.

"What was that about?"

"Nothing," I lied. How much trouble could you get in for lying to an angel? Hopefully not too much. "What can I do to help?"

"We're all set up," he assured me. "I just thought that, if it's okay with you, you should sleep next to me tonight in case any of the others let the forest's... peculiarities... overwhelm them."

My guardian angel. I gave him a smile of thanks while trying not to reveal that I wouldn't particularly mind if anyone got overwhelmed. "And you're sure it won't affect you?"

He cleared his throat as he looked away, avoiding my eye. "I am affected, Tanith, but I think it's only partly the forest. Part of it is also you."

The words were sweet, but also familiar. I had written this scene. He said his lines almost word for word, so I already knew how to respond. Flirting was a hell of a lot easier when I had the script in advance. "I didn't think that angels had those kinds of feelings."

"They don't." His eyes came back to me, their shade of green even deeper than usual. "I think it might be this place. Wherever we are, the usual rules don't apply. And if I'm struggling to control myself, I can only imagine how the others feel."

His words were still on script; a little more eloquent than what I had written, but the message remained the same, and I gave him my scripted reply. "I don't want to tempt you, Cad. I don't want you to feel uncomfortable."

His eyes travelled across my face almost desperately. "I don't think it's in your control."

With that, he turned on his heel and went back to set up my blanket next to his. We ate our small meal of fresh bread and cold meats, and afterwards, we all lay down, the forest seeming to make us all sleepy just as it made us horny.

Despite my fatigue, the aching in my body still hadn't subsided, and as I lay on the hard ground, staring up into the darkness, it only got worse. As I rolled over to try to get comfortable, my hand brushed against my nipple, finding it hard and sensitive, and I had to bite back a groan.

"Cad?" I whispered his name quietly, and no response came. He seemed to have gone to sleep, and based on the quiet snoring filling the air around us, I suspected some of the others had too.

One of them hadn't, though. One would be waiting for me back on the path, just as he did in my book, ready to keep his promise to help me ease the ache so I could sleep.

Now, I just had to decide which voice I should listen to: the angel beside me or the demon waiting to lead me into temptation.

~Zolgozig~

I didn't tell Cadriel the full truth earlier. Lying came naturally enough to me, but most of the time, I'd be honest anyway since I didn't give a fuck what anybody thought. But when Cadriel asked me if I felt any different in the forest, I told a half-truth.

I said I always felt horny, which was true. Frequent sex was the number one reason being a demon beat being an angel any year of the millennium. But the part I left out? The forest affected me too. My usual readiness for anything carnal had been bumped up a level and my body craved the delicious friction only another body could provide.

Though I wouldn't have turned my nose up at any of the group who wanted to offer it to me, Tanith was my first choice. The woman intrigued me, even if I couldn't precisely put my finger on why. Cad liked her, for one thing. He'd become protective of her, and I would even go so far as to say a little possessive, which fascinated me on its own. I'd never seen him involve himself with humans before.

She also struck me as rather innocent, a little naive, and if one thing pleased me above all else, it had always been leading humans off the straight and narrow path and helping them discover all the pleasures out there for the taking. I saw nothing wrong with indulgences that didn't hurt anyone else, and sex in particular could add some enjoyment to even the worst situation.

Tanith felt an attraction to me too, I saw it in her eyes when I made the offer, so as I waited for her on the path, I felt far more anticipation than concern. She'd turn up; I would bet on it.

And soon, she proved me right.

"Zol?" I couldn't see Tanith in the shadows, but I could hear her whispered voice.

"Over here."

At the sound of my reply, she stepped forward into the dim light of the forest, only the faintest moonlight illuminating the world around us. Night had fallen fast, but that might be typical there. The rules governing the natural order of this place seemed to be different and I suspected we would find more abnormalities as we went on.

"How do you feel?"

Her thighs clenched at the question; I could make out that movement despite the low lighting, and it answered me even before she said anything. "It's so strong," she admitted. "I can't make it stop."

"I can." With an inviting smile, I held out my hand. "We should go a little further away so the others don't hear you moaning my name."

I couldn't decide if the sound that escaped her mouth counted as a gasp or a whimper or something in between, but it definitely wasn't a refusal. Her hand slipped into mine and with a heady mix of satisfaction and anticipation, I led her further back along the path we'd come in on, my eyes scanning the darkness for a place that would suit our purpose.

After what felt like an eternity but probably lasted no longer than thirty seconds, I found a spot that would work, and as I pulled her off the path and into my arms, letting her feel how hard I was, Tanith let out a shaky breath. "Do you do this kind of thing a lot?"

Though I didn't know what she meant, I tried to guess. "Fucking in the forest?"

She laughed before she could stop herself. "I meant seducing human women. The location is irrelevant."

"Oh. Then, yes, I do this a lot. Usually I get something in return, it's part of whatever deal I make, but you can consider tonight a freebie."

"So, you're just a supernatural gigolo?" she teased, taking me by surprise. I didn't expect that kind of sass out of the quiet young woman she'd appeared to be so far. I also didn't expect her hand to move down and start to stroke my cock through the front of my pants. The woman was full of surprises.

"Something like that. Now, do you want to keep asking questions, or do you want me to fuck you so you can fall asleep?"

"No more questions," she sighed as she stretched up to kiss me.

Maybe it had to do with the forest or maybe her unexpected boldness played a part, but whatever the reason, the kiss turned me on even more than usual. Desire rushed through my body, stoking the fire that had already been smouldering, and I wasted no time in undoing her pants and thrusting my fingers down the front, checking to see if she felt just as ready as I did.

I shouldn't have doubted it. My fingers slid through her wetness easily, and the heat radiating from her matched the fire in my veins. Her fingers fumbling in their eagerness, she unzipped my pants, pulling my cock out and giving it a firm squeeze as I groaned into her mouth.

"You're not quite as innocent as you seem, Tanith."

She grinned up at me. "Or maybe you're just a bad influence."

I could definitely be that.

Now that I knew she required no further foreplay or preparation, I spun her around and placed her hands on the tree branch I'd noticed earlier, the one at the perfect height for her to support her weight. Roughly, I pulled her pants and underwear all the way down, exposing her pretty pink pussy as she moaned in anticipation.

My cock ached to be inside her but I couldn't resist the chance to taste her sweet ass first. Grabbing hold of her cheeks, I wedged my nose between them and ran my tongue around the edge of her puckered hole as she clenched around me, feeling deliciously tight even on my tongue.

"Hmmm, you haven't had anyone back here before, have you?"

"N-no."

I couldn't be sure whether she stuttered out of fear or arousal, but in either case, I didn't plan to take it any further at that particular moment. "We can keep that in mind, but right now, I know what you need."

Lining my stiff cock up against her pussy, I thrust into her in one full, long push as Tanith cried out, her hands tightening around the branch. "Oh, God."

A shudder immediately slithered its way down my spine.

"Please don't bring my father into this."

I didn't mean it as a joke; that particular phrase had always turned me off, but Tanith laughed anyway, her inner walls clenching around me as she did. "What should I say then?"

"Just Zol will be fine. 'Oh, Zol'. 'Fuck me, Zol'. 'You're the best I ever had, Zol'. Anything along those lines."

Her laughter started again, but when I thrust into her once more, it immediately died off, choked by her rising need. Fuck, she felt good. The discomfort the forest had been causing for the last few hours melted away in the perfect bliss of her warm, welcoming pussy. With each stroke, I felt more at ease and more in need at the same time. My hips slammed into her ass at a punishing pace, but she held herself steady, pushing back towards me, wanting each thrust just as much as I did.

It couldn't be called pretty and it didn't take long. In fact, as soon as I reached around to her clit, she began to tremble. No trace of laughter remained in her voice as she called out the words I'd suggested. "Oh, Zol, yes! Please!"

Her body contracted around me as I let myself go too, the feeling of surrender even stronger than usual because the buildup had been so strong.

The anticipation had been, anyway. The actual act probably took no more than five minutes.

As I pulled out of her and gave her ass a playful slap for good measure, Tanith let out one more shaky laugh. "Well, thanks, I guess."

"Anytime."

She pulled her pants back up and turned to face me, her eyes immediately darting to my forehead. "Your horns are showing."

Self-consciously, I reached up to feel them for myself. "Yeah, they do that when I come. I haven't figured out how to stop them."

That might have freaked some women out, but Tanith only smiled. "I'll have to remember that. I'd hate to lose an eye or anything."

That sounded like she anticipated this happening again, and I certainly wouldn't object either. "I've got a tail too, you know."

It also came out involuntarily during times of arousal, which proved handy if I ever needed an extra limb. To prove my point, I reached it around me to run its pointed end down her chest, and Tanith's grin widened. "You'll have to show me exactly what you can do with that."

Indeed I would. Maybe this vacation wouldn't be so bad after all.

~Tymanus~

Centaurs in general possessed a far stronger sense of smell than most humans, and mine was even more developed than most. My hearing was also very acute, so when Zolgozig and Tanith returned to the camp in the darkness, I both heard and smelled them.

In particular, I picked up the scent of sex on them both.

From the demon, it didn't really surprise me, but I hadn't really expected it from the human woman. She'd been warm and open with all of us, but I didn't expect it to go so far as physical intimacy and the idea that it might, not just for Zol but for the rest of us too, made my own loins stir, just after I'd managed to put my lust to bed for the night.

It had been a long time since I'd let myself feel anything of the kind.

In the morning, the lust inside all of us seemed to have cooled. Leith and I went for a walk and found a shallow river near the site where we'd camped. With no trees overhead, it was the brightest spot in the woods by far, and we both stripped down to have a wash. With a little practice, Leith was able to change between his legs and his tail fairly quickly, and he swam happily beneath the bright sun, enjoying being back in his natural habitat, while I lay down on my side on the shallower part of the riverbed, kicking my four legs out into the water. The cool water helped to flush away any remaining vestiges of the previous night's heat, the current washing it all away along with the dirt from the forest floor.

"Mind if I join you?" The question was innocuous enough but the way Zolgozig asked it made it sound slightly filthy anyway. His eyes scanned over us as he stepped closer, trying to see beneath the water's surface and not even bothering to hide his assessing gaze.

"There's plenty of room," Leith replied innocently, his tail splashing against the water in excitement. "Do you have another form too? I don't know what your species is."

"I'm a demon," Zol told him without a hint of embarrassment.

Leith gave me a questioning look and I nodded back at Zol. "Leith hasn't met any demons before. He needs a bit more information."

"I see."

All too happy to oblige, Zol stripped down at the river's edge, sporting a rather impressive cock even in its flaccid state. If he knew how to use it, I could imagine that Tanith had enjoyed herself the night before.

Once he had our attention, Zol transformed to his demon form. A reddish hue spread across his skin while black, curved horns sprouted from either side of his forehead and a red tail with a pointed end grew from his backside. He stuck out his forked tongue to let us see it, flexing his muscles to show off even further. His usually dark eyes seemed to flash red when they caught the light.

"Wonderful!" Leith sounded genuinely delighted, without a touch of irony, but his gaze kept returning to Zol's cock. "Don't you have anything to protect your... tentacle?"

"Tentacle?" Zol repeated in amusement, and Leith's cheeks flushed.

"I don't know what other people call it," he admitted. "Your reproductive part? Mermen call it a tentacle."

I didn't know that, but it made some sense. "There are a lot of different words people use," I told him as Zol came into the water, starting to wash himself as I spoke. "I guess the most common ones are penis, cock, or dick."

"Or trouser snake," Zol added, his eyes twinkling mischievously. "Love stick. Custard launcher. Pork sword. Uterus unicorn."

Some of those were new to me, and Leith's eyes went wide with excitement. "I tried custard for the first time the other day. I really liked it."

Zol snickered while I tried not to smile. "He's not talking about the same custard, Leith. Just call it a cock and you'll be fine."

The merman nodded in appreciation. "Thank you. But you didn't answer my question, Zol. Your 'cock' is just hanging there. Doesn't it get hurt?"

"People don't generally go around attacking it, so no, I'm fine," Zol replied, his eyes returning to the water as he tried to see what was going on with Leith's midsection. "How do you protect yours?"

"It's in a sheath," Leith explained proudly, bringing his hips to the surface so we could see his tail. As he'd suggested, no sign of his cock could be seen beneath his shiny scales.

"You look like a Ken doll," Zol pointed out bluntly, but when Leith looked to me for an explanation, I had to shrug. I had no idea what he meant either. When it became clear neither of us understood, the demon explained further. "I mean: it looks like you have no cock at all."

"I do," Leith protested. "It's just hidden."

"Show me," Zol invited with a devilish smirk, but I quickly shook my head.

"He doesn't have to do that. Leave him alone, Zol."

The demon shrugged, unbothered by the refusal, and turned his attention to me instead. "Where's your cock located? Is it down between your back legs like a horse or between your front legs like a human?"

It wasn't really any of his business, but the chances were good he'd see me naked eventually if we were going to be travelling together. Hiding it seemed pointless. "It depends which form I'm in. At the moment, it's between my back legs. When I shift to my fully human form, it's just like yours."

Leith's eyes seemed to be stuck in a permanently wide state of astonishment. "You have another form, Ty? You never told me."

"I don't use my human form, so it's irrelevant," I explained bluntly.

"Why wouldn't you use it?" Zol wondered.

"Because I don't want to." My sharp tone cut off any further questions and I tried to swallow down my irritation and return to my typical easygoing demeanour. They didn't mean any harm, and they had no way of knowing why the subject was a sore one for me. "Besides, my cock in this form is nearly twice the size. They don't say 'hung like a horse' for nothing."

Zol laughed in appreciation while Leith's eyebrows drew together. "Who says that?"

His innocence never failed to make me smile. "Never mind, Leith. I just mean it's big, okay?"

"Okay," he agreed, happy enough with that response.

"We should probably head back now," I suggested. "I can smell something cooking, and Aiqen will get his panties in a twist if he thinks we're wasting time."

"Aiqen wears panties?" Leith asked in a surprised whisper.

Zol sniggered again and that time, I laughed too. "You never know."

The three of us got out of the water, Leith changing back to his legs first. His tail still covered his midsection, leaving his sheathed cock a mystery. I noticed Zol taking a look at my backside before I could get my clothes back on, but to his credit, he didn't try to hide it. In fact, he asked me about it directly. "Have you ever fucked a human in that form?"

"No." I'd had witches ask me to, but I'd never tried it. I didn't want to hurt anyone.

"What about a demon?" I looked over at him in surprise, but he simply raised his eyebrows and smiled. "Just a thought."

It seemed the tales about the depravity of demons were true. I didn't answer, but as he bent over to pull his own pants back up, I couldn't help taking a quick glance at his ass. Now that he'd mentioned it, forgetting about it would be easier said than done. Romance didn't interest me in the least those days, but a quick fuck with someone who wanted nothing else? That sounded a lot more tempting.

So much for putting the forest's lust behind us.

CHAPTER SIX

~Tanith~

Nervously, I waited for any sign that the other men knew what happened between me and Zol the previous evening. Aiqen and Cadriel, in particular, wouldn't be pleased about it, although for different reasons: Aiqen would consider it a distraction, while Cad would be upset that he'd failed to 'protect' me. But to my relief, nobody mentioned anything in the morning, nor did they treat me any differently. If they'd heard anything, they kept quiet.

Even as I had sex with Zol the night before, part of me still thought I might be dreaming. Nothing else really seemed possible, but after going to sleep and waking up still in the forest, I felt a little less certain. No dream had ever lasted so long before, nor been quite so vividly realistic. I could still feel Zol inside me, making my body begin to ache again in a way that felt very real indeed.

With no other explanation, I decided it made the most sense to act as if it were all really happening, at least until something convinced me otherwise. Besides, aside from the gnome dying, the whole thing had been pretty fun so far. I'd never felt quite so needed or desired before, and I could definitely get used to it.

Once everyone had woken up, Leith and Ty went for a walk, Zol wandered off on his own a short while later, and I stayed behind to help Aiqen and Cad with breakfast.

"Do you have any idea why this witch would want to harm you?" Aiqen asked as he went about his tasks with determined efficiency.

"We don't know it's the witch yet," Cadriel pointed out. "Nobody knows anything about the witch at all."

"But Tanith wrote about her in this book," Aiqen argued back. "She must know something about her."

I interrupted before they could go any further, folding up the blankets we'd slept on and putting them back in the bags. "I don't know if it's the witch, and if it is, I don't know what she wants from me. Although I did write about her, I never figured out exactly what her end game was. I hadn't gotten to that part of the story yet."

Aiqen looked confused. "But you wrote the book. How can you not know how it ends?"

"I've only published the first chapters," I explained. "It's not all written yet."

He and Cadriel exchanged looks which suggested that didn't make things any clearer, so I tried again.

"It's a serialized book. I started out by publishing ten chapters at once, the chapters that brought you all here, apparently, but now it will just be one chapter a day and I plan to keep writing it as I go. The ending hasn't been set in stone yet."

"But what if you need to change things at the beginning?" Cadriel asked. "What if you write yourself into a corner?"

"Then I'll write myself back out again," I said with a shrug. "That's the nice thing about writing fantasy. Things don't always have to be plausible. You can throw a little magic in there to fix the problem and no one can argue with you."

That earned me a smile from Cadriel but Aiqen still looked a little lost. "So another chapter will come out today? What happens in that one?"

I focused on the first part of his question. "The next one is meant to come out today, yes, but is time passing in the same way at home? Is it actually tomorrow now? I don't really understand."

I'd honestly been so caught up in the mystery and excitement that I hadn't fully considered all the ramifications of me travelling to this completely foreign place, assuming I really had. Would people notice me missing? Probably not. I had no plans for the weekend, so aside from some of my online friends wondering why I hadn't responded to their messages, no one would really notice anything out of the ordinary until I didn't show up for class on Monday.

"I don't know either," Cadriel admitted. "The days seem a bit shorter here, but how time equates, I'm not sure."

It made me feel both better and worse that he seemed just as clueless about the whole situation as I felt.

"What happens in today's chapter?" Aiqen repeated. "You didn't answer me."

"Sorry." I hadn't actually forgotten he'd asked, but I'd hoped *he* would forget about it, since the next chapter contained even more sex and I didn't really want to tell them that. "It's just more of us all walking through the forest, I'm afraid. It's still going to take a while to get to where we're going."

Thankfully, he accepted that answer, and once we'd packed everything away, we got started on cooking breakfast. The smell seemed to lure the others back, and I noticed that they all looked fresh and clean.

"Did you wash up somewhere?"

Ty nodded. "There's a river just over there. We all took a quick dip."

Damn it. I wish I'd known that. After my nocturnal workout with Zol and no toilet paper in sight, I could really use a proper wash.

Cadriel noticed my disappointment and tried to reassure me. "I imagine the path will follow the river for a while. Perhaps when we break for lunch, anyone that wants to freshen up can do so."

That sounded good to me, and once we'd eaten, we set back out down the path. That time, I walked directly behind Aiqen, and the sight of his rather perfect backside proved to be a little distracting. "Will you go for a swim when we stop, Aiqen?" I asked, hoping to spend some time alone with him.

He shook his head. "Someone will need to make lunch."

"We could take turns," I suggested. "You made breakfast, so someone else can look after lunch."

He wouldn't be persuaded. "It's my responsibility. Duty comes first."

I resisted the urge to point out that it only became his responsibility when he decided to make it his responsibility. Although he was tightly wound at that moment, he would start to loosen up soon enough. I didn't need to force it to happen any sooner than it should.

Above us, the sun shone brightly, or at least it appeared that way from the small glimpses of sky we got above the tall trees. On the forest floor, however, the atmosphere remained rather dim and gloomy, and we were all feeling a little drained by the time we finally stopped for our next meal. Maybe the aphrodisiac scent had been better than nothing; we might have been horny, but at least we weren't exhausted.

"I can hear the river," Cadriel told me. "I wouldn't mind washing up too, if you don't mind the company."

"Of course not." Cad couldn't be obtrusive if he tried.

"Can I come too?" Leith asked in excitement, and although Cad's lips tightened, making it clear he'd been hoping for some time alone with me, he couldn't say no to the enthusiastic merman any more than I could.

"Didn't you already swim this morning?" he tried instead.

"Yes, but I really like the water," Leith explained, as if that were news.

Cad sighed, making me smile. "Of course you do. Come on, then."

The three of us headed to the river while the other three set about preparing a meal. Or, to be fair, Aiqen and Ty started making lunch while Zol sat down and watched.

When we reached the water, Leith was able to strip down completely, his tail still covering all of his private parts, but Cadriel stopped when he got down to his underwear. Even then, I couldn't help admiring his toned body as he pulled off his pants.

"I'll go in like this," he offered. "And turn away so you can have some privacy."

"We're all adults here," I reminded him, though in real life, I had never gone skinny dipping in my life. He didn't need to know that. Tanith in the book could be bolder than the real one. "Take your clothes off, Cad. I won't look if you don't want me to."

His eyes locked onto mine for just a second. "The problem is that what I want and what is right aren't in agreement right now."

With that, he walked into the river still in his underwear, and I could only shrug as I removed all my clothes and followed in after him.

The water that morning must have been quite cold. Beneath the daytime sun, it had warmed a little, though a chill still lurked in the deeper parts. Leith swam happily back and forth, his tail brushing against my legs as he went by while I rubbed between my legs as discreetly as I could, cleaning away any last evidence from the previous night.

After giving himself a quick wash, Cadriel got back out, not looking in my direction even though I was underwater. "I'll head back and see if the others need help. Are you okay here?"

"Am I okay in the river with a merman?" I asked sarcastically, which made him smile even though he still refused to look at me. "I'll be fine. We'll be back soon."

With a nod, Cadriel headed back the way we came, exactly as I expected him to. All of this was going according to the book. Leith and I were meant to end up in the river together, and when we were alone, he would offer to...

"Can I take you for a swim, Tanith?"

His enthusiastic expression was impossible to resist even if I hadn't already been excited about the idea since the first time I wrote about it.

"You can ride on my back and I'll take care of you."

"I would love that," I agreed, and I wrapped my arms lightly around the merman's neck, my naked body pressing against him, and held on tight as he propelled us through the water far faster than I ever could have gone on my own.

~Leith~

I already said the previous day was the best day ever, but it looked like I might have to change my mind. This one was shaping up to be even better.

Finding the river played a big part in that, since it gave me the best of both worlds. I still got to enjoy the company of my new friends but I could do it in a place where I felt completely comfortable. The water against my skin and running through my hair felt like home, and I couldn't wait to share it with the fascinating new people I'd met.

The idea of sharing it with Tanith especially excited me, and when she accepted my offer to take her for a swim willingly, wrapping her arms around me while her bare breasts pressed against my back, I couldn't remember ever feeling happier.

There were no other large marine animals to worry about in the river. The fish darted out of our way as I swam upstream, carving a path directly up the centre of the water. With my specially tuned underwater hearing, I had picked up on a rumbling noise up ahead and I wanted to investigate. Sharing the adventure with Tanith made it even more exciting, and her expressions of delight behind me sent warmth all through my body.

"Leith, this is amazing!" She laughed as we navigated around some rocks, her body swaying against mine as I tried not to focus on the feel of her slippery nakedness against my back. If I paid too much attention to it and got carried away, my sheath would open and swimming would become more difficult. It happened to every young merman at some point, but we learned to control it. It had been years since I felt as close to losing control as I did at that moment.

Eventually, the river widened into a small pool, and the source of the rumbling sound became evident. Water cascaded down into the pool from a clifftop above, creating a perfect wall of water ahead of us.

"Look at the waterfall," Tanith exclaimed from behind me. "It's beautiful. Even better than I imagined."

From the things the others had said, I knew that Tanith had a little more knowledge of this place than the rest of us did, but I didn't really understand how or why. It didn't really matter to me anyway. All I cared about was that we were there together to enjoy it.

"Do you want to swim under it?" I asked her, and to my delight, she nodded enthusiastically. "Hold on, then!"

Her grip around me tightened as I kicked my tail firmly, propelling us across the pool and directly through the watery curtain. Tanith shrieked in delight as we were both drenched. "Again!"

Happy to oblige, I turned around and went back through it again, and again, and once more for good measure. By the fourth time, her red hair stuck to her head, the water making it look even darker and more beautiful, at least from the corner of my eye. I took hold of her hand and pulled her around in front of me so we were face to face and I could see her properly. Her eyes shone in the sunshine, her expression full of happiness, and I couldn't stop myself from leaning forward and brushing my lips against hers in a light, sweet kiss, our very first one.

It simply felt like the right thing to do.

Thankfully, Tanith seemed to agree. Her arms went around my neck again, that time to pull me closer, and as my hands ran down her sides, tracing over her soft, wet skin, she sighed in happiness. Her lips tasted sweet, not at all salty like the mermaids I'd kissed before, and I inhaled her earthy scent deeply.

"Leith." She pulled back from me to look into my eyes. "In the version of this story that I know, you and I have sex here in this pool this afternoon."

My sheath began to open on its own at the idea and I quickly pulled my hips away from her so she wouldn't feel it. "That sounds wonderful,"

I told her truthfully, my heart filling with happiness. Nothing would please me more. "I'm in love with you, Tanith."

She gave me a warm smile full of tenderness, but also a touch of caution. "That's why I'm telling you this. In the story, I didn't know that you thought we were in love, and afterwards, you were upset that just because we had slept together, it didn't mean we were in an exclusive relationship. You're the sweetest man and I don't want to hurt you, even temporarily. So although I would love to experience this here with you, I need you to know up front that having sex doesn't mean we're making any kind of commitment to each other. If that's okay with you, then we can go ahead, but if it bothers you, then we don't have to."

Parts of what she said were a little unclear to me, and I wanted to make sure I completely understood. "Humans will have sex with different people even if they aren't in a relationship with them?"

She smiled ruefully. "All the time. And sometimes, they'll have sex with different people even when they're in a relationship with someone else."

My gasp of dismay made her smile even wider. Mermen *never* did that, partly because sex between merfolk left a rather distinctive underwater trail, impossible to hide. "So, it doesn't mean they're in love with them?"

"Not necessarily," she agreed. "Sometimes, it's just attraction and sometimes, it's more complicated."

"What do you feel for me?" I wanted to understand that too.

Her eyes softened as she ran her hand down my face. Her fingers felt so soft and warm. "I think you're wonderful and sweet and very handsome. I already feel something for you, but I can't call it love yet. For humans, it takes a bit longer to really fall in love, but you're definitely someone I *could* fall in love with, Leith. And I would love to make you feel good right now, if you decide you'd like that."

If I were being honest, I'd been hoping for more, but as she said, maybe things just took a bit longer with humans. She already trusted me enough that she was there with me, alone and naked. Maybe love would come later.

And in the meantime, I could show her just how strong my own feelings were and make her feel good at the same time. It sounded like a good place to start.

"I promise I won't be upset," I told her.

"Even if you found me kissing one of the other men later on?"

One of the other men in our small group of friends? Did that actually happen in her story? It felt like it must in order for her to ask such a specific question, so I did my best to really imagine it. All the other men were interesting and special in their own way. I liked all of them, so it made sense that she would too. I didn't want any of them to be unhappy, so I gave her my word. "Even then. I'm really glad you were honest with me, Tanith."

It felt like a sign of respect that she had explained things to me that way rather than just doing what she wanted and calling me naive afterwards, as some others might have.

"Me too." She smiled once more before leaning in to kiss me again, and that time, we didn't stop at a light kiss.

The sweetness of her lips fascinated me, and I had to lick them all over to enjoy their taste. She giggled happily as my tongue swept over every inch, and sighed as I slipped it into her mouth to taste her there too.

With one arm still holding onto me to keep her above water, her other hand slid down my chest, sending shivers down my spine as it drifted lower. The closer she got, the more my sheath opened, until my cock released fully and Tanith wrapped her hand around it with an appreciative sigh.

"I can see why you keep this hidden," she teased me gently. "You'd make all the others jealous."

Having seen Ty's cock that morning, I suspected otherwise, but her praise made me feel good anyway. Nothing in her expression suggested disappointment.

"I've never been with a human woman before," I admitted. "I don't know if you're made differently."

Mermaids had sheaths similar to mine that covered their opening. Tanith had no such sheath, just as the other men didn't, but I didn't know if there were any other differences.

"Why don't you find out?" she invited, taking hold of my hand and guiding it down between her legs.

I needed no further invitation. Eagerly, I let my fingers wander, exploring her just as I had explored her mouth a moment ago. She felt familiar, for the most part; the warm, wet opening, lubricated even underwater, and the spot just above it that made her sigh in pleasure. Soon, she was whimpering against me, her hips rocking against my hand.

"That feels amazing, Leith," she murmured, filling me with pride, especially since I knew the best was yet to come.

"Are you ready for me, then?"

When she nodded enthusiastically, we both laughed, at least until I pulled her down onto my waiting cock and the laughter faded into moans of pleasure.

"I don't really know how this works," she admitted to me. "You feel wonderful, but the water makes it difficult to move very fast."

"You like it fast?" I asked, and when she nodded, I smiled again. "Well, then, let me show you what this tail can do."

Since arriving, I hadn't found myself in many situations where I knew more than someone else about any subject, but when it came to underwater sex, I finally had an advantage. Holding her hips in place with my hands, I used my tail to pull my hips away, my cock stroking her channel as I did, and flicking my tail firmly in the other direction, I drove into her again.

"Oh!" She hadn't expected that, but I could tell by the way her pupils dilated that she liked it and she confirmed it for me out loud too. "Yes, Leith, just like that."

Our bodies moved together, pushing and pulling as the water swirled around us. The outer folds of my sheath brushed against her clit each time I pushed into her, which helped to keep my hands free to hold her steady. That proved useful as she began to lose control and her head fell back, floating on the water's surface. I had to hold her in place so she didn't drift away.

"Please, don't stop," she begged, and I had no intention of it. She felt so good that I was very close to my orgasm as well, and as soon as her body began to contract around me, I let go too, the whole world disappearing behind the stars I could see floating in that beautiful, secluded pool.

Keeping my promise to share her affections and not be jealous would be more difficult than I anticipated. Now that I knew just how wonderful it felt to be with her, I loved her even more than before.

~Aiqen~

Cadriel came back from the river fairly quickly, but as more time passed with no sign of Tanith and Leith, I began to get worried. We hadn't seen anyone else in the forest so far, but perhaps we'd been too complacent, especially where Tanith was concerned. Someone was out to get her, I'd been entrusted with keeping her safe, and I'd let her wander off with the well-meaning but inexperienced merman. What in the world had I been thinking?

"I'm going after them," I announced as the other men sat around digging into the lunch we'd prepared.

"I wouldn't," Zol replied with his mouth full. "Think about it: they're both naked and wet and are taking their time in coming back. You do the math."

I didn't know what math had to do with anything but very little of what the demon said seemed worth listening to so I ignored him and headed off into the woods. It didn't take long to reach the river, but when I got there, Leith and Tanith were nowhere to be seen, and my feeling of foreboding grew stronger.

Panicking wasn't in my blood, though. Situations like this were exactly what I trained so hard for. I was made to be a hero, I'd known that my whole life, and I relished any chance to prove it.

Stripping my clothes off and leaving them next to the items belonging to Tanith and Leith, I shifted into my wyvern form and took to the air, following the water downstream. The current didn't look particularly strong, but if they'd been carried away somehow, it would have taken them in that direction. With my enhanced sense of smell in my reptilian form, I sniffed deeply, looking for any sign of them or other people and scanning the riverside visually for any sign of struggle.

Nothing stood out to me, and after a few minutes, I let the air lift me higher, above the trees until the town we'd come from the day before appeared in the distance. Everything looked peaceful and familiar that way, so I turned around to head upstream instead.

As I turned back, a plume of smoke in the distance caught my eye. I couldn't tell where it came from, the trees blocking my view of the ground, but it marked the first sign of other life we'd seen since entering the forest. It lay in the direction we were heading, and I was tempted to head towards it and see where it came from and what it meant, but not while Tanith remained missing. That had to be my priority for the time being.

Swooping back down above the river, my strong wings propelled me forward as I resumed my search. Before too long, the river widened into a small pool with a waterfall, and at last I caught sight of them, laughing and splashing each other in the middle of the water. No one else seemed to be around so they must have gone there on their own, and the strength of my relief at the sight of Tanith safe and unharmed surprised me.

That relief, however, was quickly replaced by annoyance at the idea that, while the rest of us worried about their safety, they had simply been cavorting in the water as if they didn't have a care in the world.

A deep rumbling roar alerted them to my presence. Tanith shrieked as she looked up, reaching out for Leith instinctively, but the merman recognized me immediately.

"Look, it's Aiqen!" he called out in delight, waving up at me. "Hi, Aiqen!"

I dropped lower, my wings beating the air and sending ripples through the water below me, tossing the two floating figures gently in the waves. With my head, I gestured back down the river, the way they'd come.

"I think he wants us to go back," Leith guessed.

When I nodded, Tanith gave me a smile. Her shoulders and chest were bare in the water, suggesting she had nothing at all on, but the water shielded the rest of her from my view. It surprised me that I actually looked to double check. Maybe the lust from the previous night hadn't completely exited my system yet.

Even with the merman's speed, I beat them back to the spot where I'd left my clothes, and I had just finished dressing when Leith and Tanith arrived.

"I'm sorry, Aiqen," she apologized as they climbed out of the water. "We lost track of time. Have you already eaten?"

The words were on the tip of my tongue, to tell her to be more careful in the future, but the air necessary to push them out caught in my throat as she stepped fully out of the water, completely naked and glistening wet. Her red hair was sleek and wet down her shoulders, and I couldn't help noticing the hair lower down on her body matched the shade of the hair on her head precisely.

What was I doing? I didn't let women distract me. Some of my brothers had made that mistake and I'd sworn not to repeat it. However, as I stared at the bold little human woman in front of me, for the first time, I could begin to understand why they'd fallen prey to that particular diversion.

"Aiqen?" Leith said my name curiously as he pulled his own clothes back on. "Are you okay?"

"What? Yes. I mean, yes, we've already eaten but there is some left for you both. Come quickly, please."

I turned on my heel and returned to the others, keeping my head down, but Zol laughed as I took my seat again. "You look like you got an eyeful. Was his sheath still open when you found them?"

"Zol, do you need to be so crude?" Cadriel shook his head at his half-brother in disapproval. "I'm sure Aiqen didn't see anything inappropriate."

Indeed I hadn't. Nothing about Tanith's body could be called 'inappropriate', but it would be a difficult image to forget nonetheless.

Tanith and Leith ate quickly so we could resume our walk, and as I took my place at the front of the group again, my thoughts grew more and more unfocused. Why was I letting that one unexpected glimpse of a naked woman affect me so much? Did it mark the beginning of the end for me? Would I lose focus just as some of my brothers had, putting their own needs before that of the kingdom and losing their chance to rule it all? Had I already gone too far?

In my mind, I could see the whole kingdom jeering at me as I failed in the competition I'd trained so hard for, each face in the crowd somehow knowing exactly why I had let myself down.

The disappointment inside me built up so strongly that my pace began to slow, my thoughts getting darker and more depressed with each step, until finally Tanith spoke up from the back of the group. "Is anybody else feeling that?"

"Feeling what?" Ty asked, much more morosely than usual. "The lust has faded."

"It has, but this is something else," Tanith explained. "I think we've reached the Vale of Disillusion."

"What?" Cadriel sounded just as confused as I was, and nearly as sombre too.

Since none of us knew what she was talking about, Tanith gave a further description. "It's another sensory section of the forest, but unlike the aphrodisiac before, the plants here give off a scent that feeds into your deepest fears and insecurities and enhances them."

Perhaps that explained my swirling thoughts, and as I looked around at the others, they all looked like they also knew exactly what she was talking about.

"I think I preferred the lust," I admitted, and for once, Zol actually agreed with me.

"It was a lot more fun. Let's just get through this as soon as we can."

"That's not how it works," Tanith told us. "If we ignore those feelings, they'll get stronger and stronger until we end up wandering aimlessly in circles. The only way to get through it is to share our fears with each other and find a way to overcome them."

"So, this is some kind of group therapy forest?" Zol asked, sounding unimpressed. "I'll pass."

Tanith shook her head at him. "You can't pass. We need to do this together. Like it or not, we're all going to have to open up a little if we want to get through this and on to the next part of the journey."

CHAPTER SEVEN

~Cadriel~

The idea of exposing their innermost insecurities made all of my fellow travellers uneasy, and I could certainly sympathize. I didn't particularly want to share my own negative thoughts with everyone else either, but Tanith seemed to think we had to, and she had my trust. She wouldn't say it without a good reason, especially since she didn't seem entirely comfortable with the idea either. No one really wanted to air their own weaknesses that way, but knowing them would help us to understand each other better, and perhaps that was the point. We needed to be able to trust and rely on each other if we were to successfully face whatever challenges lay ahead. If we did it properly, it would lay a solid foundation for our unlikely partnership.

"Let's sit down so we can all see each other properly," I suggested. The part of the forest we were in had a number of fallen trees, as if they had also gotten so depressed that they decided there was no point in standing tall any longer. The six of us all found a place to sit on the moss-covered trunks that roughly formed a circle, their bark still slightly damp from the morning dew. "I guess I'll begin."

"Of course you will," Zol muttered, and I shot him a confused look.

"Do you want to go first?"

"No," he mumbled sullenly. "Go right ahead."

His behaviour confused me, but since I typically didn't understand why Zol did half the things he did, I let it go and dove straight into my explanation of what I felt.

"As an angel, it's my job to help people avoid things that will harm their souls. Resisting temptation and remaining focused on the big picture is my strong suit. I'm not supposed to care for any one being more than all the others, but since arriving here yesterday, I have found myself tempted more than ever before."

My eyes darted to Tanith, the source of that temptation, as I made my confession. I couldn't blame her for the fact that I found her nearly irresistible, and I suspected she didn't have any idea how I felt. I'd been doing my best not to show it.

Had I felt the same way in her book? Did I give in to my desires then? Knowing would be a double-edged sword, making things harder and easier at the same time, so I'd held myself back from asking.

"Your fear is that you will break your code of honour?" Aiqen summed up.

I nodded in agreement, his phrasing of my dilemma as good as any. "Essentially, yes."

"And what would happen if you did?" Tymanus asked.

"Nothing," Zol answered for me. "He's worried about nothing. He would be disappointed in himself but there are no consequences unless he causes others to do things they wouldn't do otherwise, and that's not what he's talking about."

He looked pointedly towards Tanith as well, making it clear that he knew exactly what kind of temptation I meant. Perhaps I hadn't hidden it as well as I thought I had, but what Zol didn't understand was that my temptation wasn't purely physical. A simple physical union wouldn't solve my problem. The larger issue was how protective of her I felt. If it came down to it, if she were in danger, I couldn't guarantee I wouldn't risk harming others to save her, and that was where the line grew dangerously blurred.

"Let's focus on all sharing our concerns first before we start looking at solutions," I suggested. "Who wants to go next?"

"I will," Leith offered. For the first time since I'd met him, he didn't have a smile on his face. In fact, his hunched shoulders almost made him look unhappy. "What's worrying me is that you all know so much more about the world than I do, and I'm afraid I'll do something stupid and someone will get hurt."

I could completely empathize with that fear. "I think a lot of us feel that way, even if we hide it well. Who else?"

Tanith hesitantly raised her hand. "I'm afraid that none of you are real and I'm having some kind of nervous breakdown."

That made us all smile, but she didn't mean it as a joke.

"Nothing exciting ever happens to me. I'm the most boring, average person you can imagine, and now I'm here in the middle of the very adventure I created to escape my boring, average life, with all of you fascinating, handsome men, and you're all treating me like I'm someone interesting and desirable. I'm equally terrified that it's real and you'll realize that you're wrong, or that it's all happening inside my head and I'm going crazy."

The desire to reassure and console her nearly overwhelmed me, but I had to stick to what I'd said before: we should all air our concerns first before we bolstered each other up.

"Thank you, Tanith. Aiqen?"

For once, the wyvern looked unhappy about being called upon, but he answered me anyway. "I'm afraid I'll let myself be distracted from the goal I've always wanted."

That sounded awfully similar to my own fear, so I asked him to elaborate a little further. "What goal is that?"

"To be chosen as ruler of my kingdom."

Ah. Therein lay the difference. I had no desire for personal glory, but I didn't begrudge Aiqen that dream. So long as he helped people along the way, ambition could be quite useful.

That left Tymanus and Zol to answer and they both tried to force the other to go first. The centaur proved the most stubborn, so Zol reluctantly stepped up, his lips pursed in displeasure.

"I'm afraid that one decision I made thousands of years ago will define me forever. People judge me for it and treat me differently because of it without ever getting to know me."

"What did you decide?" Leith asked with wide, interested eyes, his own worries temporarily forgotten.

Zol's gaze darted to me for just a second before answering the merman. "I decided to help people enjoy their lives rather than simply following a set of rules. I wanted them to know the difference between right and wrong for themselves rather than doing things because they were told to."

That made quite a poetic recounting of his fall, but not an entirely accurate one. I spelled it out a little more bluntly. "You encouraged the Romans to take part in orgies."

"Which didn't hurt anyone," Zol shot back. "Some demons exult in violence and misery, but that's never been what interests me. I simply believe in pleasure."

He winked at Tanith as he said those words and she looked down to hide her smile. Though I knew it was wrong, sometimes I couldn't help but envy the confidence he had.

"Ty? It's down to you now." The centaur was the only one left to speak, and I was eager to change the subject from my half-brother's exploits.

However, Ty crossed his arms, still looking uncooperative. "I don't need to take part."

Up until then, he'd seemed easygoing and carefree, but he couldn't look more uncomfortable with the idea of opening up to all of us.

Tanith immediately got up and went to sit next to him. "It's alright, Ty. I already know what it is. In my book, you told me all about her. No one here will judge you for it, I promise."

'Her'? Judge him? I had no idea what she meant, but her words intrigued me, and the others all encouraged him to share.

"Everyone else has been honest," Aiqen pointed out.

"We want to help," Leith added.

Tymanus obviously didn't like the attention, and he gave in more out of a desire to stop the focus on him than out of any obligation to the rest of us. When he spoke, he kept his sentences short and his words clipped. "Fine. Like Leith, I'm afraid someone will get hurt because of something I do. The last person I cared about died because of me. Since then, I haven't let anyone get close, but as I think you all appreciate, the situation here makes it more difficult to avoid getting attached."

I certainly *could* appreciate that, and it seemed the others did too. "What happened, Ty?" Leith asked, his usually sunny face lined with concern.

"I don't want to talk about it," the centaur said firmly. "You wanted to know my fear, and that's it."

"That's everyone, then," Aiqen said after a moment's silence as we each digested what had been said. "So, now that we know what's bothering each of us, how do we move on?"

~Tanith~

My heart ached for Ty as he did his best to keep all his pain inside. I hadn't been entirely certain that the back story I'd written for him in my book would turn out to be true, but from the little he'd said and how he hadn't contradicted me when I told him what I knew, it must have matched with what I'd written.

How could I have known those things about his life before we met? If all of this was real, how could I have written about *any* of these men so accurately? Their personalities, their appearances, even the way they spoke, all of it lined up with how I'd imagined it. It didn't make any sense, but neither did any other explanation I could come up with. The only thing that made any sense at all was that all of this was a dream, but if that were the case, it had been the longest, most intense dream of my life. Unless I'd somehow gone into a coma or something, even the dream theory seemed unlikely.

For the time being, I had to proceed as if what they were telling me was true and we all had our own separate lives before being brought there together.

And that, I felt, would be the key to moving on. It made the most logical answer to the question Aiqen had just asked. We each brought the sum of our experiences to the table. By pooling those, we could go farther than we ever could on our own.

"We all have our own fears and concerns," I summarized out loud to the group. "But each of us also has different skills and abilities which we could use to fill in the gaps. For instance, Leith is worried about not knowing enough. I know a lot about the human world and I seem to have some insights into this place because of my book. Cad and Zol have been around for ages so they know all kinds of things too. Anything that Leith needs to know, we can tell him. You're not doing this alone, Leith."

I smiled over at the merman as I finished speaking and he flashed me a grateful smile, his pale green eyes shining. "Thank you, Tanith. Maybe I can help Ty. He thinks he's bad luck, but merman scales are supposed to bring *good* luck. I could give him some of mine to carry."

Ty couldn't help smiling at the innocent offer, just as I did. "Thanks, Leith. Maybe that will help."

He obviously didn't believe it would, but he didn't want to hurt Leith's feelings, and I shot him a grateful smile of my own. If the events of the book held true, Ty and I would have a chance to talk about his past in more detail soon, so I would wait until then to try to see if I could do something that *would* help him come to terms with what happened. Until then, Leith's merman scales would have to do.

Ty scanned the group, trying to decide where his own skills could come in handy. "Well, I guess I can help Cadriel and Aiqen. They both take all the responsibility on themselves and take themselves too seriously. I can help to keep things in perspective, and Zol could probably help with that too. A different point of view can make things clearer."

Aiqen nodded slowly, clearly struggling with the idea that he needed any help at all, but he didn't disagree. Instead, he looked over at me. "It sounds like Tanith's fear stems from a lack of self-confidence. I've learned how to overcome any self-doubt, so I may be able to provide some assistance."

Zol rolled his eyes but I gave Aiqen a thankful nod. A little of his confidence sounded quite appealing to me. "That would be very helpful, thank you."

Cadriel still hadn't said anything, and I pointed that fact out gently.

"That leaves Zol. Cad, do you think you might be able to help him?"

The two half-brothers obviously had a history of disagreements that went back further than I could fathom, but they cared for each other too. I knew that even if they didn't, and working together might be a way to help them realize that they had more in common than they chose to admit.

"He's the last person who would understand," Zol muttered. "If I have to talk to someone, I'll talk to you. I know *you* won't judge me for my desires."

He gave me a wink that immediately brought to mind all the things we'd done together the night before, and Cadriel stiffened at the implication. "You don't know anything about her."

"I know more than you think." Zol's eyes twinkled mischievously at the chance to tease his brother, and Cad's jaw clenched tightly.

"Cad, it would mean a lot to me if you could try," I interjected, stepping in before Zol could let anything more slip. "It might be good for both of you."

The angel didn't want to say no to me, so he tried to shift the blame to his brother. "You heard him, Tanith. He doesn't want to talk to me."

"He will, though, won't you, Zol? To move this along?"

Zol groaned and rolled his eyes again. It seemed to be almost a reflex for him. "Fine. I'll agree that Cad can have my back if we can all get out of this fucking part of the forest."

"Sounds good to me," Ty quickly agreed and everyone got to their feet, all eager to keep moving now that we'd reached a resolution.

"I just want to say one more thing," Aiqen announced, making Zol groan again. I shot him a disapproving look but it didn't have quite the effect I wanted. He just winked at me, and Aiqen proceeded anyway. "As we've all just shown, each of our weaknesses can be supplemented by someone else's strength. Perhaps this is the reason why this particular group of people was brought together. Perhaps we need each of the unique abilities we all bring to the table to meet the challenges that lie ahead. By working together, we can defeat the witch or whoever is behind the threat. I therefore pledge to do my best to support you all, to the best of my ability."

He had a point. Of all the people in the world, and out of the world for that matter, who had been chosen to join this unusual adventure, there must have been a reason that each of us were among those chosen. There must have been a reason I wrote about these five men in particular, even if I didn't know they were real at the time.

Hopefully, we could band together and do whatever was required of us... as soon as we figured out exactly what that might be.

~Zolgozig~

As much as I hated to admit it, the oppressive feel of the forest *had* lifted a little after we sat down and had our chat. We still weren't moving particularly fast, but we were moving, and no one looked ready to collapse in a fit of depression anymore. Perhaps sharing our insecurities really had helped after all.

Or so I thought, until Cad caught up to me, forcing me to move over so we could walk side-by-side even though the path really wasn't meant for two.

"We promised Tanith that we'd talk," he reminded me, even though it had literally happened two minutes earlier. I hadn't forgotten. "We might as well get it over with."

"How about we just say we did?" I suggested. "She's happy, no awkward moments for us. Everyone wins."

"You want me to lie?"

Cad looked so scandalized that I had to laugh. "It's just a little white lie. It doesn't hurt anyone."

"That's where we disagree," he told me seriously. "I know you think otherwise, but there are very few misdeeds that cause no harm."

That formed the root of our disagreements, certainly. "And who would be hurt in this case?"

"Well, perhaps you would. This is obviously something that's bothering you, so if you keep it bottled up inside, it may harm you in the long run."

He was always so sure of his righteousness, so willing to cast blame on others, just like the rest of them. "And are you willing to talk about what's bothering you too? This 'temptation' you're experiencing?"

I knew exactly what kind of temptation he meant: he wanted to fuck Tanith, the same as the rest of us did, apparently. Could we blame the forest, or was it something more? I couldn't say, but I did know I had never seen Cad look at a woman the way he looked at her.

"I don't think you're the best person to help me resist temptation," he pointed out, almost sarcastically, and I raised my eyebrows at him. Sarcasm was usually my domain.

"No, but I'm the best person to help you see why it wouldn't be such a terrible thing to give in to it. It wouldn't be the end of the world, I promise you it wouldn't. You might even have some fun along the way."

He swallowed uncomfortably, looking away from me. "We're supposed to be talking about you."

I could be just as stubborn as he could. "Well, I'm not talking unless you agree to talk to me too. Tit for tat, Cad. With an emphasis on the tit in your case."

His eyes closed as he muttered a quick prayer in Latin, which I recognized immediately. *Father, give me patience.*

My lips tightened at the implication. "You can't deal with me on your own? Have to go running to Daddy for help?"

"None of us are alone, Zol," he stated firmly. "Not even you, though you act as if you were."

"You're going to try to tell me that you and the others didn't completely abandon me? Once I was cast out, you all pretended you'd never known me."

"That's part of the punishment," he reminded me. "You knew that when you chose the actions that led to your fall in the first place."

It must be nice to always be in the right. "And you really think what I did was so wrong? That it was worthy of the same punishment given to those who incite wars and genocides and torture and murders?"

Cad winced at my listing of evils, the mere words making him uncomfortable, but that was exactly my point. Those things were bad; I didn't argue with that. I just couldn't see how the temptations I encouraged fell into the same league.

"Things are either right or wrong," my half-brother replied, towing the company line as always. "There is no in-between."

"Really?" Did he honestly believe that or had he just been brainwashed so long he no longer even bothered to think about it? "So me fucking Tanith because she wanted me to would be just as bad as killing her?"

He winced again, his eyes darting to the woman walking just ahead of us, blissfully unaware of our current conversation. "They're not the same," he conceded unwillingly, "but they are both wrong."

"Why?" I demanded, refusing to let him off the hook that easily. "Neither of us are in a relationship so our actions don't affect anyone else. No promises were made, no lies were told. It was a moment's pleasure and nothing more. Why is it wrong?"

Cadriel's eyes searched my face hesitantly. "You are speaking hypothetically, aren't you?"

He didn't want me to lie, so I wouldn't. "No. We fucked each other last night. Neither of us could sleep thanks to this ridiculous forest, so we helped each other out. As you can see, she's perfectly fine. She's not moping in hurt because she wanted nothing more from me. Now tell me, who exactly have I hurt?"

Clear dismay registered across Cad's face as his eyes returned to Tanith. "I thought... I felt..."

He couldn't finish his sentence, but I began to get an idea of what he meant anyway. "Did you think there was something special between you?"

His unhappy expression as he looked back at me made it clear that I'd hit the nail on the head, and despite myself, I actually felt a little sorry for him.

"Isn't that against your own rules anyway?" I asked, trying to soften the blow.

"Of course it is. That's why I called it a temptation, Zol. I feel something for her that I've never felt before."

"I don't think she's looking for a serious relationship," I pointed out as kindly as I could. I felt pretty sure she'd also fucked the merman that afternoon, but telling Cad that wouldn't help matters any so I kept that guess to myself. "And you barely know her anyway. Maybe what you're feeling is simply lust. You don't know the difference because you've never felt it before."

"It started before the forest," he explained. "It began from the first moment I saw her."

Well, I hadn't known his feelings were that serious. Perhaps we had hurt someone after all, unintentionally, but I still didn't think what we'd done was wrong. People got hurt all the time, even with the best of intentions. You couldn't live your whole life trying to please everyone else.

Sometimes, we just had to please ourselves.

"I think you should spend some time alone together with her. If things happen, let them happen. See how you feel once you get to know her better."

Cadriel eyed me suspiciously. "Don't think I don't know what you're doing, Zol. You're trying to tempt me."

"I'm trying to make you happy." He could call it whatever he wanted, but for me, it came down to that. "Nobody else here has any claim on her. We don't know how long we're here or why. We don't even know for sure that any of this is real. You've gone thousands of years without feeling the way you're feeling right now. Don't you want to know what it means?"

I was getting to him, I could tell. His resolve seemed to be weakening before my eyes.

"I thought I was supposed to be trying to make you feel better," he tried as a last-ditch attempt to distract me.

"No, you're supposed to be showing me that not everyone dislikes me simply because I'm a demon. Show me that you don't, Cad. Trust me on this and take my advice. It would make me feel a lot better."

His lips pursed in uncertainty, but to my great surprise, he eventually nodded. "Very well. I'll speak to her the next time we stop."

I couldn't contain my shock. "Well, I'll be damned."

Cad snorted. "At least we still agree on that."

He fell back into line behind me, leaving me smiling and shaking my head and, I had to admit, feeling quite a lot better than I had before. Maybe this damned forest would turn out to be good for something after all.

CHAPTER EIGHT

~Tymanus~

Although the pace we kept as we carried on through the forest was far from taxing, my heart raced anyway. I had never spoken about what happened to anyone, not even my closest friends, and I had never planned to either. Certainly not with a group of strangers I'd randomly ended up stuck in a forest with.

Not only that, but Tanith said she knew what happened. I doubted that; if she really understood, she'd want nothing to do with me at all, so I had to guess she didn't know the full story, only parts of it. Even so, the sympathy in her eyes tempted me to want to open up to her further.

Seemed like the forest was making us all a little crazy.

It took some time, but eventually we entered a different part of the forest where the trees felt less oppressive and the gloomy mood that had been following us all afternoon seemed to lift. When Aiqen suggested we make camp there for the night, we all agreed without argument. The emotional weight of the day had taken its toll.

I helped the others to prepare our provisions, keeping an eye on Tanith the whole time. Would she offer to talk to me? I wouldn't bring it up again if she didn't, but I almost found myself hoping she would.

A moment later, Leith appeared in front of me, blocking my view with his sunny smile. "Here, Ty. I'm sorry it took me so long to make it, I didn't have any string."

My brow furrowing in confusion, I looked down at his hands where he held a shiny, blue circle of some kind. "What is it?"

Leith's smile faltered a tiny bit. "It's the scales. For luck."

Oh, right. I'd almost forgotten about his scales. I didn't for a second think they would work, but I appreciated his offer, and after taking them from him, I held them up to take a closer look. He had somehow woven the scales together to form a necklace of sorts. The blue-green scales glinted in the evening light like jewels and the whole chain smelled of the sea, just as Leith himself did. Even if they didn't bring me luck, they'd remind me of my new friend, and that provided some comfort on its own.

"It's really nice. Did it hurt you to take them out?"

"It hurts a little bit," he admitted. "But they'll grow back. I took them from all over so I wouldn't have a bald spot."

"How did you fix them together?" He'd just said he had no string, but something had to be holding them in place.

"I used pieces of grass tied together," he explained proudly. "And a thorn from a bush to make the holes."

I glanced back down at his hands, littered with cuts and scrapes. "Shit. You shouldn't have hurt yourself for me."

Nobody else should have to get hurt because of me.

Leith gave me an unconcerned shrug. "They'll heal. At least I'm not in the ocean right now. Do you know how much the saltwater stings when you cut yourself?"

I winced at the thought. "Thankfully, I don't. But thank you, Leith. I mean it. This is really kind."

I lifted the scale necklace over my head, letting it rest against my chest, and Leith's eyes lit up. "It looks great on you. You would make a handsome merman, Ty."

"Can you imagine me with a scaly tail?" I swished my own tail to emphasize my point and the thought made us both laugh.

Tanith soon came over to see what had brought on our good humour. "What's so funny?" she asked, already smiling herself.

"Ty as a merman," was all Leith had to say to set himself off laughing again, and Tanith joined in good-naturedly.

"Well, the scales really do suit you," she said to me, her eyes full of affection for the both of us. "Hopefully, they'll bring you luck too."

My mirth faded as the reason for me needing luck in the first place came back to me.

Tanith immediately noticed the shift in my mood and gestured back at the others. "You know, I think they're covered for getting supper prepared. Do you want to go take a quick walk until it's ready?"

"Oh, yes!" Leith immediately chimed in. "I like walking a lot better when you're not going anywhere in particular."

As much as I enjoyed his company, I had a feeling Tanith had been trying to make an excuse to speak to me alone, and she soon confirmed as much. "Actually, Leith, I heard Aiqen say he'd like to catch some fish for dinner so we don't use all the food he brought from the village. I'm sure you could help with that."

The merman's eyes lit up at the chance to be useful, and he quickly excused himself to run off and offer his services. I gave Tanith a knowing smile when he was out of earshot. "You know how to play him pretty well."

"It's not about playing him," she protested. "I just didn't want him to feel left out. I know you feel the same about him. He's such a sweet soul, causing him any kind of pain feels like a crime."

Since I knew exactly what she meant, I didn't argue. "So, you wanted to take a walk?"

I let her lead the way, following behind her until we could no longer hear the others. Wind rustled through the leaves overhead, but besides that, no other sound could be heard at all. No birds or insects seemed to have settled that far into the forest. Perhaps they got disoriented in the part of the forest we'd just come through too.

Finally, we found a spot with a tree stump for her to perch on and I lowered myself down onto the dry, dirt ground, sitting eye-level with her. "I'm not going to force you to talk about it if you're not ready,"

Tanith began. "But I spent a lot of time when I wrote about you trying to figure out why you'd blame yourself for something that so clearly wasn't your fault."

I had thought perhaps she didn't know the full story, and her words seemed to confirm it. "It was *entirely* my fault. I'm not sure what you think you know, but Evia is dead because of me. I thought I could protect her but I couldn't."

"You loved her." Tanith's words felt soft and supportive, her eyes searching my face with unobtrusive curiosity. "Tell me about her."

It had been a long time since I'd spoken to anyone about Evia, mostly since I found it easier not to think about her. Spending my days joking and laughing and not taking anything too seriously meant that I didn't have to feel the pain her death had caused.

"She was a fairy," I began hesitantly. Even though it made me uncomfortable, given the circumstances, if I had to confide in someone, I'd prefer it to be Tanith. "Fairies and centaurs aren't supposed to fall in love. We're big and brutish, they're petite and delicate. Nature clearly didn't intend us to be together."

"Nature doesn't always get things right," Tanith mused. "What made you fall in love with her?"

For a second, I could almost imagine I could see her, peering out at me mischievously from behind a tree just beyond the place where Tanith and I sat. As soon as my eyes focused on the spot, however, she disappeared.

"She was fearless and full of fun. I'd always been thought of as peculiar by my fellow centaurs since I liked to joke and laugh. Most of my kind are more serious and dour, focused on duty. Life always seemed rather ridiculous to me, though, and Evia saw it too. She laughed at the same things I did."

Tanith leaned forward, absorbing every word. "How did you meet?"

"We were all summoned one day to an announcement by the witches who ruled over the territory where we lived, and I saw her mimicking the witch behind her back. I'd never seen her before that, and I couldn't stop myself from laughing, which got me in trouble. She came to find me later to apologize and our friendship grew from there."

Once I started talking, I found it hard to stop. I told Tanith all kinds of stories about Evia, how she once mistook salt for sugar and baked me the worst cake I'd ever had, and how she'd ride on my back, flapping her wings at the same time. We never left the ground, but it gave me a lift that nearly felt like flying anyway. As I talked and Tanith asked curious questions, Evia felt closer than she had in a very long time.

But just when I thought I might be ready to talk about what happened at the end, Zol's voice called out from somewhere in the distance. "I don't care if you eat or not, but the others do. If you're naked, just say so and I'll leave."

Tanith didn't bother to hide her smile. "He thinks I'm some kind of nymphomaniac. I'm sorry, Ty, but we should probably go back."

The night would be upon us soon, and my stomach rumbled at the thought of food. "That's okay. It felt good to talk, though, so thank you for making me. Maybe we'll have more time to continue the conversation later."

"I'll make sure we do." With that assurance, we got up and started walking back, yelling out to Zol that we were coming.

"That's what I thought," he smirked when he caught sight of us and Tanith merely rolled her eyes not bothering to correct him.

I didn't either. We might not have been doing anything, but for the first time in a very long time, I'd actually met someone that I could imagine being with in that way, if circumstances were different.

If only Leith's lucky necklace were real, and I could be sure that no one would ever be hurt because of me again.

~Cadriel~

I intended to keep my resolution to speak to Tanith at our next stop, but once I'd finished helping to get things unpacked in preparation for the night ahead, I turned around and she'd disappeared.

"She went off with the centaur," Zol told me, obviously knowing exactly who I was looking for. "He seemed a little upset."

It surprised me that Zol had noticed, but I had seen the change in Tymanus too. Whatever secret he kept weighed heavily on him despite his usual mirth, and in her kindness, Tanith wanted to help. Just another reason for me to admire her.

My own desire to speak to her would simply have to wait. Others' needs came before my own, always. That formed a key part of my personal code of honour.

When they returned, Ty seemed a little happier, and as he and Zol joked over dinner, things seemed brighter overall. Leith's light-heartedness returned in full, and even Aiqen seemed a little more relaxed.

"It's nice to have someone else who understands that duty comes first," he admitted to me as we watched Ty and Zol engage in an arm-wrestling match once the food had all been eaten. Both parties cheated, with Tanith and Leith stepping in to try to help one side or the other, and everyone seemed to be having a good time.

How did they do it? Completely lose themselves in the moment, forgetting everything else going on in the world around them? That had never come naturally to me, and judging from the things he'd said, I suspected it didn't for Aiqen either. Did he ever wish it did?

"There's a time and place for frivolity, but we must remain on guard," he continued, unaware of my train of thought.

That gave me as good an opening as any to ask him what I'd just been wondering about. "Is there a time and place, though? I mean, do *you* make time for it? Do you ever do this?"

I gestured to the group in front of us, where the arm-wrestling had devolved to full-out wrestling. Grunts and shrieks of laughter filled the air as they grappled with each other.

Aiqen's nose wrinkled at the scene. "Well, no. Not like that."

"So, what do you do for fun?" I followed up. Although I engaged in activities which helped to relax me, I didn't know if any of them could be considered frivolous. All of them ultimately served a purpose.

"Well, I enjoy my training," he told me, almost defensively. "Flying is fun too."

I supposed it could be, but I never used my wings simply for sight-seeing. "Do you ever do anything that's not directly related to your training?"

"What are you implying?" My questions were making him suspicious, which hadn't been my intention. I asked for no reason other than my own curiosity.

"I'm just thinking about something Zol said to me. He said he wanted me to be happy, but I think we might have different definitions of what that means. He looks happy now, but in his position, I would feel self-conscious."

My half-brother clung to the underside of Ty's horse end, trying to avoid the centaur's reach. Leith had climbed onto Ty's back, trying to reach Zol from above, while Tanith had found a large fern frond somewhere and tried to reach under the centaur's body and tickle Zol with it. Despite being outnumbered, Zol grinned ear-to-ear, clearly relishing the challenge.

Aiqen's eyes narrowed as he watched. "Ty always told me he doesn't carry people on his back," he muttered, missing the bigger picture entirely.

Did I have the same problem? Did I get so focused on what I should be doing that I missed out on the other things? My conversation with Zol had opened new doubts in my mind and new questions.

When he told me he'd had sex with Tanith, it didn't upset me nearly as much as it should have. It surprised me, certainly, because I felt this unusual connection with her and had hoped she felt it too. But on the other hand, Zol saw that she was in need last night and 'helped her out', as he put it. While I'd offered to sleep next to her, he went a step further and told her in no uncertain terms what he could do for her. It turned out she wanted it too, and they'd enjoyed it, I had to assume. Tanith certainly didn't seem upset that morning. If Zol hadn't told me what happened, I never would have known.

So what would happen if I simply told her what *I* wanted? What if I tried being a little more like Zol, just this once, and didn't stress about the big picture? What if I let myself live in the moment like he did?

By the time the others had worn themselves out, I'd made up my mind. As everyone got ready for bed, I asked Tanith if we could go somewhere quiet to talk. She immediately agreed, and when we got a short distance from the camp, I offered her my hand.

"I'd like to go far enough away to give us complete privacy, but I don't want to waste our time walking. Will you let me carry you?"

I stretched out my wings to make it clear what I meant, and Tanith's face lit up. "I would love to fly with you, Cad."

I had carried humans before, but only in the course of my work. I'd never done it simply because I wanted to, but that time, when I lifted Tanith in my arms, one hand around her back and the other beneath her knees while her arms wrapped around my neck, I had no goal in mind other than spending time with her. Slowly, I aimed towards the sky, flapping my wings carefully until we cleared the trees and I could stretch them out fully.

"Oh, wow!" Tanith gazed out at the golden sunset in the distance above the canopy of trees, the whole world opening before us. "This is amazing, Cad. You must feel so free up here."

I'd never thought of it that way, but I supposed it could be freeing. With her, I felt that way. Nothing held me back unless I let it.

"Can you do any tricks?" she asked next, her eyes glinting in the setting sun. "Show me your best angel moves."

Tricks? Normally, I simply flew from point A to point B, but not wanting to disappoint her, I held her tighter against me. "Don't let go," I warned before flying straight up, putting significant distance between us and the ground before inverting back into a dive. Free-falling, we dropped back towards the trees head-first. The ground rushed towards us, the wind stealing our breath so that even if we wanted to speak, we couldn't, and at the very last second, I opened my wings again. My stomach continued to fall even as our bodies lifted upwards, giving me the same sensation of butterflies that Tanith herself did, and our feet brushed against the tops of the trees as I soared back up on the breeze.

"That was amazing," Tanith gasped, sounding just as breathless as I felt. Her heart raced against my chest, her body pressed tight against mine, and before I could second guess myself or think of all the reasons I shouldn't do it, I leaned down and brushed my lips against hers, sending my heart soaring in an entirely new way.

~Tanith~

I wrote this scene in my book: Tanith and Cadriel, high in the sky above the forest, soaring on his angel wings and locked in their first embrace, his virgin lips on hers.

I thought it seemed sexy when I wrote it, but I had vastly underestimated just how amazing it would actually be. The way my stomach flipped had very little to do with defying gravity. The wind in my hair and the feeling of weightlessness were incredible, but they didn't hold a candle to the feeling of being in Cad's arms and seeing the hopeful look in his eyes as he gave himself over to the innocent pleasure of a kiss.

For thousands of years, he'd lived without experiencing it, but after meeting me, he wanted to try, and that made me feel sexier than anything ever had before. No one had *ever* considered me any kind of temptress, and I certainly never had either, but something about Cad made me embrace the role. I wanted to show him just how good all of it could be, and how he didn't have to lose sight of his fundamental goodness just by indulging a little bit.

Knowing with certainty that he had already struggled with himself and ultimately chosen this made me bolder than I ever would have been otherwise. In the short time I'd been in that world, I already felt like a different person, someone confident and sure of herself and undeniably attractive. The feeling thrilled me almost as much as Cad's sweet kiss.

Gradually, we floated back down to the ground, our lips still locked together, until Cad's feet touched solid earth and he gently placed me down, pulling away from me with his cheeks flushed red as he took a step back.

"I'm sorry." His startled green eyes darted around the quiet forest, looking for some kind of explanation about what just happened. "I shouldn't have... I should have asked... I didn't mean to..."

For most people, a kiss like that would have been a very small thing indeed, but it had clearly shaken Cadriel. Overwhelmed with what just happened, he started to spiral, taking a step back, and another, until I stepped forward and placed my hands on his cheeks, forcing him to look down at me.

"Cad, you didn't do anything wrong. I wanted you to kiss me, and I loved it. If that's all you want to do, that's absolutely fine with me. If you'd like to do more, I'd like that too. The decision is entirely in your hands. I don't want you to be uncomfortable."

"But I've never... I don't..." He still couldn't form a complete sentence and he took a deep breath to try to calm himself, closing his eyes as he exhaled. When he opened them again, the panic had receded. Maybe his calming power worked on him too. "I've never done anything simply because I wanted to, Tanith. That's not how my life works. You don't seem surprised, so I suppose I must have done this in your book too, but it's something I never expected for myself."

His words made total sense to me, and I responded to him as honestly as I could. "I can't imagine the kind of life you've led. I mean, I tried to when I wrote about you, but there were things I never fully understood. Not just with you, but with all the men we're travelling with. I suppose it's because I only thought of you as characters whom I needed to behave a certain way, and I didn't understand all of your past experiences that made you who you are. I didn't go deep enough to try to understand how your lives shaped your motivations. So even though I know what might happen next, I don't fully understand why. In that way, I'm just as out of my depth here as you are."

As I hoped, my explanation seemed to make him feel a bit better. A smile tugged at the corner of his lips as he invited me to sit down on some rocks in the small clearing where we'd found ourselves. It looked vaguely familiar to me, and as I took a seat, I realized it must have been the same location where Zol and I had our encounter the night before. It had been darker then, but the shapes all looked the same. The tree where I'd bent over stood next to the rock that Cad sat on. Did it mean something that we'd ended up in the same spot, or was it just a coincidence?

"What happened next between us in your book?" Cad asked me straight out. "Did we come here together?"

"We did." I had no intention of hiding anything from him. "We had a conversation about how conflicted you're feeling. It's interesting: some things that have happened since I arrived here have been almost word-for-word with what I wrote and others have been close but not exact. For example, we never had this part of the conversation about what happened in my book, because my characters weren't aware that they were in a book. Does that make sense?"

It struck me as completely absurd when I said it out loud, but luckily, Cadriel understood what I was trying to say perfectly. "It makes sense to me, Tanith. It seems the basic structure is set, and even if we make small changes, the overall narrative keeps moving forward. We don't seem to have a lot of control here, other than the changes you can make with your phone to our physical surroundings."

He'd summarized it well, and I thought I understood where he might be heading. "You want to try changing something bigger?"

His pleased smile filled me with warmth. "Exactly. I think it might be worth a try. Tell me: what happens next?"

My heart beat a little faster as I looked into his deep green eyes, his firm body so close to mine. "After talking quite a lot about your duty and what kinds of pleasure are sinful, you decided it wouldn't be so bad to give in to your desires just for one night."

His eyes dropped to my lips, clearly remembering the feel of them just as I could still feel his against mine. "And that was something you wanted?"

"I've already told you it is," I reminded him. "I don't know what the point of all of this is, Cad. I don't know why we're here or for how long, but I know that you're incredible. I know that I have a connection with you, and with the others as well."

His eyes immediately snapped back up to mine. "*All* the others? Zol told me you and he already..."

He didn't seem to be able to finish the sentence, so I filled in the blank for him, wanting to be just as open with him as I had been with Leith earlier. "Slept together, yes. And Leith and I have as well. If the book holds true, before we leave these woods, I'll be intimate with both Ty and Aiqen too. I don't really know how to explain it. In my regular life, I'm not like this at all. I couldn't be even if I wanted to. I'm nobody. I'm not the girl anyone wants or anyone feels pulled towards. I'm the girl who gets left behind, the girl who gets cheated on. But here, you all see me as special. I *feel* special, and it feels natural to connect with you all physically as well as emotionally."

"So what happens here doesn't matter to you?" he asked, sounding almost hurt by the idea. "It's just a diversion?"

"No, that's not what I mean at all," I quickly corrected. "It's more like: here, the rules don't apply the same way. We feel things more deeply, more quickly. We find ourselves thrown together with people, with other species we wouldn't normally ever meet, and we connect in ways that wouldn't normally be possible. You're incredibly important to me, and so are the others. If you asked me to choose between you, I wouldn't be able to."

He glanced away from me, and afraid that I'd hurt his feelings, I tried to lighten the mood.

"Isn't that what angels believe in? Equal love for all?"

It worked. Cad's lips pursed in amusement as his eyes returned to me. "That's not exactly how we mean it."

"But the principle is the same," I prompted, and he had to concede that. "Just because I had sex with Zol doesn't mean it wouldn't be special to me with you, Cad. In fact, it would be special to me precisely *because* it's so special to you. With Zol, we both enjoyed it, but I know he's enjoyed many other women, and men, and probably other creatures too. I accept that as part of him, it doesn't make him any less attractive to me. It's just part of who he is."

Cad nodded slowly as he thought that all over. "I understand, Tanith. I think I do. But I also think it would be a good idea to try to change the narrative a little if we can. You said that in the book, we sleep together now, so perhaps we shouldn't, just to see if that changes anything else."

I couldn't pretend his suggestion didn't disappoint me, but as I promised him I would, I completely respected his decision. "If that's what you want, Cad, I understand."

He raised his hand to brush it against my cheek, very softly, as if one of his feathers had touched me rather than his fingers. "It's not what I want, and I think you know that. But I think it's what's right, for the greater good."

"And that's the difference between you and Zol in a nutshell," I couldn't help pointing out, and he conceded as much with a wry smile. "In that case, we should get back before it gets much darker."

He picked me up again effortlessly, spreading his wings once more and returning to the sky. I didn't know how he knew where to fly back to, but he didn't hesitate. In the distance, I could just make out a dim glow of lights beyond the forest.

"Is that the witch's house, do you think?" I asked him, pointing in the direction of the light.

"It could be," he agreed, looking back down at the forest, measuring how far we'd already come compared to how far we still had to go. "We're about halfway, I suppose. One more full day and night, and we should be almost there."

"That's how it is in the book, and that's as far as I got in writing it. I don't know what happens when we get there."

"Well, let's see what happens in the next day, and how closely it stays to what you'd written. If we need to make more adjustments, we can. We'll get to the bottom of this eventually, Tanith. I promise."

A promise from an angel meant a great deal, and it warmed my heart as we returned to the camp to sleep, even if my body remained frustratingly cold and unsatisfied.

CHAPTER NINE

Just as I promised Tanith I would, I tried my best not to be jealous when she went for a walk with Cadriel after supper. They might have just been going to talk, and it helped that I could distract myself by talking to Ty and Zol. The three of us made each other laugh quite a lot, and though I invited Aiqen to join us, he seemed to prefer scouting the forest for danger instead. Had I ever heard him laugh? I couldn't remember for sure.

When Tanith and Cad returned, she had her arms wrapped around herself, looking cold, so I invited her to come and sleep next to me where I could keep her warm.

"That would be nice, thank you, Leith." Her smile warmed me more than any body heat could, and as she curled up next to me, the ground felt a whole lot more comfortable. Maybe she didn't need to choose me *all* the time. Maybe these moments when she did would be enough.

In the morning, Tanith's movement woke me before anyone else had stirred. Blinking drowsily in the dim light of the rising sun, I saw her sitting up next to me, holding the strange device she had used a few other times. Ty told me it was called a phone, but I had to confess I still didn't fully understand what it did, other than giving off a soft glow that made Tanith's face even more beautiful than usual.

"What are you doing?" I asked as softly as I could, but she jumped anyway, her shoulders hunching as she held the device closer to her.

"I'm sorry if I woke you, Leith. Please, pretend you didn't see any-thing." She tapped at the screen a few more times before switching it off and putting it back in her pocket.

"Why shouldn't I have seen that?" As was often the case, I felt I had missed something.

"Cad asked me not to do what I was just doing," she admitted, lying back down next to me. "He said I shouldn't waste the phone's battery unless we needed to, but in this case, I thought it might be necessary."

"Oh." I still didn't understand but it could get annoying if I kept asking questions. Aiqen had told me so, and since I didn't want to annoy Tanith, I stayed silent instead.

Tanith turned to face me, her eyes full of affection. "You don't have any idea what I'm talking about, do you?"

I shook my head sheepishly.

Leaning forward, she placed a light kiss on my lips. "Don't worry about it. When something's important, I'll explain it fully, but you don't need to be concerned about this. Just trust me, okay?"

I trusted her completely, so I accepted that answer and we dozed off again briefly before the others all woke up. Over breakfast, Cadriel told us all about what he and Tanith had seen from above the trees last night and how he expected we had one more full day of walking to make it through the forest.

"I saw the same thing earlier yesterday," Aiqen quickly interjected, looking put out that he hadn't been the one to share the news first. "I can always go up again and check if we need to. In fact, I'd be happy to fly ahead and see what's there..."

"No, Aiqen," Tanith cut him off gently. "We need to do this as a team. It's important that we stick together. I'm sure your ability to shift and fly will come in handy later."

That assurance mollified him a little, though he obviously still would have preferred to take matters into his own hands.

"Is there anything we should know about the path ahead?" Cadriel asked Tanith. "We've already had the trees that caused lust and the Vale of Disillusion. Is there anything else between us and the far edge of the forest?"

Tanith shook her head but didn't make eye contact with him as she replied. "No. It's just a regular forest."

She glanced over at me for a moment and Cadriel followed her gaze curiously. "Leith? Do you know something?"

"I don't know anything," I answered quite truthfully.

Ty smiled as Aiqen got to his feet, ready to move on. "In that case, let's pack up and move out."

Soon, we were walking again in the forest. The day grew much hotter than the previous days had, and I missed the water's cooling touch. After an hour, I took off my shirt, figuring if Ty could go without one, I could too. Zol quickly followed suit, giving me a small rush of pride that I'd done something he considered worth copying. Aiqen and Cadriel, however, both remained fully clothed.

The vegetation grew thicker and the path became even narrower as we went, making the warm air feel even more oppressive. Several times, I brushed up against shrubs, their leaves and branches scratching at my skin and snagging on my pants.

After a little while longer, my skin began to itch.

"Stop scratching," Aiqen instructed.

"How did you know I was scratching?" From the front of the group, he shouldn't have been able to see me.

He sighed, as if I should already know the answer. "Wyverns have very good hearing and it's a very grating sound."

That explained one thing, but not why my skin seemed to be growing drier and itchier by the second.

"Could someone reach my back?" I requested as I scratched down my stomach. "It's really itchy."

"Did this just start, Leith?" Tanith moved up from the rear of the group to look over my body in concern. My skin had reddened where I'd scratched it, but otherwise, I didn't see anything to be worried about.

"Perhaps he's having some kind of reaction to the plant life," Cadriel suggested. "It didn't look like poison ivy to me, but it could be something similar."

"It's not poison ivy," Tanith told us all with a wince. "I know what this is."

"What is it?" I asked while continuing to scratch. The itching was quickly becoming unbearable.

"You said there was nothing to be concerned about," Cadriel reminded her.

"I know, but I said that because I thought I'd changed it. I went on my phone this morning and I tried to take out any mention of the Stimulating Stems. I thought it would work."

Cad's lips pursed, his eyes darting between my incessant scratching and Tanith's guilty face. "You should have told us."

"Perhaps, but it's embarrassing that I invented these things in the first place. Or at least, I thought I did. But if they're here even after I erased them, maybe I didn't make them up after all? I don't really understand."

They'd lost me with their conversation, and only partly because of how distracting the itch was.

"What are these Stimulating Stems?" Aiqen asked, looking around at all the plants suspiciously. "What do they do?"

Tanith grimaced once more as she filled us in. "Well, as Cadriel said, they're similar to poison ivy. Contact with the leaves will make you terribly itchy, but the reaction is actually happening beneath the skin. It causes an arousal that manifests as an itch. The only way to make it stop is..."

She trailed off as we all leaned forward, but the words that came out of her mouth next were not what any of us expected.

"An orgasm."

~Tymanus~

Zol snickered next to me when Tanith said that Leith had to orgasm to stop the itching. "Well, that's easy enough. He can go jerk off until he feels better and then we can keep going."

Aiqen rolled his eyes at the demon. "Why do I have a feeling that's your solution to everything?"

"Actually, in this case, it really is the best solution," Tanith explained apologetically. "Along with stopping the itching, the orgasm will make him temporarily immune, so even if he accidentally touches the leaves again, it won't bother him. The only thing is, he can't do it himself. As you can see, he can't stop scratching for more than a few seconds, definitely not long enough to make himself come."

I was actually trying *not* to watch Leith scratching himself, since watching him made me itch too. At least, I hoped the itchiness came from an empathetic response and not from having touched the leaves myself. I gave my chest a quick scratch when no one else was looking.

"So, someone else has to get him off?" Zol clarified. "That's just as easy. There's five of us and we've all got two hands and a variety of holes."

Cadriel pressed his eyes closed and took a deep breath. "Perhaps we should ask Leith what he wants."

All eyes moved over to the merman who appeared to be growing more uncomfortable by the second. "Please, just make it stop," he begged. "Tanith, will you help me?"

"Of course," she quickly agreed. "The rest of you, wait here. We'll be right back."

"Actually, I think I better come with you." Each scratch only made it itch worse. "I think I must have touched it too."

"Oh, for the love of Draig," Aiqen muttered, and Cad looked over at him curiously.

"Who's Draig?"

Aiqen's eyes widened in disbelief. "The most famous wyvern of all, you must have heard of him."

He looked set to launch into one of his long-winded tales, so I quickly motioned to Tanith that we should leave. The three of us made our way back down the path a short distance, Leith still scratching madly and my own itching getting worse all the time.

Only when we stopped did I realize Zol had come with us too. "Did you touch it too?"

He shook his head. "No, but I wasn't about to stay there with the killjoy twins. This group seems like a lot more fun. Besides, as I said, I can help."

Tanith watched my reaction carefully. "Would it be okay with you if Zol helped you, Ty?"

How she knew it, I had no idea, but I would actually prefer Zol's help. Being intimate in any way with Tanith frightened me, remembering what had happened to Evia, and even if this situation was far more clinical than sexy, I would prefer not to cross that line if I didn't have to. "That's fine," I assured her, not missing the grin that lit up the demon's face with my agreement. "You take care of Leith. Zol and I can figure the rest out."

Tanith led Leith a little further away, just out of sight, as Zol rubbed his hands together in anticipation. "I promise you've never had a handjob like the one I can give you."

I had no reason to doubt him, but at that moment, I was nowhere near turned on. If anything, my cock seemed to have shrunk with the notion that it might have to perform. I hadn't been with anyone in a sexual way since Evia. I hadn't even done anything solo. Was it possible to forget how? I felt quite unsure but I tried to put on a brave face. "How about a little less talk, Zol? Are you okay to get under me?"

I had no intention of shifting out of my centaur form, so he'd need to get beneath my horse end to reach my cock. The demon had no complaints about that, getting down onto his hands and knees willingly enough to crawl beneath me.

The itching grew stronger, but I had to admit, when the demon's hand wrapped around my cock, it provided a distraction. I definitely had no kind of romantic feelings towards Zol, and I didn't know if a demon was even capable of caring for another person.

I had no reason to feel guilty since this had nothing to do with emotion at all. The act was purely physical. Medical, even. I simply had to let myself get aroused.

On paper, it shouldn't have been difficult. Zol told the truth when he said he had plenty of experience. Once he got me out of my pants, his skillful hands got me hard easily enough, but no matter how much effort he put in, I couldn't get any closer to the necessary climax.

"Do you mind if I use my mouth?" he asked from beneath me, sounding a little confused at his lack of success.

"Go ahead." At that point, I just wanted it to be over, both the itching and the whole experience.

Again, his tongue left nothing to be desired. Other men and beasts would no doubt kill for a blowjob that good, but every time my end seemed near, Evia's face would appear and cool off my rising heat, no matter how much I tried to stop it.

"No luck?"

Tanith's voice made me jump, and I opened my eyes to see her and Leith standing just a short distance away. The merman had stopped scratching, which I assumed meant that they'd had more success than we had, and his eyes were wide as he watched Zol sucking me off from below.

It must have made quite a sight.

"I don't think it's going to happen," I admitted. "I guess I'll just have to suffer."

I couldn't ask Zol to do any more than he was already doing and I just couldn't see us getting there.

Tanith's lips pursed as she watched me scratching at my torso. "Or you could let me try, Ty."

My cock immediately stiffened at that idea, blood rushing to it almost against my will. It seemed she *might* have success, but the thought still scared me. I didn't want to feel anything for her. I didn't want her to know how to turn me on.

"It doesn't have to mean anything," she continued, moving a little closer. "It's a treatment, nothing more."

It wouldn't be only a treatment, though; that was both the problem and the reason it might work.

My resistance faded further as she placed her soft hand on my cheek. "Let me help, Ty. I know it hurts."

Did she mean the itching, or Evia's loss? Either way, she had a point; the pain had become nearly unbearable.

"Okay." I didn't even know I'd meant to say the word until I did. "Zol, thank you for trying."

With a sigh, the demon got back to his feet. "You've just ruined my perfect record, Ty. I've never failed before. Thousands of years, down the drain."

"It really isn't you." I gave him an apologetic shrug. "That tongue is something else."

That lifted his spirits, and he flashed his forked tongue for us both to see. Tanith's cheeks turned red at the sight of it even as she smiled, reminding me that she'd probably already had it used on her.

Just another reason why what we were about to do didn't mean anything. She didn't love me, not like Evia had. She was a sweet, caring, pretty girl, but when it came down to it, we were just friends and she would simply be doing me a favour.

Leith and Zol left us to return to the other two while Tanith kissed me softly. "I know you haven't been with anyone since her, and I know what it means to you, Ty, but this would be easier in your human form."

Asking the demon to crawl down in the dirt between my four legs was one thing; not only didn't he mind, he revelled in the extra depravity of it. Tanith was different. She deserved to feel comfortable, even if it brought my painful memories even closer to the surface.

My heart pounding, I closed my eyes and began the shift. It felt stiff and awkward, like stretching out a muscle not used in a long time, but eventually, I stood before her on only two legs instead of four.

Almost immediately, I lost my balance.

"Here, come and sit down."

Doing her best to support me, Tanith led me to a fallen tree and helped me take a seat on it. My cock, smaller in this form, was still stiff, and once I was seated, Tanith knelt down between my legs.

"This is a lot more manageable," she said with a warm smile, taking my cock in her hand. "Still impressive, but not scary."

The itching seemed to subside as all the sensation in my body centered in the organ she stroked so gently. Tired of the emotional weight I'd been carrying for so long, I let it go just for a minute as I leaned back and closed my eyes. Maybe it wouldn't hurt to forget, just for a moment.

Taking that as an invitation, Tanith began to stroke my cock harder. She spit into her hand several times, trying to keep it lubricated, but eventually, she asked me just as Zol had, "Is it okay if I use my mouth?"

I simply nodded, not wanting to break the spell that had descended over me. It felt like floating, sitting there in my human form, focused only on the moment. I had no past and no future, nothing other than this moment, and when her warm, wet mouth covered me, blood pumped through my body even harder, taking me even closer to release.

Tanith hummed with satisfaction as she felt me hardening, and the vibration of her mouth around my sensitive head sent shivers of pleasure through me. As she sucked and stroked me eagerly, knowing me in all my forms and all my vulnerabilities and wanting to please me anyway, I finally let myself go.

~Aiqen~

I had only just finished telling Cadriel the story of Draig and his most famous exploits when Leith and Zol returned to us. I had many more stories I could tell but at least he'd gotten the gist of it. Draig was my idol and one day, hopefully, people would tell stories of my adventures in the same way.

"Where are the others?" I asked, peering down the path behind the two who had just returned. We kept wasting time in this forest, and now that we knew our goal lay within reach, if not that night then definitely by the next morning, I was more eager than ever to keep moving. The sooner we got there, the sooner we could overcome the challenge that awaited us, and hopefully with that accomplished, we would all return to our individual realms and lives, making this whole strange situation nothing but a curious memory.

"Ty got itchy as well," Leith explained. He seemed to have stopped scratching, thankfully. "Tanith is helping him."

Cadriel's lips tightened at that news. It seemed he wanted to move on as much as I did. I understood him far more than I did any of the others. "Has anyone managed to identify what this plant looks like, so the rest of us can avoid it? Leith, which ones did you touch?"

The merman looked around helplessly at the various plants surrounding us. "Most of them?"

"There's an easy enough way to tell," the demon claimed. "These three are the most common in this part of the forest."

He pointed to three different plants, and I had to agree those did seem to be the most prolific ones surrounding our path.

"The three of us haven't been affected yet," he continued, gesturing to himself, me and Cadriel. "So, we each rub one on ourselves, and whoever gets itchy will have the winner."

Cadriel's jaw clenched. "Or we could just avoid touching *all* the plants."

"In a fucking forest?" Zol scoffed. "The path is getting narrower all the time. In fact, we're probably all going to touch it eventually, so maybe identifying it doesn't even matter. We might as well get it over with and get the immunity so we can get through the rest of the day with no further distractions."

His suggestion held a certain amount of logic, though the idea of having to rely on someone else to 'help me' with the treatment went against all my natural inclinations. Generally, I preferred to be the one doing the helping, but in this case, that didn't appeal to me either, at least not so far as the other men were concerned. Perhaps if Tanith were the one in need of assistance...

My body reacted to that thought against my will, but while I would usually push that kind of response down, this might actually be the perfect time to indulge the thoughts and feelings I'd had about Tanith. Nobody could really call it a distraction if some intimacy between us was required in order for us to keep progressing.

Cadriel, however, didn't seem to agree. "I want no part in it," he insisted, and Zol shrugged.

"It's your call. Aiqen, are you with me?"

The demon picked some leaves off the closest of the plants and began to rub it across his chest. Not wanting to let him show me up, I quickly followed suit, rubbing the leaves along my neck while the angel watched us both, his arms crossed in disapproval.

We were just finishing with the third plant when Tanith and Ty rejoined us. "What are you two doing?" Tanith asked in bewilderment, looking at me and Zol.

"Purposefully infecting ourselves to gain immunity," I explained while Zol gave her a flirtatious wink.

"I hope your wrist isn't too worn out yet."

Tanith rolled her eyes, but I could see her thinking things over. "It does make sense, but this didn't happen in the book," she told Cadriel, who still hadn't moved. "So maybe we should? Change the direction of the story, as you suggested? Maybe this is because of the change you made last night?"

"I'll just avoid the leaves," he told her, still sticking to his position. "But you may do as you like."

With a shrug, Tanith took the leaves Zol offered her and rubbed them on her neck, following my lead.

"How quickly will we know if it worked?" I wondered out loud. Thus far, I felt fine.

"I think it will be a few minutes," Tanith guessed. "We can keep moving forward in the meantime if you like."

That *did* appeal to me, so we continued on forward, me at the front again. I couldn't help peering back at the others from time to time to see if they were starting to scratch. Cadriel walked very carefully, ensuring no exposed part of his body came into contact with anything.

After about ten minutes, my skin began to tingle.

"I think I'm feeling it now," Zol announced from behind me, and Tanith and I both nodded in agreement.

"It's mild at first," she explained. "If you scratch it, it will get worse."

"What, like this?" Immediately, Zol began to scratch on his chest as Tanith shook her head in amusement.

"The rest of you, wait here," I instructed. "We'll return as soon as we can."

"Hopefully not *too* soon," Zol added, giving the others a smirk.

I would have preferred not to have him along, but I already had a plan: Tanith could take care of him first so that Zol could leave us, and then she and I would mutually treat each other's symptoms.

Zol, however, had a different plan, which he made clear to us as soon as we found an appropriate spot in the forest with enough room for the three of us.

"Tanith needs to come too, so it's more efficient if we all work together. A spit-roast should work perfectly."

Tanith's cheeks flushed as I tried to figure out what he meant. Eventually, I had to admit defeat. I'd never heard the term before, at least not to refer to anything other than cooking. "What's that?"

Zol replied as bluntly as always. "One of us fucks her mouth and the other takes her pussy. Since I'm a gentleman, you can have first pick."

Heat rose in my cheeks to match Tanith's blush. I'd never heard of such a thing, but they both seemed to regard it as something common and acceptable. Humans and demons differed from wyverns in a few ways, it seemed.

"No one has ever accused you of being a gentleman, Zol," Tanith admonished him, but I noticed she didn't object to his suggestion. Instead, she looked over at me with an apologetic shrug. "It *would* be more efficient, but it's up to you, Aiqen."

I certainly hadn't anticipated anything like that, but I could see the benefit. My itchiness had increased and I assumed Tanith felt the same. If we waited for her to treat Zol first, it would only get worse.

"If you're sure you don't mind, then it's okay with me." She would be the one having to deal with both of us.

A tentative smile crossed Tanith's face. "I think I won't really mind at all."

Zol took the lead, telling us both to remove our pants as he pulled his own off. Just the anticipation of what was about to happen had me growing harder despite my itchiness, and when Tanith reached down to start to stroke both of our cocks, me in her right hand and Zol in her left, I had to admit I found the whole situation rather arousing.

So did she, clearly, from the way her thighs clenched. "I'm ready when you both are," she told us, sounding a little more breathless than she had earlier.

I could sympathize. Although we were doing this as 'treatment', my focus was on scratching a very different itch instead.

In a surprisingly thoughtful gesture, Zol arranged our discarded clothing on the ground for Tanith to rest her hands and knees on as she got into position. "Which end are you taking?" he asked me as we stood above her.

If this was going to be my one moment of indulgence, which was all I intended it to be, I might as well make the most of it. I therefore moved around to her backside, running my fingers over her smooth, rounded cheeks lightly before slipping my hand between her legs. She hadn't been kidding about being ready. I wouldn't need to do much at all to prepare her.

Zol made no complaint about my choice as he stood in front of Tanith, placing his cock against her lips while I got down on one knee, finding the best position for myself.

I'd had sex before, but not often, and never quite like this. Wyvern females were dominant and sexually demanding. Men might rule the battlefield, but in bed, women usually caused the shots. Tanith, however, could hardly look more compliant as she knelt there, taking Zol in one end with her legs spread for me.

When I slid my hard cock slowly into her wet hole, it only got better. Tight and warm, her pussy felt even more perfect than I'd imagined. From my vantage point, I could watch my cock sliding in and out of her, coated in her wetness, and the sight combined with the physical sensations turned me on even more. She let me set the pace, giving me full control, and as our mutual enjoyment increased with each stroke, I forgot all about being the hero. I forgot about quests and witches and thrones and focused entirely on this unusual woman and the pleasure I could give her and she could give me.

She moaned in approval as I moved within her, the sound muffled by Zol's cock as he thrust into her mouth, and for some reason, that only turned me on more. I'd never been in an intimate situation with another man there, and it surprised me that it not only didn't bother me, it almost enhanced the experience.

Together, the three of us worked ourselves to a fever pitch that had nothing to do with the stimulation stems. Tanith's body took us both beautifully as we complimented her skill and beauty. I never knew anyone could look so enchanting while being ravaged by two different men at the same time.

When I felt myself getting close, I let them both know. It only felt right that we should try to reach our climax together.

"I can go on command," Zol told me. "You just worry about Tanith."

Reaching around her body, I rubbed her clit as I continued to thrust into her, faster and harder as my eruption grew closer, and when I felt her beginning to clench around me, I groaned in satisfaction.

"Now," I told Zol, and he exhaled loudly, letting himself go at the same time I did. Every feeling in my body seemed to concentrate in my cock, exploding in a release of pleasure that flooded back out through every part of me, erasing everything else in its path.

It took a moment before I could move again, and as I pulled out of Tanith, my body felt much lighter even as my mind reeled. I really hadn't expected that to be anywhere near that good. I didn't even realize the itching had stopped until we all got back to our feet.

"Everyone feel better?" Zol asked as we put our pants back on. I put my arm around Tanith to help steady her as she stepped into her underwear. She seemed a little unsteady on her feet.

"I feel great," she told us both, smiling between us. "How about you?"

"I feel great too," I admitted. In fact, I couldn't remember the last time I felt so relaxed. "It seems to have worked."

"You're not so bad when you stop talking," Zol told me with a laugh. "That was fun. We should do it again sometime."

Tanith shook her head again, finding Zol as amusing as she usually did, but what surprised me most of all was just how much his suggestion appealed to me.

CHAPTER TEN

~Tanith~

Warm satisfaction filled me as Aiqen, Zol and I returned to the rest of the group, and not only because of the amazing orgasm I'd just had.

As I told Cadriel, this part didn't happen in my book: Aiqen and Zol didn't purposely infect themselves and the threesome had never taken place. It had been in the back of my mind to write that kind of scene eventually, but I hadn't built up to it yet, and I was pretty sure that nothing I could have written would have lived up to the reality of it anyway.

Not only did these two unique, intriguing, handsome men both like me, and find me sexy, they were starting to trust and like each other too. In my book, that had been the point of the forest: to bring us all together in a way that made us vulnerable to each other, not only sexually but emotionally too, so that when we were called upon to face the challenges that lay ahead, we were all invested not only in our individual success, but in each other too.

So far, that seemed to be working even better than anticipated, as Aiqen and Zol laughed together, enjoying each other's company for the first time since they'd met.

The only holdout was Cadriel.

He was proving to be a harder nut to crack than I had anticipated, and although I knew he would give his all to help our cause, we were still missing that deeper connection that had started to form between the rest of us. It didn't come down to sex; well, it didn't *only* come down to sex, but the fact that he refused any kind of intimacy suggested he hadn't connected with me as much as the others had, or as much as he had in my book.

He said he wanted to change the narrative, but I didn't want to miss out on the connection we were supposed to have and the benefits that came with it. It had a wider purpose beyond the physical pleasure we would both get from it. Cadriel was supposed to learn that letting his guard down and doing things simply for the enjoyment he might get from them could be a good thing, which would help him have a more fulfilling life going forward.

He avoided eye contact with me as we all resumed our walk, moving to the back of the group and keeping his distance from everyone. Did he disapprove of what I had done with the others, even if he only had a vague idea what it might be, or was he secretly jealous? How could I break through the wall he'd erected around himself and help him towards a different kind of erection instead? He gave me no clues about how I should proceed.

Other than Cad's aloofness, the rest of the day's walk proved enjoyable for all of us. The atmosphere felt light and easy as we all laughed and joked with each other. The other men took turns speculating as to what other crazy plants might be hidden in the forest, which turned into a speculation of what secret kinks I might have that would have made me write about them.

"We already had the lust trees, but maybe there are some flowers that give you more romantic feelings instead," Leith suggested innocently.

"I think there might be vines that tie you up," was Zol's contribution. "I think Tanith would get a kick out of a little bondage in the forest."

His wink did things to my body that should be illegal, and the other men, seeing my blush, immediately joined in the teasing.

"Some of the tree branches are just the right firmness for spanking," Ty pointed out.

"The smaller ones could be used for tickling," Aiqen added. "Or for a gag."

"I did not create a BDSM forest!" My denial only made them laugh. Zol and Aiqen continued to suggest other uses for the trees and vines as Ty quietly explained to Leith exactly what BDSM was.

By the time we were ready to stop for the night, it felt to me as if the day had flown by, but Cadriel remained uncharacteristically quiet as the group began to set up camp for the night. A few times, I noticed him grimacing, and after a while, he quietly excused himself and wandered off into the woods on his own.

He might just need to relieve himself, but I didn't think his bladder was the issue, so I followed after him, leaving the other four still chatting together.

"Cad?" He had stopped for a moment, leaning against a tree, and he startled when I said his name. Apparently, he hadn't realized I was behind him.

"Go back to the others, Tanith," he requested politely, in a restrained, quiet tone. "I'll be there in just a moment."

"Cad, you're infected, aren't you?" He must have incredible discipline to have lasted this long without doing something about it. The itching would have been unbearable. "You can't just endure it. You have to treat it."

"I know," he admitted softly, both physical and emotional turmoil painted across his face. "I have never... done this... but I must."

"You've never had an orgasm? Not even on your own?" How was that even possible?

"Our bodies were not meant to be used that way," he said, still speaking in that restrained way, as if every word was a struggle to get out. "Orgasm is meant for procreation. Angels are not allowed to procreate, which means there is no need for it."

"Then why would you have the ability?" I couldn't help asking. "If your body wasn't meant to, why can it?"

"By that logic, why shouldn't we murder everyone we come across, since we are able to?"

Masturbation was hardly comparable to murder. It hurt no one. "I am not about to argue theological semantics with an angel, but you really have to do something about this, Cad. I'll leave you on your own if you prefer, but if you don't know what you're doing, it might take longer. I can help you if you'll let me."

"Since you definitely know what you're doing." Those words were slightly defeated and, I was almost certain that time, tinged with jealousy.

"I do," I admitted freely. "Although I have had much more practice at it over these past few days than I ever have before. I think we're meant to be something slightly different than ourselves in this place, Cad. Whatever the reason is we were brought here, there must be a reason we were specifically chosen. The others are all growing closer together and we want you there with us too. We want to know the real you, not just the angel doing his job. What makes Cadriel different from all the other angels?"

"Nothing," he answered me almost sadly. "There is nothing that makes me special."

His confidence in that response nearly broke my heart, and I moved towards him more out of necessity than desire. "I already know that's not true, but I'd like to know more. Let me help you with this, Cad. Trust me the way I already trust you. Take a chance and open yourself up to me. Please."

~**Cadriel**~

I had never known this kind of agony, either physical and spiritual. Many times, I visited people going through torture or other suffering on earth and advised them to endure it, to hold out as long as they could, never fully understanding their situation. Now, faced with a form of torture I had never anticipated, I could finally begin to comprehend what they had gone through..

I could finally understand the temptation to simply give in.

Yet, no matter how much I tried to convince myself that letting Tanith help to cure me of the terrible itch consuming me would be only medicinal, I knew better. Part of me wanted her to do it. Part of me craved it, and that part terrified me.

If I gave in, what would make me any different from Zol? I would be just one more angel who turned his back on the rules that made us what we were.

Tanith asked what made me different from the others, and I told her truthfully that there was nothing. I was simply a soldier doing my job, nameless to all but a very select few, and I was content with that. I had wanted nothing more, not until this place. Until her.

Her hand reached up to stroke my face gently as I continued to fight against the forces at work inside me. "If you tell me to go, I'll go," she promised softly. "I don't want to cause you any discomfort, Cad. I only want to help."

I knew she did, and that made my decision even harder. If she were merely a temptress, someone whose only desire was to see me fail, it would be easier to resist. But as she said, she truly cared for me. She felt something for me; maybe not exactly what I felt for her, since she had also forged a similar connection to all the other men here, but more than any woman ever had before. She was the first one to ever look at me and see more than just an angel. From the moment we met, she had treated me as a man first, and that might have just been the most tempting thing of all.

First and foremost, however, I had to make the itching stop. In my present condition, I was no good to anyone. Although Tanith said it would be difficult for any man to perform the necessary maneuver to relieve himself because of the itching, I would have to try. It still wouldn't be right, and I would need to confess and atone for it, but at least I wouldn't be involving anyone else in my shame.

"Please, go," I whispered back. They weren't the words I wanted to say but the ones I felt I must, and as she promised she would, Tanith nodded in understanding even as disappointment clouded her eyes.

"Alright. I'll see you back at the camp."

As she turned and began to walk back to the others, loneliness flooded through me, stronger than I had ever felt before through all the centuries on my own. In my desire to maintain my code of honour, I was pushing away someone I truly cared about, and the idea of being able to make myself orgasm through that despair seemed even more impossible than before. Although I had never experienced it myself, I knew there was a mental component to sexual fulfillment. In my guilt and sadness, there would be nothing to provide the kind of stimulation required.

The prospect of attempting it on my own and not succeeding appealed to me least of all. Perhaps I needed to reconsider.

"Tanith, wait."

I said the words so quietly that someone else might have missed them, but she stopped immediately, tuned into me as she always seemed to be. "Yes?"

"I... I changed my mind. I need your help."

She turned back without hesitation, not in the least put off by my wavering. "Of course, Cad. I'll help you however I can. Just tell me what you want me to do."

"I don't know what I want you to do." I felt foolish saying the words, but they were true. As much as I understood the mechanics of the various acts, I had no idea which one would work best for me. I had no idea how any of them felt.

She understood me without me needing to explain that in any further detail. "Well, I can use my hands or my mouth or my body. All of them would work so it depends what you would prefer. Are any of them less wrong?"

As I told Zol earlier, I didn't believe in degrees of right or wrong. Things were one or the other, and all the things she suggested fell into the category of wrong. But if they were all as bad as each other, then perhaps I might as well just go for the one I wanted most of all, if I let myself be completely honest.

If I was going to fall anyway, what difference did it make how fast I went down?

"Your body, please." Again, the words were whispered so quietly that I barely heard them myself, but as soon as they were out, as soon as I fully comprehended that I had said them out loud, a rush of desire ran through me, settling straight into my groin in a way I'd never experienced before. It nearly knocked me off my feet.

If I shocked Tanith, she didn't show it. She simply nodded, focused on the task at hand. "In that case, I think you should sit down over here, your back against this tree if that's comfortable. You can keep your clothes on if you prefer, but you'll need your cock out."

Her clinical approach to the situation helped to set me at ease. Guilt and excitement still warred within me, but the idea that we were only doing this because of the medical necessity gave me a bit of relief.

Was this how other people justified their own actions?

Was this how Zol did?

Pushing him out of my mind, I followed her instructions, undoing my pants and pulling them down just enough to release my swelling cock, which had never been in quite this state before. If I ever felt any kind of arousal in the past, I quickly pushed it down. but now, as Tanith's eyes went to the most private part of me, it seemed to grow even bigger beneath her gaze. Painful in its own way, I couldn't deny there was a pleasurable component to the hardening process as well.

She said nothing as I sat down on the mossy grass beneath the tree, leaning back with my legs flat on the ground and my thickened cock lying flat against my stomach. The itchiness that had consumed me for the past few hours left my mind almost entirely as Tanith removed her own pants, giving me a perfect view of her smooth, curvy legs and the junction between them.

I had seen naked women before in the course of my work, perhaps millions of them, but I had never wanted to touch one as much as I did her, even though I had no idea what I was doing.

Thankfully for me, Tanith took the lead.

"You don't need to do anything, Cadriel," she assured me as she knelt down next to me. "I'll take care of you."

I knew she would.

Slowly and gently, giving me plenty of time to change my mind, she reached down and stroked my cock lightly with her fingertips. Even that small amount of contact sent a firestorm of arousal through my body, far stronger than I anticipated. Tanith watched me closely, waiting for me to say that I wanted her to stop, but I couldn't bring myself to speak. I closed my eyes instead, letting the sensations overwhelm me.

If that was the moment of my fall, I may as well enjoy it.

Growing bolder with my compliance, Tanith began to stroke me harder, just for a minute or two, before she removed her hand and I almost cried out in desperation, not wanting the pleasure to stop. She only did it so she could wet her hand though, coating the head of my cock with her saliva before straddling me with her body, her knees on either side of me.

"Cad." She said my name softly, but its meaning was clear: she wanted my confirmation that I still wanted this. I could picture the look of concern and affection in her eyes even as I kept mine closed.

I whispered my consent. "Yes. Please."

With that, she sank down onto me, enveloping my cock in the warm, wet depths of her body, and the pleasure was so intense, my eyes flew open as an unintelligible sound came out of my mouth, a sound of both praise and surprise.

Tanith smiled down at me, her hands cupping my face gently. "That good, huh?"

"It's... miraculous."

She smiled wider before kissing me gently on the lips. Then, her body began to move.

As she promised, I didn't have to do anything. I simply sat there in a stunned stupor of pleasure as she worked her magic, stroking my cock with her body, making me forget everything but the feel of her and the way our bodies fit together so perfectly. Each movement sent fire through my veins, warming me and driving my need for her higher even as it brought me satisfaction.

We were designed for this, just as she'd said.

Her breathing grew shallower as I struggled to catch mine too, making me realize that she was enjoying this as well.

"What do I do?" I asked, feeling rather useless as she did all the work. "How can I satisfy you?"

"Don't worry about that," she assured me, moaning a little as she sank firmly down on me again. "I've got it."

Her hand went between us, touching herself in a way that made her bite her lip in restraint, and the sight of her, so in control yet just as lost to the moment as I was, gave me the final push I needed to lose any control I had left. Pleasure washed over me as my orgasm hit, and Tanith collapsed against me a moment later, her body pulsing in response to the rhythm of my own.

Part of me expected the skies to open and condemnation to rain down upon me, but it didn't. Nothing changed at all, except that in the quiet, calm aftermath of our union, I felt closer to her than I ever had before, and closer to heaven too, which left me wondering: if we both felt this good, why exactly was it wrong?

~Zolgozig~

It didn't take a genius to guess what Cad and Tanith had been up to. When they returned to the camp, her cheeks still flushed with that post-orgasmic haze that seemed strongest in redheads, and my half-brother looked both more relaxed and more wound up than ever before. I said nothing while we ate our meal, but after we'd finished, I asked him to join me for a quick walk.

The wary look he gave me made it clear he didn't want to talk, but I didn't care. Whether he realized it or not, he needed to. The guilt and worry would slowly eat away at him otherwise.

I should know.

I wasted no time diving in as soon as we were out of earshot of the others. The forest closed in dark and thick around us, but after the last three days, I had almost grown accustomed to it. Being in the open after this would take some getting used to. The darkness made it easier to hide.

"The first time I fucked a human, I thought my life was over."

Cad stumbled over his feet, not expecting those words. When he regained his balance, he gave me a look somewhere between curiosity and trepidation. "I don't want to talk about this with you, Zol."

"I know, but we're going to do it anyway. You won't lie to me if I ask you if you slept with her, will you?"

He swallowed, keeping his gaze down at the ground as he told me a half-truth. "The itching drove me crazy."

"That's bullshit, Cad. You were thinking about it before, this just gave you the excuse. At least be honest about it."

At the implication he had lied, his eyes snapped back to me, blazing in indignation. "Fine. I thought about it, I knew it was wrong, and I did it anyway. I was weak. Is that what you want to hear?"

"Not at all." Everyone always assumed demons liked to see people suffering, and for some of them it might be true, but it didn't appeal to me in the least. I got much more pleasure when people enjoyed themselves, even my holier-than-thou pain-in-the-ass half-brother. "Was it as good as you imagined?"

He sputtered a moment longer, trying to maintain his air of righteousness, but finally, his shoulders slumped and his eyes closed as he gave in and answered me not as an angel, but as a man. "Better. So much better."

I clapped him on the shoulder in solidarity. "Good. Now, we're getting somewhere."

With a grimace, he pushed my hand away. "I truly don't mean any offense, Zol, but I don't think you can possibly understand what I'm going through right now. I'd rather deal with this on my own."

As he turned to walk away, an anger I rarely let myself feel began to bubble up inside me and I called out after him in a harsher tone than either of us expected. "You think you're the first angel who's ever been through this? You think you're the first one to feel temptation and to lose the battle? You really think you're that fucking special?"

He turned back to me, his face lined with both hurt and confusion. "I don't think I'm special at all. That's the whole problem. The one thing that defined me was how well I did my job, and without that, I don't know who I am anymore."

He could have been describing me a couple of thousand years earlier. I had been through this exact same moment of self-loathing, he just didn't realize it because he'd never bothered to ask. "That's because we were never *allowed* to be more than the job. We were never allowed to be ourselves at all. You're more than you've let yourself think, Cad. You just don't know it because you've pushed it down for so long."

"How do you know?" The question could have been accusatory, but it didn't come out that way. It sounded plaintive instead, as if he would be willing to believe me if I could only convince him.

"Because I've been there, Cad. You might not remember, but I came to you the first time I 'strayed'. I didn't tell you what had happened, not in so many words, but I came to you for advice. I tried to open up to you."

Cadriel looked even more confused than before as he stepped back towards me, the moonlight that drifted through the trees above falling directly on his face. "When?"

"We were assigned to a battle during the Han dynasty, just the two of us. Do you remember?"

Angels were often sent to watch over battles, supervising the carnage though we were generally not permitted to intervene. It had never been a part of the job I enjoyed. Suffering had never appealed to me.

Cad nodded slowly. "We had just been promoted so that we could go on our own, without supervision, and your fall occurred not long afterwards."

He had the timeline correct, but I wanted to know if he remembered our conversation in particular. "We sat on the mountain looking out over the battlefield, and I told you about the young concubine in the emperor's court."

I could see the moment he pulled it from his memory. "I commented on the beauty of the moonlight across the plains, so at odds with the bloodshed to come, and you compared it to the young woman's form in the cool garden of the palace."

His recollection of the details flattered me, and I found it strangely touching that he would remember so clearly the words I'd spoken two thousand years earlier. "That's right. What I didn't tell you was that I had slept with her the night before. My first time, and the guilt ate away at me, just as it's doing to you right now. I wanted to tell you about it, to talk through the confusion I felt, and do you remember what you said?"

Cad winced as he thought back. "I said that kind of beauty only led to danger, that it had no place in our hearts, and that you cheapened yourself by taking notice of it."

He had it word-for-word, and it stung me almost as much two thousand years later as it had then. "You also told me if I said another word on the subject, you'd report me."

Cad sighed in acknowledgement. "I can see that was harsh. We were young then, Zol. A lot younger than we are now. I hadn't been trusted with a partner before and I wanted to do a good job. I also wanted to help you resist temptation. I thought 'tough love' was the way to go. Obviously, I failed, and when news came of your fall, I felt responsible. That was why I avoided you for so long afterwards. I thought I should have done more that night."

"You abandoned me, along with all the others." My anger had gone, replaced with the betrayal and hurt I'd felt in those lonely decades following my fall. I had no place among the angels but the demons didn't accept me either. They found me 'soft' since I refused to delight in pain the way they did. Humans were my only companions for a long time, and as much as I enjoyed their company, it could never fully compare to the understanding that came from my own kind.

"You knew the consequences, Zol." He had said those words to me before, but they were softer this time, more understanding. "Just as I did tonight. I knew it may lead to my own fall, but I couldn't resist. If it comes to that, I have no one to blame but myself, just as you had to deal with it yourself."

"Fucking the emperor's plaything didn't lead to my fall," I told him crudely, anticipating how uncomfortable the words would make him but knowing they would have more impact that way. "Nor did the dozens of other women and men after her. That's what they don't tell you, Cad: so long as it was just me and willing participants, there *were* no consequences."

My brother's brow furrowed in confusion and disbelief. "That can't be true."

"It is. My own pleasure didn't bring about my fall, and the more I realized it, the angrier I became. I had denied myself for so long, we *all* had, and for what? My anger made me reckless, and I started taking part in the orgies you heard about. One of them attracted a rather sick bastard who not only brought his whole family to it, but his slaves as well, insisting that they take part. They had no choice, and it was the harm brought to *them* that led to my punishment. That was my crime, Cad. I never meant for it to go that way, but up until then, nothing

I had done came to the attention of our superiors. Either they didn't know or they didn't care, so unless you've done Tanith any harm, I truly don't think you have anything to worry about. For once in your life, Cad, you've done something for yourself. That's not something to be ashamed of."

He remained silent for a long while, thinking things over as the last twilight faded around us.

"I'm sorry, Zol."

When he finally spoke again, his words were so quiet, I almost missed them.

"For what?"

"For not listening to you when you tried to open up to me. For not trying to understand."

I'd waited a long time to hear those words from him, or any of them, and though I could barely see his face in the darkness, his tone told me he meant it sincerely.

"Thanks." I cleared my throat as it unexpectedly started to close up. I rarely let my emotional side out and obviously, I needed more practice controlling it. "I'm not sure it would have changed anything that happened."

"Maybe not, but at least you wouldn't have been alone for it. Thank you for not judging me now."

"I'm in no position to judge anyone, Cad. And you know what? Life's a lot more fun when you stop worrying about everyone else anyway."

"And that's a good thing?" A little of his confidence had started to seep back into his voice, but the new softness remained, a gently teasing vibe that made me smile.

"It's a very good thing. Trust me, Cad. The world isn't ending because you gave into temptation, and if you take things a little slower than I did and don't go off the deep end, I honestly think you have nothing to worry about."

That time, he was the one who clapped my shoulder, and we returned to the camp together for our last night in the forest, closer than we had been in millennia and ready to see what the next day would bring.

CHAPTER ELEVEN

I expected guilt or anxiety to overwhelm me once the day ended and I had a chance to fully process everything that had happened, but to my surprise, those familiar feelings didn't make an appearance. Zolgozig took the spot closest to me as we both lay down for the night, looking happier too.

"You doing alright, Ty?"

He asked it casually, not making a big deal of it, but I could tell he meant it sincerely and it felt nice to have people around who cared enough to ask. "Yeah, I'm good. Today was good."

"Surprisingly so," he agreed with a small chuckle. "Who knew a forest could be so much fun?"

I wouldn't go that far, but it had certainly been enlightening. "Let's hope what's waiting on the other side isn't going to spoil it all."

Until that point, I hadn't been too worried about the witch who apparently awaited us. The whole situation with all of us being pulled out of our lives and brought to this odd realm seemed preposterous, and though the gnome had died a few days earlier, it felt like a distant memory. For three days, we walked through the forest unimpeded. If someone were really out to get Tanith, or any of us, wouldn't they have tried to strike at us during that time?

The odd irregularities in Tanith's book that she could correct with her phone and this forest with its sexual proclivities gave the whole thing an air of absurdism that I couldn't quite reconcile with any real threat of danger, even if I knew exactly how dangerous witches could be. Making sense of any of it would take more energy than I had left after an emotionally draining day, and I soon fell into a deep sleep instead.

In the morning, Aiqen had breakfast waiting for us when we all awoke, obviously eager to move on. "We've had some good times in the forest," he acknowledged. "But we need to be sharp today. We don't know what lies ahead. Everyone eat and get yourselves prepared."

Even though he still considered himself in charge, his instructions felt a little less annoying than usual, and not even Zol put up a fight. Tanith made a comment about her clothes starting to smell less than fresh, and Aiqen suggested she wash them as best she could in the river that still meandered next to us, and he would use his wings to dry them. I took him up on that offer too, and everyone else quickly jumped in too. Soon, we were all naked in the river, laughing together, as if this were some kind of holiday. Even Cadriel seemed to have loosened up a little; he still kept himself covered by the water in front of the others, but he smiled and joined in with the good-natured teasing that went on.

When Aiqen shifted to his wyvern and began to beat his wings to dry the clothes, I made a bet with Leith to see which of us could last longest against the wind until he blew us over.

"That's not fair," Tanith protested. "You've got four legs and he's only got two, which he hasn't even had very long."

"Shift to your human form instead," Zol suggested. "You're not used to it either so it'll even the playing field."

For the second time in two days, I ended up in my human form, standing next to Leith as Aiqen tried his best to blow us both over. The others shouted out in encouragement and laughter as they watched us try and fail not to fall over.

By the time I had shifted back and we were all dressed again and packed up to go, a strong feeling of camaraderie had settled between us. If forming a bond between us had been the point of this forest, I had to admit it had been a success.

It truly really didn't feel as if anything too bad could happen while we were all getting along so well.

It took another three hours of walking until the trees began to thin and Aiqen slowed to a halt at the front of our group. "Do you smell that?"

I hadn't until he pointed it out, but after taking a deep breath, I could smell smoke faintly, and another bitter smell I knew far too well: a mix of incense and earth and other, nastier things which could only have one source.

"A witch."

Everyone turned to look at me curiously. "You can smell a witch?" Leith asked with his usual wide-eyed astonishment.

"Not the person, but her magic. Those scents, they're all things used in spells. It's what it smells like when they're working."

As I'd already told them, there were plenty of witches in the realm where I lived. I'd know the stench anywhere.

"Well, it fits what we were told," Aiqen pointed out. "And it also explains the smoke I saw a couple of days ago. Perhaps Cadriel and I should fly up again to scout for any dangers."

The fact that he included the angel in his proposal marked a positive step for Aiqen, and we all agreed it made sense. Aiqen shifted to his wyvern form and both the winged creatures flapped their way to the top of the tree line, not going too far up as they didn't want to attract attention.

When they returned to the ground, Cad was able to fill us in first as Aiqen still had to shift back and get dressed again. "It's just a small cottage. There doesn't seem to be anyone else around but we should still proceed with caution."

"What's the plan?" Zol wondered. "Are we just going to go knock on her door?"

"She wants me," Tanith reminded us all. "I have a feeling we won't need to find her. As soon as she knows we've arrived, *she'll* find us. Hopefully, we can find out exactly what she wants and why, and if she had anything to do with bringing us all here in the first place."

That sounded good to me, and since the path had widened around us, we arranged ourselves into a rough circle: Aiqen and Tanith in the front, Leith and I to the sides, and Zol and Cad bringing up the rear. If threatened, we could quickly turn our backs to each other in self-defense.

Moving as quietly as we could, we continued walking forward until the small cottage came into view, just as I imagined it from what Cad had said. And just as Tanith had suggested, the door opened before we could reach it. Two large ogres stepped out first as we all immediately drew to a halt. Crossing their arms, they stepped to the side to reveal a petite brunette, and as my eyes fell on her, the whole world seemed to spin around me.

It was *her.*

Not just *a* witch, but the witch who killed Evia.

My heart pounded as I blinked quickly, hoping my eyes were playing tricks on me, but the closer she got to us, the more certain I became of it.

And to my great surprise, I didn't seem to be the only one who recognized her. Several of the others had equally quizzical looks on their faces, and at the front of our small group, Tanith watched the witch's approach with her eyebrows drawn tightly together.

"Amanda? What the hell is this?"

~Tanith~

I had tried to prepare myself for anything that might come out of the door. Although I hadn't gotten to this point in writing the story, I knew the world I'd created, or that I *thought* I'd created, and I knew the types of beings in it. The ogres, therefore, although fearsome to see in the flesh, didn't come as a surprise.

What *did* shock me was the woman who walked out after them. It took me a moment to recognize her with brown hair instead of blonde, but her face looked exactly the same, right down to the condescending look in her eyes and the sneer on her lips.

"Amanda?" This couldn't be for real, could it? The woman who had made it her personal mission to torment me for my entire first semester of college? The woman who seduced Blaine into cheating on me? Was she actually the witch in my story, or did the witch simply look like her, the same way Cad bore a strong resemblance to my TA and Aiqen to my ex-boyfriend? "What the hell is this?"

"She's not Amanda," Aiqen growled beside me. "Her name is Gutha."

"I know her as Lila," Zol piped up from the back.

"Koia?" Leith sounded just as confused as I felt.

The woman in front of us simply smiled, enjoying our confusion. "I've had a lot of different names and spent time in a lot of different places. This, however, is my home, and my true form."

She gestured to the world around us and back to her own body, running her hands down her hips as if we were meant to be impressed.

I still didn't understand what was happening. "Are you actually the girl from my college?"

"I *pretended* to be a girl at your college," she corrected. "Does this look more familiar?"

With a snap of her fingers, she transformed in front of us, her hair changing to the sleek blonde style I knew and her clothes morphed into her sorority sweater, designer jeans and boots. She laughed as a shudder worked its way down my spine.

"What do you think? Is this better, or do you prefer me like this?"

Another snap, and another version of the woman appeared, her hair light blue and wavy, her chest bare with a shiny mermaid's tail that ended at her feet. We all glanced over at Leith, who blinked in confusion, looking completely lost.

"Or this?"

Suddenly, black hair fell down past her waist, her clothes dark and heavy, a wand in her hand.

From my left, Tymanus let out a growl of pure fury, startling us all. I'd never heard a sound like that from anyone and I certainly didn't expect it from him. "You'll pay for what you did, you evil bitch."

His hooves pawed at the ground as if he were getting ready to charge, but the witch only laughed. "Don't be foolish, centaur. You have no power here."

To make her point, she waved her hand which held the wand, and the ground beneath Ty immediately turned soft, his hooves sinking into a thick mud which held him in place no matter how he struggled against it, huffing and snorting.

"What do you want?" Cad spoke up for the first time, his eyes fixed on the woman in front of us. He hadn't said whether he recognized her or not, but she certainly had his attention. "Why have you interfered in our lives? Why have you brought us here?"

"Tanith is the only one who can answer that," she claimed.

All eyes turned to me as my brow furrowed even deeper than before. "What are you talking about? I didn't do any of this."

Her nostrils flared at my denial. "This bumbling, innocent act might work in the human world, but you can drop it now. Let's be honest with each other."

I honestly had no clue what she meant. "I don't know any more than anyone else does. I only arrived here three days ago."

Her eyes narrowed, not a trace of amusement left on her face. "And what about all the changes you made to my realm before that? Are you going to pretend not to know anything about that either?"

Changes? Did she mean...?

My hand went instinctively to my phone in my pocket. Apparently, I could change things in this place by simply writing about them. Had I unknowingly been making changes the whole time? Even those stories I started back in high school and never finished? They'd always been set in this place, which I thought only existed in my head. What if it had been real the whole time?

Even if that were true, it didn't explain why she'd done her best to make my life miserable for months, not to mention apparently showing up in the lives of all the men with me as well.

"Get us out of here," Cad whispered to me under his breath, moving around me to block me from the witch's view. "Use the power you have to buy us some time."

What did he mean? I thought I could only change the environment; our earlier experiment had seemed to prove that. Even though I didn't understand what he wanted me to do, I tried to obey anyway, powering on my phone while Aiqen scowled beside me. "So, because Tanith added a few houses and creatures to your land, that gave you the right to disrupt our lives?"

I had no idea what she did to Aiqen, but he clearly didn't appreciate it. However, his anger paled in comparison to Ty's, who still struggled against the quicksand at his feet, looking as if he'd tear the witch limb-from-limb given the chance.

The woman in front of us continued to look affronted, as if *she* had been done wrong. "No one knew this realm existed before Tanith. It's supposed to be my sanctuary. Now, others are trying to take it from me."

I did my best to listen to the conversation as I pulled up the story on my phone, blinking in surprise at the text on the page. What we were experiencing at that exact moment had never been part of the story. I hadn't gotten that far in writing it, but as I watched, words began to appear on the screen on their own, dialogue being placed into the characters' mouths as they uttered the words out loud.

"And how does bringing us here help?" Zol challenged. "How does any of this help?"

Tentatively, I pressed the delete button, erasing that question.

"And how does bringing us here help?" Zol repeated. "How does any of this help?"

I cast a furtive glance around to see everyone's reaction, but no one acted as if anything strange had just happened at all. No one else seemed to realize he had already asked it.

Emboldened, I deleted more lines, back to the point where Ty became stuck in the mud, and sure enough, the witch once again changed the ground beneath him, trapping him there. Just as before, everyone else seemed to be experiencing it for the first time, even though I had my phone in my hand which I hadn't the first time around.

"What's that?" the witch asked, noticing the device immediately, and as everyone else turned to look at me, I pressed the delete button once more, holding it down until we got to the point where Cad and Aiqen went into the air to check what lay ahead of us. Back in the forest, they landed in front of us as I shoved the phone back into my pocket.

"What's the plan?" Zol asked. "Are we just going to go knock on her door?"

"No." Everyone looked at me in surprise as I answered firmly. "Not yet. First, we all need to have a serious talk."

~Leith~

Thankfully, I wasn't the only one baffled when Tanith said we needed to talk.

"All we've done is talk for three days," Aiqen pointed out as he finished pulling his clothes back on. "It's time to confront this witch."

"Talking's not *all* we've done..." Zol muttered under his breath, earning him an exasperated look from Cadriel.

"What do we need to talk about, Tanith?" the angel asked her, taking charge as he often did so naturally. I couldn't help wondering what it would be like to have people listen to me so seriously the way they always did to him. It must be a little scary. "I've just seen the witch."

Tanith made eye contact with each of us, making sure we were all listening carefully. "She's someone I know, and apparently someone you all know too. Cad, you asked me to buy us some time, and so I brought us back here. I think we need to compare stories so we can come up with a plan before we go talk to her."

She had completely lost me again, but as I looked around at the others, everyone else looked equally bewildered. "Start from the beginning," Cadriel suggested. "How did you see her?"

Tanith took a breath, trying to speak more slowly. "We all went to see her, just a few minutes from now. I recognized her and so did all of you. You asked me to buy some time for us with my phone, and I found that if I deleted the words on the screen, it actually turned back time, at least for me. The rest of you don't seem to remember any of what happened."

That didn't clear much up for me. "You went back in time?"

"Kind of?" She didn't sound completely sure of it herself. "I complete-ly *deleted* time, I think. It didn't happen for anyone else except for me."

"I've never heard of anything like that," Aiqen said warily.

"We've never heard of half the stuff that's going on here," Zol countered. "Doesn't mean it's not happening."

"If Tanith says it happened, I trust her," Ty added, and I quickly nodded in agreement.

"Me too."

Tanith gave us both a warm smile. "I appreciate that, but I don't want you to have to take my word for it. Maybe I can prove it," she mused, drumming her fingers on the edge of the phone she held in her hand. "Hold on."

She tapped at the screen for a second before holding it up for all of us to see. Displayed on it was an image of the six of us, me and Ty and Tanith smiling, Zol smirking, Aiqen posing regally and Cad looking slightly uncomfortable. Aiqen spoke first, looking from the screen to Tanith in confusion. "When did you take this?"

"A few minutes from now." When nobody reacted, she explained further. "I took it and then I deleted the part of the story where I took it, bringing me back here so I could show it to you before it happened. I thought that way, you might believe me."

The details of how it happened still weren't completely clear to me, but there seemed no doubt that her words were true, since I certainly didn't remember posing for any picture. "You tried to delete the part where the gnome died earlier," Cadriel reminded her. "It didn't work."

"No, but that part had already been written. None of what's happening now was in my manuscript. It's being added to the story as it's happening, but I seem to be able to edit it. Or delete it, at least."

Cadriel seemed to understand, at least more than I did. "In that case, your phone just became even more valuable. We should save it until we truly need it. Please, put it away."

Tanith did as he asked, turning the phone off and putting it back in her pocket before turning to the rest of us with determination. "Now that we've established I'm telling the truth, we need to talk about this witch."

"You said we all knew her?" Zol said, repeating what Tanith had told us before we got distracted by the matter of her moving through time.

Tanith nodded. "We all had a different name for her. Aiqen, you called her Gutha."

The wyvern's eyes went so wide, I worried they might pop out of his head. "Gutha is here?"

"Who's Gutha?" I asked, finding this conversation very difficult to follow. Hopefully, someone could explain it all to me again, a little more slowly, later on.

Aiqen's lips pursed as if he'd tasted something sour. "She showed up a few months ago, out of nowhere, and seduced a couple of my brothers. Though I can't be certain, I thought she was giving them some kind of unfair advantage in their training. It felt like she wanted me to fail in our competition, but I never understood why. I thought she was a wyvern, though, not a witch."

Tanith nodded again, listening intently as if storing the information away for later use. "Zol, you said you knew her as Lila."

The demon snorted dramatically. "I should have guessed Lila was a witch."

"How do you know her?" Cadriel asked.

"She summoned me, wanting to make a deal, but every time we would get close, she'd change her mind. She's been jerking me around for months."

Tanith turned to me after we'd all absorbed that. "Leith, you called her Koia."

Involuntarily, I took a step back, my surprise overwhelming me. "You all know Koia?"

"I don't think any of us actually know her," Tanith corrected me gently. "I don't think she's shown any of us who she truly is. Who was she for you?"

In my mind, I could see the first time the blue-haired beauty appeared in the ocean in front of me. Mermaids rarely travelled outside their own part of the ocean, and never on their own. Worried that she might be lost, I offered to help her.

I summed that up as succinctly as I could. "She's a new friend I made recently."

"You were actually friends with her?" Tanith sounded confused. "She wasn't awful to you?"

I tried to think back over conversations we had and things she said. *Why would I want help from someone like you? You're no good to anyone here. Haven't you noticed how no one cares if you're here or not?*

"Well, she mentioned things about me that aren't perfect, but I took them as suggestions for improvement. I thought she was trying to help."

Zol snorted again. "So, basically, she was a bitch to him too but it went over his head." Tanith placed her hand on my arm supportively, shooting Zol a disapproving look.

"Who did I know her as?" Ty's quiet question could have been missed if it weren't for the almost desperate undertone to it.

Tanith's expression turned sympathetically cautious as she answered him. "You didn't mention her name, but you were furious. You said she'd pay for what she did. I can only assume it had something to do with Evia."

His jaw clenched tightly, his hooves pawing restlessly at the ground. "I knew it. Somehow, as soon as you said we all knew her, I felt it must be her. And I didn't kill her on sight?"

I had never seen him looking so angry. If he weren't my friend, I would find him rather terrifying at that moment.

Tanith moved from me to Ty, placing her gentle hand on his shoulder. "You probably would have, but she has magical powers, at least in this realm. She stopped you. That's why we need to have this conversation first about how to approach her. If we just walk up to her, she has all the power."

"Who is she to me?" Cadriel asked, the only one left who hadn't made the connection yet, and Tanith's brow furrowed as she searched his memory.

"Actually, you never said. You seemed to know her too, but you never used a name."

That didn't please him, I could tell. "Well, what does she look like?"

I could help with that part. "She has blue hair and bright green eyes."

Ty shook his head. "No, she's dark-haired and dark-eyed. Black, like her heart."

"Lila's a redhead," Zol chimed in.

Tanith held up her hands to stop us. "That's the thing: she appeared differently to each of us. I don't know what she would have looked like to you, Cad. I'm sorry."

"It's not your fault." His lips were tight, but he looked upset with himself more than anyone else. "I don't open up about things, and this is the consequence. I suppose I'll know her when I see her. So, she appeared to all of us in different guises before we came here, but why? What does she want?"

Tanith obviously wished she could answer that, but she shrugged instead. "I'm not entirely sure. She said I started making changes to this world and that it brought it to the attention of other people who are now trying to take it away from her. But who those people are and what that has to do with all of you, I honestly don't know."

I didn't know either, so hopefully one of the others would. As Koia had told me, figuring things out had never been my strong suit, and it seemed she had a point. I really wasn't much use to anyone at all.

CHAPTER TWELVE

~Aiqen~

The fact that Gutha had been behind all of this, that she had entered our lives to disrupt them before bringing us to this place, made me see red, but I tried my best not to give in to my fury. Emotional responses often caused more problems than they solved. The more detached and logical we could be, even if we all had reason to take it personally, the more likely we'd be to reach the best decision about what to do next.

"She doesn't seem to want us dead," I pointed out to the group, reviewing everything in my head. I had never spent time alone with her, but if she had wanted to, it wouldn't have been hard to find me. "She had plenty of opportunity to cause us harm in our own realms."

"And we know she's capable of it," Ty added darkly.

"So whatever she's up to, she wants us alive," Zol agreed. "That's an advantage for us."

"Unless she only needs us alive up to fulfill a certain purpose, after which we're expendable," Cad countered. "We can't assume we're safe. We can't assume anything."

Frustratingly, he made a good point.

Tanith agreed, though she made a further adjustment. "When we confronted her in the future I erased, she didn't immediately attack us. She wanted to talk, so if she needs us for something, it's still coming up. I think Zol's right that it gives us at least a small advantage. She needs us, but we don't need her."

"Unless we need her to get home?" Leith suggested timidly. "Maybe I don't understand it right, but if she brought us here, maybe she also has the power to send us back."

Tanith put her arm around him supportively. "I think you've understood it perfectly. We haven't met anyone else who knows anything about this realm, whereas she seems to be able to move in and out of it. It makes sense that she would be able to transport us too."

"So I can't just kill her on sight?" Ty asked, more serious than joking, though I could detect a hint of his usual humour behind the question too. He seemed to be doing his best to control his anger too.

"Not yet," Tanith told him apologetically. "Not until we know more, though I certainly understand why you want to."

There was a lot more we still needed to know, and I tried a different tack to bring us back on course. "Let's take a step back. She came to each of us, not to kill us and not to befriend us either, with the possible exception of Leith. In fact, she seemed to go out of her way to make sure we all hated her. Why?"

"Maybe she wants us to fight her?" Zol suggested. "She said there were others trying to take the land from her. Maybe if we attack her, she can show off her power and it will scare the others off."

"It's an interesting thought," Tanith mused. "But I think it might be simpler than that. In each case, she made our lives harder in a particular way, a way that seems to be connected to the fears that we all shared with each other back in the Vale of Disillusion."

Cadriel took a step closer to her, his brow furrowed in concentration. "What are you thinking?"

"Well, for example, with me, my fear was being average and uninteresting, and as the girl who always made fun of me, she did her very best to make me feel that way. Ty's connection is even more direct; his fear of people he cares about getting hurt stems directly from what she did. Maybe he had no fear she could exploit before then?"

As I applied her theory to my own situation, I had to agree it fit. "She preyed on my fear of losing the competition and letting everyone down."

In supporting my brothers, she had always implied that they had nothing to fear from me, and that no matter how hard I trained, I couldn't beat them.

"She made me doubt my deal-making abilities," Zol admitted. "And if I'm not any good as a demon, which is all anyone sees me as, then what am I?"

Tanith nodded as if she had expected those responses and turned to Leith, whom she still had her arm around. "Did she make you feel that you weren't smart?"

The merman nodded sheepishly. "She said it pretty much in those words."

Tanith certainly seemed to be onto something here, and I looked over at Cadriel. "Does that help to give you any idea of who she might have been to you, if she tried to exploit your own fears?"

He obviously *wanted* it to make a difference, but ultimately, he shook his head. "I'm still not sure."What kind of life did he have if he hadn't even noticed someone who turned up specifically to make his life difficult?

"So she wanted us to all arrive here feeling bad about ourselves," Zol summed up. "Then why give us the time to get to know each other?"

"I don't know if she had a choice in that," Cad guessed. "She might control some things in this realm but Tanith's book seems to control others. She's not all-powerful."

"Maybe she didn't know about the Vale of Disillusion," Tanith added. "I wrote about it in the book so maybe it's one of the things I changed here without meaning to, and she doesn't know it exists. She didn't know we would open up to each other that way and try to help each other get over those very weaknesses she had tried to exploit."

I agreed it didn't seem like any of our adventures in the forest would be beneficial to the witch, so I put them to one side. "So, let's assume, like Zol said, she wanted us to be feeling insecure when we arrived here. How does that help her?"

Everyone else fell silent as they thought it over, no one seeming to have any more idea than I did what the point of any of this might be.

"I think she's the only one who can explain it to us," Tanith finally said when no one else came up with an answer. "And I think I should go and speak to her, alone, to try to figure it out."

Words of protest came out of not only my mouth but the other four men as well. We were there to protect each other and especially her. Sending Tanith in alone wasn't an option.

Tanith held up her hands to try to stop the refusals coming at her from all sides. "With all six of us, there are too many different dynamics, too many different stories. She asked for me to come, so I'm the one who should go. And besides, I have my phone, so if I run into trouble, I can find a way out."

"You have to take at least one of us," I countered. "I'm happy to volunteer. I will protect you."I didn't say it out loud, not wanting to hurt anyone's feelings, but I was the obvious choice. Ty's situation made him too emotional, Leith was too kind-hearted, Zol not serious enough, and Cad was a step behind with not remembering the witch at all. He might have been too distracted when he made the connection.

"Thank you, Aiqen." She gave me a smile that brought me right back to the previous day and the intimate moments we'd shared. "But actually, I think I should take Zol."

"Zol?!"

I couldn't help spouting the name in surprise at the same time Cadriel did. Glancing over at the demon, I could tell he hadn't expected it either. He looked just as surprised as the rest of us.

"Me?"

Tanith transferred her smile to him. "Yes, you, Zol. You're able to remain detached from things in a way that the rest of us can't, but you pay attention too. You'll pick up on anything I miss, and we can report it all back to everyone else after we've spoken to her."

"What makes you think she'll let you go?" Cad asked, his jaw clenched tightly. "What if she just holds you there, or takes you away, or even kills you?"

Tanith could only shrug. "I'm not sure why, but I think right now she really just wants to talk. She's confused too, and she wants to get to the bottom of this. I can't explain it, Cad, but I have a feeling this is the way the story's meant to go."

~Zolgozig~

An unexpected warmth filled my body when Tanith announced me as her choice to accompany her to meet the witch. It had been a very long time since anyone praised my abilities to someone else, especially to a group of people whom, I had to admit, I had kind of started to respect.

People found me charming, certainly; that explained the success rate of my deals. But my superiors always found me lacking compared to the other demons who delighted in causing chaos and bloodshed. No one ever described me in positive terms to other people. No one saw me as more than just a demon.

Until her.

And the exact things she said were a further source of pride: she thought me capable of keeping a level head and of picking up on small details. Those were qualities I'd attribute to myself, and the fact that she'd noticed them after such a short time together made me feel truly *seen* for the first time in centuries.

I could tell the others weren't thrilled about it, though. Ty and Leith had no objections, perhaps, but Aiqen looked put out that he hadn't been the one chosen and Cad had reservations about the whole idea of going in without the whole group as backup.

I did my best to put them both at ease. "I won't let anything happen to Tanith. I've got some tricks up my sleeve if things get out of hand, demonic powers and all that. I'm not just a pretty face."

Although I might not be able to fly anymore, having lost my wings during my fall, I had some other abilities at my disposal. Showing off with them just wasn't my style, which was why none of them had seen them yet.

Aiqen looked to Cad for confirmation, since Cad had known me longer. Before the last few days, if we had found ourselves in a situation like this, I had no doubt that Cadriel would have announced I couldn't be trusted. That day, however, my half-brother gave me a searching look that I met as confidently yet humbly as possible, and finally, he nodded to the others.

"If this is Tanith's decision, we should give them a chance. Zol can take care of himself and her."

So much praise all in one day might start to go to my head.

"What's the plan?" I asked Tanith, trying not to smile. When was the last time I actually fucking smiled because I felt *happy?*

"We just need to get her talking. The more we can find out about her and her connection to this place and everything that's going on, the better."

With our goal in place, Tanith and I set out towards the forest's edge as I thought over my past interactions with Lila. Getting her to talk had never been an issue. The problem seemed to be that everything she'd ever told me had been a lie.

It had been a little over two months since she first summoned me. She even requested me by name, which rarely happened. Many other demons were better known than me, their names written in books hidden just out of sight of the general public, but Lila told me she had a friend who'd been very satisfied with the arrangement I'd made for her and that I'd been personally recommended. That sounded entirely plausible. My customers were almost always satisfied, at least in the short term.

"I'm in love with someone who's off-limits. He won't even look at me that way," she explained. Again, it sounded perfectly realistic. A lot of my deals started that way. Unrequited love - or, more usually, lust - could be a bitch. "He kind of looks like you, actually, but hotter."

Perhaps that should have been my first clue she was only messing with me.

I explained the rules of my deal: I couldn't actually make anyone fall in love with anyone else. Free will still reigned supreme, even among demons. My business didn't involve non-consent. What I *could* do was make her nearly irresistible so that all but the strongest of men would be moved to raging desire at the sight of her.

"What if he's not a man?" she asked with a sly smile.

As that memory crossed my mind, the pieces began to fall into place in my head. Had she been talking to me about one of the other men here? Was one of them the one she wanted to seduce? She had refused to tell me the species of being we were dealing with, which formed just one of the sticking points that led to our deal never coming to fruition.

Or had the man never existed at all, and she invented the whole thing to screw with me? I couldn't say. As Tanith had pointed out earlier, we needed more information, and it looked like our opportunity had come to get it.

As we reached the end of the forest, a small cottage appeared, smoke billowing from its chimney and a rather bitter, rancid smell filling the air.

"Ty said that's the smell of witchcraft," Tanith whispered to me as we continued to walk closer. "He told us that in the future I erased."

Before I could make any kind of response, the cottage door opened and two hulking, green-skinned creatures appeared, bending down so they wouldn't hit their heads on the way out. From behind them, a petite brunette appeared, and thanks to Tanith's forewarning, I recognized her as Lila immediately. With the different hair and clothing, she looked both different and yet exactly the same as I remembered her, right down to the smug look in her eyes.

That look quickly vanished, however, her brow furrowing at the sight of us, and she scanned the surrounding trees before her gaze returned to us. "Where are the rest of them?"

"The rest of whom?" Tanith asked innocently, and once again, I had to fight back a smile. Though I enjoyed Tanith in all the situations I'd known her in so far, the confident, mischievous side of her was by far my favourite.

Lila, or whatever her actual name was, didn't appreciate that answer nearly as much as I did. She scowled at the both of us. "Don't you recognize me?"

"I always thought you had a slight stench around you, Lila," I replied, wrinkling my nose. "Now, I know why."

She gave a huff of amusement. "You had no complaints about it the night you fucked me, Zol."

Shit. I hadn't told Tanith that part, and I could see in her eyes as she turned to me that it both surprised and dismayed her. It hadn't meant anything to me. I only did it because I thought it might speed the deal along.

It didn't.

The witch's smirk grew wider as she noted Tanith's reaction. "Didn't he tell you, Tanith? You're nothing special. He'll fuck anything on two legs."

"The two legs part isn't a strict rule." I tried to make light of it, even though, for the first time in a very long time, I felt something an awful lot like guilt pressing down on my chest.

"What do you want?" Tanith asked, her teeth gritted as she refused to take the bait. I was proud of her, even though she probably didn't care about my approval at that moment. "Why did you bring me here? Why did you bring any of us here?"

"Why don't you come in?" the witch suggested, gesturing at the house behind her. "With only two of you here, we might as well sit down and discuss things like civilized beings. Even if one of us is Zol."

"Hilarious." I glared at her before turning to Tanith and speaking under my breath. "What do you want to do?"

"We might as well," she whispered back. "Maybe we can get some clues inside, as long as you keep your dick in your pants."

"I'm a lust demon," I reminded her. "It goes with the territory."

"I know, and I don't care about anyone else you might have slept with, but... *her?*" Tanith gestured towards the witch in disgust. "Ty's not going to be happy."

Fuck. I *really* hadn't thought about that. It had been a long time since I'd had to consider anyone else's feelings. Maybe there were benefits to not having friends after all.

"I'll follow your lead," was all I said as Tanith and I headed inside the witch's cottage to see what we could learn.

~Tanith~

The thought that Zol had slept with Amanda made my skin crawl. I didn't want to have a thing in common with her, and certainly not the fact that we'd both slept with two different men. On the one hand, I saw his point that I shouldn't be surprised based on his nature, and he hadn't known at the time about all the things she'd done, but on the other hand, however irrational it might be, I felt like he *should* have known. He should have felt her ill-will and general bitchiness just as clearly as I always had and steered clear of it.

In any case, I had to put it out of my mind as we walked into the witch's living room, as if we were there for coffee and a chat rather than to find out why she'd yanked us all out of our lives and why. The house felt larger on the inside than it seemed from the outside. We had a choice of seats in the living room, so I took an armchair while Zol sat on a couch next to me, both of us taking a look around as we got settled. The decoration wouldn't have been my choice, far too much black furniture and animal horns on the wall, but she definitely wasn't living in squalor. It looked clean and well-kept.My hand brushed against my pocket as I sat, making sure my phone was still there and within easy reach in case we needed to get out of here in a hurry.

"What are we supposed to call you?" I asked as she sent the two ogres out of the room, leaving the three of us alone. "Zol called you Lila but I know you as Amanda."I didn't mention that the other men all knew her too. She didn't know I knew that yet.

"My proper name is Aris," she replied, taking a seat on the couch next to Zol. He immediately shuffled further away from her, making her smile. She seemed far less defensive than she had in the alternate timeline, sitting here with just the two of us. It seemed coming here without the full group had been the right decision. "What's your true name?"

Zol gave me a curious look, but I had no idea what she meant. "It's Tanith. You should know, you've made fun of it enough times over the last few months."

"I mean your real name," she said, her eyes narrowing. "And your real species. You're obviously not fully human."

I hadn't encountered that accusation before. "What else would I be?"

"That's what I want to know." She leaned forward, scanning me from head to toe. "You blend in remarkably well, but no human could do the things you've done to my realm. Now that you're here, we might as well be honest with each other. As you see, I'm willing to talk. I haven't harmed you or anyone else, even though I certainly could."

She meant that to sound intimidating, but I heard the tiny hitch in her voice at the end. Something held her back from attacking me, something other than merely goodwill or a desire to talk.

Saying she hadn't harmed anyone felt like a stretch, anyway. "You killed a gnome with your message to get me to come here and you killed Tymanus' friend in his home realm. Forgive me if I don't trust that you only want to talk."

Aris' eyes narrowed even further, her nostrils flaring. "How do you know about what happened with Tymanus? What are you?"

Damn it. I shouldn't have brought up Ty yet. I couldn't explain how I knew her relation to him without mentioning that he had already seen her there, and I had no intention of giving away any of that.

"Lucky guess," I lied instead. "He described the woman who killed Evia and she sounded an awful lot like you. Looks like I was right."

"Why don't we cut to the chase?" Zol suggested, stepping in before she could question me further, to my relief. "You've got us here, so why don't you just tell us what you want? Maybe we can come to a deal and all be home before dinner."

His distraction worked, thankfully. Aris sat back and turned to him, an amused smirk returning to her face. "It's always a deal with you demons. You think you can get whatever you want through a little negotiation."

"You seemed to enjoy the process," he reminded her, leaving a bitter taste in my mouth once again. "But I'm guessing what you really want has nothing to do with love. So why don't you tell us what you're really after?"

Her good humour fell away once again. "All I want now is this space for myself. No one was supposed to know it existed, and no one did until *she* turned up."

She looked back at me in disapproval, and finally, we were back to the point at which the other conversation had been cut off. Why did she think I'd been there before?

"I don't know what you mean," I told her truthfully, trying to keep my voice level. Despite the months of torment she'd put me through, I didn't want to argue with her. I only wanted some answers. "I had no idea this place existed outside of my imagination until I arrived here three days ago. I've never been here before."

"Don't lie to me." Her eyes flashed in anger. "I saw you multiple times. I even saw you with him."

She gestured back towards Zol, who looked equally confused. "I've never been here either until you brought me here," he told her.

"I didn't bring you!" Aris burst out. "I don't want you here, any of you. Why would I bring you here?"

If only because she seemed equally as frustrated and confused as I did, I actually believed her. Maybe she hadn't brought us there after all. But even if that part were true, it still left me with a lot of questions. "Then why did you come into our lives? Why did you pose as Amanda and make my life miserable?"

"Because you had already interfered in my life!" Her frustration grew so strong, electricity seemed to spark from her fingertips, and Zol and I exchanged worried glances. My hand moved towards my pocket almost subconsciously.

Zol tried to calm her down. "Listen, Aris, if you didn't bring us here, and Tanith didn't bring us here, then someone else did. Maybe we can work together to figure out who's behind it all and why. There's no reason we can't all get along."

"The fact that she killed Evia might make that difficult," I pointed out. Based on Ty's reaction when he saw her, I couldn't imagine him agreeing to let bygones be bygones, even if the rest of us could.

Before either of them could respond to that, a loud rumble went through the house, shaking the walls around us. The horns rattled in their mountings and Aris' face went pale.

"What was that?" I asked in alarm. It almost felt like an earthquake, but we hadn't felt anything like it during our time here so far.

"I have to go," she whispered in reply, and with a snap of her fingers, she disappeared from in front of us. I quickly turned around, checking the entire room, but there was no sign of her.

"Well, that was a waste of time," I exclaimed in frustration. "We're no further along than we were in the first place, and now we don't even know where she is."

"Not entirely," Zol countered. "We found out a few things, and even better, she just left us alone in her house. I think it's time to give ourselves a tour."

CHAPTER THIRTEEN

~Tanith~

Zol looked so pleased with himself as he suggested snooping around the witch's house that I had to smile, even if his proposition sounded completely unrealistic.

"What about the ogres?" I asked. We could still hear them lumbering around in the kitchen on the other side of the wall. Wherever Aris went, she didn't take them with her. "You think they're going to just stand back and let us rummage around?"

"Of course not," he assured me. "That's where my demonic gifts come in handy."

Clearing his throat, he placed a hand on his chest. When he spoke again, the voice that came out of him sounded completely different.

"I need some more newt eyes. Get me twenty-five, as fast as you can."

His impression of Aris was uncannily good and the shuffling in the next room immediately stopped. "Newt eyes?" one of the ogres replied through the closed door. I raised my eyebrows at Zol but he simply winked at me.

"Are you deaf now as well as dumb? That's what I said. Twenty-five of them, now."

I could almost feel their hesitation. They obviously had their doubts, so Zol turned up the urgency.

"Are you trying to make me look bad in front of my guests? If you don't go now, I'll find replacements for you both who know how to obey their mistress."

That did the trick. Mumbling under their breaths, they stomped out the door as I shook my head at my grinning companion. "There's no reason that should have worked."

He shrugged, not the least bit concerned as he reverted to his regular voice. "If it didn't, I'd have come up with something else. There are a lot of things I can do, Tanith. You don't know the half of it."

I didn't doubt that he could still show me a few things. "Well, let's hope you don't have to pull out that voice again. That was creepy."

"Do you prefer me like this?" This time, he spoke in my own voice, and I shuddered in dismay.

"No! That's terrible. How are you doing that?"

"Demons have the gift of mimicry. Many of my colleagues use it to fool the people they deal with, but that's never been my style. I prefer to be honest in my dealings. People are depraved enough on their own without resorting to cheap tricks."

An honest demon. I shook my head at the ridiculousness of all of it. "Let's get moving before they come back." We started to head for the hallway that led further into the cottage, but I stopped short before reaching the door. "One more thing: why twenty-FIVE eyes? They come in pairs. Are they supposed to just take one eye from one of them?"

He grinned his devilish smile. "Exactly. They'll be wondering the same thing."

I didn't know whether to laugh or groan, so I simply shook my head once more and headed into the hall. Two more large rooms made up the back of the cottage: a bedroom and another room that seemed to be a workshop of some kind. The bitter smell we'd picked up from the forest was a lot stronger there, and jars of various ingredients lined the shelves and tables, making it look like a school science lab from the Middle Ages.

"Ha, you see!" Zol picked up one of the jars triumphantly and held it up to me. "Newt eyes."

That time, I had to laugh. "The jar is full. Maybe that's why they were so confused."

We looked around the workshop, pointing out a few particularly disgusting things to each other, but I couldn't see anything that would be helpful to us. Maybe if we knew anything about magic, we might be able to tell what kind of spells she did and why, but neither of us had any kind of expertise on the subject. It felt like trying to decipher a foreign language.

"Let's check the bedroom," Zol suggested, and I followed him down the hall to the other room. Its decoration complemented the living room, dark wood walls with large, dark, heavy furniture, but as soon as we stepped inside, it became clear we would find a lot more useful information there.

Photos of me and all the men I'd been travelling with filled one wall, jumbled together with maps and notes with our names, species and locations. Under mine, she'd written: "Human?" with a question mark, making it clear her earlier question to me had been a legitimate one.

"Well, this doesn't feel like a serial killer's lair or anything," Zol joked, but I could tell it rattled him a little, just as it did me. If it hadn't already been clear from the way she'd turned up in our lives, this would confirm she'd definitely been tracking us.

Was she trying to solve the mystery of what connected us all, the same as we were, or was there something more sinister behind it? Why did she kill Evia? What did *any* of it mean?

Zol lifted some of the pictures on top to reveal even more photos and notes underneath. "Can you take pictures of some of this stuff with your phone? The others might pick up things we miss."

He had a point, though Cad's warning about not wasting the battery life echoed in my head again too. After debating with myself internally for a moment, I agreed. "Alright. Let's be quick about it, though."

We worked together, Zol arranging pictures and directing me where to take the photos while I snapped them. When we got to the information about me, Aris had a copy of my class schedule and my home address, and even a picture of me with my ex-boyfriend, Blaine. His face had been circled several times in red ink.

"Is that Aiqen?" Zol squinted at the photo. "It looks like a younger version of him."

"It's not him, but they do share some similarities," I agreed. "Hurry, keep going."

We took a few more photos until Zol flipped up a page to reveal another picture that made us both stop and stare. It showed a younger Aris with someone who looked an awful lot like Blaine or, as Zol suggested, a younger version of Aiqen. The main differences were that the boy's ears were pointed and his physique slimmer than both of the others.

"They could almost be twins," I muttered, pulling the picture of me and Blaine off the wall to compare.

I didn't ask Zol what it meant because I knew he wouldn't know any more than I did. One more mystery to add to the pile. It felt like we'd come up with even more questions and not very many answers.

"Are you two enjoying yourselves?"

Zol and I both froze as Aris' voice sounded from the bedroom door. Her arms were crossed as she glared at us, caught red-handed.

"Tanith?" Zol asked under his breath, looking for direction.

"I'm on it," I promised, switching from the camera on my phone to my writing app.

"What are you doing?" Aris demanded at the sight of my phone, just as she had in the other timeline, and just as I had then, I deleted the words before I had to answer them.

A moment later, I sat back in the living room with Zol, just after Aris had disappeared.

"I think it's time to give ourselves a tour," Zol said, but I shook my head at him.

"We already did. I'll explain on the way. Let's get back to the others and tell them what we've found out."

~Cadriel~

Although I had given Zol my vote of confidence, I couldn't help breathing a sigh of relief as he and Tanith returned to the group looking none the worse for wear. Whatever had happened with the witch, they seemed to be unharmed, even though they both looked back over their shoulders a few times, checking that they weren't being followed.

It frustrated me more than I could say that I didn't know who the witch could be. While Tanith and Zol were away, I asked the others to describe her to me again but the conflicting reports of her appearance made it impossible to pin down. They all agreed that she had first appeared to them within the last few months, but I couldn't think of anyone who had recently shown up in my life and made an impression on me, not until I arrived there and met Tanith.

Aiqen immediately leapt to his feet at the sight of them, ready to spring into action. He had only just sat down after pacing most of the time they'd been away. "What happened?"

Tanith answered first. "We spoke to her. She invited us into her house." Together, they told us about the conversation they'd had in as much detail as they could. "Then, something made the house shake, a loud, rumbling sound. It seemed to frighten her and she disappeared. We came back as soon as we could, but she may be looking for us now. She'll know we're close by."

We'd heard it too; the ground beneath us shook as the sound rolled across the air like thunder. Though none of us had spoken our fears out loud, we had all probably had the same worry, that the witch had caused the sound by doing something to Tanith and Zol.

"It was all surprisingly civilized," Zol added. "And apparently, Tanith took some photos in her house too, but I don't remember that part."

She had taken photos *and* manipulated time again? That phone battery wasn't going to last forever. She had to be more judicious with it or it could fail right when we needed it most.

"I know, Cad." Tanith gave me a sheepish smile even though I hadn't said anything out loud. "But she was furious when she caught us in her bedroom. I had to do it."

Immediately, shadowy images of Tanith and Zol together on a bed filled my mind, an accompanying jealousy spreading through my chest, and I had to shake my head at myself. Obviously, she hadn't meant it that way, and I had no reason to be jealous anyway. I had to be reasonable.

"What are the pictures of?" Leith wondered, and Tanith immediately pulled the phone out of her pocket.

"She had information on all of us. I took a few photos of it to see if anything might be important, but as far as you're concerned, Cad, this one will be the most interesting of all. This is the witch, a few years ago. She said her real name is Aris."

She held the phone out to me and I took it reluctantly, still not thrilled about using it at all, but as soon as I laid eyes on the photo, all other concerns flew out of my head.

I definitely knew this woman, but I hadn't only met her in the last few months. I had known her for her whole life.

"Who is she to you?" Tanith asked softly. She must have seen in my reaction that I recognized her.

"She's one of my protectorates."

"Seriously?" Zol gaped at me in surprise while the others exchanged uncertain glances, unsure of the significance of my words. "But she's a witch. Protectorates are human. I've never heard of a supernatural one."

"I know. I assumed it must be incorrect when I received the assignment, but my superiors assured me there had been no mistake. She was born on Earth, despite being a witch."

Ty stepped in on behalf of the others. "Okay, back up a second. What the hell is a protectorate?"

Zol smiled at the choice of words while I answered the centaur. "A protectorate is an individual who gets assigned an angel to watch over them. It's usually because they have a specific purpose to achieve, a destiny, if you will, although sometimes, through their own choices, it doesn't come to pass. Sometimes, our job is to prevent them from doing whatever they are destined to do, or they might simply be seen as more likely to be vulnerable to demonic dealing and need extra protection for that reason. Angels like me aren't told the reasons; we simply accept the assignments we're given and do our best to watch out for them alongside our other duties."

"You're her guardian angel?" Tanith asked.

"In a sense, yes." That was probably the easiest way to describe it.

"No offense, Cad, but I think you've missed the mark a bit," Ty pointed out sullenly. "She's killed at least two people."

"It has been challenging," I admitted. Although I didn't know she'd killed anyone, I had felt her slipping away from me. "With humans, we have ways of reaching them. Since she's a witch, many of my usual methods didn't work. She seems to move between realms. I can only visit her when she's on Earth, and I suspect she can even shield herself from me then if she chooses to."

"So what was the point of assigning you to her, then?" Aiqen asked, and I shrugged in frustration.

"I honestly don't know. The one time I questioned it, I was told to keep my head down and do as I was told. Their records indicated that a girl born at precisely the stroke of midnight on the 7th of December in the town of Greenville needed a protector."

Tanith let out a sharp gasp that made us all jump. I almost dropped the phone but managed to catch it at the last second.

"What was that for?" Zol asked, not pleased at having been startled.

Tanith's bewildered stare pierced into me. "Cad, *I* was born in Greenville, at midnight on the 7th of December."

That seemed extraordinarily unlikely, but it didn't sound like she meant it as a joke.

"It must mean something, doesn't it? Aris and I were born at the same time. And look: this guy she's with in the photo, he looks just like someone I used to date."

"He looks like Aiqen!" Leith exclaimed as he leaned over to examine the photo closer.

I'd been so distracted by the sight of Aris herself, I hadn't even noticed the man in the picture, but he certainly did bear a strong resemblance to the wyvern.

"Good-looking young man," Aiqen acknowledged, making Zol roll his eyes. "Could he be the same one you dated? We all knew Aris as someone else, so maybe this person also travels between realms."

Tanith took a moment to think it over, but ultimately shook her head. "I don't think so. I've known Blaine since we were kids. I think I would have noticed if he had a double life."

She meant it half as a joke, and most of us smiled, but clearly, something very unusual lay behind the coincidences.

"It certainly looks like your lives are linked somehow," I said, turning the phone off to the protests of everyone assembled. "We have to be smart about this. I'll hold onto the phone until it's needed again."

Although I said nothing about not trusting Tanith with it, she obviously took that message away from my words, giving me a hurt look as I tucked the phone into my own pocket.

I tried to change the subject as a means of distraction. "Let's focus on you and Aris. Does anyone have any suggestions about what these connections might mean?"

I had one, and Zol quickly suggested the same thing. "Soul shadows?"

As before, the words meant nothing to anyone beside the two of us. "What's that?" Ty asked.

I looked over at Zol to see if he wanted to handle the explanation, but he shrugged, telling me to go ahead. "Souls can become linked to each other in several ways. The most common one that you've probably all heard of is soulmates."

They all nodded in acknowledgement.

"In that case, patterns are made in the soul, like puzzle pieces. When you meet the person who matches yours, you feel a sense of completion. It's a good thing. Soul shadows are different, though; even if the people never meet, what one does in life affects the other. Sometimes, they feel the same things, so if one's happy, the other will be happy, and sometimes the inverse is true. When things go well for one person, the other has bad luck."

"Why would anyone want that?" Tanith asked, and I had to agree it didn't sound very good from my definition.

"It's usually a glitch," I admitted. "Something happens prior to birth and they're linked together in a way they're not meant to be. Regardless of *why* it happened, though, it might explain how you knew about this realm after she created it, and how she saw you here when you visited in your imagination."

"So the worse my life gets, the better hers is?" Tanith pressed, trying to understand the implication. "Does she know that? Is that why she bullied me? Is that why I'm here?"

"I don't think she knows about it." From everything Tanith had told me about their interactions so far, it sounded like the connection confused Aris too. "But maybe someone else does. Maybe they brought you together because of it. Maybe it's why I was assigned to Aris in the first place."

The stakes kept getting higher. Whatever was happening here, we needed to start figuring it out and fast, before anyone else got hurt.

~Aiqen~

As flattered as I might be that Tanith and Guntha - or Aris, apparently - had both dated someone who looked like me, making it clear that I was definitely their type, we were all losing sight of the bigger issue.

"We need to decide if we're moving forward or falling back," I reminded the group. "The longer we stay standing here, the better chance we'll be discovered."

Our enemy apparently had the ability to appear and disappear at will. We didn't know yet how far that ability extended, and by staying in one place, within easy striking distance of her home base, we were making easy targets of ourselves.

"I say we go back and confront her, all of us," Zol suggested. "In the future Tanith erased, Aris came back within half an hour of leaving. She's probably back there by now. Let's find out what she's up to, once and for all."

"We can tell her what we've figured out," Leith added enthusiastically. "Maybe she'll want to help us work out the rest."

"I wouldn't trust her to have anyone's interests at heart but her own." Ty crossed his arms firmly. "If we go there, it should only be to capture her, or worse. She needs to pay for what she's done."

"I think we have more to discuss before we can choose how to approach her," Cadriel summed up, giving me a nod. "I guess for now, that means retreat."

That disappointed me, since I'd been primed and ready for some action, but a good strategy was important too. Rushing in without thinking things through could have disastrous results. "In that case, we should move quickly, back into the forest. She must have known we were in there these past few days but she didn't come in. It feels like the safest place until we decide on our next move."

"That's an interesting point," Tanith mused. "I wonder why she didn't come into the forest."

"Maybe she didn't want to touch the itching leaves?" Leith suggested tentatively.

He winced as if he thought we would all tell him that was a stupid idea, but actually, it made a lot of sense to me. "I think you're onto something. She said that Tanith had been changing things in the forest. If the things we encountered there didn't exist until Tanith added them, she might be afraid to go in. She wouldn't know the antidote as we did."

"In which case, it will definitely be the safest place for us," Cad concluded, giving Leith a nod of approval. "Can you swim back up the river? Aiqen and I can move the others quickly."

"Move us? How?" Zol instantly had his back up. "I'm capable of moving myself."

"We need to go quickly," Cad reminded him. "Flying will be fastest, but we'll need to stay below the tree line so Aris doesn't see us. By flying over the river, we can stay low and hopefully remain undetected."

"And you're going to what... *carry* me?" Zol couldn't sound more put out.

"Actually, I'm going to carry Tanith. Aiqen can take you and Ty in his talons, and Leith can swim."

Ty gave me a curious look and I nodded proudly. I could definitely do that. As strong as I might be as a human, as a wyvern, my strength was tripled.

"Come on, Zol, it'll be a lot faster," Tanith pleaded with him. "It won't take long either. We should stick together. Please?"

He couldn't resist her any more than I could have, but he gave in less than gracefully. "Fine, but if he drops me, I reserve the right to kick his ass later."

I returned his scowl with an innocent smile. It would be tempting to let the demon go over the river and claim it had been a slip, but luckily for him, I took my responsibility more seriously than that. I always had.

We headed to the river on foot where Leith shed his clothes and Tanith folded them up to carry for him. The merman extended his tail in the water as he climbed in, splashing happily. "This way," he called to the rest of us. "Try to keep up!"

He headed off upriver as I quickly removed my own clothes to shift. Tanith took those too, and Cad took her, lifting her in his arms as he extended his wings. In my wyvern form, I picked up Ty in my right talon and Zol in the left one, taking care not to squeeze too tightly. When they were both secure, I took to the air, following the angel and the merman back up the river.

The sun shone overhead, casting its light onto the water below like a golden path lighting the way. Cad's angel wings seemed to glow ahead of me while Leith's merman scales sparkled like jewels in the water below every time his tail came to the surface. The whole scene would almost be idyllic under different circumstances, if we were all there for pleasure instead of against our will.

"Hey, Zol, how ticklish do you think Aiqen's feet are?"

Ty's question pulled me out of my head and back to the present with a start. I couldn't see him at the moment, but I could feel him turning to look over at the demon.

"I think we should put it to the test." The demon sounded more like his usual, mischievous self as he answered, and a second later, I could feel something start to brush against my toes.

Don't do that, you idiot! You're the one who didn't want me to drop you. Those were the words in my head, but since I couldn't speak in my wyvern form, it came out as a grunt instead, which they both seemed to find hilarious.

My other toes began to feel itchy as Ty's tail brushed across them. Zol grew bolder, reaching for the sensitive skin between my toes, and I had to squeeze a little harder so I didn't let go. We dipped to one side as my left wing twitched, and the two of them practically howled in laughter.

They really wanted to play this kind of schoolyard game, did they? If so, I could play with the best of them. Swooping low, I held them both just above the water's surface as my wings continued to propel us forward. They had to lift up their legs to keep from getting wet.

"He won't actually do it," I heard Zol say. "It's a bluff."

He tickled me one more time, and I immediately dunked him completely, soaking him in the river from head to toe.

"Son of a bitch!" he sputtered as I pulled him back up again. Ty laughed even harder than before and I let out a throaty chuckle, or at least as close to one as a wyvern could make.

"Incoming!"

Cad's shouted warning startled us all, and I looked up just in time to see an arrow heading straight for me. Tucking both Ty and Zol against my body for protection, I dodged it just in the nick of time.

More arrows soon followed, making it even clearer that we'd been spotted.

"Into the trees!" Cad ordered. "Leith, you go first, we'll draw their fire."

The merman gave him a thumbs up and Cad circled back towards us. I understood him immediately, and the two of us began to fly in circles around each other to form a layer of protection as the naked merman hopped out of the river on his legs and ran into the cover of the forest.

I couldn't see where the arrows were coming from, but they must have come from Aris, the same way she had used an arrow to deliver the note that led us to her in the first place. They came thick and fast as we circled, and one nicked my ear as it went whistling past.

"Now!" Cad instructed as soon as Leith had safely disappeared, and the two of us flew into the forest, dodging the trees until we found a safe place to land. I had just spotted a flat, empty spot when my wing caught against a branch and me and the two men in my claws all went tumbling onto the forest floor.

Cad made a much smoother landing, setting Tanith down gently as I shifted back to my human form and she handed me and Leith our clothes back.

"What happened to you?" she asked Zol with a laugh as he sat there dripping wet.

"Shhhh." Cad shushed her as he listened intently, watching the sky for any further sign of trouble. We all sat in silence as the seconds ticked by until finally, he sighed. "I think we've lost her. Or them. Whoever was shooting at us."

He gave me a pointed look that I had to admit I'd earned. I had lost my focus, which wasn't like me at all. At least we made it back to safety and all in one piece.

I may have spoken too soon, though. After another minute, Ty began to scratch on his chest. "Did we ever figure out exactly what that itching plant looked like?"

Warily, we all took a look around. In our rush into the trees, we had probably brushed against pretty much every plant in the forest, and it seemed like our immunity to the plant had reached its limit. No sooner had Ty mentioned it than I began to feel the itch too.

Shit. How many of us were infected at once?

CHAPTER FOURTEEN

At first, I thought my itchiness might be empathy-induced. I'd always been the kind of guy to yawn when someone else yawned, and watching Ty, Zol and Aiqen start to scratch at themselves, I couldn't help scratching at my stomach too.

"Are you infected too, Leith?" Tanith asked. So far, she didn't appear to be, or Cadriel either, though he never seemed to let anything affect him.

"I'm not sure," I told her honestly. "I feel itchy, but it could be in my head."

"Turn around and don't look at them," she advised, putting her hands on my shoulders to spin me around in the other direction. "Take a deep breath and think about the water instead."

Following her instructions, I closed my eyes and imagined the cool, silky feel of the ocean against my skin. It worked for a few seconds, but the itchiness came back, coming from within that time, and I had to admit defeat. "I must have touched it. I'm still itchy."

"That's four of you," Tanith summarized, looking around at all of us who couldn't stop scratching. "Unless you are too, Cad, and you're just not telling me?"

The angel shook his head. "I feel fine. I don't think we touched anything."

He and Tanith had a much smoother landing than the other three. I hadn't rolled around on the forest floor like they had, but I did run across it in my bare feet after getting out of the river.

"I think it must be something on the ground, or close to it," I guessed. "Maybe this one?"

A snaking plant wove its way through the area where we stood, its leaves sitting just on top of the grass, and I picked it up to show it to the others. Looking around, I could see it also climbed up tree trunks and other shrubs. Now that I'd noticed it, it seemed to be everywhere.

Tanith's encouraging smile made my chest swell with pride. "I think you might be right, Leith. There's one way to find out for sure."

With those words, she walked over and took the plant from my hand to rub it against her exposed skin.

Cadriel let out a loud sigh. "What are you doing?"

"It's better that we know which one it is," Tanith pointed out. "And since they're all infected anyway, they're going to need my help. I might as well get the same immunity again. This kills two birds with one stone."

It made sense to me. Better than worrying about it, or worse, getting infected when we were in a dangerous situation. "Maybe you should do the same?" I suggested to the angel. I hadn't spoken to him very much directly yet, finding the controlled, intelligent man slightly intimidating.

"No." He snapped the word so harshly that I winced, and his eyes closed for a second. When he spoke again, his tone was milder. "Thank you for your concern, Leith, but I'll pass. I'll go and set up a safe space for us while you all... take care of this. I assume it worked and you're infected now too?"

He directed that question to Tanith, who had started to scratch the back of her neck, and she gave him a nod. "Looks like Leith was right. We know which plant to avoid now."

How about that? I actually figured something out before anyone else did.

"I'll be sure to avoid it, then," Cadriel answered before walking away and leaving the five of us alone.

Tanith looked almost disappointed as she watched him go, but a moment later, she turned to the rest of us, still scratching her neck. "Does anyone other than Zol have any ideas about how we can all help each other without making anyone wait?"

"Why 'other than Zol'?" the demon in question demanded. "I have several ideas."

"I know, and that's why I want to give someone else a chance." Although Tanith shook her head at him, I could see the affection in her eyes. "If we can't figure anything out, I promise we'll come back to you."

"I suppose we could form some sort of chain where we all jerk each other off," Aiqen suggested, though he didn't sound thrilled about it. "I've never done anything like that to another man before, but if it's required, I will try, in the name of duty."

"Hands up: who *doesn't* want Aiqen touching them?" Ty raised his own hand while I sheepishly added mine. Nothing personal against the wyvern, I just wouldn't be particularly comfortable with any of the other men touching me, especially if they didn't really want to. It didn't sound very sexy at all.

Secretly, I hoped this might give me the opportunity to experience some pleasure with Tanith again, although with only one of her and four of us, that seemed unlikely.

"I'm not sure it would work anyway," she said. "All of us concentrating on trying to get someone else off while we're supposed to be orgasming ourselves? Could be tricky. There's a reason we can't do it to ourselves, remember?"

"Are you ready for my suggestions yet?" Zol smirked, but Tanith still shook her head.

"Not yet. Ty? Leith? Any ideas?"

"I'd be okay with fucking Zol, since he's already made it clear he'd be willing," Ty offered. "That gives you one less of us to worry about, Tanith."

"That was already part of my plan," Zol piped up, but Tanith shushed him.

"That's helpful, Ty, thanks. Leith? What do you think?"

I honestly didn't know. I'd never done anything involving more than one person at a time, and the idea of sharing Tanith with everyone else felt a little strange, even if I knew our situation made it necessary. In this case, I had to defer to the expert. "I think I'd like to hear what Zol has to say?"

Tanith turned to the demon with a smile. "Alright, I guess you're up. What have you got?"

"Well, in my ideal scenario, we'd have some lube," he began, and Aiqen rolled his eyes.

"I don't think you're going to magically stumble across some in the forest."

Actually, I could help with that, and I put my hand up again to get everyone's attention. "Merman can produce their own lubrication. It's needed in the water because the salt water can actually dry things out, ironically."

The demon's eyes flashed red for a moment. "That's perfect. That means you can take Tanith's ass."

"Excuse me?" she squeaked.

"As long as you want to," Zol quickly amended. "I know you haven't done it before, but if you're willing and I'm taking Ty, you've got three cocks to worry about and three holes. Seems like easy math to me."

Tanith thought that over, trying to work it all out in her head. I tried to visualize it too, even as my cock already began to harden at the idea of being inside Tanith again. I'd never used a woman's other hole before, but if Tanith hadn't either, it would be a new experience we could share.

I quite liked the sound of that.

"I don't understand how it's going to work," Aiqen finally admitted, looking frustrated with his inability to picture it. "Who's going where?"

Zol had it all worked out. "Once Leith has got Tanith used to him, he can lie down with Tanith on top of him. I'll take her from the front while Ty has me from behind. You can have her mouth."

I still couldn't fully imagine it, but as long as they told me what to do and where to go, I'd be okay. "What about Tanith herself?" I asked. "If we're all just focused on ourselves, who's going to worry about her?"

Zol gave her a heated smile. "Don't worry about that. She's going to love it."

Tanith's cheeks had turned red, not from the itching but from the flush of anticipation. Now that it had all been laid out, she looked as eager to begin as I felt.

"Everyone strip," Zol ordered. "There's no time to be shy."

Everyone else started to remove their clothes, so I quickly followed suit. My cock strained against my sheath as the others all released theirs and Tanith shimmied out of her pants. Shamelessly, Zol reached between her legs, making her gasp in surprise, and he lifted his fingers to show the rest of us how they glistened in the afternoon light.

"Look how much the idea of being completely filled has turned her on."

Tanith's thighs clenched as the rest of us took a moment to appreciate her in all her naked beauty. Her creamy skin, her bright red hair, her freckles on her face and her chest, every single part of her appealed to me, and obviously to the others too.

Surprisingly, it didn't bother me to see them looking at her. In a way, it almost made me feel closer to them, like we all had something in common by finding her irresistible.

"Now, we just need the other hole ready. I'll help you," Zol offered. "Leith, get down on your knees and eat her out while I do some prep work. It'll help distract her."

When Tanith looked over at me with excitement in her eyes, I couldn't resist. Kneeling before her as if I were about to worship her - which in a way, I was - I began to lap at her, right where Zol's fingers had just been, inhaling her sweet scent and letting her perfect taste linger on my tongue.

She moaned and shifted against my face, her fingers threading through my hair as Zol gently pushed her over. "Relax as much as you can," I heard him whisper to her. From the corner of my eye, I could see Aiqen stroking himself as he watched the three of us, and I couldn't blame him. I was rock hard too but trying to ignore it as I focused on Tanith.

Zol's hand brushed against my chin as he pressed a finger into her ass, using her own natural lubricant to ease his way. I could feel her tensing against me so I moved my tongue faster, trying to distract her with pleasure from any possible discomfort.

Zol dipped a different finger inside her pussy, nudging my tongue out of the way, then returned to his own work while I sucked and licked her even harder.

"Oh, fuck," Tanith gasped from above, sending a wave of pleasure through me at the knowledge that she was enjoying herself.

Zol praised me too. "Keep going. Make her come with my finger inside her."

I tried my best. My own fingers went to her pussy as my tongue teased her clit, and as I pushed them inside her, her tightness made me groan. That sound seemed to trigger Tanith's orgasm, and as soon as she started to come, Zol pulled me back to my feet, bending Tanith over even further and gesturing to her ass.

"Nice and slow, with plenty of lube. Stop if she says stop."

With him guiding me the whole way, I unsheathed my cock and rubbed it with my own secretions before starting to press into her. It didn't seem like it would fit into her tight hole, and I waited for her to tell me so, but once the head disappeared inside her, the rest followed surprisingly easily.

"How does it feel?" I asked her breathlessly. It felt incredible for me, but I wanted to be sure she enjoyed it too.

"Different," she managed to gasp. "I think it'll be good, but I could use some more distraction."

Zol grinned beside me, clapping me on the shoulder. "That's where I come in."

~Zolgozig~

At last, I was totally in my element.

Helping people find pleasure had been my entire purpose in life for the last two thousand years, and I relished the chance to put those skills to use with a group of people I had actually come to care about. Every one of us would enjoy this experience if we could all let go of any inhibitions or worries; I had no doubt of it, but I had a feeling I would enjoy it most of all.

So far, we had Leith's cock buried in Tanith's previously-virgin ass, and both of them seemed more than satisfied with that arrangement. The ability of mermen to provide their own lubrication was something I would definitely have to learn more about. It could come in handy in so many situations.

Until then, my attention remained entirely focused on the task at hand. "Leith, get down on the ground. Here, I'll get something for your head."

A pile of discarded clothes lay strewn across the area, so I bunched some of those up and placed them beneath the merman's head to make it a bit more comfortable for him. As he pulled out of Tanith and lay down on his back, he gave me a grateful smile. "Thanks, Zol."

"No problem." People always seemed surprised when I did something nice even though I was a nice fucking guy. Most people just didn't get to know me well enough to figure that out. "Now, Tanith, you're going to sit down on top of him. Don't worry, I've got you."

Putting her trust in me completely, she took hold of my arms as Leith held up his cock, lining it up with her ass as I lowered her down. She gasped as he filled her again, but thanks to his lube and the work we'd already done, she went down smoothly.

"Lie back now, as much as you can. Keep your legs spread. We all want to see that pussy right now. Look at Aiqen, he can barely take it."

At my prompting, she glanced over at the wyvern who alternated between scratching himself and rubbing his cock. Ty was just scratching since he couldn't reach his cock in his centaur form, but I could see by the size of him that he found the whole situation titillating too.

"Let me help, Aiqen," Tanith offered, calling him over to her, but I shook my head.

"Not yet. We've got to get the positioning just right first. He'll be the easiest one to fit in."

When she had leaned back and started to relax, Leith's hips moving against her ass like he couldn't fully control it, I squatted down over them both, placing the tip of my cock against Tanith's other entrance.

"Do you need any more warm-up?" I didn't think she did, but I wanted her to be fully comfortable, so I flicked my finger across her clit a few times, smiling as her legs twitched.

"No," she moaned. "Just do it, Zol. Fill me up."

Fuck, yes. With a groan of my own, I pushed into her tight pussy, made even tighter by the presence of Leith's cock pressing against her internal walls from inside her ass.

"Holy shit," Tanith gasped, making me smile again.

"There's nothing holy about this. That's why it feels so good. Ty, are you ready?"

I called back over my shoulder to the centaur as I bent over further, exposing my ass to him. His eyes zeroed in on it as he walked over and I could see the heat in them. I got the feeling he hadn't done this before, but he was open to it, and that was all we needed.

"Do you want me to shift?" he asked.

For whatever reason, he didn't seem to like being in his human form, and I had no intention of making him uncomfortable. More than that, I had been eyeing that centaur cock of his for a few days, and I really wanted to know what it felt like.

"No. You should fit on top of all of us just like that. Just spit on my ass a bit first so it's not totally dry." I had done this enough times that I didn't need all the lubrication that Tanith did, but with a cock that size, it would still require a bit of help to go in smoothly.

As Ty followed my instructions, bending over to spit directly into my ass, Tanith groaned from beneath me. "Men are gross."

I smirked at her while I rolled my hips, pressing my cock deeper into her. "Is that really what you think right now?"

"I can think you're gross and hot at the same time," she panted back, her body clenching against both me and Leith, making us both inhale in pleasure.

Soon, the centaur's dick began to press into me and it really had to be the biggest one I'd ever had. With over two thousand years of experience, that was saying something.

"Alright, Aiqen, you're up." My voice came out slightly strangled as I adjusted to the very full sensation of being mounted by a horse.

The wyvern approached our multi-layered sandwich warily, looking for the best position for him to take, but he found it naturally enough without any direction from me, getting on his knees over Leith and Tanith and pressing his cock downwards until it found her lips. She took it in eagerly while he groaned in satisfaction.

Finally, we were all lined up and ready to go. "That's enough foreplay. Time to fuck."

Tanith groaned again, the sound muffled by Aiqen's cock as Leith and I began to move at the same time. My own movements weren't entirely in my control, not when Ty's pumping against me pushed and pulled me away from Tanith, letting me give and take at the same time. Using and being used, fucking and being fucked, it couldn't get any better for me. Connected to them all through the power of pleasure, I loved every second of it.

No one else had any complaints either. Leith's hands rested on Tanith's hips, holding her steady as he thrust into her from behind. Ty's hands held my shoulders for the same reason, giving him some leverage as he slid in and out of me, grunting in an almost primal way that sent a hot wave of pleasure through me. I'd always loved a man who let his animal side out, and Ty more than fit the bill.

Tanith herself looked completely overwhelmed in the best possible way, giving herself over completely to the pleasure of providing pleasure. Only Aiqen looked even the slightest bit unsatisfied, and only because the angle Tanith had for him wasn't the best. His cock kept popping out of her mouth, despite her best efforts to keep sucking on it.

"I can help, if you want," I offered, looking him straight in the eye. Since I faced down rather than up like Tanith, I could take him more comfortably for us both, but I didn't know if he'd agree. We were getting along better, certainly, but this would still be a big step for him.

His eyes wandered above me, to the centaur currently fucking my ass and enjoying it, and finally, he nodded. "Alright."

Spreading my legs wider to keep my balance, I took Aiqen's cock from Tanith and gave her a kiss. "You're taking us all so well," I praised her, not wanting her to feel like I was taking over with Aiqen because she'd failed. She hadn't at all; it just came down to simple physics. "Don't forget to enjoy yourself."

With that prompting, her head fell back onto Leith's shoulder, her eyes closing, and I squeezed her breast with one hand while the other brought Aiqen's cock to my mouth. My forked tongue slid along it, exploring each ridge and groove as the wyvern moaned in surprised pleasure.

By that point, I was so turned out that my horns had come out, and when Tanith opened her eyes and saw them, she grinned, reaching up to take hold of them. "Demon isn't the right word for you, Zol. I think we need to crown you a sex god."

Fuck, I felt like it with my cock buried inside her, Ty's inside me and Aiqen's in my mouth. As all of us writhed together on the forest floor, pushing and thrusting and pulling and touching, kissing and licking and sucking, I had never felt more alive. My orgasm came like a freight train, running me over and knocking me down as we all began to climax, one by one, leaving a panting, heaving pile of bodies in its wake.

I fucking loved that forest.

~Tymanus~

I enjoyed that a lot more than I expected to.

Maybe I needed the release after all the emotions of the last few hours, learning that the witch who killed Evia was nearby and all the repressed feelings that surfaced inside me with that revelation. Aris seemed to have been involved in all of our lives, but she had altered mine most of all. She called Leith stupid, bullied Tanith and refused to make a deal with Zol, but she actually killed the woman I loved. How were those things even remotely comparable? What had I done to earn the very worst she could do? What had Evia done?

I didn't blame the others. None of it was their fault, but I couldn't help being envious anyway, and a little resentful when they didn't immediately offer to help me seek revenge. They even talked about forming some kind of alliance with her, working together to figure out this world we'd found ourselves in.

I didn't care about any of that. I only wanted her to suffer, the same way I did when she killed my love.

I'd spent the past few months pushing those kinds of thoughts down. The witch had disappeared after Evia's death, and no one knew where she'd gone, or even where she'd come from in the first place. Every road I tried turned out to be a dead end and I finally had to accept there was nothing I could do. Nothing would bring Evia back.

Punishing the witch still wouldn't, but at least I could feel that I'd done *something*. If no one else here would help me, I'd have to find a way to do it myself.

I didn't want any of them to know that, though. They would try to stop me for one reason or another: Aiqen and Cad because they didn't want me to ruin whatever master plan they had, Tanith and Leith because they didn't want me to get hurt. Maybe Zol would take my side but I couldn't risk that he'd mention it to the others. Instead, I pretended to go along with what they wanted, joking with Zol as Aiqen carried us in his wyvern form away from the witch's house, and taking part in the orgy we'd just had in the middle of the forest.

The orgy had been a good distraction as well as a new experience for me. Centaurs were far more open to crossing gender and species lines than a lot of other creatures were, partly because there weren't all that many of us left and females were rarer than males. Groups of male centaurs often travelled together over great distances and would have sex with each other when there were no other options. I'd personally never taken part myself, but I didn't see anything wrong with it. Sex was sex, and if both parties were willing, why not?

Having sex with any human or humanoid creature, man or woman, in centaur form was far rarer. Injuries could and did happen due to our size. I'd personally never done that before either, so fucking Zol that day counted as two firsts for me. He seemed convinced he could handle it, and it seemed he could. I'd gotten plenty of physical enjoyment out of the whole thing, not to mention the arousal of watching everyone else enjoying themselves too. Even Aiqen let himself go, to my surprise. I would have never guessed even a few days earlier that he'd be standing naked in the middle of the forest with his cock in a demon's mouth and, by all appearances, loving it.

Still, as much fun as we all had, as soon as we were done, I made my excuses to slip away. "I'm going to see if I can go find some berries or edible roots in the forest. We need to eat and we're almost out of food."

All of that was true, so I didn't expect any resistance. Aiqen even nodded at me in approval. "Leith can try to help me catch some fish, after we check that the river's safe now." "I'll meet you by the river when I've got something, then," I offered, and when he agreed, I took one last look at the group of strangers who had become my unlikely friends. If things went badly with Aris, I might not see them again. If I managed to kill her and we couldn't ever leave this place because of it, they might not *want* to see me. Either way, my actions would probably change things between us, but I had to do it anyway.

For Evia, and to ease my own guilt, I had to.

As soon as I got out of sight and earshot of the group, I picked up my pace. The trees were too densely packed to get into a gallop, but I could move quicker than we had been travelling as a group without expending much more energy. It might take me an hour to make up the distance that Aiqen had managed to fly us in less than ten minutes, but I was determined to reach the witch's house before anyone realized I'd gone and tried to stop me.

"Ty!"

The voice sounded faint at first, so faint I thought I imagined it. In my head, it sounded like Evia calling for me, urging me on.

"Ty, stop! Please, wait."

Stop? My brow furrowed as I slowed down and looked over my shoulder. Evia wouldn't be telling me to stop, so maybe someone else was actually there?

It took a second for them to appear: Tanith and Zol, running through the forest after me.

"What is it?" I tried to sound as jovial as usual, as though they hadn't just caught me running away. They couldn't know what I was planning, so maybe they just wanted to help me look for food. I'd have to come up with an excuse to get rid of them.

Tanith struggled for breath as she came up to me. "You're really fast," she complained, her cheeks flushed. She must have been sprinting on her human legs to keep up with me. Zol looked out of breath too, though he hid it better.

"You haven't seen me run in the open yet," I reminded her, my eyes darting between her and Zol as I tried to determine the best way to get them to leave me alone. "If you want to help, I think there were some blackberry bushes back that way..."

"Ty, we know where you're really going." She gulped for air at the end of her sentence, gesturing for Zol to take over as she bent over to catch her breath.

"I totally get it," Zol assured me. "What Aris did to you was brutal. I've never been in love, not really, so I can't know exactly how you feel, but I understand the need for revenge. I've seen it consume way more people than you can imagine. Rushing in there and letting her capture or kill you isn't going to help anything. Even if you kill her, it won't change anything, and chances are you won't succeed anyway. I'm just being honest. How will it honour Evia's memory if you let this bitch kill you too? Not to mention, Tanith would miss you if something happened to you."

"*Just* me?" Tanith challenged him, and Zol gave a playful shrug.

"Alright, I'd miss you too. I'm going to be dreaming about that cock of yours for weeks."

His teasing made me smile, even though I felt completely lost. "How did you know what I planned to do?"

Zol looked over at Tanith, who gave me a soft smile. "I could see it in your face, Ty. As soon as we all finished, you withdrew. You went somewhere else. Maybe other people wouldn't see it, but you lost that spark that makes you *you*. I've only seen you look like that when you're thinking about Evia."

How was it even possible she knew me that well after the short time we'd spent together? We had a connection that I couldn't fully explain. "If you know all that, then you know why I have to go. I can't sit back and do nothing while listening to Aiqen and Cad debate the pros and cons of allying with her. I just can't."

"Then we'll take that into account," Tanith promised. "No one's feelings or opinions are any more valid than anyone else's. Aiqen and Cad don't get to make all the decisions, no matter what they might think sometimes. You just need to tell them exactly how you feel and we'll do what's best for all of us, because we're a team. We need you on our team, Ty. We *all* care about you.."

She gave Zol a warning look, and that time, he actually nodded seriously, without his usual mischievous look. "She's right. I'll back you up if you say a deal's off the table. And deals are my whole thing, so that's huge coming from me."

"You're not alone anymore," Tanith added, reaching over to take my hand. "I know it's felt that way since you lost Evia, but you've got us now. We can't take her place, but we can be there for you as you deal with it. When you come face-to-face with Aris again, I want you to have all our support. I want you to have all the power."

I wanted that too, and my shoulders slumped as I let go of the adrenaline that had been racing around inside me. If I looked at things rationally, I knew they had a point: Aris had magic on her side and I had none. I had brute strength and I had passion, but those things on their own might not be enough. When we combined all our skills together, we stood a much greater chance.

"Alright. I'll talk to the others and try to come to an agreement."

Zol broke into a smile while Tanith threw her arms around my waist. "Thank you, Ty. We're all on the same side, and we'll have your back. I promise."

Together, the three of us headed back to the others, stopping to pick up some berries and plants for lunch so no one else would have to know where I had actually been going. They promised to keep my secret and I trusted they would.

I just had to convince the rest of them that Aris didn't deserve a second chance. Negotiation wouldn't do. We needed to attack.

CHAPTER FIFTEEN

~Cadriel~

As soon as I walked away from the others, I began to second-guess myself. As Zol predicted, having sex with Tanith hadn't brought about the end of the world. None of my superiors appeared to cast me out or throw judgement at me. And though I felt some guilt when I thought back on it, I had a hard time summoning up much regret. Overall, I preferred to have the memory rather than never having experienced it.

Given all that, why couldn't I let myself go like the others all seemed able to? I honestly couldn't imagine what they would be doing, five of them together all at once, but other than Zol, I had to guess that none of them had been in a similar situation before. It must have been a little frightening for all of them, and yet, they were all being open and vulnerable with each other. Why couldn't I do the same?

Part of me felt tempted to turn around and go back to them, but just as I would make up my mind to do so, the guilt and fear would come back, and I'd turn around again. I must have looked like a madman, muttering to myself and turning in circles all alone in the forest.

Finally, I had to accept that I'd missed my chance. Whatever they were doing, they must have already started, and coming in half-way seemed even less appealing than being there from the start. Therefore, I put it out of my mind and began to set up the few remaining things we had left from our initial travelling supplies. As I worked, I thought back on Aris and our relationship, trying to understand where I had gone wrong with her. I must have messed up at some point, since protectorates weren't supposed to go around killing people. Where was my punishment for *that* failure?

Maybe because it didn't happen on Earth, my superiors weren't aware of it. After all, we didn't patrol the magical realms. Perhaps that explained why I'd faced no repercussions for my sexual slip either. I didn't even know where we were, so maybe anything I did there lay beyond the knowledge or control of those in charge.

That was a dangerous thought indeed. A lack of accountability could lead to all kinds of trouble. I pushed it away with all the other unhelpful thoughts swirling around in my head and focused back on the problem at hand.

Aris had been frustrated earlier that year. She told me herself, since she often had one-sided conversations with me. Even though I never revealed myself to her, she always seemed to know I was there. That in itself didn't seem unusual to me; often, protectorates had a stronger connection to the spiritual world than regular humans. Now, I had to wonder if it had been because of her magic that she could sense me. I would have to reevaluate every interaction I'd ever had with her.

"Everything was so good and now it's a mess," she complained at the start of the new year. "Ever since my birthday, nothing has gone right. It feels like there's a curse on me, like someone is doing this on purpose."

I hadn't put much stock in her words at the time, assuming she was being overly dramatic in the way that young humans often could be. She didn't go into any specifics about what had gone wrong, but with the new information I had, it left me to wonder: did Tanith have a string of good luck at the time? Were their lives actually connected in that way? Was the soul shadow theory correct?

It seemed extraordinary that these two women should have been born at the exact same moment as each other, in cities with the same name. It almost made me wonder if...

"Fuck!"

As soon as the thought entered my head, I let out a loud curse before immediately covering my mouth in horror. I'd never spoken that word before in my whole life, and luckily for me, no one had been around to hear it. I just hadn't been able to think of any other word to do justice to the thought that had just occurred to me.

What if I should have been assigned to Tanith all along?

Did that explain the way I felt drawn to her? It had never happened with any of my other protectorates, but I had heard of other angels who developed stronger than acceptable feelings for the ones under their care. They usually ended up being reassigned after confessing those feelings to their superiors.

But could such a mistake really have been made? If Tanith had been my assignment all along, what destiny did she have that put her in need of protection? Or was Aris my true assignment, but I was meant to protect Tanith *from* her? I had a lot of questions and no one to answer them. For the first time in my long life, I had to trust my own instincts and make the decision for myself.

"Hi, Cadriel."

Caught up in my thoughts, I missed Leith and Aiqen returning until they spoke. The merman gave me a friendly, slightly awkward wave as I looked up.

"We're going to go get some fish from the river. Do you want to come with us?"

"No, thanks. You're a much better swimmer than I am." I gave him a smile to let him know I was joking, and he grinned back. "Where are the others? Where's Tanith?"

"They went to go find some other food," Aiqen explained. "They should be back shortly."

As they turned to walk away, I couldn't help asking the obvious question. "So, you're all immune again?"

Aiqen and Leith exchanged a look that somehow combined embarrassment, amusement and satisfaction. Aiqen answered me, looking far more relaxed than usual. "Yeah. We're all taken care of."

With no more details than that, they walked away, leaving both my curiosity and my unwanted arousal unsatisfied.

I started a fire while the others foraged for food, and by the time everyone had returned, we had a decent feast of fresh fish, berries, and some roots that Ty said he could turn into a broth. Surprisingly, it didn't taste that bad, but when we finished eating, I pointed out the obvious.

"We can't survive out in the woods forever. We're going to need to decide what to do about Aris."

Tanith looked over at Ty and gave him a nod, and the centaur cleared his throat.

"I understand why you think talking to her could be important, but I refuse to sit down with her. *She* should talk, once we've captured and restrained her, but we don't owe her any consideration. If we can't all agree to that, then I can't be a part of this."

He spoke calmly and carefully, but I could hear the conviction underlying each word. Clearly, he didn't make the ultimatum lightly, and from the look Tanith gave him, I could tell she'd already chosen a side.

"We have to remember she's a witch," Aiqen pointed out. "We don't know what powers she has. It might not be possible to capture her, and if we try and fail, we could just piss her off more."

Ty didn't back down an inch. "Then we piss her off. I'll go down fighting, but I'm not going to ask for any favours from her. *She* owes us, not the other way around."

"I agree with Ty," Leith spoke up. "It means a lot to him, and an attack on one of us should be an attack on us all."

"I'm in too," Zol added. "Tanith and I already tried talking to her and she wanted to ask all the questions, not answer them. She thinks she's in charge. Time to shift the balance of power a bit."

That left me and Aiqen sitting on the fence, and I glanced over at the wyvern as he shrugged at me. "You're the one who's supposed to be protecting her. What do you think?"

Thankfully, I'd had a lot of time to think, and at last, I'd made up my mind. "I respect Ty's passion and his position. I'd like to avoid any unnecessary violence, but I agree that we'll get more information if we turn up the pressure on her. Let's go and get some answers."

~Aiqen~

Finally, we were going to get to the action. After almost ten days in this world without accomplishing anything, I couldn't be more ready, so once Cadriel agreed that capturing Aris would be our best move, I immediately switched into strategizing mode.

"We'll need the element of surprise. Since she can disappear at will, we either need to take her completely off guard or lull her into a false sense of security."

"Hold up. If she can disappear at will, what's to stop her from disappearing even after we capture her?" Zol countered.

"Mistletoe." Ty's blunt reply took everyone by surprise, and I exchanged glances with Cad, not sure if the centaur was serious. "That'll stop her from teleporting herself, and St John's Wort will force her to answer our questions truthfully."

When his answer was met with surprised silence, he sighed.

"You don't grow up in a realm with witches without learning a thing or two about their weaknesses."

That would be helpful indeed, but I saw one problem. "Do those plants even grow here? I haven't seen anything that looks like mistletoe around."

Everyone's heads turned as they scanned the plants growing around us in the forest. Although plentiful and varied, I couldn't see any that looked like the two Ty had mentioned.

"Maybe Tanith could add some?" Leith suggested hesitantly. "She can change the forest with her phone, right?"

"That's brilliant, Leith." She reached over to squeeze his hand, and I could have kicked myself for not thinking of it first. "Cad, can I have my phone?"

The angel reluctantly pulled it out of his pocket and handed it over. "I suppose this is a necessary use, but please, be quick."

Tanith's lips pursed as she took it from him, obviously not pleased with the reminder. By that point, everyone knew how important Cadriel thought the phone battery was.

We all watched as she opened her book and tapped on the keyboard, reading aloud as she typed: "Along with the poisonous plants in the forest, mistletoe and St John's Wort were the most common, growing through all the regions of the woods."

Sure enough, as soon as we looked around again, those plants had suddenly appeared where they definitely hadn't been before. Tanith switched off the phone and handed it back to Cadriel with a smirk.

"Fast enough for you?"

"Yes. Thank you." He pocketed it again, completely immune to her sarcasm, while I tried to move the conversation back to our overall strategy.

"So, we have a means of restraining her and forcing her to talk, but we still have to figure out how we're making our approach without alarming her or tipping her off about our intentions."

"Night time would be best," Zol suggested. "Darkness always helps when you're trying to make trouble."

He gave me a wink that previously would have irritated me, but that time, a warm heat spread through my body as I remembered his tongue and mouth on me. I hadn't expected to enjoy that particular experience nearly as much as I had.

Clearing my throat, I pushed those memories down. They had a time and a place, which was definitely not that particular moment. "We have to consider that she has some kind of alarm or perimeter defense set up."

"Zol and I can help with that," Cad offered. "I'm able to undo any ill enchantments over a location while Zol can neutralize any beneficial ones. We can't affect the person herself, but we can make the location safe."

"Excellent." I hadn't anticipated they would have those kinds of powers any more than I had expected Ty's knowledge of plant life, but between the five of us, we might just have all the skills needed to pull this off. "I can take out any physical security she has. Tanith mentioned ogres and I have experience dealing with them. That only leaves the approach to Aris herself. As I said, we don't want her to be too suspicious too quickly."

"Leith would probably be the least threatening," Tanith suggested. "He and I can go together. Ty can tell us what we need to do with the mistletoe to keep her from disappearing before the rest of you get there."

I looked around the circle to ensure that no one had any objections, and when none were forthcoming, I gave them all a nod of approval. "In that case, let's get to work."

By the time night fell, all the arrangements had been made. Tanith and Leith had worked with Ty to come up with a way of rooting Aris in place with the mistletoe. Ty also created a drink using the St John's Wort that should act as something of a truth serum once we got her where we wanted her. He would bring it with him once we had Aris in hand.

Under the cover of darkness, the whole group of us returned through the forest back to where the trees began to thin. Cad put out his arm to stop us, not making a sound, and the whole group stopped right on cue. Holding his hands up, he closed his eyes as the air around him seemed to hum, his hands taking on a golden glow. Just as I began to worry the brightness might give us away, the light faded and he nodded.

"It's done," he whispered. "Anything that might have harmed us has been eliminated. Zol, you're up."

Taking a breath, Zol repeated his half-brother's gesture, raising his hands and closing his eyes, but no light came from his hands. After a moment, he opened one eye and grinned at the rest of us. "Just kidding."

With a wink, he snapped his fingers, and a red light sizzled through the air, like a spark of electricity.

"There. No more alarms."

Cadriel shook his head. "Do you always need to show off?"

"The protections have all dissolved?" I interrupted, more concerned about our current endeavour than their sibling rivalry. When they both nodded, I quickly stripped off my clothes and shifted to my wyvern form. I would draw out Aris' security, leaving her alone and vulnerable for Tanith and Leith to make their approach.

With a great swoop of my wings, I lifted off, heading into the open space in front of the witch's cottage. It didn't take long for my appearance to catch the attention of the two ogres patrolling the perimeter of the house, especially since I used my powerful wings to send gusts of wind directly at the house. Inside the house, Aris would simply think there was a storm.

"Hey! How'd you get there?" The first one sounded confused as he shouted at me, gesturing with his large, unwieldy arm to his counterpart. "Get the net!"

A net would work perfectly. While they were distracted, I flew to the top of the house and blew a gust of air down the chimney, extinguishing the fire that burned within, reinforcing the idea that a storm was responsible for any commotion Aris might be able to hear. When I returned to the front of the house, the ogres had a net between them which they tried to throw up and over me as I flew by. They had tied the ropes at the end around themselves for leverage.

They were making it far too easy for me.

As they tossed the net into the air, I rose up out of its reach and grabbed it with my talons instead. With the net firmly in my grasp, I soared higher, pulling the hapless ogres off the ground with me. Too startled to do more than grunt, they clung onto the ropes for dear life as I quickly flew out of earshot of the cottage until I found an open space where I could set them down. As soon as they were on their feet again, and with the net still clutched firmly in my claws, I flew in circles around them, wrapping the net tightly to tie them together. Once I was sure they weren't going anywhere soon, I flew back to the others and shifted back to my human form.

"The coast is clear," I told Tanith and Leith. "She's all yours."

~Tanith~

I had a little trouble walking straight as Leith and I made our way out of the trees towards the witch's cottage. Although I enjoyed every second of our group menage earlier, I'd be lying if I said I didn't feel some after effects. Having Leith inside my ass had been an entirely new sensation, and when Zol added his considerable girth to the mix, it left me feeling fuller than I could have ever imagined.

That was even before Aiqen filled my mouth.

The whole thing had left me feeling filthy and adored, degraded and worshipped, used and wanted all at the same time.

Incredible didn't even begin to cover it. The sex was amazing and completely fulfilling, but it meant more than that too. We were all truly starting to care for each other, not only me for them and each of them for me, but all the men for each other too, in at least a platonic way if not a sexual one.

The only thing that would have made it better would have been having Cad involved, but that might be a step too far for him. I could still barely believe we'd actually slept together at all, especially since he knew I'd been with the others and had every intention of being with them again. For that one moment, he let himself go, and I could have sworn he enjoyed it. But since then, he'd withdrawn back into himself again, unlike Aiqen, who seemed to be loosening up more with each passing minute.

I didn't know how to break through Cad's reserve again, but it would have to wait. With Leith at my side and Aris' door in front of me, I had other things to worry about.

I knocked firmly, keeping my other hand in my pocket where I hid the mistletoe bracelet I'd made earlier with Ty. I would have to find a way to get it on Aris, at least temporarily. Ty told us that the essence of it would remain on her skin even if she pulled it off, grounding her long enough for the others to get her and restrain her properly. I just had to get close enough to slip it on.

When there was no reply to my knock, I tried again, louder. Leith leaned forward, listening as I did for any sign of life within and eventually, we heard Aris muttering as she came to the door. "Where are those stupid ogres?"

She opened the door a mere crack, peering out at us in the darkness. "What do you want?"

Even as she spoke, I could see her eyes darting around, still looking for her bodyguards who were, of course, nowhere in sight.

I kept my tone as pleasantly neutral as possible. "You disappeared this afternoon when we were talking. We didn't get to finish our conversation."

"You had a different companion then," she reminded me, giving Leith an appraising look. "Are you just trading one for the other whenever it suits you?"

The bitter undercurrent of her tone made me smile since I had a pretty good idea what it meant. "Are you jealous?"

"Of *you*?" she protested, snorting a little too strongly. "Never."

"You *are* jealous." It seemed so obvious, I didn't know how I'd missed it before. "That's why you came and bullied me. You wanted me to feel unlovable because you'd seen me with these men in your visions. You knew they would all care about me."

"I've noticed that sometimes, people accuse others of the things they feel themselves," Leith added thoughtfully before addressing Aris. "You always told me no one cared what I thought, but maybe that's how you actually feel about yourself? And you told Tanith no one would like her because you think people don't like you?"

"I think you're absolutely right, Leith." As far as I was concerned, he'd hit the nail squarely on the head. He was far smarter than he gave himself credit for, especially when it came to emotion and empathy.

"He's not right, he's never *been* right in his whole life, and I am not in the mood for a psychology lesson in the middle of the night," Aris practically growled. "I have nothing more to say to you right now. Come back in the morning, *all* of you, and we can talk."

She moved to close the door, but I stuck my foot in its path just in time, wincing as the solid wood pinched my skin against the door frame. "Not so fast. You sent that note asking me to come here. I'm here now, and I want to know what's going on."

"You are not calling the shots here!" She removed her hand from the door so she could point them both in my direction, intending to cast some kind of spell on me, no doubt, but what she actually did was give me a perfect opportunity to achieve what I came there to do. As her arms raised, I pulled the mistletoe bracelet from my pocket and forced it onto her wrist before she had a chance to react at all.

"What the hell is this?" she demanded before getting a proper look at it. When she did, her face paled. "How did you know... no, never mind. We're done here."

Pulling the bracelet off and throwing it back in my face, she shoved the door closed on us. That hadn't been exactly the plan, but at least she couldn't leave, so I let out the agreed whistle, a signal for the others to join us.

They arrived in no time at all, Cad flying in carrying Aiqen, and Zol riding on top of Ty. "She's inside?" Cad asked as he landed and set Aiqen down. Zol slid off of Ty's back, giving the centaur's ass a playful swat on the way down.

I nodded. "I got the bracelet on her for a few seconds so she knows we're up to something. She tried to get rid of us."

"We'll need to move fast," Cad said. "We've removed the magic protecting the house and she can't teleport, but she could still cast spells on any of us. Ty, do you think you can break this door down?"

"With pleasure."

We all stepped aside as Ty backed up a few paces, his hooves pawing at the ground like a runner taking his mark, and with a loud roar, he barrelled into the door with all his strength. The wooden barrier never stood a chance, creaking and cracking beneath the force of his weight.

"Split up!" Aiqen shouted as he ran inside. "Someone stay at the door so she can't escape. Shout when you've found her."

Cad quickly took the spot by the door, urging the rest of us to follow Aiqen, and since I knew the layout of the house best, having already explored it earlier that day in the deleted timeline, I headed straight for the workshop. Sure enough, I found her there, hurriedly throwing some ingredients into a bubbling liquid, looking like the most stereotypical witch imaginable.

I tried once again to reason with her. "We're just here to talk to you, Aris. You're the one who wanted to talk in the first place! We need to get to the bottom of what's happening here. How did we all end up here and what made that noise this afternoon that scared you so much?"

She glanced up at me for just a second when I mentioned the noise, that glimmer of fear still in her eyes, before she looked back down at her potion, muttering some words as she gave it a stir with a long, wooden spoon.

Obviously, she planned to ignore me, so I shouted to the others as Aiqen had instructed. "She's in here! I've got her."

Aris looked up at me once more, but this time with a hint of a smile. "Or maybe *I* have *you*."

She brought the spoon to her lips, whispering some words I couldn't make out, and as soon as the liquid hit her tongue, something seemed to pull at me from deep inside. I tried to cry out, but my voice wouldn't work. In fact, I couldn't seem to move my body at all, but I could see it, from the outside, for just a second. In the next instant, I felt slammed back against a wall, though I still hadn't moved an inch. Something bitter stung my mouth, and I dropped the spoon that I was now somehow holding, looking down in horror.

I stood exactly where Aris had been standing, hovering over the potion. And when I looked up, I could see... *me*, standing in the doorway, smirking while the men all rushed into the room. Aiqen came over to my current location, his handsome face hard, and he grabbed one of my arms while Zol took the other, yanking them firmly behind my back as they tied the longer mistletoe rope we'd made earlier around my wrists.

"You wanted to do this the hard way, Aris, so that's what we'll do. One way or another, you're going to give us the answers we want."

Aris? He looked right at me as he said the name, and my eyes returned to the Tanith by the door again, the one not even bothering to hide her satisfied smile.

That bitch was in my body. Somehow, she'd switched us, her soul and mine.

How was I going to explain that to the others?

CHAPTER SIXTEEN

~Leith~

I put my arm around Tanith as the others tied Aris up. "Are you okay? She didn't try anything before we got here?"

She leaned into me, making my whole body flush simply from her proximity. "No. She was making some kind of potion, but whatever it is, she drank it herself."

Ty, who stood on my other side, heard every word. "What did you do to yourself?" he demanded, his muscles tense and on edge as he addressed the witch. Although he tried his best to hold himself back, we could all see how deep his hatred for her ran.

"I didn't... it wasn't... I'm not her," Aris blurted out, her eyes panicked as she looked around the room at all of us. "Guys, it's me. It's Tanith. She switched us somehow. I'm in her body and she's in mine. That's not me."

Since her hands were already tied behind her back, Aris used her head to gesture towards the woman at my side.

"What are you trying to say?" Tanith asked, sounding just as confused as I felt.

"You know exactly what I'm talking about." Aris narrowed her eyes, her jaw clenching before she turned to Cadriel, who stood on Tanith's other side. "Cad, can you feel it? My soul got swapped with hers. It has something to do with this potion, I think."

Cadriel's response was wary. "How do you know my name? We've never spoken before."

"Because it's *me*," Aris repeated. "It's Tanith. I know everything about you."

"She's been having visions of all of us," Tanith reminded us. "She probably knows a lot more about all of us than we think she does. This is obviously some kind of trick so we won't hurt her, or maybe so you'll turn against me."

My arm tightened around her. "That will never happen," I promised. "But there's an easy way to check if she's telling the truth, isn't there? We have Ty's drink."

He told me as he created it that it meant any witch would be unable to lie. Having a foolproof lie detector should put the whole question of body swapping to rest pretty easily.

"You give it to her," Ty told me, holding out the pouch he carried. "If I get any closer to her, I can't promise I'll control myself."

Reluctantly, I let Tanith go to take the drink from Ty. With the pouch in my hands, I walked over to where Aiqen and Zol held Aris, and her dark eyes watched me intently as I approached. "Leith, you believe me, don't you? It really is me in here."

I avoided the question as I held the nozzle of the pouch up to her lips. "Just drink this and then we can find out for sure."

To my surprise, she didn't try to avoid it. She drank it willingly enough, and when I pulled the pouch back, a small trickle ran down her chin. With her hands tied, she had no way of wiping it away herself, so I did it for her and, just for a second, something in the way she looked at me seemed familiar. Or did I imagine it?

Before I could get confused, I took a step back.

"How quickly does this work?" Aiqen asked Ty.

"Immediately," he replied, still glowering at Aris. "Let's get some answers."

With a nod, Aiqen turned back to the witch. "Alright, let's start with the basics, then: what's your name?"

"It's Tanith," she repeated firmly. "I know this is confusing. I don't understand it myself but I'm telling you the truth. Aris is over there. She's in my body."

The rest of all exchanged confused glances. "Are you sure it's effective?" Zol asked Ty, gesturing at the pouch I still held in my hands.

"It always has been," he growled in reply. "Unless she's got some way of counteracting it?"

"The potion," Tanith suggested with a gasp. "I bet that's what it's for. It's protecting her against the St John's Wort."

Something about that didn't entirely make sense to me. "But how would she have known we were going to use this particular drink?"

Tanith had an answer for that too. "She's seen us, remember? Maybe she had a vision about it."

That could be possible. Looking around at the other men, I could tell no one had any other suggestions, unless she really *was* telling the truth, but that seemed even less likely. Wouldn't we be able to tell the difference?

"Why don't they give *you* the drink and ask you the same question?" Aris suggested, glaring at Tanith.

Tanith blinked in surprise. "Does it work on humans? I've never heard of that before."

"No, it doesn't," Ty confirmed. "It's for witches only."

"But if a witch really is in her body, maybe it would work on that witch?" I asked tentatively. What made a witch? Something in her body, or something in her soul?

"Do you really think I'm her?" The plaintive look in Tanith's eyes felt like something sharp poking at my stomach. I never wanted her to feel bad because of me.

"We should cover all our bases," Cad said, backing me up. "Unless there's a reason you don't want to drink it?"

Tanith quickly shrugged. "No, of course not. If you want me to, I will."

I handed the pouch to her, letting her take a mouthful, and when she'd swallowed it down, Aiqen asked the same question he'd asked Aris. "What's your name?"

"It's Tanith." Something flashed in her eyes before she smiled. "You see? It's all a distraction."

"You're using my humanity to avoid our questions. You're using my body to protect yourself!" Aris tried to move towards Tanith, but Aiqen and Zol were right there to hold her back.

"Alright, let's think about this logically," Cad suggested, holding his hands up to calm both women. "There are two possibilities as far as I see it: either Aris is lying and she made a potion that helps her avoid the St John's Wort, or she's telling the truth and that really is Tanith in there, in which case the potion works on the Tanith version of Aris, but not on the Aris version of Tanith."

I mostly followed that, but I couldn't see his point. "How do we tell which it is?"

"I can tell you things," Aris offered. "Things you've all said to me, things we've done over the past few days. I can prove I was there."

"Except you could have got all those 'memories' from your visions or through magic," Tanith pointed out, her arms wrapping tighter around herself with each word. "I can't believe we're even talking about this!"

"Then don't ask me. Ask *her* those questions," Aris suggested. "See if she can answer them."

"Whatever we do, we shouldn't stay here," Aiqen added. "Those ogres might come back, and we don't know what other defensive backups she might have. We should head back to the forest."

"After helping ourselves to a few luxuries." Zol gave Aris a smirk. "Some food from your cupboard will come in handy, and I could use a pillow after three nights of sleeping on the hard ground."

"Take whatever you want," Aris replied. "It's not mine. It all belongs to her."

Tanith shrugged. "I was about to say the same thing."

My head had started to hurt from all the confusion, so when Cadriel told me and Ty to go to the kitchen and find some food, it came as a relief. "Do you think they might really be in each other's bodies?" I whispered to my centaur friend as we filled up some bags we found with both fresh and canned food from the witch's larder.

"I'm not sure. I can't look at Aris without wanting to kill her. If Tanith really is in there, I don't know what we'll do."

Neither did I. How could something like that be undone?

As quickly as possible, we finished grabbing what we could carry and joined the others back in the workshop. Zol really did have some pillows under his arms and some blankets and other fabrics too.

"Alright, let's..."

Aiqen started to give us our next instruction, but before he could finish, the same deep rumbling noise from earlier surrounded us again, the windows rattling and the ground shaking beneath us.

Aris' eyes darted around the room as Tanith went pale. "We need to leave," Tanith told us. "Whatever that is, it can't be good."

It certainly didn't feel good, but before we could do anything, a bright light flashed, and a tall man appeared in the room with us. He wore clothes that looked similar to Cadriel's, professional and put together, but his ears were pointed and his long, dark hair was pulled back at his neck. He looked almost equally as surprised to see us as we were to see him, but as his gaze swept the room, it fell on Aris, and he gave a grim smile.

"There you are. You couldn't hide from me forever. It's time for us to have a talk."

"I think we were here first," Aiqen protested, but it made no difference. The man walked over, put a hand on Aris, and the white light flashed again. The next instant, they both disappeared.

"Who the fuck was that?" Zol grumbled, his hand grasping the air where Aris had been just a second ago. "Where did he take her?"

"I don't know, but we better get out of here before he comes back," Tanith suggested.

At least, it *looked* like Tanith, but what if the other woman had been telling the truth, and the strange man actually took Tanith instead? Something about all of this felt very wrong.

~Tymanus~

I had rarely felt so frustrated. Not only did the potion not work, but we lost Aris. The man who took her looked like a fairy from the brief glimpse I got of him, though I'd never known any fairies with the kind of power he seemed to have. Whoever he was, he seemed to have his own grievance against Aris, but it couldn't compare to mine.

So fucking close. I should have taken the opportunity while I had it to get my revenge and let her feel even a fraction of the pain she put me through. Two things stopped me: one, the deal I'd made with the others to get information out of her first, and two, the odd claim she made about actually being Tanith in Aris' body.

Leith asked me if I thought that could be possible and I honestly didn't know. I'd never heard of anything like that, but this place kept throwing up things none of us had encountered before, so how could I say it couldn't be true?

I asked Zol about it as we made our way back to the forest without Aris. "Could you tell if someone's soul had changed? Aren't souls your currency?"

I might not know all the ins and outs of what demons or angels did, but they dealt in souls, I knew that much.

"I don't have any kind of soul x-ray, if that's what you're asking." Zol's answer sounded as sarcastic as ever, but a hint of uncertainty underpinned it. He really didn't know whether to trust Tanith either. "I can't see or feel anything more than you do. Neither can Cad. We're like delivery men; we guide souls towards heaven or hell, but we don't get to see what's actually in the package."

"So we'll have to get her to answer questions that only Tanith would know," I surmised, which was, I had to admit, just what Aris suggested.

Zol shrugged. "If Tanith answers correctly, Aris could claim she'd used a potion to get the information. Or maybe she *is* Aris but whatever spell she used to switch bodies also gave her access to Tanith's memories? Whatever happens, it could be twisted. Witches are fucking slippery, Ty."

He didn't need to tell me that, but I would pin Aris down eventually, even if it was the last thing I did. "I'm going to try to get her alone to talk. I might be able to goad her into saying something incriminating, if there's any truth to this idea at all. Can you be on standby if I do?"

"I've got your back," he promised, and funnily enough, I really believed that he did.

"That's far enough," Cadriel announced once the trees surrounded us again. "It's too dark to go any further. We can't see what we might be running into."

"If you'd just infected yourself with the rest of us this afternoon, you wouldn't have to worry about that," Zol reminded him. "Right, Tanith?"

He gave her a wink in the darkness, and Tanith flashed him a smile in return. "Right. I'm happy to stop here. I'm really tired, actually. We should rest and regroup in the morning. It's been a long day."

It certainly had, but did she actually remember any of it, or was she just trying to get out of talking to us? No matter how late the hour, I had no intention of going to sleep until I could put my mind at rest. "Tanith, could I talk to you while the others get everything set up?"

"Can it wait until the morning? I can barely keep my eyes open."

"No. It can't." Her trying to put me off made me more suspicious and everyone else watched us closely, waiting to see what she would do.

"Alright," she gave in. "If it's important to you, of course we can talk."

That sounded more like Tanith but I still had my doubts, and as I told Zol, I had an idea about how I could trip her up if it actually *was* Aris talking to me.

After we walked a short distance away from the others, I turned to face her. "I don't want to keep you long, I know you're tired, but I need to talk to you since you're the only one who knows more than the bare essentials about Evia."

The darkness prevented me from seeing her expression clearly, but I could tell she watched me closely. "I'm here for you, Ty. What is it?"

"When I saw Aris today, I remembered something Evia said the first time she saw her. She said she looked familiar to her, that she had a feeling they'd met before but she couldn't quite place it." I had actually forgotten all about that until I saw Aris for myself. Like the others described, she looked the same as I remembered her, but different too. It gave me an odd sense of déjà vu, and perhaps Evia felt the same thing. "I wonder if she interfered in Evia's life before we even met.""I suppose it's possible they met before," Tanith agreed. "Or she could have just reminded her of someone. I wouldn't worry about it."

There she went again, attempting to wrap up the conversation. Tanith never did that. When she talked to me, I always felt I had her full attention.

I refused to stop there. "This whole time, I thought she killed Evia because of me. When we found out she messed with each of us, it seemed to confirm it. But then I wondered: why did she hurt me so much worse than she hurt anyone else? Why did she hurt Evia?"

"We're not going to get answers to those questions tonight," she said, stifling a yawn. "Let's sleep on it and we can talk about it in the morning."

I carried on as if she hadn't spoken. "Did you notice anything strange about the man who took her?"

Tanith shrugged. "You mean besides the fact that he appeared out of nowhere and made the ground shake?"

Touché. "I mean that he looked like a fairy. Evia's race. Maybe he's a relative of hers?"

"Isn't that a little bit racist? Or species-ist?" she asked with a laugh. "Just because they're from the same species doesn't mean they're related."

Tanith wouldn't be laughing, not after everything that had just happened. She would take me seriously and help me work through my concerns. With each word, I became more convinced that the person in front of me wasn't Tanith at all.

"Do you remember what I told you that Evia said about witches in general? About how they're all delusional, thinking they're so much smarter than everyone else?"

Even in the dim light, I could see Tanith's jaw clench. "Of course. I'm starting to think she was right."

She must have thought that disparaging witches would convince me she was Tanith, but she'd missed one important thing. "That's funny, because I never said anything like that. Neither did Evia."

Her eyes widened for just a second before she turned to run.

She didn't get more than three steps before Zol blocked her path. "Going somewhere, Aris?"

She backed up, heading in the opposite direction instead, but Aiqen stood there, his arms crossed. "You really think we're that stupid, do you?"

She looked left and right as Leith and Cad came up on her other sides, blocking her in. Zol must have filled them in and brought them all for backup, and I gave him a grateful nod.

"You can't do anything to me while I'm in this body," Aris tried, dropping the pretense while grasping at straws. "Not if you ever want her to get it back."

That might be true, but there was plenty we could do that didn't involve physical torture. Information would be more valuable to us than causing her pain. "Just tell us one thing: where is Tanith right now? Who took her?"

She snorted in derision. "Are you really that dense? You basically just told me who it was."

Had I? I said I thought he might be a relative of Evia's, but I'd only been guessing. If it were true, maybe that explained *why* he had come for Aris. Maybe he was someone very closely related indeed.

"Is he Evia's father?"

~Zolgozig~

Apparently, Ty just had some kind of epiphany, but he'd lost me along the way. "Remind me who Evia is?" I asked while grabbing hold of Aris' arm so she couldn't try to make a break for it. I took care not to hold it *too* tightly since I didn't want to leave Tanith with any bruises. Not ones that weren't caused by pleasure, anyway.

"Evia is the woman Aris killed. The woman I loved. I thought she killed her because of me, but now, I'm not so sure."

"Alright, Zol and I will take it from here," Cad told the others. "Go and get some rest. I know we're all worried about Tanith, but we can't do anything to find her until we know more about what's happening."

"You think you can make her talk?" Ty stared at Aris with a withering mix of hatred and disdain. I didn't know if I'd ever felt as strongly about anyone as he seemed to feel about her.

"We'll do our best," was all Cad would promise. "Go and rest. We won't let her go."

Taking my half-brother at his word, Aiqen and Leith turned to leave, Leith putting his arm around Ty to gently pull him away. When they'd gone, Cad's voice echoed in my head in a way it hadn't done in thousands of years.

She's had very different relationships with the two of us. If we play off that - a little 'good cop, bad cop' as it were - we might be able to get her talking.

The words he said were far less interesting to me than how he said them. *You can still communicate with me telepathically?*

He gave an almost sheepish shrug. *We're not supposed to talk to anyone who's fallen. You all think we can't simply because we don't.*

He had to be fucking kidding. Losing the ability to tap into the minds of my fellow angels had been one more way I'd been cut off by those I considered my family. That meant they would have heard me calling out to them in those first days and weeks, pleading for help, asking for mercy, and they all simply tuned me out. Bastards.

And yet, by telling me this, Cad held out an olive branch. Nothing stopped me from spreading that information to every fallen angel out there, but he trusted I wouldn't, and that trust meant a great deal to me. Little by little, he was opening up to me again. *Alright. You start, I'll follow your lead.*

"Do you know who I am?" Cad asked Aris aloud, pacing slowly in front of her while I continued to hold her by the arm.

"You're Cadriel. The angel."

At least she answered, if not the answer he wanted. "I mean: do you know who I am to you?"

To make it easier for her to see him, he held up his hands to his face as they produced a heavenly glow, a soft and warm light. My hands used to do the same; now, they only gave off a red heat that might be sexier, but not nearly as comforting.

Aris kept her eyes on him. "I've seen you with Tanith, but that's all. I couldn't track you down like the others."

"How *did* you track us all down?" I interrupted. She found me by summoning me, but Ty, Leith and Aiqen wouldn't have been as easy to locate. She would have had to go to them.

"One thing at a time, Zol. We don't want to overwhelm her," Cad chastised me gently, taking his 'good cop' role to heart. When I said nothing further, he focused back on Aris. "You may not have seen me before, but you've felt me. I know you have."

It took a moment, but eventually, realization dawned on her. "You're the watcher."

"You could call me that," Cad agreed. "I've been watching you since you were born, Aris. I planned to step in when you needed me, but apparently, I missed the signs that you already did."

"Needed you for what?" She managed to sound both curious and put out at the same time, her voice softer than it had been in her own body. Hearing her speak in Tanith's voice couldn't be any stranger.

"I didn't know at the time, but I think now that I should have prevented you from going down the path you have. We need to talk about Evia, but first, I want to know more about you. How did you end up being born on Earth when you belong in another realm?"

I couldn't say if Cad's gentle, calming presence did it, or if she really just wanted someone to confide in, but to my surprise, Aris began talking. "My mother was expelled from our realm when she got pregnant with me. Apparently, my father already had a wife, a powerful one, and when she found out that her husband had been unfaithful, she blamed my mother for it and cast her out."

The words 'cast out' gave me a jolt, and Cad's eyes moved to me in empathy. *Still a touchy subject*, I tried to joke in my head, playing it off, but I appreciated that he'd noticed my reaction.

Unaware of our interaction, Aris continued. "I was born on Earth instead, and it seems to have given me both advantages and disadvantages."

"In what way?" I kept my voice harsh so that Cad would seem even nicer by comparison.

It seemed to work, since she kept her eyes on Cad as she answered me. "I can move between realms in a way most witches can't, but it also seems to have limited my magic. I'm not as strong as I should be when it comes to spells and other magic."

"And you resent that?" Cad's probing questions were meant to try to understand her, when I would much rather get to the point and figure out what Evia's father wanted with Aris and where he'd taken Tanith in her body.

"Of course I do!" Anger burned through Aris' words. "It's not fair that my power was diminished by something out of my control. It's not fair that I always had to hide my identity when travelling to the magical realms. It's not fair that this nobody gets the things that should have been mine."

She gestured down to Tanith's form as she talked about a 'nobody', and I latched on to that. "What do you know about Tanith? How do you know about her?"

She didn't answer me until Cad nodded. "I would like to know that too."

"I had nothing to do with her until she showed up here. I created this realm, no one else should have known about it, but I saw her here with all of you. I tracked her down to try to figure out who she is and what she wants, but I haven't been able to. I've been going to that stupid college, trying to get to the bottom of it, but she's a nobody. I don't know how she fooled all of you into thinking she's something special, but she's pathetic and spineless and..."

"That's enough." My grip tightened on her arm, making her gasp, and I quickly released it as I remembered I actually held Tanith's arm. Fuck, this was complicated. "*How* did you track her?"

"It's another of my gifts." She smiled smugly, the expression looking strange on Tanith's face as she continued to speak to Cad as though I weren't there. "I can move between realms and I can see where people are, all except the two of you. I couldn't track you using my usual methods, so I summoned Zol. But you, I couldn't find at all."

"And you played with us, like a bully does," I summed up. "Except for Ty. With Ty, you went a lot further. Why?"

"Let's talk about that now," Cad agreed. "Why did you kill Evia? Did Tymanus do something to you?"

I knew he didn't believe that, he was just trying to sound empathetic, and it seemed to work as Aris snorted. "It had nothing to do with that stupid centaur."

It took all my self-control not to squeeze her arm again. "What did it have to do with, then?"

"What it always comes down to," she replied in an overdramatic style that sounded all wrong coming out of Tanith's mouth. "Love."

CHAPTER SEVENTEEN

Finally, we were making some progress. The more Aris opened up, telling me things I never knew despite having been present through many parts of her life, the more I understood her. Not to say that I agreed with her conclusions and decisions, because of course I didn't, especially when it came to causing harm to others. Still, I had seen many people become twisted by bitterness or jealousy, carrying a chip on their shoulder when they believed they were entitled to things they were denied, so I could start to understand why she behaved the way she did, even if it didn't excuse it.

Her motivation was slowly becoming clearer, and although she didn't realize it, she had told us something that not only seemed to back up my theory that she and Tanith were soul shadows, but it actually explained something else that had heretofore been a complete mystery.

She thought being born on Earth resulted in her being less powerful than other witches, but I didn't think that was the case at all. What I suspected actually happened was that at the moment of their birth, when her soul and Tanith's collided somehow and became linked, part of their souls were swapped in a completely unintentional way. Like two photographs stuck together, when they were pulled apart, the images became mixed, part of one picture sticking to the other.

What that meant in practice was that a little bit of Tanith's humanity got 'stuck' to Aris. *That* accounted for her magical weakness rather than the location of her birth. And on the flip side, if Tanith ended up with just a tiny bit of Aris' magical ability, it might explain how she was able to write our story before it happened, and even how she could use her phone to control things within our world. It seemed far more likely that the ability came from within her rather than from a random phone purchased at the mall.

Aris had been convinced that Tanith couldn't be fully human, and it seemed like she might be right. What she didn't know was how the two things were connected, and I had no intention of telling her. She already resented Tanith, and if my suspicions were correct, knowing the rest wouldn't make her feelings any warmer.

That much, I had figured out. What I didn't understand was what she had just said about killing Evia for love. Obviously, we were still missing part of the story.

"You *loved* Evia?" Zol asked, sounding just as confused by her answer as I felt, and Aris snorted again, throwing him a disparaging look.

"Of course not! She stood in the way of the love that belonged to me."

"Start at the beginning, please." I did my best to keep my tone calm and soothing. She seemed to respond well when she felt she was being listened to and understood. "It sounds like it must have been a difficult experience for you. I'm sorry I couldn't be there to help you through it. I'm assuming the person you loved wasn't human."

I never saw Aris with anyone on Earth, and the photo Tanith found in her house showed a boy who clearly belonged to a different species. Could he be the person we were talking about?

Her next words confirmed as much. "Lysanthir is a fairy. I met him in one of the realms I visited, one without any other witches in it. He thought the things I could do were incredible and he never made me feel defective in any way, like other witches always did."

Zol's lips grew tighter and tighter, struggling to control his temper as Aris continued to paint herself as the victim. She wanted us to feel bad for her that other witches had bullied her, when she went out of her way to bully Tanith and Leith? Those were all the earmarks of a classic narcissist.

"He cared for you too?" I prompted, trying to move her along to the meat of her story. "You were in a relationship?"

"Yes. We knew it wouldn't be easy because he came from an important family and they looked down on just about everyone but especially me. He promised me he didn't care about any of that, though. We were happy together and planning our future. I even created this world just for us. We were going to live here away from everyone else who might judge us for being together. Those were the best days of my life."

Mortals are so fucking overdramatic, Zol's voice said in my head, and on this occasion, I had to agree. She spoke as if her life had already ended.

"What happened?"

"Evia happened." Her face darkened as she said the fairy's name, the scowl looking completely out of place on Tanith's face. "Her family was also important, and their parents agreed that Lysanthir and Evia should be married to combine their family lines."

"Arranged marriages can be a bitch," Zol agreed. "Let me guess: fairy boy wanted out of it so he asked you to off her?"

"No." In the dark shadows of the night, Aris' eyes seemed to burn. "He was actually happy about it! After months of telling me how special I was and how he couldn't imagine being with anyone else, he dropped me just like that. Said he couldn't do anything about it, but I could see the truth. He was actually excited about it."

A piece of the puzzle remained missing. "If they got together, where does Tymanus fit in?"

Aris got more worked up with each word, the volume of her voice growing louder and shriller. "That's the thing. Although Lysanthir was perfectly happy about it all, Evia didn't want to marry *him*. She ran away. She must have had someone transport her to another realm where another tribe of fairies lived so she could hide with them. It caused a huge uproar, and I thought for sure Lysanthir would give up on her then, but he didn't. He got angry at *me*, thinking I must have done something to her since he knew I could move between realms. He told me so long as there was a chance she'd be found, he wouldn't give up on her."

At last, the remaining pieces fell into place. "And then you bumped into her, completely by coincidence when you tracked down Ty, and you made sure she would never be found."

"What else could I do?" she whined. "I'd been so close to happiness and it all fell apart. First, this world I created that no one else was supposed to know about it starts getting populated by creatures I don't want here, then I meet Tanith who has a whole group of men hanging off her *and* a boyfriend at home who looks just like Lysanthir, even though there's nothing special about her at all, and then I see Evia with one of Tanith's men? I'm not stupid. I put it all together. Somehow, Tanith is involved in all of this. She has some kind of power I don't understand, and by getting rid of Evia, maybe I could disrupt the whole scheme. At the very least, I could get Lysanthir back. It made sense."

I noticed her use of the past tense. At some point, it had stopped making sense, and I could guess when and why. "You didn't expect Evia's father to be able to track you down here."

Her pressed lips told me I'd got it right. "He shouldn't be able to. I know he's royalty, but he shouldn't have the power..."

"Royalty?" Zol interrupted. "Are you telling us you killed a fucking princess and didn't expect any repercussions?"

My stomach sank as my eyes met Zol's and we both reached the same realization at the same time: a powerful fairy king knew that Aris killed his daughter, he tracked her down, and now he had Tanith, thinking she was Aris.

How much danger was Tanith in, and what could we possibly do to stop it?

~Tanith~

For a moment, I felt like I might throw up. When the man took hold of my arm, the room began to spin around us, and a second later, we seemed to drop, the ground giving way beneath our feet while my stomach stayed behind. As quickly as it began, the movement stopped and a bright white light shone on us, so bright that I had to close my eyes against it as I tried to push the nausea down and get my bearings.

What the hell just happened?

The man let go of my arm and I stumbled back, feeling dizzy and off balance until strong arms grabbed me from behind and I forced my eyes open.

"What did you bind her with?" a voice asked from behind me, the voice belonging to the arms, and as I tried to look back at him, I only got a glimpse of some pointed ears before he turned me roughly back around.

The man who brought me there answered his question. "I don't know what it is. She was already restrained when I found her and it seems to be controlling her abilities, so we might as well keep it on. Between that and the metal lining in the room, she shouldn't be able to harm anyone else."

As my vision cleared, I could see the room we were in bore no resemblance to the small cottage I'd just been standing in. White, smooth, bare walls surrounded us and the ceiling glowed with a kind of light I had never seen before. A bed stood against one wall and a small, curtained-off corner seemed to contain a toilet and sink. It looked for all the world like some kind of hospital or prison, neither of which filled me with any kind of confidence about what they meant to do to me.

Clearing my throat, I tried to reason with them. "Look, I don't know who you are or what you want, but I'm afraid you've made a mistake. I know that I look like Aris right now, but I'm not her. She switched our bodies to avoid having to answer for what she'd done to me and my friends and now it looks like she's managed to evade you too. I don't know if that was part of her plan, or just a happy accident on her part."

I tried to keep my voice calm so they wouldn't dismiss my words as panicked self-preservation, but I could see it didn't make much of an impression on them anyway. And why would it? Not even the men who'd spent several days with me in the most intimate of circumstances could tell the difference once Aris took over my body, so why should complete strangers be any different?

"Keep her here," the man who abducted me said, his eyes filled with cool contempt as he looked at me. His ears were pointed too, I noticed. They must belong to the same species. Did it have something to do with the picture in Aris' house, the one with the boy who looked like Blaine? "I'll bring some people to get her talking."

That sounded bad, but I tried to remain calm as he left me alone with the other man in the clinical-looking room. I had to try to get some information. I needed to figure out what was going on before I could decide how to proceed. "Where is this? Where are we?"

"You've never seen the inside of His Majesty's cells before, have you?" The man chuckled, as if any part of this were funny. "You'll get to know them very well before long, *if* he lets you live."

Fuck. 'His Majesty'? What kind of world had I stumbled into, and what did Aris do to this man to deserve this kind of treatment?

Most importantly, how could I possibly convince them I wasn't her?

"What's your name?" I asked the man holding me. I still couldn't see him; every time I tried to turn around to look at him, his grip tightened, keeping me in place.

"You don't need to worry about me. I suggest you spend your energy figuring out what you can offer to keep your life."

He seemed determined to scare me with the possibility of my death, and of course it frightened me. Anyone would be terrified, but I tried to think about things logically. If they simply wanted to kill Aris, they'd have done it already. The fact that they brought her there - or in this case, me - must mean they wanted something else from her. That gave me a very small window of opportunity to convince them they had the wrong woman. It wouldn't be easy, but I had to try.

Soon, the king returned with a woman carrying a basket filled with plants and vials. They looked like the things from Aris' workshop, so I could only guess the woman was also some kind of witch.

"I should have known you'd end up in trouble sooner or later," the woman sneered at me, though I'd never seen her before in my life. "But starting a war, Aris? That's impressive."

"A war?" I repeated out loud, unable to contain my curiosity. "What are you talking about?"

"I'll be asking the questions here," the king answered for her. "First, bring in the boy."

Those words were called back into the open doorway, and a moment later, another fairy appeared, dragging along with him a young man in chains, his face bruised and swollen.

"Aris!" Unlike everyone else in the room, his eyes lit up at the sight of me. "At last. You can tell them the truth. You have to tell them. I didn't ask you to do anything. Please, tell them."

None of this made *any* sense to me, but at least I finally recognized someone. He was the one from Aris' photo, the young man who looked like Blaine. It looked like I'd been right that these other people were connected to him somehow.

"I'm not Aris," I told him truthfully, looking between him and the king. "I don't know what you're talking about. I know it sounds crazy, but she *was* there in that room where you found me except she had switched her soul with mine. She's in my body and I'm in hers. If you go back, you might still find her there. I'm not a witch at all. I'm human, and I don't know what any of this is about."

Would the others have stuck around to see if I'd come back, or would they have gone back into hiding, believing they still had me with them? I honestly couldn't guess.

In a flash of light, the king vanished from our view, and a few seconds later, he returned again. "They're gone. The room is empty."

Damn it. Now what? At least he had done me the courtesy of checking, so I tried to build on that. "There must be some way I can prove it to you. You obviously have some kind of powers, is there some way you can tell that I'm human?"

His lips pursed, but he didn't dismiss my request out of hand. Instead, he turned to the woman and asked for her opinion. "Do you have some kind of litmus test for magic?"

She nodded, eager to help. "Of course, Your Majesty. There is a very basic one."

From her basket, she picked up a small round object, the size of a large marble and held it up for everyone to see. Then, without warning, she threw it at me with all her strength, straight at my face.

With my hands still bound and the man holding onto me, I couldn't move out of the way. I could only close my eyes instead as I waited for the inevitable impact.

It never came.

Tentatively, I opened one eye and then the other, blinking in disbelief as I saw the small ball hovering in the air in front of my face. "What just happened?"

The woman ignored me, addressing the king. "That's a test of magical instinct. As a human would instinctively try to protect themselves, a witch will stop it. Their natural magic responds to the desire not to get hurt. It's almost impossible to cheat against."

The king's face hardened once more as he glared at me. Apparently, any doubt I had managed to plant in his mind had just been erased. "No more of these games, Aris. Answer the question: did Lysanthir plot with you to kill Evia?"

"This is about Evia?" Once again, I asked the question out loud, too stunned to keep my thoughts bottled up as the ball flew back across the room into the witch's outstretched hand. How had I stopped the ball when I didn't have any magic? What the hell was going on?

His nostrils flared angrily. "Let's leave them alone together for a while," he said to the others. "They can get their story straight and then we'll decide what to do with them."

The man holding me finally let me go and so did the man holding the young man, apparently named Lysanthir. The witch shot me one more smug look as she left the room with the others, and as it closed behind them, the outline of the door disappeared entirely, leaving no sign of where it had once been. There was literally no way out.

"I can't believe you would do this," Lysanthir said, his pleading turning to anger once we were alone. "You must be completely insane!"

"I don't know who you are!" I shouted back at him, my patience starting to wear thin. Why couldn't anyone see beyond what their eyes told them?

"Always another plot with you, another scheme." He looked so angry as he walked over to me that I took a step back, afraid he might hit me. However, he took hold of my arm instead and pulled me towards him. "Maybe this will jog your memory."

With that, his lips pressed against mine, feeling so much like Blaine's kiss that I thought I must be losing my mind.

Maybe I was. Maybe I had invented all of it. Maybe it had only ever been in my head, some kind of intense fever dream created from Blaine's betrayal, Amanda's bullying, and the book I'd been writing.

That made a hell of a lot more sense than anything else I could think of, but if it really was just a dream, I was ready to wake up.

~Aiqen~

It felt like my eyes had just closed when suddenly, Cad's hand pressed on my shoulder. "Aiqen, wake up. We need to go."

"Go?" I mumbled back sleepily. "Where?"

"To find Tanith."

My eyes shot open to see the angel standing over me, the night sky behind him still dark. Not very much time could have passed since we left him and Zol alone with Aris..

"Do you know where she is?" I asked, but Cadriel didn't answer, moving on to wake Leith next.

"I'm still up," Ty's voice said from further in the darkness. "I couldn't sleep. What did you find out?"

When Cadriel had our full attention, he gave us a synopsis of what Aris told them about Evia. The news interested us all, but obviously meant a lot more to Ty than to the rest of us.

"A princess?" He couldn't sound more confused. "I never knew that. She told me she had a fight with her family and that's why she came to live in our town, but I just assumed it had something to do with her not taking things seriously enough. She didn't believe in rules. I can't imagine her being forced to marry someone against her will."

"Neither could she, apparently," Cadriel agreed. "She had no intention of it, which is why she ran away. It sounds like she found exactly what she wanted with you."

Ty's lips pressed together, in sadness or in anger, or perhaps both, and his nostrils flared. "If Aris wasn't in Tanith's body right now..."

Cad cut him off before he could finish that thought. "I know, but she is, so we need to focus on that. Evia's father took her, and if he thinks, like we did, that she's really Aris, she could be in a lot of trouble."

"Do you know where she is?" I repeated since my question had been ignored the first time. I would be happy to go and rescue her, but we'd need to know where to go first.

"Not exactly," Cadriel admitted. "However, Aris can track people across realms. She can travel between them, and she could take us too, just as Evia's father took Tanith. That's how Aris was able to find all of you in the first place."

"And she's going to help us?" That seemed very unlikely from what I'd seen so far. "What's in it for her?"

"This." Cad held up Tanith's phone from his pocket. "I'm going to tell Aris about how Tanith can control and delete things using this phone. If she agrees to help us, Tanith can delete all of it so that Evia's father never finds Aris."

"No," Ty protested. "I can't agree to that. Aris should have to answer for what she did, whether it's to me or..."

"And she will," Cad interrupted again. "We're going to *tell* her that Tanith will delete everything, but I have no intention of actually asking Tanith to do so."

"You're going to lie?" Leith gasped.

That did seem rather out of character for the angel, but Cadriel gave us all a sheepish shrug. "Zol came up with the idea, but I think it's a good one. In rare cases, bending the rules a bit might be forgivable. Coming from me, she'll be more likely to believe it."

I couldn't argue with that. No one would expect to be double-crossed by an angel. Just a few days ago, I couldn't imagine Cad saying bending the rules would be acceptable, but then, I couldn't have imagined taking part in an orgy and letting a demon suck my cock either. It seemed the time spent in this realm had given us both a new perspective on things.

"So, we get Aris to take us to this fairy king's home," I summarized. "Then what?"

"I'm not sure," Cadriel admitted. "But I think we all have to go. I think this is the reason why we were all brought here."

I didn't entirely follow, and I wasn't the only one. "What do you mean?" Leith asked.

Cadriel shared his theory about how Tanith had taken a bit of Aris' magical ability when they became soul shadows. "I think that magic explains not only how she could see us all come together, but *why* the five of us in particular were chosen. She must have known subconsciously that we were the people she needed to help when it got to this point in the story. Unfortunately, that part isn't written yet, so I don't know how it will play out, but I'm convinced that we all need to be there, working together, each playing his part, so we can stop whatever Aris has set in motion. This is why I was meant to watch over her, or perhaps both of them. This is what it's all been leading to."

He sounded utterly convinced of his theory, and since I had nothing to refute it with, I simply gave my agreement. "You know I'm willing to do whatever it takes to see Tanith back safely."

"Me too," Leith quickly agreed.

"Tanith safe and Aris punished?" Ty summed up. "I'm in."

Leaving our belongings where they were, we followed Cadriel back to where Zol and Aris stood. Aris listened carefully to Cadriel's proposal, her eyes darting warily to the rest of us from time to time.

"What guarantee do I have that she'll actually help me?" Aris wanted to know, exactly as I'd anticipated she would.

"I'm sworn to watch over you," Cad reminded her. "And angels cannot lie."

By saying so, he was, in fact, lying, but none of the rest of us pointed that out, and Aris seemed to buy it. "Maybe I can just do it myself," Aris suggested, holding out her hand for the phone. "I can go back to before the king found us, then there will be no need to go and rescue her at all."

Cadriel wasn't that stupid. "It only works when Tanith does it," he claimed, though I didn't know if we actually had proof of that. "It's her story, she's the only one who can change it. But if you take us to him and switch your souls back to their proper bodies, we'll make sure everyone gets what they want."

He left that ominously vague, but Aris didn't seem to notice it. "I'm not even sure I can travel in this body," she pointed out next. "Your St John's Wort didn't work on me. My magical abilities are subdued."

"You said this ability of yours isn't something other witches can do," Zol jumped in. "Whatever magic dampening is happening shouldn't affect it."

Aris had run out of excuses, and with a sigh, she acquiesced. "Fine. I want my own body back rather than... this." She gestured down as if Tanith's body was somehow undesirable, which made no sense to me at all. "But if things go wrong, I'm getting out of there. You're on your own."

"Sounds like we have a deal," I said, eager to get going. "How will you transport all of us?"

"You all need to be touching me. I've never moved so many people at once, but I'll try."

Not wanting to waste any more time, we all crowded around her, making sure at least part of our bodies touched hers, and in a bright white flash, the world around us disappeared.

CHAPTER EIGHTEEN

~Leith~

I sure was getting to see a lot of interesting places. For someone who had never left the ocean until ten days ago, I'd now visited two different magical realms and met more kinds of people than I ever knew existed.

This realm didn't look anything like the place we had just been with its small town, forest, and Aris' cottage. All the buildings surrounding us seemed to be made of glass and smooth stone, like sand had been poured into exactly the shape they wanted and frozen there. The sun had already started to rise and a heavy dew sat on the bright green grass, soaking into our shoes as we all stepped away from Aris.

In front of us, a tall, narrow building rose up into the sky. That must be where the king lived. Other than the lack of water, it bore a strong resemblance to the merking's castle. The building seemed to defy gravity, parts of it hanging out over thin air, as if they'd been added on later when they were found to be necessary. Its white walls glistened in the early sunlight, the glass of its many windows sparkling like diamonds.

"Fairies have their own kind of magic," Ty said, looking equally impressed with the structure. "I guess this is where she grew up."

I really couldn't imagine what my friend felt, learning so much about the woman he'd loved after she was gone, but I did know one thing, and I shared it with the others before I could forget it.

"Ty should speak to the king. They both loved Evia, so I think the king will listen to him."

Cadriel hesitated, but Zol backed me up. "You said we were all chosen for a reason, right? Ty's the only one who has any connection to this place and its people. Seems to me that might be the reason he's here."

Turning that over in his head, Cad eventually nodded. "Very well. We'll try a diplomatic approach first. We'll stick together, but Tymanus can do the talking."

"Thanks, Cadriel." As Ty gave the angel a grateful nod, I noticed his fingers drift to the scale necklace I'd given him, maybe hoping to get a bit of extra luck before speaking to his former love's father for the first time.

The six of us walked across the damp grass, Zol still holding firm to Aris' arm, even though we knew she was capable of vanishing at any time and leaving us in this realm. Perhaps it made him feel a little more control to have his hand on her.

Two tall men with pointed ears stepped out to block our path as we approached the castle itself, looking between our assorted collection of features in confusion. "Who are you? *What* are you?"

We must have looked as foreign to them as this whole place felt to us.

"We're here to see the king," Ty explained. "I knew his daughter, Evia."

The men whispered to each other for a few seconds before turning back to us. "How did you know her?"

"I was with her when she died."

That certainly got their attention. After another quick, whispered exchange, one of the men went inside while the other turned back to us. "Who are the rest of you, then?"

"They're with me," Ty said firmly, as if that explained everything, and the man asked no further questions.

It didn't take long before the first man returned and we were checked for weapons and ushered inside. The interior of the castle looked even more fantastical than the outside. Walls appeared to shimmer and the rooms seemed to expand as we walked through them and contract again as we left.

We were taken to a comfortable room with several chairs and a table, not completely unlike the table where we first all sat together in the wizard's house before we began our quest through the forest. The man we had seen briefly in Aris' house stood at the head of the table, his eyes passing over each of us in turn as we entered. Next to him stood a woman I had never seen before, but I had a feeling Aris had. Her eyes widened in surprise at the sight of her, but naturally, the woman didn't recognize Aris in her present form.

She *did* seem to recognize Zol, though, her cheeks flushing at the sight of him. It appeared there were still more connections for us to uncover.

"Which of you knew my daughter?" the king asked, and Ty stepped forward.

"She came to live in my realm just a short time before her death. I didn't know she was your daughter until just a few hours ago."

"You are the creatures who were with the witch, Aris, in her house," the king deduced, either recognizing us or simply putting the pieces together. "How did you get here?"

Distrust began to darken his expression, so Ty did his best to calm him. "We will explain everything to you, Your Majesty, but the reason we've come to see you now is that the woman you took is not actually Aris. She's a different woman in Aris' body."

The king remained skeptical. "That's what she claimed, but she also claimed to be human and we proved that she is not."

"How did you prove it?" Zol interjected. "Did you have this hack prove it for you?"

He gestured to the woman next to the king, who sputtered out an indignant reply. "How dare you? He doesn't know what he's talking about, Your Majesty."

The king ignored her, his eyes focusing on Zol instead. "How do you know her?"

Zol answered him as flippantly as he spoke to everyone. "She made a deal with me. She sold her soul so she could pass the magical standards exam, just barely. Normally, I don't handle those kinds of deals, but my counterparts were all busy."

"I should have known," Aris smirked from beside him. "Everyone always thought you screwed the professor, but not even he would be that desperate."

The woman's face turned red as she looked between Zol and Aris, still not knowing Aris' true identity.

Cadriel stepped in before things could get any more heated, addressing himself to the king. "The woman you are holding *does* have some magical ability, but she's not aware of it. Most importantly, however, she didn't kill your daughter. She had nothing to do with it."

"What is it you want?" the king asked stiffly. Obviously, he still had his suspicions about the whole situation.

"We want you to release the woman you have. We want to help you find Evia's real killer. And we want to..."

He didn't get to finish before a loud rumble filled the air, the ground shaking beneath us just as it had back at Aris' house. I thought that disturbance had been caused by the king's arrival, but he didn't seem to have done anything this time.

"What was that?" I gasped, holding onto the table to keep my balance.

"The sun is up," the king told us grimly. "The fighting has resumed. Our whole realm is at war, and Aris is the only person who can answer the question that will stop it."

~Tanith~

Lysanthir's lips continued to press against mine until I twisted out of his reach. With my hands still tied behind my back with the mistletoe, I couldn't push him away. "Get off me! I don't know who you are. I'm not Aris!"

Just because I slept with five men in the past few days didn't mean I wanted anything to do with this one, and not just because he looked almost exactly like my cheating ex-boyfriend.

"They didn't buy that," he reminded me, scowling as he grabbed hold of my shoulders and spun me back around. "If you want to talk your way out of this, you'll have to do better than that."

My head had started to hurt from trying to figure out what everyone was talking about. "Can you just back up, please? I know a tiny bit about Evia, but I don't know who she was to you or to the man who brought me here. I definitely don't know anything about any war. If you tell me what's going on, maybe we can come up with a plan."

"Stop wasting time!" His face lost all its charm as he snarled at me. "He'll be back soon and if you don't tell the truth…"

"You're the one wasting time." I had never been the kind of woman to give orders, but I'd had just about enough of this. This was *my* story, wasn't it? Maybe the time had come for me to take some control of the narrative. "Stop arguing with me and answer my question so we can move on."

He gave in sullenly, his expression almost the same as Blaine's when I caught him cheating red-handed. "You want me to say it? We used to be together. I loved you, Aris! I know you think I didn't, but I did. But you started to scare me with all your talk about creating our own world where we'd never have to see anyone else. I never wanted that life. I would have been happy with you here. But you were lost in your own plans, and when the king decided I should marry his daughter, it seemed so much easier. Besides, no one says no to the king. Do you know why not? Because if you do, you end up with a fucking war!"

As he shouted the last words, the ground beneath us shook and that same rumbling sound I heard in Aris' cottage rolled through the air around us. "What is that?"

His nostrils flared in frustration and anger. "That's the sound of people dying. The whole kingdom is in a civil war because of *you*, because you killed her and they think I asked you to. They captured me and they want me to confess, but if I do, my life is over. My parents and their supporters are fighting to get me back. They believe me, but the king doesn't. You have to tell him the truth, Aris. Tell him you killed her for any reason other than because of me."

Finally, the pieces began to fall into place. "You dumped Aris to marry Evia? That's why she killed her?"

A vein throbbed on his forehead, looking ready to explode. "It wasn't my fault! The king won't stop until he has someone to blame. My family were planning to send me to Earth when the king's forces caught up to me. Apparently, they found someone in some out-of-the-way town who looks like me, and they were going to hide me there until this all blew over."

If we weren't in such serious danger, I would have laughed. Could he be talking about Blaine? It seemed we were all connected somehow, and connected to a war that threatened that spill over into my real life. If the fairy king could move between realms, what would stop him from going to my hometown and tearing it apart until he found where Lysanthir was hiding?

All of this had gotten completely out of hand, and it all came down to Aris. "What if Aris tells him you didn't put her up to it? What happens to her then?"

"Would you stop referring to yourself in the third person?" he growled at me. "And what do you think happens? They'll kill you, or lock you up so they can drain and use your power. But if you think you're getting out of here any other way, you're even crazier than I thought. Now that they've got you, you're stuck, but if you ever actually loved me, please, do the right thing and tell them the truth. I never asked you to kill Evia."

I believed him on that, actually. Lysanthir might not be completely blameless, but I felt fairly certain he hadn't wanted Evia dead. Now, if I could only convince him that I wasn't actually Aris...

Tanith?

I spun around as I heard Cad's voice, so close it almost sounded like it came from inside my head, but the room behind me was empty.

"What are you doing now?" Lysanthir asked as I heard another murmured word in my head.

"Be quiet! I'm trying to listen."

The fairy snorted in disbelief. "You really are completely crazy."

"Shut up!"

I couldn't cover my ears with my hands still tied but I closed my eyes and put my head down, trying to block things out as much as I could.

Cad? Can you hear me?

I couldn't say what I expected. I'd never been able to talk to anyone in my head before, but either he answered me or my imagination was really taking over.

Yes, I can. Thank Go... well, you know who. I don't want to say his name and get his attention right now.

I smiled despite myself. *How are you doing this?*

Angels have some telepathic ability, but I think you're doing it as much as I am. You have magic inside you, Tanith.

The king said that too, but I had no idea why Cad would think so. *What do you mean?*

When you were born, you got some of Aris' magical ability and she got some of your humanity. It linked your souls together. You're going to need to use it now. We need a reason for the king to bring us to you.

I almost followed the first bit, but he lost me in the second half. *Bring you to me? What do you mean?*

We're here in his castle. We're trying to get to you.

Warmth and relief flooded through me with those words. They came for me. They believed me and they came to get me. *So what do I do? I still have this mistletoe on me.*

I don't think that should matter. Your humanity overrides your magical essence, so I think it will cancel out the effects of the mistletoe.

Even if that were true, I could still see one big problem. *I don't know how to do any magic.*

I think you need to draw on emotion. The stronger you feel...

"Are you just about finished yet?" Lysanthir's voice cut into the conversation in my head, drowning out the rest of Cad's sentence. "We're running out of time."

"Would you leave me alone?" I glared at him, directing my anger about the whole situation at him, fuelled on by his resemblance to Blaine, and the next thing I knew, he keeled over, hitting the ground as if I'd physically pushed him.

Tanith? Can you still hear me?

I stared at Lysanthir in disbelief as he stumbled back to his feet. "I thought they said your magic wasn't working," he grumbled.

I ignored him to respond to the angel in my head. *I hear you, Cad. I think I can make it work.*

I knew you could. You've always been special, Tanith. There's nothing average about you at all.

Pride, along with a strange new sense of power, swelled inside me as I looked over at the walls around us. I didn't have any potions or magical words, but I did have a lot of built-up emotion, and I directed it at the walls, imagining them filling with all the anger inside me, making them vibrate as all the frustrations and disappointments of the last few months flowed through them.

Soon, they began to physically shake.

"Hey!" Lysanthir called out, his eyes wide with terror. "Help! Someone help me!"

Maybe his cries did it, or maybe just the movement of the walls got their attention. Either way, the door reappeared in the wall, and the king walked through it once again.

~Tymanus~

Being in the house where Evia must have grown up felt completely surreal. The sterile, white rooms didn't feel like her at all, nor did her cold father remind me of her in the least. She had been warm and colourful, quick to laugh and impossible to contain, not like this place at all.

I always knew she was special, always felt it deep in my bones, but I had never imagined anything like this. A secret princess. A pawn in an arranged marriage. A woman that a war would be fought over.

Okay, the last point didn't really surprise me; I would have fought for her too, given the chance.

I glanced over at Cadriel to see how he would react to news of the fact that we'd entered a war zone, but he seemed distracted. His eyes were focused on something far in the distance and it seemed his mind was there too.

Someone else would need to take the lead.

As usual, Aiqen stepped in, but, I had to admit, in a less obnoxious way than usual. He had truly mellowed in the last couple of days. "What's the question that needs to be answered?" he asked the king. "Who's attacking you?"

Evia's father quickly filled us in on how factions had formed following Evia's death between those who believed Lysanthir and his family should be held responsible and those who believed them innocent. "We need Aris to confirm whether or not she acted alone. We need to know the truth."

That would be easy enough to achieve once Aris was back in her own body. I still had some of the drink I'd brewed earlier. It hadn't worked on her in Tanith's body, but it would when she returned to her true form. That much, I felt certain about.

My certainty faltered a little when it came to whether or not Aris would happily go back into her body, especially now that she knew more about the whole situation and what she had done to these people and their world. She had Cad's promise that we would turn back time for her, but given everything that had happened between all of us, she had to be suspicious that it wouldn't be quite that easy. I worried she had something else up her sleeve.

We would need luck on our side to pull off the switch and ensure Aris got what she deserved.

"Forgive me, Your Majesty, but I don't see what good fighting each other is doing?" Leith was getting bolder about speaking up. He had always been too hard on himself, letting his lack of knowledge hold him back even when his instincts were good, so it pleased me to see him gaining in confidence. "No matter what happens, it won't bring your daughter back."

He had a point, but the king didn't hesitate in his response. "Her murderers must be punished. They want my throne, that's why they killed my heir."

His *heir*? Evia should have been a queen? Just when I thought nothing else could surprise me, one more piece of the puzzle fell into place and I understood more than ever why she wouldn't have told me. That kind of life had never appealed to me. Perhaps it explained why she liked me in the first place; the time we had together couldn't have been more different from her old life.

"I know a thing or two about fighting over a throne," Aiqen reminded us all. "Perhaps I can reason with the other side and get them to stop attacking while you get this question of liability sorted out."

The king gave Aiqen his full attention for the first time, frowning as he did. "You look like Lysanthir, actually. An older version of him."

Aiqen cleared his throat awkwardly. "Yes, well... I think this might be why I have been brought here."

None of us knew what that meant, but he quickly explained.

"I learned not that long ago that my father, the man I always *thought* was my father, wasn't actually my biological father. My mother had a brief love affair with a man from another realm. The wyvern genes are dominant, so I never knew what my other half was, but having seen the resemblance for myself, I have to wonder if this explains it."

It explained a lot more than that. Suddenly, Aiqen's insistence on proving himself, his overcompensation and his need to always be in charge, made a lot more sense. Knowing he was illegitimate and a half-breed, he felt inadequate in a similar way that Aris did, never quite fitting in.

The same way I hadn't fit in with the other centaurs, and Evia hadn't fit in with her family.

It seemed a lot of us could relate.

And Cadriel did say he believed we had all been chosen for this adventure for a particular reason, so maybe Aiqen had come there to find the missing side of his family.

Before the king could respond to that, another rumbling shook the air around us, but that time, it felt different. Rather than coming from above, it seemed to start below us, like something bubbling up through the walls.

"The witch," the king muttered, getting to his feet, and Cad immediately jumped up too.

"We're coming with you. We can prove to you she isn't who you think she is."

The king hesitated for a moment, torn between arguing with us and wanting to see what was going on as quickly as possible, and finally, he gave in, turning to Aiqen first. "You: go and make overtures to the other side if you want, but I take no responsibility if they kill you on sight. The rest of you: come with me."

We all wished Aiqen luck as we quickly followed the king from the room and down another white-walled corridor, Zol still holding onto Aris the whole way. A handful of the king's guards fell into line with us, our group now numbering nearly a dozen. At the bottom of a flight of uneven stairs, we were confronted with a solid wall, but as we watched, the king held his hands over it and a door appeared where there hadn't been one before.

The walls continued to vibrate as he pushed the door open to reveal some kind of holding cell, a frightened Lysanthir, and, at last, Tanith, still within Aris' body. Her eyes lit up at the sight of us, sending a rush of guilt through me that we had ever doubted her.

"How are you doing this?" the king demanded. "I thought they bound you."

Tanith held up her hands, showing us all that the mistletoe we'd tied around them had burned clean away. "I guess it didn't work because I'm not a witch. I tried to tell you before."

I saw her mistake almost immediately, and so did Cad. Without the mistletoe holding her back, Aris' body was now free, and there was no reason for her to stay in Tanith's body any longer. She didn't need to wait for us to keep our word. She could make her own move, and a moment later, she did.

Both Aris' and Tanith's bodies jolted, apparently with the force of their souls being switched once more, and a second later, Aris disappeared from view.

~Zolgozig~

As soon as Aris disappeared, we all knew what had happened: she switched bodies again and took off, taking advantage of the fact that Tanith had broken her bindings. She saw her chance and she took it. I actually had to kind of admire her perseverance, even though it worked against us.

"I knew it!" the king growled at the young man who must be Lysanthir. "You set this up! You helped her escape."

"No!" The younger fairy's face looked pale and frightened and frustrated. "I didn't do anything! I was trying to get her to confess but she started talking to herself and made the walls shake and then you all came in and she just disappeared. I didn't do anything."

He mumbled the last words beneath the king's withering glare, since His Majesty didn't look very impressed with his excuses. The king really needed to lighten up.

"What's the big deal?" I wondered out loud. "You tracked her down before, just go and find her again."

He turned his thunderous glare on me. "Do you know how long it took me to find her the first time? I'm trying to fight a war here, I can't be chasing her across every realm in existence."

"You don't have to." Tanith's assertion got everyone's attention, and only then did I realize I still held her by the arm, as I had ever since we realized Aris took over her body. I quickly let go. "She can try to hide all she wants, but she's forgotten one very important thing. Cad, I assume you still have my phone?"

My half-brother's face broke into a smile as he put together what she had in mind. It took me a second, but I got there too: with her phone, Tanith could simply erase the part of the story where Aris got away, and bring her back.

"We won't have a lot of time between when she returns to her body and when she vanishes," I pointed out. "And she won't necessarily go back into her own body if she thinks she's still bound."

The timing would have to be just right for Aris to believe she could be free but not actually allowing her to escape. How could we stop her from leaving? No one brought any extra mistletoe with them. We hadn't considered that we'd need it.

"Those scales he's wearing should do," the other witch spoke up from the door. I hadn't even realized she'd followed us down there, but she seemed to have a full grasp on the situation as she pointed to the necklace Leith had made for Ty, the one he said would bring him luck. "Mermaid scales have a dampening effect on all magic. Witches are taught to avoid them. I remember *that* much from my classes."

Her self-deprecating comment made me smile. I called her a hack earlier, and I meant it, but I had never had anything against her personally.

Not like Aris did, apparently.

"I never knew that about my scales." Leith sounded just as surprised as the rest of us, but his face lit up at the realization. "Maybe that's why they're lucky!"

"I think we're lucky to have you." Ty gave him a warm smile before turning back to the rest of us. "But how will we get the scales onto her? If Tanith takes us back in time, I won't remember that I need to give the necklace to her."

He had a point. So far, every time Tanith had deleted part of her story, we all forgot everything that had happened.

"I'll remember though," Tanith reminded us. "Ty, if I ask you to give me the necklace as soon as you enter the room, while I'm still in Aris' body, do you think you'll do it, no questions asked?"

The centaur considered the question carefully before nodding. "I think so. I trust you."

"We only get one shot at this," Cadriel pointed out. "When Tanith moves time back, the phone goes with her. That means she'll be holding it while she's in Aris' body. If we don't manage to stop Aris and she disappears again, she'll take the phone with her and then we're completely fucked."

My eyes met his in surprise as he swore, and he gave me a sheepish shrug.

"As they say."

He really had started to change, and only for the better as far as I could see. He could still be a good person even if he didn't do everything completely by the book. If nothing else came of this whole crazy adventure, I hoped he would remember that.

"So, how sure are you that you'll do as Tanith says?" Cad asked Ty, getting back to his point.

The longer he thought about it, the more certain he seemed to become. "I will. If she tells me it's for Evia's sake, I'll do it."

"Alright then," Tanith said, taking a deep breath. "Let's do it." She held out her hand as Cadriel handed her the phone.

I wasn't quite ready to go yet, though. "Just so I'm clear, none of us are going to remember any of this happened, right?"

Tanith looked up from the phone screen with a wary expression. "Why am I afraid to ask why you want to know?"

"You always think the worst of me," I teased, since I knew it couldn't be further from the truth. Tanith had always given me the benefit of the doubt, unlike so many others, but in this case, I did have something up my sleeve.

As everyone watched, I walked over to Tymanus, reached up and grabbed the back of his head. Lust, my familiar friend, flowed like fire through my veins as I watched his eyes darken with the realization of what I meant to do, and he made no attempt to resist me. In fact, he kissed me back just as firmly, his lips and tongue demanding pleasure from me in equal measure to the satisfaction he gave me.

"What the fuck is happening?" I heard the king shout, but I didn't care and neither did Ty. When I pulled back, a smile pulled at his lips.

"I'm almost sorry I won't remember that."

That made two of us. I went to turn back to Tanith to tell her to go ahead, but Leith stepped into my path. "Do you think I could try too? Since it doesn't matter?"

Just because we wouldn't remember didn't mean it didn't matter, but I happily obliged. "Of course."

I kissed the merman more gently than I had Ty. His lips were softer too, and slightly salty with the taste of the sea that would probably never fully leave him. It made it feel like we were floating, and I would have happily floated there a little longer if we didn't have a war to stop.

"Cad? You want a turn?" I offered in jest, and he knew I didn't really mean it. His lips twitched in amusement.

"I'm good, thanks. Tanith, are you ready to go?"

"I'm ready," she confirmed. "I'll see you all in the past."

CHAPTER NINETEEN

I had to time this very carefully. As Zol said, we wouldn't have a lot of extra time to play with once Aris entered the room in my body. I also couldn't go too far back; if I returned to the time before I managed to make the walls shake, I might not be able to conjure the necessary emotion to do it a second time. Now that I knew my group of protectors and lovers were there to support me, most of my frustration had melted away.

We were missing Aiqen, but as nobody seemed concerned about it, I didn't make a big deal of it either. I had to believe Zol wouldn't have gone around sticking his tongue down everyone else's throat if something had happened to our friend.

Scrolling back through the text that still continued to populate in my book, I got back to the point where Lysanthir called for help, just before the others arrived in the room. Taking a deep breath to steady myself, I hit the delete button, and the next thing I knew, I stood back in Aris' body as the door appeared in the wall, the phone still in my hands.

"How are you doing this?" the king demanded as he burst through the entrance. "I thought they bound you."

Rather than holding up my hands as I had before, I immediately turned to Ty. "I need your scale necklace. It's for Evia."

He blinked in surprise, but a moment later, he moved towards me, pulling it off his neck and slipping it over mine, no questions asked, just as Aris' gaze fell on my unbound hands holding my phone. The screen went to black, the battery finally giving out, and my stomach sank.

We were all stuck in this timeline, like it or not.

A moment later, I seemed to be floating as my soul lifted out of her body, drifting for just a second before it painfully jolted back into my own form. I looked up to see a flash of triumph in Aris' eyes but it quickly faded as she stayed in one spot.

Her eyes narrowing, she looked down at her unbound wrists and the useless phone in her hands, tossing it to the floor. "No! Why isn't it... what did you do to me?"

She shouted the words as her gaze returned to me, and for a moment, my heart seemed to stop as I realized she might just take over my body again and disappear that way. We hadn't considered that, and without any power left on my phone, we wouldn't be able to bring her back easily. The thought of being stuck in her body for an indeterminate length of time filled me with dread.

I'd never really loved my body before, but after having it worshipped by different men over the past few days, and the experience of living inside someone else, I appreciated it more than ever. Maybe I'd been too hard on myself before.

However, a second later, Aris' scowl grew even darker. She couldn't do it! The mermaid scales must have blocked her magic, just as the other witch had said.

In the end, Leith saved the day.

With everyone else still unaware of what just happened, I shook my arm free of Zol's grip, and turned to throw my arms around the startled merman. "You did it. She's trapped."

"Tanith?" he asked tentatively.

"It's me," I assured him. "You remember how you felt you weren't as smart as the others in the group?"

His eyes lit up as his arms wrapped around me, trusting now that it really *was* me. "I remember."

"You might just be the smartest one of all. You said the necklace would bring us luck and you were right. You're magical, Leith."

His cheeks flushed in response to the praise as the flustered fairy king stared at us both. "Will someone tell me what the fuck is going on?"

I pointed to Aris. "That's Aris now, the *real* her. Tie her hands again and I'll tell you everything."

The king's guards quickly did just that and only once they'd restrained her did I explain about the merman scales and how they prevented her from escaping.

"If Ty still has some of his drink, you should be able to get the answers you want."

With his lips set in a firm, determined line, Ty walked over and held the bottle to Aris' lips as the king's men held her in place. Although she tried her best not to swallow, her struggle proved to be in vain as they forced it down her throat. Finally, she had no choice but to confess.

"Did Lysanthir ask you to kill Evia?" the king demanded once we'd established the drink had taken effect.

"No," Aris answered miserably. "He didn't know. He was furious with me when he found out what I'd done."

Under the king's questioning, she relayed the whole story. Cad whispered to me that they already knew most of it, that Aris had told them herself once they realized she wasn't me, but to hear it for myself still shocked me. She had gone so far over the line of what was reasonable that she didn't even seem to recognize the line existed anymore.

The king's anger melted into despair as he heard the words straight from her mouth, about how she attacked the fairy for no reason other than her own jealousy. Though it hadn't been his intention, forcing her into the arranged marriage had led to her running away and, ultimately, to her death. As his shoulders sagged, I could see the depths of his guilt, which helped to explain his extreme actions. He'd been looking for someone to blame, someone like Lysanthir, so he wouldn't have to bear the blame alone.

Knowing that Aris acted alone didn't ease the sense of loss he felt, or that anyone else felt, for that matter, but I put my arm around Ty as Aris finished talking. "I know it doesn't change the fact that she's gone, but at least you know she didn't die because of you."

He nodded solemnly. "I think that will help. Not right now, but eventually."

A little time would do us all some good. I could see how Aris' confession weighed on Cad too, how he felt responsible for her failings even though they were entirely her own doing.

"Maybe I could have been nicer to her?" Leith whispered to me, his green eyes looking watery as he took in all the grief surrounding us.

I squeezed his hand with mine. "I really don't think you could have." Leith was already the nicest person I'd ever met.

"Does this mean I'm free to go?" Lysanthir wanted to know once Aris had been taken away to an even more secure area to await her punishment, the scale necklace secure around her neck.

"Yes," the king agreed, though he didn't sound overly happy about it. "I'm willing to make terms with your family, if they agree to a ceasefire."

"Actually, I think there already might be one," Zol pointed out. "There haven't been any more attacks since we got down here."

I didn't see the connection. "What do you think that means?"

His devilish grin looked more enticing than ever. "I think Aiqen might have found his daddy."

"What?"

He simply laughed. "You'll see. Let's go and find him and finally wrap this whole fucking thing up."

~Aiqen~

As I shifted to my wyvern form and took to the sky, I probably should have felt at least some fear. I had no idea what fairy warfare looked like. Maybe they'd shoot me right out of the sky at the sight of me, but I couldn't bring myself to worry about it. Finally, it felt like the pieces had all started to come together. *This* was why I'd been pulled out of my life, and along with stopping the fighting, maybe I could finally get the answers I'd wanted for so long, answers to questions I'd tried to hide away from most of my life.

I'd always been the runt of the family. Even my egg was small, my brothers liked to tease me. I hadn't thought much of it until I found out they weren't lying; it actually *had* been small, because I was only half-wyvern.

In our wyvern forms, we only mated with other wyverns, and children were often conceived that way. But in our human forms, we could mate with any other humanoid creature, as my recent activities with Tanith proved well enough, and occasionally, hybrids were born. When my mother confessed to me that her wyvern mate was not my father, she wouldn't tell me who my biological father was, and at the time, I didn't think it mattered. All it meant to me was that I would have to work even harder, twice as hard as my brothers, just to compete with them.

And I did.

But after spending the last week among other species, I had to admit that there were good points to each of their species too. Ty's strength and levity, Leith's skill in the water and his empathy, Zol's confidence and understanding of our instincts, and Cad's leadership and honesty had all made an impression on me, as had Tanith's tenderness and generosity. I'd always considered wyverns the best species, which contributed to the need I had to bury my other half, whatever it might be, but after that week, I had to confess that having a few attributes from another species might not be the end of the world.

Was I half-fairy? What would that mean for me if I was? Would getting to know the other side of me help to quell the need I'd always had to prove myself?

Those thoughts were all spinning around my head as I flew over the unfamiliar terrain, but my immediate challenge would be locating the attacking forces and getting them to speak to me in the first place. It wouldn't necessarily be easy. All too often, people got caught up in their own struggles and didn't step back to see the big picture.

And a large flying reptile might not be entirely welcome.

Another rumble passed through the air, and with my wyvern eyes, I could actually see the ripples as they travelled towards me, throwing me briefly off course. Narrowing in on the ripple's source, I flew even faster until I saw the group gathered with their weapon, some kind of machine I'd never seen before.

Shrieks of surprise and fear filled the air as I landed right in the middle of them, and I quickly shifted back to my human form before they could attack me. Naked and unarmed, they would feel a lot less intimidated by my human self.

"What the... who are you?" an older woman asked, stepping forward from the crowd. With her long, dark hair, flowing dress and pointed ears, she looked almost regal.

"My name is Aiqen. I've just spoken to the king, and my friends are still with him. They're doing their best to convince him that Lysanthir had nothing to do with Evia's death."

The woman's brow furrowed as she considered my words. "How do you know any of this? We've never seen your kind here before."

"I'm from another realm. I didn't know anything about any of this until just a few days ago, but I believe I was brought here for a reason. I believe I'm connected to this place somehow..."

I didn't get to finish my sentence before another figure emerged from the crowd, a man who, though older than me, looked an awful lot like me.

The woman turned to him with several questions burning in her eyes. "Do you know anything about this, Taeral?"

Wincing beneath the accusation in the woman's voice, his eyes scanned me intently. "You're wyvern?"

I nodded, though it should have been obvious enough after my entrance. "My mother is Udroh."

Recognition flashed in his eyes, and the woman next to him noticed it at the same time I did. "Is there something you need to tell me?" she demanded, jealousy infusing every word and making the relationship between them quite clear.

"She's the one I already told you about, before we met," Taeral answered her under his breath, trying not to be overheard by the crowd behind them. "There has been no other."

It seemed my suspicions were correct, which didn't even really surprise me at that point. Nothing else made sense; there was no other reason for me to be involved in any of this if I hadn't been meant to come there and find my father. I'd already discovered far more about myself on an emotional and physical level than I'd expected during our days in the woods, and now, it seemed I would have a better understanding of myself on a biological level as well.

"What brings you here, Aiqen?" Taeral asked me, with some trepidation but also something that almost looked like pride. "Your mother made it quite clear when I left that I was to play no part in your life."

Obviously, I needed to know more of the story, but for the time being, I stuck to the more immediate reason for my visit. "I came here with the witch who killed the king's daughter."

A murmur ran through the assembled crowd, everyone speculating on what that might mean. "Did she tell the king that Lysanthir is innocent?" Taeral's wife, who must also be Lysanthir's mother, asked me, gripping onto her husband's arm for support.

"Not yet, but I believe she will soon. I left my comrades there to deal with that while I came to speak to you. The king is grieving and looking for someone to blame, but there's no reason that it has to lead to war. Please, tell me how I can help you."

And so it was that through simply talking and listening rather than any show of my strength, I got Lysanthir's family to stop attacking and explain their position to me. There were grievances outside of Lysanthir's capture but they were not, as the king had accused them, trying to take his throne. We were still discussing the whole political situation when a small party approached in the distance. Everyone immediately took up positions, ready to defend themselves, but I recognized the members of the group immediately simply by the shape of them.

The centaur was especially hard to miss.

"Wait! They're here to help."

The fairies held their positions but didn't attack, waiting as the group drew closer, and finally, Lysanthir's mother let out a cry of relief as she saw her son amongst them. Amidst the joy of their reunion, Lysanthir explained to everyone gathered how Aris had confessed and the king had released him.

"He should pay for this insult to our family!" someone in the back shouted. "We must demand retribution."

"And where does it stop?" I called back. "The man has lost his daughter and heir. He has already suffered."

"I agree," Lysanthir backed me up. "He was not himself. This whole situation got completely out of control."

It had indeed. It had drawn me and all of the others in, from all over the realms, connecting us all and now that it seemed to be coming to an end, I wasn't quite sure where we went from there. The only thing I knew for certain was that none of our lives would ever be quite the same again.

~Cadriel~

As we watched Evia's father and Lysanthir's father - who was also Aiqen's father, apparently - agree to a ceasefire later that day in the royal garden, Tanith came to stand next to me. The peaceful setting felt completely at odds with all the tension of the past few days and she seemed to feel it too.

"So, I guess that's really the end of it. Did that feel a little anticlimactic to you?" she wondered. "I expected a big battle, life-and-death stakes and all of that. That's how these kinds of books usually go."

A chuckle slipped through my lips. Surely, we'd proven to her by then that we weren't in a book at all. "I'm not at all sorry we avoided that. In fact, I think we were all brought here to avoid precisely that outcome. The stakes were a lot higher than we realized."

She turned to look at me curiously. "What do you mean?"

It had taken me a while to make the connection, but when we accompanied Lysanthir back to his family and saw the weapon the ferries were using, it all fell into place. I had seen one before, more than a hundred years earlier, when a different set of warring fairies set off one of the biggest earthquakes Earth had ever known. The weapon shook the air and rumbled the ground, and it had the unfortunate effect of rippling across realms.

That was why we had been able to feel it even in the world Aris created, and, if left unchecked, it could have caused a great deal of damage not only in the fairy realm but in our own worlds as well. Perhaps that explained why I'd been assigned to Aris in the first place. I was meant to stop this from escalating, perhaps saving an unknown number of lives in the process, with the help of the rest of our small band of unlikely comrades.

Tanith listened carefully as I explained it all to her. "That does make sense, but there's so much I still don't understand. Like how I knew about you all in the first place and how we were all brought to Aris' world if she didn't do it intentionally."

Since I didn't have those answers either, I could only shrug. "Sometimes, it just comes down to magic."

It was her turn to laugh. "That's a cop-out authors use when they've left a plot hole they can't fill."

"Perhaps, but the fact remains that you have magic inside you, Tanith. I think *you* brought us all together somehow, and you've helped us all grow, even in the short time we've had together."

The way she pressed her lips together told me how much it meant to her to hear that. I could read every emotion that played across her face because I'd learned so much about her over the past week, and yet there was still so much more I wanted to know. I wanted to continue to be by her side, but with the danger passed and Aris apprehended, we would all have to focus on getting back to our own lives.

Even though the life I'd led for thousands of years now felt almost foreign to me. It astonished me how quickly things could change.

The fairy king came over to us when the treaty had been signed and all the formalities concluded. "Thank you all for your help. You're welcome to stay the night, if you like, before you head back to your homes."

Tanith and I exchanged uncertain glances. "We don't actually have any way of returning to where we came from," she admitted to the king. "I wanted to ask, since you're able to move between realms, if you could help us all get home? If it's not too much trouble."

"How did you get here in the first place..." he started to ask before shaking his head. "Aris, I presume?"

"Possibly. It's all a bit of a mystery." We couldn't explain it to him when we didn't understand it ourselves. I also didn't want to let go just yet. "It is getting quite late, though. If we could take you up on your offer of accommodation for the night and you could help to transport us in the morning, it would be very much appreciated."

"Certainly," he agreed. "You've earned my thanks and my hospitality. I'll make the arrangements now."

As he walked away, Tanith looked up at me curiously. "Don't you need to be getting back?"

I did, but I also didn't want to, at least not without a proper farewell. "Do you *want* me to leave now?" I replied, putting the question back to her.

She leaned into me, her arm slipping around my waist. "No. I don't."

That made two of us, then.

"What's the plan now?" Zol asked as he walked up to us. He'd obviously seen us speaking to the fairy king, and Leith, Aiqen and Ty were right behind him.

I quickly filled them in. "The king has offered to return us all to our own realms in the morning. We can spend the night here and enjoy each other's company without any threat hanging over our heads before we part ways."

"Enjoy each other's company?" Zol repeated, giving Tanith a wink. "That's a euphemism if I ever heard one."

"He didn't mean it that way," Tanith admonished.

"Actually... I kind of did."

Her mouth fell open as Zol's eyes lit up. He looked like a kid in a candy store, and I couldn't help smiling.

"We can simply talk and see how it goes. There don't have to be any expectations, but if something happens, it happens."

Tanith looked stunned by my words, but in the moment, they felt right. If we were all going to be separated the next day, I wanted her company one last time, but I knew each of the others did too. It felt selfish to demand she spend the night with only me. We had each played an equal part in this - different, but equal - and no one was more entitled to the particular pleasure of her attention than anyone else. These men were all good people in their own way, and Tanith cared for each of them.

In my own way, I did too.

They had already been intimate together back in the forest without me and it didn't seem to have made the relationship between them awkward. In fact, they seemed closer than ever and if this really was the last night we would all have together, I had a feeling that if I didn't take the opportunity, I would regret it.

In fact, my heart had already begun to beat a little faster in anticipation, the blood flowing faster through my veins as the sky above us began to darken.

Before long, one of the king's men came up to our small group. "I've been asked to show you upstairs. Your rooms are ready."

CHAPTER TWENTY

The king went all out to make us comfortable. We were each given a bedroom, six rooms spread out around a central staircase, and offered food and drink to be brought up to us. It would make a nice change to sleep in a bed again, though there were things I would miss about the forest.

"Please bring all the food to this room," Cadriel requested, pointing at the room that had been assigned to Tanith. "We should share one last meal together."

Based on what he'd said down in the garden, I had a feeling we'd be sharing more than just food, but I didn't blame him for not saying so in front of the king's men. That could be our secret.

Just like the rooms downstairs, Tanith's bedroom got bigger with each new person who walked in, so we all had plenty of space to sit down and relax. "This could be useful in other situations," Zol said, taking a seat on the bed itself. "Things that keep getting bigger the more you put in them."

He gave Tanith a wink that had her rolling her eyes as she tried not to laugh. "You want me to blow up like a balloon?"

"Only certain parts of you."

We all talked and laughed as we ate the food brought for us and drank the sweet liquid from crystal bottles. They called it nectar, but whatever was in it left us all with a pleasant buzz. After the stress of the last week and the emotion brought about by all of the day's revelations, it felt damn good to let it all wash away and just enjoy the moment. I even shifted to my human form to sit on the couch with the others since some spare clothes had been provided for us all.

Since Evia's death, I'd avoided taking my human form since I'd been human when she died. I thought at the time that if I had been in my centaur form, I might have been fast enough to save her. I blamed myself, but now that I knew why Aris went after her, I could see that nothing I did would have been enough. A selfish witch wanted her out of the way and *that* was the reason she died, not because of me or anything I did or didn't do.

"Ty?" Leith had somehow ended up leaning on my shoulder as we drank the last of our bottles. "Do we *have* to go home?"

I knew just what he meant. After Evia died, I thought I'd never find that kind of feeling of belonging again. It might not be exactly the same with Tanith and the others, but it was good all on its own. I didn't want to lose it either.

It seemed our story had come to an end, though. I didn't know what other choice we had, so I tried to look on the bright side. "You must be a little bit excited to go back. Don't you miss the ocean?"

His nose wrinkled in a rather adorable way. "Not really. Not as much as I'll miss you."

I threw my arm around him and pulled him in tighter. "I'll miss you too, Leith."

"What about me?" Zol piped up from the bed. He'd been talking to Cadriel and I hadn't thought he was paying any attention to us, but obviously, he'd overheard.

"What *about* you?" I shot back, teasing him since I knew exactly what he meant.

The demon put his hand on his heart in mock offense. "I'm hurt, Ty. You can't pretend you won't miss this ass, at least."

He leaned over to give us all a better view, rubbing his hand down it for good measure, as we all chuckled.

"I won't miss your ass as much as the rest of you," I told him, and his eyebrow drew together, trying to figure out what I meant. I wouldn't make him guess though. "You showed me that it's okay to keep living. That all the rest of life - the jokes, the friendship and yeah, the sex - it can keep going even when things aren't perfect. Hell, sometimes that's when you need it most. You *all* helped me see that."

I had everyone's full attention, and I made eye contact with each one of them as I spoke.

"I'm not really good at the sappy stuff, but thanks for that. I'll miss all of you. Hell, I'll even miss Aiqen."

The wyvern chucked a pillow at my head, but I managed to lean back at the last minute and it hit Leith instead, making everyone laugh again as the merman blinked in bewilderment.

"You know, before I turned back time the last time, you and Zol kissed each other," Tanith said, grinning over at us both. "It was very sexy."

Did we? My eyes immediately darted to Zol, who gave me a devilish grin of his own. "I'm sorry I don't remember that," he practically purred, licking his lips with his forked tongue for added emphasis and a shot of desire rushed through my body. He was so utterly over the top and completely unashamed of it, and fuck, life was short. Why not go for it?

Zol's eyes widened in surprise as I got to my feet and walked over to him. Without a word, I pushed him down onto his back, pinning him to the bed with my hands on his arms, and pressed my lips firmly against his. His surprise only lasted a second before he kissed me back, teasing, playful and seductive. Where my hips leaned against his, my cock began to harden at nearly the same time his did.

By the time I pushed myself back up, we were both panting, and a quick glance at Tanith told me how much she'd enjoyed watching it too. Her flushed cheeks were the first sign of her arousal, turning nearly as red as her hair.

I turned to Cad who sat next to us on the bed. "Have you noticed how Tanith's cheeks turn red when she's turned on?"

His eyes immediately went to her, and her face flushed even deeper. "Hey, this isn't about me. We were talking about the two of you."

"No, I'd rather talk about you," Zol agreed, sitting back up and giving me an appreciative nod. "You're the only one in the room who's kissed every one of us. Who's the best?"

We all wanted to hear her answer to that, but Tanith shook her head. "I'm not answering that. It's way too subjective."

"Alright, let's be objective, then," Aiqen suggested. "Who's got the best cock?"

Tanith gasped in surprise while Zol let out an impressed whistle. "Going for the big question right off the bat. I like it."

"I can't... you don't... there isn't... you're all different, but equally great," she managed to splutter as we all grinned at her discomfort. Aiqen's hand had moved to his groin while Leith shifted in his seat. It had definitely started to feel a little warmer, and our clothes a little too tight.

"Well, I think we can all agree that Tanith has the best tits," Zol offered next, while Tanith groaned, covering her face with her hands, both flattered and embarrassed. "And I don't know about everyone else, but I'd love to get one last look at them."

Nobody disagreed. Even Cadriel swallowed hard in anticipation.

"Come on, Tanith," the demon encouraged her with that smooth tongue of his. "Let us all worship you one last time."

~Tanith~

The atmosphere in the room shifted as soon as Ty and Zol shared that amazingly sexy kiss. Even in his human form, Ty was the biggest man in the group, the tallest, broadest and strongest one, and to see him dominating the usually cocky demon easily took one of the top spots on the list of the hottest things I'd ever seen.

I knew what it felt like to kiss both of them, so to see them kissing each other stirred something inside me that I hadn't even known existed. I would have been happy to watch more, but they turned the focus back on me until all five men in the room watched me hopefully as Zol asked me to let them 'worship' me one last time.

Who in their right mind would say no to that?

Even so, it felt different that time. Being with them all individually was one thing. The frenzied groupings in the forest, fed by necessity and lust, had been something else. But with no more threat hanging over us, with no reason we *had* to do this other than because we all wanted to, with each of the five amazing men I'd come to know and care for so much in such a short amount of time all ready and eager to take part, the air around me seemed to sizzle with electricity. It ran down my skin, leaving goosebumps in its wake, and shot straight to the deepest parts of me, setting off a base, pulsing need.

I wanted them all and I wanted to give all of them what they wanted. If this really would end in the morning, why not make our last night count?

With five pairs of eyes watching me, I got to my feet. My heart pounded with both excitement and nerves as I slowly began to undress, knowing my every move was being devoured from five different angles. I had never stripped for anyone before, let alone a whole group of men at once. No one had ever made me feel so safe and so adored at the same time that I wanted to.

When I got down to my underwear, they couldn't hold back any more. Suddenly, I was surrounded, hands brushing against my skin as they pulled off the last few scraps of fabric. Mouths sucked at my breasts as soon as they were free of my bra, one on each nipple, while insistent hands pushed my legs apart just far enough that a tongue could get between them. I knew *whose* tongue from the way its forked end teased my sensitive clit, and Ty's strong arm held me up as he kissed my mouth and leaned me back, giving Leith and Aiqen better access to my chest.

Pure fire seemed to race through my body with all the attention it was being given. So many hands were on me that I could no longer tell which belonged to whom. The sensations overwhelmed me in the very best way, but something was still missing.

Gently, I pushed Ty back so that I could raise my head and look over to where Cadriel sat, watching us all from beneath hooded eyelids, his deep green eyes heavy with need. His hand rested close to his groin but not touching it, even though I could see the swelling bulge in his pants. He obviously wanted to be part of this but he didn't quite know how.

Disentangling myself from the others, I walked over to him, completely naked, feeling the weight of his stare upon me.

"Are you willing to do exactly what I say?"

I had never been the type to take charge sexually, but in this case, he needed it. It seemed to work too, as he nodded slowly. "Tell me what to do," he breathed.

"Keep your eyes on me at all times," I instructed first. "And take your clothes off."

~Cadriel~

I wouldn't have thought I would like watching Tanith be touched and kissed by the others, but to my surprise, my body reacted almost immediately. She looked incredible: confident and sexy, giving herself up to them but also having them all completely at her mercy.

I felt just the same: utterly unable to resist.

But I didn't know how to take the next step. They all seemed to move like a choreographed dance, with assigned parts, and I didn't see where I fit in.

I might have sat there, frozen with hesitation, all night, but Tanith, with her unerring ability to sense what each of us felt, realized how lost I felt. She made a point of drawing me in, asking me to put myself in her hands, and I willingly agreed. I would do anything she told me to, so long as it meant being with her.

Although I knew the others could see me, I kept my eyes on her as I took off all my clothes, exhaling in relief as I freed my stiff cock from my tight pants. With her eyes still on my face, Tanith reached down and stroked my cock tenderly, sending shivers of longing through my body. Her touch felt electric, but even more than that, the look in her eyes held me captive. Even though there were four other men just behind her, waiting for the pleasure of her company too, that look told me that this meant more to her than something purely physical.

It always had.

"Come and lie down on the bed," she whispered, still with that commanding edge to her voice. In my peripheral vision, I could see that the other men had all started to undress too, palming themselves as they watched Tanith's hand on me, but my eyes didn't stray from hers as I lay myself down on my back, my hips at the edge of the bed, my feet still on the floor.

Her eyes full of the same anticipation I felt, Tanith climbed up after me, positioning herself on top of me as she took my cock and rubbed it along her warm slit, coating it in her own arousal before slowly, breathtakingly, sinking down onto me.

"Yes," I exhaled in wonder. "That's... perfect."

How could one small act feel quite so incredible? I'd never understood what made people do the crazy things they did in the name of lust, the people who made deals with demons like Zol just to sate their desires, but in the feel of her body enveloping mine, it almost began to make sense. The physicality on its own was pleasant, no question, but combined with the emotion in Tanith's eyes, the moment of pure connection between us elevated it to a whole other level.

It became almost divine.

"Don't get too carried away yet," I heard Zol say as Tanith slowly rolled her hips against mine, our bodies moving together as I thrust up into her. "There's more to come."

"Just look at me," Tanith whispered to me. "Ignore whatever he's doing."

"I've had a lot of practice at that," I managed to stutter through my breathlessness. "And don't worry. All I see is you."

She gave me one of her stunning smiles just before hands appeared on her shoulders, pushing her down so her chest rested on mine. A moment later, the warm, wet, tight feel of her pussy around me got even tighter as someone else began to push into her other hole. Tanith tensed, and I immediately jumped at the chance to help her relax as she'd helped me.

"I'm right here. Just look at me."

Her shoulders relaxed as I gently stroked her face, pulling her down to me to kiss her lips. I could feel the other cock sliding into her, against mine, and surprisingly, I didn't mind at all. We were all getting what we wanted, and as long as Tanith enjoyed it, I would enjoy it too.

~**Aiqen**~

I'd asked Tanith which cock she liked best because I had seen all the others during our earlier group session in the forest, and I felt pretty confident about how mine compared, at least when Ty wasn't in his centaur form.

However, when Cadriel dropped his pants, I had to admit to having a brief flash of envy.

"Don't worry," Zol whispered to me with his devious grin. "He doesn't have a clue what to do with it. It isn't all about size."

Something in the way the angel and Tanith whispered to each other, her hand on his cock, both teasing and encouraging, had me growing harder by the second. Zol had his pants off already, though I hadn't even seen him undress, and the others were following suit. I quickly shed mine too, stroking myself while Tanith got Cad onto the bed and climbed on top of him. We'd all had a little bit to drink, sure, but it still surprised me how comfortable I felt being naked in front of the others. Maybe it shouldn't have, though. We were all there for the same reason, with the same purpose: to celebrate our victory and to revel in the connection we'd created with each other.

"Aiqen, you should take Tanith's ass this time," Zol suggested. "She loved having two of us at once."

She certainly had seemed to, I had to agree. "What about lubrication?" I wondered.

"I'm on it," he assured me. "Leith, may I?"

He reached down to the merman's cock, stiff and hard, but paused before touching him, waiting for permission.

"Yes?" Leith agreed, though he didn't sound entirely sure what he was agreeing to.

With a satisfied grin, Zol began to pump him, activating whatever biology produced the lubrication Leith had told us about earlier. Once Leith's surprise passed, he closed his eyes in enjoyment until Zol's hand was well coated, the occasional moan slipping past his lips.

The demon walked over to me next. "Well?" he asked, cocking an eyebrow at me in challenge as he held out his hand towards my cock next.

Unlike Leith, I knew what he meant. He wanted to use Leith's lube to get me ready, and it made sense. Besides, he'd already had his mouth on me, so what harm would his hand do?

With my nod, Zol took a firm hold of my cock and rubbed it slowly, twisting as he went, his fingertips running all the way along my shaft and back up again, giving the head a slight squeeze as he reached it. Fuck, he knew what he was doing, if I'd had any doubt from the blow job he gave me before.

"Being different isn't a bad thing," he whispered to me just before letting go. "You don't have to prove yourself to anyone."

With that, he released me and stepped away, leaving me blinking in surprise and unexpectedly touched as he moved over to the bed and pushed Tanith down on top of Cad so that her ass was exposed to me, the small hole beckoning to my aching cock.

"Except for Tanith," Zol amended with a smirk. "You can prove to her how much you want her."

That, I could certainly do.

~Leith~

When Tanith first told me that as much as she enjoyed our time together, she didn't want to be with me exclusively, I didn't really understand. I thought it would hurt to see her with anyone else or that I would be jealous at the thought of another man touching her or bringing her the kind of pleasure that we shared together.

But watching her with two different men inside her, one beneath her and one behind, all three of them lost in the satisfaction they gave each other, jealousy didn't factor in. It made me happy to see her so happy. And since I liked both Cad and Aiqen, I liked to see them enjoying themselves too. I didn't feel left out, especially since I knew Tanith wanted me there and I knew she wouldn't forget about me.

Zol, ever the stage manager, directed me and Ty onto the bed next to the threesome already there, Ty on one side and me on the other, both on our knees. Just like the room had, the bed seemed to grow bigger as we all climbed onto it. With hazy, sex-soaked eyes, Tanith looked up at me, her lips curling into a satisfied smile.

"We need your hands, Tanith," Zol told him. "Cad can help you keep your balance."

The angel immediately did just that, his hands on her waist while Aiqen's hands rested just below, on Tanith's hips, as he continued to thrust into her from behind. Balancing on her knees, Tanith lifted her arms off the bed, her left hand wrapping around my cock as she continued to smile up at me. A moment later, she transferred that smile to Ty, taking his cock in her right hand as he inhaled in pleasure.

"You're incredible," she whispered to him, her hand slowly pumping him in rhythm with the movements she made on mine, and she turned to me again. "You too, Leith. Fuck, you make me feel so sexy."

Could she really doubt that she was? "You look amazing," I told her, sighing as her hand slid along my length, her touch firm and adoring.

"Enough talking," Zol instructed. "I'm going to fuck that pretty mouth now. Don't worry about doing anything. You just stay still, Tanith. Let us share you."

She whimpered her approval as he took hold of her head, placing the tip of his cock against her lips, and pushed his way in.

Her hands stilled, obviously overwhelmed with everything her body felt, so I began to move instead, sliding my cock back and forth within her grasp, my hips moving just like each of the other men on the bed, each of us enjoying a different part of her, like a group of musicians all playing the same instrument together.

And we made beautiful music, a great symphony of moans, grunts, sighs, and muttered words.

Tanith's first orgasm seemed to take her by surprise, her body convulsing with no warning as she moaned around Zol's cock, her grip on me tightening as pleasure coursed through her.

"That's one," Zol said with a grin, pulling his cock from her mouth and running it along her lips. "Now, we switch."

~Zolgozig~

I had never felt more completely at home. All the hesitation and uncertainty had gone and we were all completely focused on just one goal: making each other, and especially Tanith, feel as fucking good as possible.

We rotated a few times, changing the positions, changing who filled which hole, taking a break when we needed to. Finally, her limbs refusing to function anymore, Tanith whispered something to Ty and he gave her a gentle kiss before coming over to me.

"She'd like to watch me fuck you so she can have a rest," he told me bluntly. "In human form this time."

I couldn't refuse an offer like that. "Does anyone else want in? I've got a mouth too."

Aiqen had just come so he declined, and Cad was obviously a no. He lay on the bed with Tanith propped against his chest so she had a better view. That left Leith, and when I raised an eyebrow in invitation, his cheeks turned slightly red.

"I guess it's good to try new things?" he said hesitantly, looking for assurance from the others.

"Only if you want to," Ty told him. "But if you're at all curious, you couldn't do better than Zol."

I appreciated that. It always felt good to have your skill recognized.

With Leith's agreement, we arranged ourselves in a classic spit roast position as I climbed up onto the couch on my hands and knees. Ty helped himself to a little of Leith's lube, pressing his fingers into my ass to stretch me out before his cock followed. He was smaller in his human form, but still an impressive specimen, and I groaned in pleasure as he pushed all the way in. One of the few regrets I had in my long life was that I would never know exactly what a woman felt as she took a man into her pussy, but this had to be the next best thing.

Reaching out to Leith, I pulled him closer to me, letting my tongue dance down the length of his shaft first before I really got started. I couldn't say what I expected his lubrication to taste like, but I was pleasantly surprised anyway. A little salty but also slightly sweet, it made my mouth water and also made me curious about whether his cum would taste different too. I couldn't wait to find out.

As I lost myself to the pleasure of getting fucked by two hot and likeable men at the same time, I had to admit this might just be the best vacation I'd ever had.

"Hold on. We can't forget about you." With my eyes closed, I missed Tanith walking over to me. She bent down to kiss my cheek and whisper in my ear. "Thank you for starting us off, Zol."

My mouth was too full to reply, and when she positioned herself beneath me to begin sucking my cock too, I pretty much lost the power of speech anyway. In thousands of years, I had never enjoyed myself so much, and that was fucking saying something.

We came one after the other, Leith first, then Ty, and finally me before we all collapsed into a sweaty, panting pile on the sofa, sated and fully satisfied.

Tanith had just got back to her feet when someone knocked at the door, making us all temporarily freeze.

I recovered myself first. "What are we afraid of? We're all adults here and we aren't doing anything wrong."

"True," Tanith agreed with a shaky laugh. "But I better see who it is. This is my room, after all."

As quickly as she could, she grabbed a bathrobe from the adjoining bathroom and went to the door, opening it just a crack so the five naked men behind her wouldn't be visible.

"Forgive me for disturbing your rest," the voice from the other side said. "The witch has asked to speak with you."

Aris wanted to talk to Tanith? I didn't like that idea, and neither did any of the others.

Tanith, however, had other ideas. "Just give me a minute to get dressed," she told the person before closing the door and turning back to us all. "Not a word. I know what you're going to say, but she's restrained and wearing Leith's scales. She can't hurt me, and this might be the last chance I have to get the rest of my questions answered. I'm going to talk to her."

"I'll go with you." We all spoke almost at the same time, all of us getting to our feet.

"No, you won't. None of you. I can do this alone." Tanith smiled affectionately around the room. "I won't be long. Will you wait here for me? I want to come back to the five most amazing men in the universe, naked in my bed."

With a great deal of grumbling, we all reluctantly agreed to stay put while Tanith went to clean up and put her clothes back on. Blowing us all a kiss, she headed out the door.

~Tanith~

My legs still felt a little wobbly as I followed the guard down the winding staircases of the king's castle, down to the underground room where Aris had been locked up. If I didn't want to get a bit of closure, I wouldn't have let myself be pulled away from the incredible time I'd been having with the others. Although I'd given myself a quick rinse and freshened up, the sensation of being completely and utterly filled still lingered. Not a single part of me hadn't been touched or sucked or adored. I could still taste Zol's cum in the back of my mouth; he hadn't been the only one to finish there tonight, but he had been the most recent.

I'd lost track of my own orgasms. Sometimes, it felt like another one started before the last one subsided. It overwhelmed and awed me how they could all make me feel so incredibly special and I wanted more of that before I returned home the next day. I couldn't quite imagine going back to my old life after all of this. How could anything ever compare again? How could I pretend none of it had ever happened?

We would have to find a way to see each other again. I didn't know how it would work, but there had to be a way. We would talk about it as soon as I got back, presuming we could all control our lust for a little bit longer. I couldn't just let them go.

When we reached the bottom of the stairs, the guard opened the door for me before stepping aside. "I'll be right here if you need me," he said, but I noticed he didn't seem eager to go inside himself.

The room I walked into looked similar to the one I'd been held in earlier while in Aris' body, but smaller and more secure. She had literally been chained to the wall, one end of the chain around her ankle so that she could move around but not very far. Far enough to reach the bed where she sat. I had to assume the chain had been enhanced with some kind of magic inhibitor, and the scale necklace still lay around her neck, even though her hands were now free. She caught me looking at it as I walked in and gave me a sarcastic smile.

"They've got it alarmed somehow. If I touch it, they'll know."

Good, I wanted to say. She deserved to feel powerless, and more, but I held my tongue. I didn't go there to rub her defeat in, no matter how awful she had been. I could be gracious in victory. "You wanted to see me?"

All traces of a smile, real or not, fell from her face. "I just want the truth," she claimed, those eyes that had mocked me so many times in the past looking completely earnest. "What *are* you, really?"

She still didn't get it and, completely unexpectedly, a tiny twinge of sympathy for her surfaced from somewhere deep inside me. Taking care to stay out of reach of where her chain could go, I took a few steps forward. "I know you don't want to believe it, but I'm just a human. I have a little bit of magical ability, apparently, that I got from you. Cad thinks our souls crossed paths before we were born and I took a touch of your magic while you got a touch of... whatever I have, I guess. But whatever magic I have is nothing compared to you. It never was."

That answer didn't seem to satisfy her, no matter how true it might be, so I tried to explain it another way.

"We're the same in a lot of ways, Aris. Not just being the same age and sharing this soul connection or whatever, but I know what it's like to feel like you're not good enough. I know what it's like to feel like everyone else has it easier than me, and I definitely know what it's like to have the boy I thought I loved cheat on me with someone else. You made sure of that."

"Your boyfriend looked just like Lysanthir," she pointed out, sounding confused about that fact, and I could only shrug.

"I don't know why that is. Just a coincidence, I guess? Or maybe it's not. Maybe it has something to do with us and soul shadows and magic and fairies, and who knows what else. But he's not my boyfriend anymore, and you know what? I couldn't be happier about that. I always felt like he was out of my league and I should be thrilled just to have someone like him, but now that I've met people who make me feel like *they're* the lucky ones for getting to be with me, I can see just how backward my thinking was before."

She didn't respond to that but I could see her thinking about it. Hopefully, she would take it to heart, though for her, it had come too late. Actions had consequences, no matter how hurt we might have been to make them. If I had killed her after finding her in bed with Blaine, I would have to pay for that too. The world just worked that way.

And though the betrayal of my boyfriend had crushed me at the time, all I needed was a little time and five gorgeous men to understand that I was better off without Blaine. I wouldn't waste another second pining over someone who didn't put me first.

I also didn't want to waste any extra time with Aris, so I got to the reason I had agreed to see her in the first place. "I have a question for you too while I'm here. There's one thing I still don't understand: you said you saw me and the others in the forest but we were never there. How could you have seen us?"

Aris sighed, the mermaid scales glimmering in the light as her chest moved. "I think it had something to do with the book you were writing. Cadriel explained to me how you had written parts of it before it happened. I think, somehow, I could see it while you were writing it, even though it was only happening in your head."

I supposed it wasn't any crazier than me writing the book in the first place before I had met any of them, or my phone controlling our surroundings and the timeline. Like Cad said, it all came back to magic in the end, and the strange connection that Aris and I seemed to share.

"They'll take my magic from me," she added, her voice quiet and full of self-pity. "They can do that. They'll drain it somehow and use it for themselves, and then I'll be nothing."

Just when I started to feel a little bit sorry for her, she added one more sentence to remind me of who she really was.

"I'll be just like you."

I had nothing left to say to her. "Goodbye, Aris."

Maybe I would never fully understand everything that had happened, but I knew the important parts: there was magic inside me, and perhaps, inside all of us. When we found the right person, or people, who appreciated it, there was no limit on what we could do.

The guard locked the door behind me and I began to head back up the stairs, my whole body starting to hum in excitement again at the thought of the men waiting there for me. As much as we needed to talk, hopefully they were still naked too. Hopefully, nobody wanted to get any sleep that night.

In my enthusiasm, I forgot to watch my step on the spiral staircase.

My foot slipped.

For a moment, my body seemed to hover in the air as I scrambled to regain my balance, but it was no use. I fell forward, my head smacking against the balustrade with an echoing thud, and the world around me went dark.

Floating in blackness, I was vaguely aware of voices, of a soothing touch on my forehead, and then, only silence.

The ding of notifications on my phone woke me up fully. Blinking into the sunlight streaming through my window, I tried to fight through the fog in my head as I looked around the familiar surroundings of my dorm room.

"What the hell?" I mumbled aloud as my phone continued to ping like it had been possessed. It sat on my bedside table, plugged into the wall, the screen barely turning off as message after message popped up.

How did I get back there?

My stomach sank as the reality began to set in that I really *was* back. Where did the guys go? Had I missed my chance to say goodbye?

Or had any of it really happened? Maybe I had dreamt the whole thing, just as I thought at the start.

Disoriented, and with a great pit of loss settling in my stomach, I picked up my phone to see who on earth was trying to get a hold of me so desperately.

OMG, I loved this book so much! The sex scenes were so hot! Where do I get my own multi-species harem?

Please tell me there's going to be a sequel! That ending had to be a decoy. I need more of ALL of them (but especially Zol).

Zol is fun, but Leith is my favourite! We need more Leith!

They went on for pages and pages, comment after comment of nothing but praise, and my heart raced as I opened up the serialized app and saw my book there with a big, bold '**complete**' next to the title.

How could it be complete? I hadn't finished writing it yet. The story wasn't over.

My fingers trembled as I pulled up the last chapter. There was Tanith, slipping on the staircase and hitting her head, and in the next scene, she woke up in bed, realized it had all been a dream, and vowed to live her life with new confidence and find men just like the ones from her dream in real life.

"No," I whispered to the phone, into the empty air of my room. It couldn't end like that. I wanted to see them all again. I wanted them in my life somehow. They had to be real.

They *had* to be.

Frantically, I went to the editing app instead, to the working version of my story, and highlighted the last chapter to delete it. I could take more care on the stairs this time. I could get back to the room where they were all waiting for me and they would tell me they had always been real and we would come up with a plan to stay together.

I hadn't just made them up. I couldn't have.

A red message box popped up on my screen as I pressed the delete button.

Completed stories can no longer be amended. Please contact customer support for assistance.

Slowly, I lowered the phone, tears gathering in the corners of my eyes as the positive comments on the book continued to pop up. There was even one from Melissass, the popular author who had trashed my book after the first few chapters, saying she would happily take back her earlier comments.

This book ended up going against all my expectations of what would happen, and took us on a fun ride to get there. Well done.

I couldn't care less.

I started writing the book because I wanted to escape from my reality. Now, I wanted nothing more than to go back to the reality I'd been living for the past week.

Wait a minute.

My heart beat faster once again as I thought about how long I had been gone. Far too long for it all to have just been a dream. What was the date?

I tapped a few more times on my screen and brought up the calendar, and saw that it had indeed been a week since my birthday, a week since Cad had knocked on my door. I couldn't have slept *all* that time. There had to be some truth to it.

But if it really had all happened, why did the ending of my book say it was a dream? Why would they have left me on my own?

Would I ever see them again?

CHAPTER TWENTY-ONE

One week later

~Tanith~

As I handed in my last exam before the Christmas break to the professor who hadn't been able to look me in the eye since I brought up why-choose romance in his class, I breathed a sigh of relief. Studying had been nearly impossible since all I could think about was the week I'd been away.

Nobody even seemed all that concerned that I'd been missing for a whole week. The resident adviser in my dorm said she thought I'd gone home early for Christmas. She admitted she'd half-expected me to drop out and not come back. My family had sent the occasional text, but when I didn't reply, they assumed I was busy studying for my exams. It didn't inspire a lot of confidence that anyone would have come to my rescue if anything bad had actually happened to me.

And what *did* happen during that week? I still didn't know for certain. My writing friends were in awe, saying I must have written day and night to get the whole book finished so quickly. Was that what happened? Did I go into some kind of intense meditative state where I got so wrapped up in writing the book that I thought I was actually living it? It didn't seem likely, but then, the longer I spent back in my regular life, the less likely it seemed that any of it had actually happened either. It seemed unreal that the world should just go on around me like nothing had changed, when for me, everything felt different.

I truly didn't know how to feel as I shoved my belongings into my truck and headed out on the highway, heading for home. Snow covered the fields on either side of the road, a far cry from the warm summer nights in the forest with my five men around me. Every now and then, I would catch myself looking up at the sky, hoping to see Aiqen's reptilian form flying among the clouds or a glimpse of Cad's white, feathery wings. As I crossed over a river, I couldn't help glancing down, wishing for a glimmer of Leith's scales shining beneath the surface. Passing by a field with horses, I searched in vain for a centaur among them, and sometimes, I could almost swear I saw Zol's smirk in my peripheral vision, but when I turned, there was no one there.

If it had all been in my head, I would have to move on, and I spent most of the drive thinking about what that looked like. I didn't have any passion for the courses I'd been taking, so maybe I could change my major and enroll in a creative writing class instead. Thousands of people every day were still reading my book, but I couldn't bring myself to look at any of the comments. It only made me miss the men contained in its pages even more.

The lights were off when I arrived at my family's house, and I found a note from my parents in the kitchen saying they'd gone to my younger sister's school for a Christmas fundraiser and would be home in about an hour. Grabbing a cookie from the counter, I headed up to my room and emptied my bags before bringing the presents back downstairs to put under the tree.

As I stood back up, the angel at the top of the tree caught my eye, and even though it looked nothing like the angel I'd fallen in love with, I couldn't help thinking of him anyway. "I miss you, Cadriel," I whispered into the silence of the room.

As soon as I said his name, a soft, fluttering noise, like the quiet flapping of wings, came from behind me and I spun around, my heart racing, wondering if I was truly starting to go crazy.

If I was, at least the delusion was a good one.

Beside my sofa stood the very man I'd just been thinking about. Those bright green eyes and red lips were just as I remembered them, but his clothing had changed. He looked almost impossibly casual in jeans and a cream sweater that made his dark hair look even darker than usual.

"Did I scare you? I'm sorry." An apologetic smile accompanied his words. "I only finished my debrief this morning, and I wanted to see you as soon as possible, but I had to wait until you called for me."

"Debrief?" I repeated in confusion, afraid to move or even blink in case this turned out to be another dream.

Cad grimaced. "That's the polite word. Interrogation would be more accurate. My superiors weren't pleased about me going AWOL for a whole week. They wanted to know everything. That's the bad news, but the good news is: they wanted to know everything, which means they didn't already know anything that had happened."

As much as I truly tried to follow along with what he said, I was also still trying to process the fact that he was there at all, and I couldn't do both at the same time. "I don't understand," I had to admit.

He laughed softly, his eyes warm and affectionate. "It means they don't know anything about what happened between us, or with the others. I told them all about Aris and Evia and the fairy war and all the rest, but some parts I kept to myself."

"You mean you lied?" I couldn't help teasing him, and he chuckled again.

"I omitted certain things," he amended. "And I requested that with Aris unlikely to return to Earth, I be assigned to you instead, as your protector."

Could this really be happening? After the last week, it felt dangerous to let myself hope, and Cad immediately sensed my reluctance, although he misinterpreted the reason for it.

"Of course, I don't have to if you would rather not…"

"No!" I blurted out, too loudly. "I'm just… I don't understand. I thought… I didn't even know if you were real. I thought I made it all up. I was afraid I would never see you again."

His expression softened as he took a step closer to me. "What's the last thing you remember?"

"I was going back up the stairs to see you all and I slipped and hit my head. The next thing I knew, I was back in my bed."

Cad groaned as he reached out to take my hand, bringing me to sit next to him on the sofa. "The king warned us that might happen. He said the magic might mess with your short-term memory."

"Magic?" He had lost me again. "What magic?"

Cad looked me straight in the eye, speaking nice and slowly. "You did slip and hit your head; that's true. It took a while for you to wake up, and while we waited for you with the fairy doctor, I talked to the king about Aris' punishment. He said they would drain her of her magic, that they had ways of doing that and they could make use of her abilities in various ways. I asked if they could transfer any of them to another person, and he and the other witch believed that would be possible, presuming the person receiving them had some magical ability to begin with."

"You're not making things any clearer."

He grinned his devastatingly handsome smile. "Be patient, I'm getting to the point. When you woke up, I suggested that we try to transfer Aris' ability to move between realms to you, as your reward for helping to stop her. The king agreed, but the witch warned that it might overwhelm your system for a little while and potentially affect your memory."

"I don't remember waking up there. I don't remember any of that."

"I can see that." He gave me another smile, this one of encouragement. "I thought that might be the case, because when we took you home and put you in bed, I plugged your phone back in and the end of the story appeared. In it, you thought everything had been a dream. I didn't know if you truly believed that, or if you would remember on your own when you woke up. Apparently, you didn't."

"So... it really did happen? All of it?" It seemed a ridiculous question to ask the man who had been there with me, who clearly remembered everything I did, but I needed to hear him say the words anyway. I needed to know I wasn't crazy.

"It all happened," he assured me. "And with your new ability, you can start writing a new story now, Tanith, one where you get to set the parameters."

His words were slowly starting to make sense in my head but before I got too excited, I wanted to make sure I had it right. "So... I can travel between realms and track people, just like Aris could?"

He nodded, pleased to see me catching on.

I tried to think things through logically. "So, let's say I took you to another realm, one outside of the jurisdiction of angels..."

"... then we could do whatever we liked, away from anyone else's prying eyes."

That sounded almost too good to be true. I could pinch myself to see if I was dreaming, but if I was, I didn't want to wake up. I wanted to stay in the dream as long as possible.

"And the others?" I wondered.

"You should be able to visit them in their own worlds and transport them with you, just as Aris took us all to the fairy's realm. Zol is different; he and I can't be tracked, but I'll be watching you as much as I can. You can call for me when you need me, like you did now. When you say my name, I'll hear you. And Zol, you can summon."

"How do I summon him?" The idea of seeing Zol's mischievous, handsome face again filled me with joy, and Cad smiled indulgently.

"It's literally this easy." He turned and addressed himself to the empty air. "I'd like to make a deal, Zolgozig."

Nothing happened.

I let a few seconds tick by before asking Cad, "Are you sure..."

"Just give it a minute," he promised. "He probably had to put his pants back on."

That made me laugh, and sure enough, a few seconds later, Zol appeared, an almost bored look on his face until he caught sight of the two of us, and a grin spread across his face. "Tanith!"

He pulled me to my feet, picking me up in his strong arms and spinning me around as I clung to him, laughing.

"What took you so long?" he asked once he'd put me down.

"She didn't remember that she could reach out to us," Cad explained for me, getting to his feet. "Where to next, Tanith?"

The possibility of seeing everyone, all of them together again, left me giddy. "Ty. Let's go find Ty. How do I do it?"

"The witch said you could control it all through your phone to start with, since that's how your power initially manifested itself. Maybe you just have to call him?"

It couldn't be that simple, could it? Pulling my phone from my pocket, I flipped through my embarrassingly short contact list until I saw an entry that had never been there before under Tymanus.

"I think we better hold onto you," Cad suggested, and he and Zol both placed their hands on my arms as I pressed the call button.

In a bright flash, the room vanished, my stomach flipping as we travelled through space until we arrived in an open field with no sign of snow. A group of centaurs were gathered together, building some kind of structure, and a few of them glanced over in our direction as we appeared out of thin air, but only one of them responded with a grin of pure delight.

"Ty!" I called out his name, waving to him, and he immediately ran over to us, looking as pleased to see us as we were to see him. After we embraced, I gestured to the construction site behind him. "What's happening here?"

"It's a playground," he explained, shrugging almost bashfully. "Evia always thought everyone took things too seriously, and I thought that maybe, if we let children here have more fun, centaurs and witches and fairies and everyone else all playing together, they might grow up to be happier adults too. I think she would have liked it."

"I'm sure she would have. It sounds wonderful."

Seeing him moving on and making something good out of Evia's memory brought tears to my eyes.

"I'm ready for a break, though. Are we getting the others?" he asked, looking around at our small group.

"We're going to try. Hold on."

I had no idea what would happen when I called Leith's entry. Would we all end up at the bottom of the ocean, drenched, and my phone ruined? Aris hadn't drowned, though, so I figured it would be worth the risk.

After another brief, nauseating journey, we arrived at the shore of a vast body of water, and before I could even ask the others what we should do next, Leith's head popped up from the water. "You came!" He sounded so pleased, but also like he had never really doubted it. "Hold on just a minute."

He transformed from his tail to his human legs, stumbling out of the water, and came over to stand next to us. "Where's Aiqen?"

"We're about to find out." With all four of them holding onto me now, I called the last new entry in my phone, and we soon found ourselves on the side of a mountain, watching as dozens of wyverns flew past, almost like they were in some kind of race.

"Which one is he?" Leith asked, and I couldn't tell either. They all looked a lot alike.

"Is this the competition he was training for?" I wondered.

"It was, but I decided not to take part." Aiqen's voice came from behind us, and we all turned to see him standing with a small group of other people, in human form, watching the tournament. "I decided there were more important things to do than simply accumulating power."

He shook hands with all the other men and gave me a hug, everyone looking pleased and excited to be together, and as they caught up on what they'd all been doing for the past week, I opened a new document on my phone and began to type.

With Aris' former personal realm now empty, the fairy king
having returned all its inhabitants to their original homes,
Tanith was able to use it whenever she wanted as a retreat
from the monotony of everyday life. Sometimes, she met

with one of the men at a time. Other times there would be two or three, and occasionally, all of them would be together, just as they had been on that night in the fairy king's castle. Sometimes, they just talked and spent time together, and other times, they made use of the very large bed that they built together for that purpose.

Though their lives might be worlds apart, their hearts remained connected, and the bonds that had formed between them never wavered, even though they could never be fully explained.

Sometimes, it just came down to magic.

EPILOGUE

~Leith~

Tanith handed me a stack of plates amidst the bustle of activity in the cottage kitchen. "Those are for the table. Thanks, Leith."

Her lips brushed against mine quickly before she got distracted again. "Zol, get your hand out of the turkey's ass!"

Ty chuckled as he walked past me with a handful of knives and forks. "Come on, let's go and finish the table before things get ugly in here."

I followed him to the new dining room we'd just finished building a couple of weeks earlier. The cottage that once belonged to Aris was hardly recognizable anymore. Over the course of the last year, we'd expanded and enhanced it, making it a home for all of us. It beat anything the sea had to offer by a long shot.

It was my favourite place in all the realms, especially when we were all there together.

"What does this holiday mean?" I asked Ty as we set the table between us. Merpeople didn't use plates or cutlery or tables. It had been a steep learning curve for me, but most of the time, I knew what was going on these days. However, Thanksgiving was still a new concept to me.

Ty couldn't offer much help either. "I'm not really sure, other than an excuse to get together and eat some good food. Tanith has a few days off, so we aren't in any hurry to get back. Sounds like a perfect holiday to me."

Me too.

Cadriel entered the room just as we finished arranging all the place settings, carrying a bow of red mush.

"Jellied cranberries," he told me when he caught my curious look. "I don't know why, so don't ask."

Aiqen followed with potatoes and green beans before Zol appeared, carrying a large roasted turkey and wearing a look of pride. "Who's ready to eat?"

Tanith brought up the rear, with two bottles of wine in her hands. "And drink!"

Over our meal, we caught up on each other's lives since the last time we'd all been together. I never had much to tell compared to the others, but they always listened to my stories of life under the sea with interest.

"Someday, we need to figure out a way to come and see you down there," Tanith said, her eyes shining with excitement at the idea. "Aris did it, so there has to be a way."

"Ty would make a pretty funny-looking merman," Zol snickered. "Would you have two tails?"

"Even underwater, I'd still be faster than you," Ty shot back.

Tanith told us about the new book she was writing, all about a group of wyvern brothers competing for their father's throne.

"It's about time wyverns got some recognition," Aiqen sniffed. "Dragons have had the spotlight far too long."

As the meal wound down and more wine was opened, Tanith stood up from her seat. "We still have the best part left. Who's ready for dessert?"

The five of us exchanged glances, every last one of us on the same page, and Zol answered for all of us.

"We thought you'd never ask."

~Tanith~

My body flushed beneath the heated looks the men gave me, and I hurried to explain myself. "I meant pie. There's pumpkin pie in the kitchen."

Nobody paid me any attention. As if they'd planned it in advance, Ty and Zol pushed all the dishes to one end of the table and Leith wiped the surface clean while Cad and Aiqen approached me on either side, each taking one of my arms as they turned me around so my back was to the table. Strong hands circled my waist, lifting me up until I sat on the solid oak, and another pair of hands, gentler but still firm, pushed me down onto my back.

Every nerve in my body sparked with excitement, every inch craving attention, and I knew they intended to give it to me. They had never let me down.

"Whose turn is it to go first?" Cadriel asked the others. He always wanted to make sure no one felt left out.

"Leith," Zol answered. Somehow, he managed to keep track of those things. "Just leave some for the rest of us, okay?"

With that, more hands appeared, unbuttoning my jeans and tugging at my shirt, slipping off my panties and unhooking my bra until I lay completely naked on the table, staring up at the ceiling above me. My nipples stiffened in the cooler air even as my body throbbed. Wetness had already begun to pool between my legs, and when Leith gently pushed them open, exposing my pussy to the group, their murmurs of appreciation made me even wetter.

His head bent down between my thighs, Leith inhaled deeply. "I think I like Thanksgiving."

I did too, and I'd certainly never had one quite like this before.

His tongue connected with my clit while Cad leaned down from beside me, his lips trailing across the peak of my nipple. On my other side, Ty nuzzled into my neck, sucking at the sensitive skin there. My hand reached for Aiqen's cock, but he caught my wrist in his hand, holding it against the table.

"Not yet. First, we'll feast on you."

His words sent a shiver down my spine, and as Leith began to pump his fingers into me, I let out a moan that was immediately swallowed up in Zol's kiss, his forked tongue slipping into my mouth and stealing my breath away.

The pressure built at a furious pace, my body overstimulated from all sides, and when I came, I only got a brief respite while they changed positions. Aiqen took the spot between my legs and Zol used his tail to tie my hands above my head as they all began to devour my body again.

And again.

And again.

My legs shook, my muscles seeming to melt beneath the onslaught of pleasure, until all five had taken the chance to eat me out.

I'd already come five times and none of them even had their cocks out yet. It seemed like I had an awful lot to be thankful for.

~Cadriel~

With Tanith still woozy from the aftereffects of her orgasms, I lifted her from the table and carried her down the hallway to the bedroom. Although I laughed when I first saw the bed Ty and Zol constructed, big enough to fit all of us at once, it had come in handy many times and would do so again that night.

By the time I placed Tanith down onto it, the others had already entered the room behind me and begun undressing. Ty shifted to his human form and Leith opened his sheath, all of us eager to continue what we started in the dining room.

Over the course of the past year, the other four had all become very comfortable being intimate with each other as well as Tanith, but it had never appealed to me. I still wanted only her, and the others respected that. We all respected each other, which was part of what made our group so enjoyable.

So when I undressed myself and lay down next to Tanith, no one else protested. "You ready for more?" I whispered to her, and she nodded, her eyes only half-open but full of contentment.

Gently, I rolled her over on top of me. Her earlier orgasms had left her dripping wet, so my cock slid into her easily, and with her ass exposed, the other men could all take their places.

Leith's self-lubricated cock took Tanith's ass, and for the others, they grabbed one of the many bottles of lube we kept handy in the bedroom, ready for a moment just like that one. Leith's scales opened in the back too, exposing his ass for Zol, and Ty formed another link in the chain, placing his stiff cock inside the demon.

Aiqen knelt beside me, his cock at lip-level with Tanith, who took it in eagerly.

Every movement caused a chain reaction. Ty thrust hard into Zol, whose cock pressed into Leith, who moved inside Tanith. That pushed her forward, her pussy sliding along my cock and her mouth taking Aiqen in deeper. With my hands on her hips, I slid her back down until I bottomed out inside her, and the whole wave moved in reverse.

In and out. Up and down. Bodies writhed against each other, within each other, each working towards our common goal of mutual and communal satisfaction, and when Tanith came on my cock, her body tightening around me, it felt just like heaven.

I prayed it always would.

~~THE END~~

MORE FROM THE AUTHOR

<u>Contemporary Romance – 18+</u>

Callahan Series
A Matter of Time
A Piece of Land
A Change of Heart
A Work of Art

Christmas in the City Series
Mistletoe Mistake
Candy Cane Challenge
Tinsel Temptation
Gingerbread Gamble
Stocking Standoff
Eggnog Experiment

Standalones
Leading Lady
A Set of Three
Charity Case
Hired Lover

<u>Contemporary Romance – New Adult/Clean</u>

It Figures duet
It Figures
Figuring It Out

<u>Historical Romance – 18+</u>

Lady in Waiting Series
Lady in Waiting
King in Training
Princess in Hiding

<u>Paranormal Romance – 18+</u>

Standalone
Out of My Depth

Cold Lake Pack Series
The Curse and the Prophecy
The Spell and the Legacy
The Dream and the Destiny

Mismatched Mates Series
Mismatched Mates
Misguided Motives
Mistaken Meanings

Serena's Story
The Alpha's Second Chance
The Returned Mate
The Vampire's Consort

Sacrifice Series
Blood Donor
Life Giver

Paranormal Romance – New Adult/Clean

The Alpha's Prey

KEEP **IN TOUCH**

Daily updates from my works-in-progress, bonus chapters and more can be found on my Ream account, Chilli & Chocolate, along with Emma Lee-Johnson:
https://reamstories.com/chilliandchocolate

You can find and follow me on Facebook at:
facebook.com/melodytyden

Join the Facebook group Melody's Romance Corner for fun games, interaction with the author and exclusive news and excerpts.

You can also sign up to my newsletter at www.melodytyden.com for all the latest news.